THE SHADOW GIRL

INSPIRED BY A TRUE STORY

JOHN LARKIN

WOOLSHED PRESS
An Imprint of Random House Australia

*For my children Chantelle, Damian and Gabrielle,
and of course to the girl who rode the trains, wherever
you are. I hope you're well. I hope you're safe.*

ACT ONE

BEFORE

Nothing exists but you. And you are
but a thought – a vagrant thought, a useless
thought, a homeless thought, wandering forlorn
among the empty eternities.

— MARK TWAIN

The End

I'M LYING IN THE BATH SHAVING MY LEGS BY THE DIM GLOW OF candlelight when the doorbell rings.

In most houses this wouldn't be a biggie. Someone else would get the door or, if it was a salesperson on foot or God-botherers or whatever, you could keep quiet or hide or say you were with Optus or atheists or something. But things are different in my house. No one lives here. Not even me.

The thing that surprises me most is that the doorbell actually works. Of course I'd seen it there by the battered and warped screen door. A big old clunky wooden thing with a weather-beaten brass button in the centre. But I figured it would have seized up by now, or gone to doorbell heaven, or whatever it is that doorbells do when they haven't been used for decades.

So it's the doorbell itself – its resonating *dong* seeking out every cobwebbed nook and cranny of the house – that jolts me upright in the bath, rather than any intrigue about who might be on the other side of it. I drop my razor, which sinks poetically to the bottom, taking my happiness with it. Actually it doesn't. It's one of those yellow plastic el-cheapo ones, so it just bobs on the surface like something bobbing on top of something else. It's hard to be poetic and construct complex metaphors (okay, similes) when you haven't enough money to afford decent razors that sink when you drop them.

I take a breath and lower myself deeper into the bath so that just my eyes are above the water, like a sort of suburban crocodile.

The doorbell *dongs* again. Louder this time. Or so it seems. I imagine it's like sonar: the sound waves cannoning into the bathroom, vibrating off my chest and giving away my location.

Lying there, with the water getting colder by the second, I try to come up with a list of who it might be:

The owners – Possibly. Though according to Miss Taylor, the house has been abandoned for years. And besides, owners tend to use keys. They wouldn't ring their own doorbell, surely. Not unless they were expecting to find someone in. Squatters, maybe. Me.

Delivery guy – You would need to have the mental capacity of a rabid rabbit's dropping to deliver your pizza to a house that has no lights and is practically boarded up and slowly rotting back into the earth.

Friends – Don't have any. Not close, anyway. Although I'm tight with my group at school, they live in ivy-covered houses with swimming pools and atriums and vestibules and generally a full complement of parents. I could never bring them here.

Flowers – It's my fifteenth birthday – I've already celeb-rated with fish and chips, a cupcake and a Bacardi Breezer, which was just too disgusting for words and ended up down the sink – but who would send *me* flowers?

Creepo – Ditto on the doorbell ringing.

Homeboys looking for a derelict house to plan their next gang war or play their DOOF DOOF music – God I hope not, especially considering what I've got on. But I suppose ditto with the doorbell ringing again. I'd rather it was the:

Police – Bloody nosey old bag next door. The house wasn't doing anything. Just sitting here. Unloved. Neglected. Rotting. If I'd been a rat, or a cat, or a possum, she wouldn't have said anything. But I'm human, so I'm not welcome.

My heart leaps up my throat and I feel my intestines coil around each other like mating pythons when I hear the murmur of voices and the clatter of footsteps coming up the side of the house.

I realise almost too late that my lavender and ylang ylang scented candles are going to give me away. Even through the frosted glass of the bathroom window, whoever or whatever it is that's lurking about out there will surely see the flickering glow of the candles.

I reach out and pull them into the bath with me. The sizzle of the wicks hitting the water sounds as loud as the *dong* of the doorbell and I'm certain the game is up.

There is a heavy knock on one of the bedroom windows along the side of the house. Who knocks on windows?

'Is anybody in there?' A gruff voice. Definitely authority figure. Police. Social worker. School principal. Vigilante.

I hold my breath and try not to blink, figuring that the sound of my eyelids banging down will give me up.

The flicker of torchlight illuminates the bathroom window and I know for sure that it's either the cops or one hell of a persistent pizza delivery guy.

'She's in there, all right.'

My stomach lurches when Gruff Voice says this.

'Can you smell that?'

'Marijuana?'

'Smells more like lavender.'

And then they're gone. Not back down the front, unfortunately, but around the back.

They say that if you lose one of your senses, your others become more heightened to compensate. So here I am, lying in the bath in the pitch-black with everything but my eyes set to hyper-alert mode. I can hear the clump of their boots on the back verandah. I sense they've stopped at the back door. Feel that my life is about to change. Again.

I pray to God that I've locked the back door, but then I remember that I'm not religious and, from what I remember, God doesn't bother with piddly little stuff like locking doors anyway. Miraculously locking back doors so that cops can't spring teenage girls having a candlelit bath on their birthdays might prove His existence – and we couldn't have that now, could we?

Oh shit! I didn't lock it. I remember. My hands were full when I came back from the shops and I made a mental note to go back and lock it when I got myself organised. Note to self – stop making mental notes.

Then, barely audible above the pounding of my heart, the back door creaks open. I can hear and feel the vibration of their voices. They're in the kitchen, checking out the evidence of my dinner.

Thanks, God. You couldn't just do that for me? Give me one minuscule break and lock the friggin' back door? It wouldn't have even proved your existence. I would've just assumed that I'd done it myself. And maybe that's the point. He knows that I wouldn't have given him credit for it so now he's sulking.

What sort of previously unclassified subspecies of idiot am I? How many fifteen-year-olds living by themselves would come home, have a little birthday party, go for a nice, relaxing candlelit bath and fail to lock the back door?

I'll tell you how many – one. Me. The idiot actually still in the bath.

They're clomping down the hallway now, towards the lounge room. I can sense their torches on my sleeping bag, my backpack, my clothes, my books. My life.

'Hello!'

Don't move a muscle. Don't even breathe.

If I had my clothes in the bathroom with me, I could quietly slip them on and then slide out the window.

'We only want to talk. You're not in any trouble.'

So why are there police in my house?

Oh crap! My clothes. They'll see my clothes lying there and know someone's here.

Slowly, almost sloth-like, I ease myself up and out of the bath. The water cascading off my body sounds like Niagara Falls in the rainy season, but I have to risk it.

I clear the water just in time. They're clomping over towards me now. I can see the approaching torchlight under the door. Thank God (or Buddha, Allah, Krishna or some of the lesser known Indonesian deities) that I'd closed the bathroom door.

'Hello.' There's a gentle tap on the door, the sort you might make if your grandmother is in the bath and you're sent in to tell her that dinner's almost ready or to make sure she hasn't drowned.

I hope to my non-existent God that I haven't locked the bathroom door because then they would know for certain that I'm in here. That would be pure genius, wouldn't it? Leave the back door unlocked but deadbolt the bathroom.

The door swings open and their torchlight fills the bathroom. Fortunately (or unfortunately, depending on how you look at the world, I suppose) through years of neglect I'm actually as skinny as an anorexic broomstick and there's room for me behind the door, which they obviously think is hard up against the doorstop.

'Well, she's not here,' says Gruff Voice.

'She has been, though. The water's still in the bath. Kind of creepy in a way. Like that yacht they found in the middle of the ocean with the coffee still warm in the mugs but no one on board.'

Their torchlight plays upon the water but they don't seem to notice the bobbing candles and el-cheapo razor. If they shine their torches on the floor, they'll see my footprints and the water dripping off me and then I'm gone.

'Neighbours don't want squatters,' says Gruff Voice.

There's a pause. I'm on tiptoes so my feet couldn't get wedged under the door and scraped back to the bone when they opened it. I will my heart to stop, my lungs to still, so as not to give away my position. I use thought control to stop any more water dripping off my body and under the door. I even stop my spleen from doing whatever it does that spleens do. I'm a ghost. A wraith of atoms. A shadow.

'Er, yeah, yeah,' says the young female cop. 'She'd better be gone in the morning or we'll come back with the sniffer dogs.'

There's a snort from Gruff Voice. And then the torchlight fades and they're clomping down the hallway and out through the kitchen. The back door closes and they're outside.

'Sniffer dogs,' laughs Gruff Voice as they make their way back down the side of the house. 'You've been watching too many American cop shows, sweetheart.'

'Don't call me sweetheart.'

'Hey. Don't burn your bra just yet, darling. You're still on probation.'

'What century are you living in, Sarge?' laughs the female cop. 'Bra burning happened in the sixties. The *nineteen*-sixties. I suppose you were just getting your sergeant's stripes then.'

The banter continues all the way down the side of the house until they're out of hearing range.

When my pulse has settled, I slide out from behind the door. I remove the plug halfway so that the water drains slowly and doesn't make that strangling sound at the end. Then I dry myself and, still in tiptoe mode, creep out to the lounge room.

They haven't touched my stuff. They could have taken it. Thrown it out or confiscated it. But they didn't. They were nice. They knew I was here. Hiding. Somewhere in the house. They probably sussed that I was behind the door. That whole 'sniffer dog' bit was for my benefit. Luckily they didn't realise that I was a kid. I'd be sitting in the back of their car now if they had. Off to a hostel. Or to emergency foster care. Or back to that sack of shit uncle's place. I slip on my tracksuit and jumper and two pairs of bed socks. Then I crawl into my sleeping bag. I pick up my old friend *Bleak House*. But I decide not to read tonight. My mind's too churned up with wondering what I'm going to do in the morning. Where am I going to go?

A tear rolls down my cheek. I lick it off, enjoying its salty tang.

I was happy here. The happiest I've ever been. I could read, do my homework, cook (I replaced the fuses after I'd spoken to a bearded guy in an apron at the hardware store), sleep, have candlelit baths, breathe. Live.

That haggard old sow next door. I've seen her pottering around her garden. I wasn't hurting her. There's no reason she had to call the cops.

The light from the passing cars steals in through the curtains (*my* curtains. I paid for them myself) and briefly illuminates the ceiling. I love the sound of cars as they pass. The Doppler effect, I think it's called. An incomplete Doppler means that someone has pulled up outside. Potential trouble. Like tonight. But a full Doppler means I'm safe. The car has gone on its way. I love full Dopplers.

You'd think that the ghosts in the walls would visit me tonight. To say goodbye. But they leave me alone. There's just the sound of the dying gum tree scratching on the tin roof to get in. The comings and goings of the possums in the ceiling. A storm brewing to the south.

Sleep creeps up on me slowly, like hypothermia at sea, and I'm happy to be carried away. This will probably be the last good night's sleep I'll have for a while, so I better make it count. Tomorrow I'll be back. Back on the trains.

CAFÉ

Okay, that was your last night in the house. Before we go any further, though, I need to ask you a question. Why me?

I don't understand. Why not you?

That's not really an answer. There are loads of writers around who could do this . . . so why did you choose me?

You don't remember me, do you?

[Pause]

It's okay if you don't. I tried to be forgettable. That's how I survived.

We've met?

You gave me a book. Signed it too. I sold it on eBay.

Really? How much . . .?

I'm joking. I've still got it at home. You came to my school for an author talk and workshop when I was in year eight. I'd only just started there.

Which school?

Out west.

I do a lot of school talks. Where out west specifically?

Just out west.

Look, if we're going to do this, you have to be honest with me.

I will. Mostly.

I gave you a book? I don't do that very often.

I think you felt sorry for me.

I hope I didn't embarrass –

No, you didn't. But you saw through me. You saw me. So I thought if I ever survived this . . . this shit, I would find you to see if you were interested in, well, writing about it. I tried doing it myself but, I don't know, it wasn't working too well.

I remember now. You went to [deleted from transcript] High.

That's right. But you can't put that in.

When I told my daughter about you she cried. Said I should have brought you home to live with us.

I would have liked that.

Schools generally don't approve of visiting guests taking students home with them.

You knew I was a street kid?

Not really. I sort of remember your librarian saying something.

Mrs Lee.

She told me you were doing it tough. She didn't say anything about you being homeless, though.

But you forgot me.

I meet thousands of students each year. I guess I figured you would be okay because you were so smart . . . and I was right.

It wasn't as easy as it sounds.

What are you now, eighteen, nineteen?

Something like that.

And how old were you when you found the house?

I was in year nine; so, fourteen.

We need to go back. Before you found the house. I'm interested in how you came to be . . . on the trains in the first place.

You can say it.

Say what?

Homeless.

Okay. When you were homeless.

[Pause]

Wait a minute. Is the bit about the house and the cops and everything going to be, like, the epilogue – I mean, prologue?

It might. I haven't decided how I'm going to structure it yet.

Cool. But you can't use my name.

I know.

My uncle would kill me. I'd be fish bait.

I won't mention you by name. Or him.

Or any of the places. Schools and suburbs and stuff.

That's going to be really hard. Making up fictitious names for schools and everything. Readers like to feel connected. Even if . . .

You don't believe me, do you?

Of course I do. You found *me*, remember?

He'll kill you too. He's a total psycho.

Well, that's a risk I'm going to have to take. My name has to go on the cover.

Couldn't you put 'Anonymous' or something?

It's been done. You always get found out. And then it seems like a publicity stunt.

No names!

You won't even know which country it's set in. Okay?

Thank you.

So can we go back?

First homeless day?

Is there one?

It's not something you try out.

What I mean is, isn't it gradual? Things start to fall apart. You leave, come back, leave again.

Not with me. I had a home and then I didn't.

How about earlier? I'd like to get some more background on you first. What were you like at school?

Smart . . .

Yes, I can see that.

You didn't let me finish. I was going to say smart-arse. At least that's what everyone said. I went to a Catholic school before it all . . . went wrong.

Primary or high school?

Both. It was K to twelve and it was great. The teachers were fantastic, the principal was cool. Or at least she was until I started causing trouble. I didn't realise that I was causing trouble, obviously, or I would have stopped. And it only happened twice. The second time I had to leave.

You mean you were expelled?

I don't know. That's what my aunt and uncle said. I was living with them then. They said that I had to go.

So what happened? The first time, I mean.

Too much God. Not enough reason. Or at least, not enough questions.

Miracle in ~~South~~ Central America

'HER NAME WAS MARIA LOPEZ AND SHE LIVED IN ONE OF THE POOREST areas of Tijuana. Or maybe it was Guadalajara. Anyway, it was somewhere in South America. And so one day –'

'Central America.'

'What was that?'

'You said South America, but it's actually Central America.'

'I was referring to Mexico.'

'Which is in Central America.'

'No it's not, missy! But if you want a geography lesson I'm happy to give you one. Central America refers to America, or the USA as we call it. North America is Canada and Alaska and perhaps Hawaii. And anything below the USA is South America.'

'Hawaii? That's in the middle of the Pacific Ocean. The US and Canada, along with Alaska, make up North America, and Mexico is the start of Central America, which includes countries like Guatemala, Honduras and Nicaragua. South America actually starts at Colombia and . . .'

'Sorry, Father. You'll have to forgive her. She reads a lot.'

'Maybe she reads too much. Perhaps we should look in the school library to see if there's a book on manners.'

'We could get you an atlas while we're there.'

'What did you say?'

'Nothing.'

'Nothing what?'

'Nothing . . . Father.'

'Please continue with your story, Father. And no more interruptions, boys and *girls*.'

'Despite being poor, Maria Lopez was a good and kind woman. She went to church every day and three times on Sunday and prayed for the soul of her late husband who had tragically died on board a flight to the United States, which of course is in *Central* America.

'And so one day, just as Maria and Jesus had returned home from mass, a terrible earthquake struck the city. It was nature at her worst. Or perhaps it was God's wrath. Who knows? When the earthquake struck, Maria and Jesus' apartment block collapsed. There was nothing but rubble where once a fifteen-story building stood tall. People emerged from their homes and started digging, using nothing but their bare hands. Trying to find survivors. Some workmen from a nearby building site joined in the search. All through the night they dug, always conscious that an aftershock might bring about a further collapse and bury the rescuers along with those already buried. And then just as dawn was breaking, the rescuers heard a faint cry. Somehow, through God's good grace, an air pocket had formed around Maria and little Jesus. The rescuers doubled their effort and by midmorning they had opened up a small gap through which they could communicate with her.

The rescuers asked Maria Lopez what she wanted. And do you know what she asked for, boys and girls?'

'A Big Mac?'

'A Coke?'

'Nintendo DS?'

'An atlas?'

'She asked for a priest. And so the priest was summoned and he prayed for Maria and little Jesus. And others joined in the prayers. And they sang hymns and held hands and prayed for this miracle that was unfolding before their very eyes. And just before nightfall –'

'You shouldn't keep starting sentences with "and".'

'Ssshhh!'

'– everyone's prayers were answered. And Maria and Jesus were plucked from what had almost become their tomb. And do you know what, children? When Maria Lopez emerged from the rubble with her tiny miracle in her arms, she refused to lay on the stretcher –'

'*Lie* on the stretcher.'

'– and instead she walked up to the priest and got down on her knees and thanked God for saving her and her baby. Now isn't that a wonderful story of how God looks after us, children? Are there any questions?'

'How come she thanked –'

'Hands up!'

'How come she thanked the priest, and not the people who'd risked *their* lives digging her out? It sounds like the priest just stood there singing and holding hands and stuff when everybody else was doing all the work and then *he* goes and gets the credit.'

'Sorry, Father Kelliher.'

'Not at all, Mrs Henry. Despite her conduct today, it's a fair question. You see children, God knew that Maria Lopez was a good woman and so he saved her and little Jesus by creating an air pocket for them when the building collapsed.'

'So weren't there any other good people in the building?'

'Apparently not.'

'How did God know?'

'He knows all.'

'So only bad people die in earthquakes?'

'On this occasion, yes.'

'But good people die in bus crashes and house fires and September eleven and floods and other earthquakes and tsunamis and stuff.'

'You don't believe, missy, like the rest of us, that God was looking after Maria Lopez and baby Jesus that day?'

'Not really. No.'

'So how do you explain Maria and Jesus Lopez's survival if God hadn't created an air pocket for them?'

'Luck.'

'Luck?'

'If God really wanted to save them he wouldn't have let the building collapse in the first place. Or when she was out at church or something he could have been a voice from the sky or a burning cactus plant or something and said don't go home, go for a walk in the country or something where no buildings can fall on your head. Or he could have just not had the earthquake at all. Saved everyone a lot of trouble.'

'Sorry, Father.'

'Anyway, children. I really must be going. Thank you, Mrs Henry.'

'Say thank you to Father, boys and girls.'

'THANK YOU, FATHER.'

'Thank you, children.'

'*You* can see me at recess.'

CAFÉ

SO YOU WERE PUT ON DETENTION?

No. Mrs Henry said that I was right. About Central America and all that. She also said that it was okay to question him about his miracle story. She just said that I had to be more respectful to him. To Father Kelliher. He'd done a lot for the parish. He'd built the school, worked in Africa, blah blah blah. But he was just such a know-it-all. Wandering around telling his stupid stories about how God saved this person and that person and yet when this girl in year four's mother died of cancer he told her that God had a plan. What sort of fucked-up plan involves taking a mother from a ten-year-old kid? Sorry.

That's okay; I can edit it out later. So you don't believe in God?

I didn't say that. I just don't think he's involved in the day-to-day stuff. I mean, he's either involved all the time or not at all. You just can't say he's involved in this bit to support your argument, but he's not involved in that bit. You can't make it up as you go along.

So praying is pointless?

Absolutely.

What if a person finds comfort or gains strength through prayer, or meditation?

Well, then the strength came from them. Not from some magic man with a beard floating around on a cloud.

Does it matter? I mean, surely the important thing is that people find the strength, the comfort, whatever it may be.

I just don't think it's right for God or priests to take the credit for it.

What about you?

What about me?

Did you pray? When you first became homeless. On the trains?

Yes I did.

Did it work?

You mean did my parents get back together and suddenly start to give a shit about me and my schoolwork and buy me a pony for my birthday? No, they didn't. Because then that really would have been a miracle. Back from the dead. Lazarus and all that. But I did pray for God to get me out of it. Off the streets. Off the trains. Away from those creeps who just wanted to mess with me. That Creepo would never find me.

And then you found the house.

That's right. *I* found the house, with my teacher's help. If God had found it for me, how do you explain the old woman from next door springing me and phoning the cops?

He moves in mysterious ways. Or maybe he had a plan. Testing your faith.

Yeah, right.

You mentioned that the area you grew up in was a bit rough.

Yeah, it sucked. It wasn't as bad as some places I've lived since, but you never really felt safe.

What about at school? Was that safe?

Yeah, it was like a sanctuary.

Your teacher – Mrs Henry, was it? – said that you had to be more respectful to Father Kelliher because he'd built the school.

In the sixties or something. He'd gone to Africa first, from Ireland, and then he was sent here.

And he built a school? The sanctuary that you enjoyed? So he wasn't all bad?

Yeah, all right. I see what you're getting at. I just hated the way he wafted around thinking that he knew everything and brainwashing kids with these made-up stories. I bet the whole Maria Lopez thing was total bullshit.

He gave the children of your area a sanctuary; a place to learn and reflect. Listening to a few stories, which you could choose to ignore anyway, seems like a small price to pay.

Are you supposed to be interviewing me or making me feel like crap? I was in year five, what the hell did I know about anything? I know that Father Kelliher was a good person, but that wasn't obvious until later.

You said before that there were two incidents at your school.

I've had enough today.

Okay. Can we meet up again tomorrow?

You don't think it looks a bit suss? You meeting a teenage girl every day and buying her coffee?

That's why I insist we meet publicly.

Are you going to write this up tonight?

I'll make a start.

Can I read it tomorrow? Before we begin the interview?

Yeah, okay. Where did you say you were living now?

I didn't. See you tomorrow.

[Tape stopped]

[Interview resumed]

So?

Yeah. I like it.

It still needs some work with the language. I can't imagine a teenage girl thinking 'barely audible above the pounding of my heart'.

I didn't think you would write it in first person, but it works. I love the image of the dying gum tree trying to get into the house. That's what it felt like.

Now, you said yesterday that there was another incident, at your school, and that you had to leave because of it. Could you tell me about that?

It happened a few years later when I was in year eight. We had to do a creative writing exercise in English, which I normally loved and got top marks for. But this time it was different. We had to write about someone close to us. I'd been living with my aunt and uncle since I was nine but things were starting to get scary. Get bad. With Uncle Creepo, I mean. So I wrote about my parents. I didn't really think it through, though, and almost ended up digging my own grave.

My Parents

I'M SITTING IN THE SMALL RECEPTION AREA OUTSIDE THE PRINCIPAL'S office looking at photos of ex-students and a bunch of dead priests and nuns. There's an overly large trophy cabinet, its contents padded out with inter-house shields and ribbons to make up for the fact that we've only ever won one trophy – some minor diocese football tournament about twenty years ago.

The office ladies keep casting me disapproving looks so that I know that they know that I'm in deep shitola. But how would they know what I've done, anyway? They're not in the chain of command – teacher, deputy principal, school counsellor, principal, Father Kelliher, police. I wouldn't say office ladies are omniscient, but they're as close as a mortal can get.

The principal's door is closed, which is never a good sign. But it'll be worse when I'm on the other side of it. There's murmuring coming from under the door and the shadows of the powers-that-be move behind the frosted glass. I can hear the school counsellor's monotonous drone, and I wonder how long they'll let her waffle on about attention-seeking, calls for help and Ritalin before they lapse into a coma themselves.

They're all in there talking about me, of course. I just wish they were saying nice things. But nice things don't generally involve closed doors, murmuring, school counsellors and disapproving looks from omniscient office ladies.

'You can go in,' says office lady number one, whose name, I think, is Joy. Talk about ironic. 'They're ready for you now.'

I don't know how she knows this because I didn't hear a phone ring or intercom go off or whatever, but no sooner has she finished her sentence than the principal's door swings open, as if operated by some celestial force.

'Sit down,' says the principal in her best so-it's-come-to-this tone. She doesn't use my name. I don't think she actually knows it. She's not great with children, which I suppose is why they moved her out of the classroom and into the principal's job.

Things are worse than I thought. Out of my chain of command list, the only one missing is the cops, though it's early yet and they could still make an appearance. There's a chair in the middle of the room, which I assume is the one I'm supposed to sit on. My captors are gathered in a semi-circle around the chair. They are either going to interrogate me about my 'story' or interview me for a teaching position. I can feel my bowels slowly beginning to liquefy. Father Kelliher absently touches the small silver cross that's pinned to his collar. I wonder briefly whether, if Jesus had died of old age or been trampled by an animal rather than being crucified, would Father Kelliher wear a walking stick or a camel around his neck instead? Maybe I'm missing the point. I didn't think I was missing the point of the creative writing exercise – *Write a Brief Profile, Using any Style or Voice, of Someone Close to You.* The principal hands me my draft book and asks me to read it.

I pause for breath, look around and hit the launch button. '*My father arrived here . . .*'

'Not out loud,' snaps the principal. 'We've all read it. Read it to yourself.'

This seems a bit pointless because I know what I've written. However, I don't want to upset anyone – more than I have already – so I stare intently at my writing, as if hoping that it will somehow reveal why I'm in trouble, though of course I know. I'm just playing dumb for their benefit.

My Parents

My father arrived here from Eastern Europe about twenty years ago. I don't know what sort of beatings he took from his father when he was a boy but they must have been pretty bad. We are nothing if not the sum of our parents, as somebody wise once said.

Most of the Eastern European men I've met through my family or at kids' parties are lovely and gentle and would die for their family. My father wasn't like that. Neither was his creepo brother, whom I now have the misfortune to live with. My father and Uncle Creepo were in the building game, supposedly. Kind of like the Mafia were in the horse-racing game. And I know what I'm talking about. I've read *The Godfather*. I was going to say they must have read it too but the idea of Uncle Creepo actually reading a book is about as moronic as an oxymoron gets. Not that he would know what that means. My father was a reader, but he's gone back to live in Europe now. Which is a gentle family euphemism for 'he's dead'. Not that I'm one hundred per cent certain. But having a carving knife embedded in your neck and the blood from your severed artery spray-painting the kitchen walls would probably put a kybosh on plans to emigrate back to the old country.

I stop and look up at my audience, figuring that it might have been the last bit that caught their attention. I don't even get to Mum's profile, which is the really interesting one. She's gone back to live in Europe too.

As if to hammer home the point, the principal snatches my book off me and does exactly what she asked me not to do. Reads it out loud. She also stops at the bit about my father having the knife in his neck. So at least I'm right about that.

'God . . . father?' says Father Kelliher, narrowly avoiding blasphemy. 'What is a fourteen-year-old girl doing reading *The Godfather.*'

'Actually, I'm thirteen.'

'Be quiet, missy!' he snaps. 'You're in enough trouble as it is.'

My poor English teacher, Miss Feathershaw, is sitting transfixed like a rabbit in the headlights. Fresh out of uni and they give her year eight. That's a tough gig for anyone, let alone a newbie.

'Yes, well,' interjects the principal, because Miss Feathershaw appears to be thinking about a career in retail. 'This one's never without a book in her hand.'

'Then I think it's high time that we started monitoring what she's reading.' Father K rubs his crucifix again and for a moment I wonder if they're going to perform some sort of exorcism on me.

'I think,' intones the school counsellor, 'we need to focus on the real issue here.' You can actually feel the room yawn at this point.

'And what, Miss Sigmund Freud, do you think *is* the real issue?' Her name is actually Mrs DeSouza (though everyone calls her Mrs DeSnooza behind her back), but the way Father K spits 'Sigmund Freud' at her lets everyone know his opinion of psychologists.

'I'm not entirely certain. I would need to spend a few sessions with her alone. If we could make some time next week there are some things . . .'

'Do you think,' interjects the principal quickly before we all fall asleep, 'that it was appropriate to share your work with the class? To read it out loud? Shirley Jennings has gone home sick.'

'Shirley Jennings is always sick,' I reply. 'She should be living in a bubble.'

Miss Feathershaw snorts at this and everyone looks at her, but fortunately she manages to turn it into a cough.

Father Kelliher shakes his head. 'What an imagination.' He says this like it's a bad thing.

'I think the real issue –' begins Mrs DeSouza but she is soon cut off.

'Will you stop it with your touchy feely "real issues", woman,' snaps Father Kelliher, reminding us all that in a Catholic school at least, the Church still rules the roost. 'The REAL issue, as far as I can see, is that she's either making all this up for attention, or she's telling the truth. If it's the former then I think a few sessions with Mrs DeSouza *are* in order. If it's the latter, then God help us all.'

Father Kelliher directs his attention to me. 'Well, missy. What do you have to say for yourself?'

I decide that now would be a good time to focus on the tessellating pattern of the carpet. I wanted to push this because of what happened last night, but now that I'm past the point of no return, I want to go back. I can deal with Uncle Creepo. Why *hadn't* I just made something up? I'm the best writer in the class. I could have said that my father works hard and Mum bakes cakes and helps out in a soup kitchen on the weekends. Or Mum works hard and my father bakes cakes, blah blah blah. But now I'm either going to score some counselling sessions with Mrs DeSnooza, or find myself in a shallow grave in the forest this afternoon.

'Well, her parents *did* move overseas when she was in year three,' offers the principal when she realises that I've been temporarily struck mute. 'She lives with her aunt and uncle now. We've contacted them and they're on their way.'

Oh no. I've done it now.

Father Kelliher turns to the principal. 'Do you think she might be being . . . you know?' Then he turns to me. 'You can wait outside now, missy.'

The door mysteriously clicks opens and once again I come under the hateful glare of the office ladies.

Father Kelliher doesn't think I knew what he was going on about with his suggestion that I was being 'you-knowed'. Priests can be so naive at times. He was asking whether I was at risk of my uncle slipping into my room at night and reading me bedtime stories that finish with a happy ending – for him at least. So I decide to let them run with it. To see how far it goes. He might be rubbish at geography, but Father K is smarter than I gave him credit for. Except now my aunt and Uncle Creepo have been summoned up to school and I'm in serious trouble.

My aunt and uncle sidle into the reception area looking like they've been forcibly torn away from a bling and pimp convention. My aunt's hair appears to have been fluffed out with static electricity and then set in quick-dry cement, while her flashy wedding ring seems a bit out of place in the school's dowdy reception, especially considering the almost-vacant trophy cabinet and the area that we live in. She belongs in that cabinet. The perfect trophy wife. Her advice to me when I was put in the top class and given extension work was: 'Don't act too smart. Boys don't like it when you're smarter than them.'

She ignores me and wobbles up to the glass window. Her shiny skin-tight pants make her butt look like a couple of baby hippos fighting in a garbage bag. Uncle Creepo gives me the death stare, but I avoid his eyes by gazing at the floor again. He sits down next to me and mumbles something under his breath. Something about me being like my mother.

'Are you going to send me back to live in Europe too?'

'There's something seriously wrong with you.'

'And you're perfectly normal, shower boy.' If I wasn't past the point of no return before, then I definitely am now.

'If you've said anything, I'll . . .'

'You'll what?'

'You'll see.'

I look at my watch. It's two o'clock in the afternoon. I'll probably be dead by tea time.

CAFÉ

SO WHAT HAPPENED NEXT?

Well, they were summoned into the office and even though I couldn't hear the conversation, I got the gist of it. 'She's always had an active imagination . . . reads too much . . . Parents are fine . . . they're living back in Europe but they wanted to give her a better chance because she doesn't speak the language . . . we're raising her like she's our own,' and on and on until you could almost hear the violins. And that was it. They came out smiling and laughing and it was handshakes all round.

Creepo said, 'Come on, you,' and ruffled my hair, which almost made me vomit. He even picked up my backpack and slung it over his shoulder, like it was the sort of thing he did all the time, and I wanted to scream at Father Kelliher and the principal and the counsellor and everyone that he'd fooled them all. That he'd got our house and all our money and I'd never see a cent of it because he'd buried it out in this forest somewhere.

Why did you think that?

Because just after it happened, the first night after my parents went back to live in Europe and I moved in with Creepo and Serena, I was looking out of my bedroom window and I saw him packing a shovel and a couple of big garbage bags in the boot of Serena's car. The bags were so heavy that she had to help him lift them in. And she was crying. So I figured he's been to my parents' house and stolen their stuff, and now he wants to hide it. And then he came and got me. Gave me a hot chocolate and said we were going for a little drive. I always thought it'd been a dream.

Can we hang on a minute? What happened to your parents?

I can't even remember what they looked like. Not without photos.

How old were you when they – left?

I was in year three, so I would have been . . . nine.

Do you want to talk about it?

They weren't the best parents in the world. Mum was okay. A bit lost if I think about it. But my father wanted boys. Or a boy at least. Instead he got me. They kind of left me to it. Or I let them leave me to it. I read this book when I was in year two – *Matilda* by Roald Dahl – and then I saw the movie in vacation care and I wanted to be her. I wanted to be Matilda. So I used to read everything and anything. Had my mum buy me books and join the local library. I even tried telekinesis but nothing ever happened. I asked Mum if I could change my name to Matilda but she cracked the shits and said that I had a lovely, traditional Eastern European name. I wasn't quite as smart or as innocent as Matilda but I still became pretty cluey because I read the same books that she did, even if I didn't entirely get most of them. So we were a lot like the Wormwoods. Up to a point.

I can't remember Matilda's dad being killed by his wife. Though he probably deserved it.

I think I'll order you decaf tomorrow.

No. This is good. Isn't it what you writers call being in the zone?

All right, keep going.

Parents?

The night they went away.

The Night They Went Away

I STAGGER IN FROM SCHOOL LUGGING ANOTHER STACK OF BOOKS THAT Matilda recommended. Mum's slouched over the breakfast bar. Although she doesn't work she's usually out in the afternoons and I'm kind of a latchkey kid so it's a shock to see her here. I'm actually a bit annoyed, because I like having the house to myself and I wonder if she's been walking into doors again, which happens a lot around our place. Well, it does to her.

She's rocking backwards and forwards like crazy people in movies do. And although I just want to go up to my room and read, I feel that I ought to do the mother–daughter thing.

'Are you all right, Mum?'

She's just had the kitchen completely redone in a sort of Neanderthal man meets *Better Homes and Gardens* theme. It's all granite and stainless steel, so my voice seems to get absorbed by the rock and heavy metal.

I try again. 'MUM!'

She looks over at me but her mascara is making a run for freedom, her eyes all blotchy and black.

'Are you okay?' Clearly she's not, but what do you say? 'Is something . . .'

'It's okay, sweetie,' she replies. 'I'm fine. Go and do your homework and I'll fix you a snack.'

I feel like saying, 'Oh, duh! I did my homework at lunch-time like I always do.' But I don't want to ruin my mum's little bonding moment so I let it go.

She's toying with something on the breakfast bar. I step closer and see that it's her mobile. Actually, it's my father's mobile. He must have forgotten it this morning. I get the feeling the mobile is responsible for Mum's smudged mascara, but I'm not sure how. I've got to read more adult books to get the hang of this sort of stuff.

'Things are going to be different from now on,' she says as I gather up my backpack. 'You'll see.'

As I'm dragging my backpack up the stairs I hear Mum call out 'Bitch!' and for a minute I think that I might not get that snack after all. But then I realise the 'bitch' has probably got something to do with my father's mobile and the runny mascara.

I slump onto my bed and open my backpack.

Out of Matilda's list of books I managed to get:

> *Oliver Twist* by Charles Dickens
> *Jane Eyre* by Charlotte Brontë
> *The Old Man and the Sea* by Ernest Hemingway
> *Animal Farm* by George Orwell

When I plonked the books on the counter, the librarian gave me a funny look, so I told her that they were for my grandmother who was sick in bed with a fatal disease. The librarian made a sort of 'harrumph' noise but then I looked sad because of my grandmother and her disease and everything, so she cheered up a bit and said that if my grandmother liked 'those' sorts of books then she would love this one. She handed me another book by Charles Dickens which was called *Bleak House*. It was about the size of a brick.

I arrange the books on my bedroom floor and decide to start with *The Old Man and the Sea*. It's about twenty times shorter than *Bleak House*.

I'm just getting into *The Old Man and the Sea* – you can actually taste the salt air and feel the cold as Santiago gets up mega-early to go fishing – when Mum comes into my room with my snack. It's a glass of soy milk (yuck) and a honey and oat muesli bar (gross).

She sits down on the bed and strokes my face. 'Whatever happens,' she sniffs. 'I'll always love you.'

She looks like she wants to talk, which is weird. She's never been as cuddly as the mums who do the school pickups. Sometimes she seems sad, or kind of disappointed. I once overheard her ask my father why she couldn't get a part-time job – something in a clothes shop or a salon. My father got mad and said it would shame him. I wasn't sure why. Lots of kids at school had mums who worked. Maybe it was because, unlike her, he was born in the old country. Or maybe he was just weird and old-fashioned.

She once told me that she had wanted to be a nurse but she kept skipping school to hang out at the shops with her friends, and when her father found out he burned her school uniform along with her 'useless' report cards and screamed at her that her only hope was of finding a rich husband. Because she was useless at that too, he went out and found one for her – one of *his* so-called business associates not long off the boat from the old country. So she walked down the aisle with her head bowed and me along for the ride, to be greeted by the cold stare of my middle-aged father. She was eighteen. However, my mother was far from being the baby machine that my first-date conception had promised. My premature arrival led to complications. Apparently my father wept like a baby when I was born. Not for my safe arrival, but for the sons that would no longer follow me down the birth canal.

I think the reason he's never divorced us is because the only thing that matters to him more than family is money. Mum told him once that she would take a big fat slice of the pie if he ever packed us off or she caught him cheating. She was entitled to save face too, she reminded him as he stood over her with his fists clenched. And following this argument, just like every argument, she had to use strategically placed make-up in order to show her face in public. The stupid doors again.

'What are you reading?' she asks, which is totally out of the blue. She stopped reading to me in kindergarten.

'It's called *The Old Man and the Sea*.'

'Ah,' she says. 'Hemingway.'

To say that I'm stunned is a major understatement. My mum's reading stretches to supermarket checkout magazines. And even then she probably only looks at the pictures.

'You've read it?' I try not to sound too surprised.

'No,' she says, and suddenly we're back on familiar ground. 'Didn't he shoot himself?'

'The old man?'

'Hemingway.'

'I don't know.' I turn to the small author bio in the front and scan down. 'It just says that he died in 1961.'

'I'm sure he shot himself,' she says. 'Death comes to all of us in the end.'

I wonder how she knows this. Maybe there was a magazine article about it at the checkout – 'The Somethingth Anniversary of Author Blowing Own Head Off' pullout special. But

Mum has a distant look in her eyes and I'm not sure that I want to be talking to her about this stuff. I'm nine years old. Shouldn't we be discussing homework, or upcoming birthday parties, or my first holy communion in two weeks' time?

She pats my hand, stands up and smiles, but there's that look in her eye again.

'When your father comes home from work, you might want to stay up here.'

I never saw her again.

CAFÉ

Let's take a break.
 I'm okay.
 Tissue?
 Thanks.
 Another coffee?
 Hot chocolate please. With soy milk.
 Soy milk? I thought . . . I'll shut up.
 [Tape stopped]

 [Interview resumed]
 So you were closer to your mother than you let on?
 No. We weren't close at all and that's what upsets me. She didn't know how to be close to me because of her family life and stuff and so she never taught me or showed me how to be close to her. To anyone. She had a crap life. Her father practically pimped her out to my father, probably to pay off a debt or something.

Do you ever see them? Your grandparents, I mean.

No. Why would I? My grandfather on my father's side was a widower and lived in [deleted from transcript] and we never really saw much of my mum's parents anyway. The few times that we met they were always trying to hook me up with some mutant cousin.

Very few Hallmarks card to cover that particular wedding. Sorry, this is serious.

No, that's funny.

[Pause]

Can we get back?

If we have to.

We can stop for the day if you want.

No. Let's keep going. I only want to do this bit once.

So we finished up with your mother warning you not to come downstairs when your father got home from work.

Yeah. She knew it was going to kick off. Or that she was going to kick it off. I think she also knew that once it started, there'd be no going back.

The Thrashing

WHEN MY FATHER'S CAR PULLS INTO THE DRIVEWAY A COUPLE OF hours later, I automatically switch to reading with my fingers wedged in my ears. It's hard to turn the page with your elbow, but I've had enough practice to be quite skilled at it.

Santiago's marlin has just been hit by the first shark when the yelling from the kitchen hits *me*, and I know that this is going to be a bad one. Even through my la-la-la-ing I can hear furniture hitting walls and crockery smashing. And then just as abruptly it stops and I figure that maybe I'm wrong. That maybe he's backed off and apologised and that he is holding her face in his hands, tenderly stroking her rapidly swelling eyes and promising never to do it again. Again.

I unplug my fingers and listen to the deafening silence. And then it hits me. A sound I never want to hear again.

Once, on a school excursion to the city, one of the ADHD kids got hold of an apple and chucked it out the train's window. The apple hit a pylon with a wet smack. I don't know why but it wasn't the sort of sound that I expected an apple to make.

That sound comes smacking up the stairs from the kitchen now. Two of them. In quick succession. And I know that my mum's eyes will need some serious plastering over, possibly even surgery, before she can go out to the shops again. Or she can show her face in church. Or *he* can.

I quickly stuff my fingers back in my ears, and even though they're wedged in there quite deep, I hear it kick off again. It sounds like Mum's giving as good as she's getting. And when she screams, 'You'll never hit me again, you bastard!' with no response from my father, I figure that she's somehow got the better of him. Which is pretty amazing because he's twice her size and used to be a semi-professional boxer back in the old country. Then this weird silence falls over the house.

I put down *The Old Man and the Sea* and creep out of my bedroom towards the stairs. I step silently over the creaking sixth step and tiptoe the rest of the way down. I peer into the kitchen and see that the floor around my father is completely covered in tomato sauce as if he and Mum have had a huge food fight. My father is leaning on the breakfast bar, like he's just trying to steady himself for a minute. There's something sticking out of his neck and he's covered in tomato sauce or red cordial. He's holding his mobile to his mouth and although his jaw is going up and down, up and down, there's no sound coming out, only more tomato sauce. I don't know where Mum is but I figure she's going to be pretty angry with my father for making a mess of her nice new granite floor. Then he drops and now he's thrashing around wildly on the ground.

I know that Mum is going to be really mad with him and the mess that he's making and she'll probably have a couple of black eyes in the morning for telling him off, so I race back upstairs and go back to my book.

Santiago desperately wants to get his marlin back to shore while it's still got some value but the sharks keep coming in and are tearing it to pieces. There's just the carcass and torn flesh left and the sharks are ripping ripping ripping. And downstairs in the kitchen my father is thrashing thrashing thrashing.

CAFÉ

DO YOU NEED A BREAK?

No. I'm okay.

I think *I* need one. So where was your mum?

I don't know. Maybe she was there. Curled up in a corner or something. Or maybe she went out the back for a smoke. She'd only do that when he wasn't around. He'd tell her off when he caught her, of course. Said it was a disgusting habit and she should be ashamed of herself for smoking in front of 'the girl'. He sucked down about eighty a day.

So then what happened?

Well, I was up in my room reading or pretending to and then about half an hour later someone came and started banging on the back door. And then I heard breaking glass and even though I had my fingers wedged in my ears again, I heard my uncle yelling, 'What have you done, Bridgette? What the fuck have you done?' And my aunt was screeching like a cat until suddenly she stopped and I figured that my uncle had covered her mouth with his hand or something else. Then I heard these two muffled bangs and my aunt was screaming again and this time it was a loud smacking sound that made *her* stop, a bit like that apple hitting the pylon again, and then this smoky smell wafted up the stairs.

Was this in your creative writing piece?

Not that bit, no.

Sorry. Please carry on.

It went quiet so I thought maybe they'd gone. But then I heard the sixth step creaking. Someone was coming up the stairs. Coming up the stairs for me. And I thought there'd be a couple more muffled bangs and the air would be smoky again. I stared at the door as it slowly opened and a face peered around the corner and even though her cheek was quite red she looked like an angel.

She ran over and hugged me and told me that everything was going to be all right. Then she opened my wardrobe and pulled out my little suitcase. She was stuffing in clothes, although she didn't have a clue which ones fitted me and which ones I hated. She told me to pack my backpack and that she would get my toothbrush, because I was going to be living with them for a while. I asked why but she started sobbing again and it must have hurt to wipe her tears away because the red mark on her face reached up to her eye, so I thought maybe that's why she was crying.

Once she'd packed my toothbrush, comb and my pink hair dryer, she sat down on my bed and held my hand. She called me princess and stroked my hair. She told me that Mum had accidentally hurt my father and that Uncle Tony had taken them to the hospital and that everything was going to be okay. But because my mum had done a really bad thing, she would be in trouble with the police and would probably have to go to jail, so when they come out of the hospital they were going back to [deleted from transcript] for a while.

As soon as things had settled down they would send for me and we would all be together again.

I put my head in my aunt's lap as she stroked my hair. I asked her to tell me about Europe, about the old country, but she didn't really know much because, like me and Mum, she was born here. I tried to imagine what it would be like living over there. I'd only ever seen it in glossy posters in the travel agent's window or on late-night movies that I shouldn't have been allowed to watch anyway. Maybe we'd have a glistening white house overlooking the ocean and my father would work as a fisherman, just like Santiago, only there wouldn't be any sharks to rip his marlin to pieces. And Mum would go to fashion school or become a hair or nail expert and have her own salon and everyone would be mega friendly and I'd sit in the sun and read and do my homework in two languages and we would be really happy and Mum wouldn't walk into doors any more.

[Pause]

So did your father go to the hospital?

I doubt it. I'm just telling you how I saw it and what I was told. When you're young and adults tell you stuff, you don't think they're lying because they're always going on about how you should tell the truth, so you kind of assume that's what they do too. And by the time you realise that adults are liars too – probably even bigger ones than kids – then it's usually too late.

But what makes you think they didn't go to the hospital?

Well, at the time everything was sort of jumbled up. Aunt Serena told me that Uncle Creepo had taken them to hospital. After we finished packing she carried my suitcase and school backpack down the stairs. When we got to the bottom, Uncle Creepo was sitting in the doorway, just kind of slumped there. He asked my aunt what she'd told me and she went through it again. She had her jacket covering my face so I couldn't see into the kitchen, kind of like a mother swan tucking its kids beneath its wing, but I noticed that she changed her story from him having *taken* them to hospital to that he was *going* to take them to hospital. She had to say that because he was still there. My uncle said it was good, what she'd said, as if I wasn't even there, so I kind of figured it out. Well, I did later.

Uncle Creepo told my aunt that she had to take me home and that he would be there a while cleaning up and that he had some friends, 'the boys', who were coming over to help, and even though I was buried beneath Aunt Serena's wing, I sort of laughed at this, at the image of Uncle Creepo cleaning up with, like, a bottle of Pine O Cleen and a mop, because he didn't seem like the sort of husband to pitch in with the housework. More like one of those Neanderthals who sits there on the lounge watching TV with his feet on the coffee table while wifey vacuums around him.

You know what? I've been saying their names. You can't use this bit.

It's okay, I'll change them when I have the transcript typed up.

What to?

I'll just make up some names.

Can I do it?

It's your story.

[Pause]

Who's the biggest ever psycho in movies? Kind of like a wannabe gangster?

[Pause]

Probably Al Pacino's character in *Scarface*. In my opinion.

What was his name? In the movie, I mean.

I don't know. I'll have to look it up.

Use that then. Unless it's something silly, like Bubbles or something?

You don't get many psychotic Cuban drug lords called Bubbles. I think it was just an ordinary name. Anthony or something. Tony. I'll look it up. What about the others?

Make Mum Bridgette. I had a really great teacher in year four called Bridgette so I love that name. I think if I ever have a daughter I'll call her Bridgette or Serena. Make my aunt Serena.

And your father?

I don't want him to have a name. He doesn't deserve one. I don't want you to even have me calling him 'Dad'. Just make him 'my father'.

You're not making this easy.

I bet it was harder to live it than write about it.

Sorry.

[Pause]

What about the country? I can't just make up a country. It'll sound silly.

That's okay. I'll just have it deleted from the transcripts.

Thank you.

So you went to live with Serena and Tony. Did they have kids of their own?

No. I don't think he wanted any. I think Aunt Serena would have liked them, but he was the boss of everything.

So what was it like? Living with them?

It was okay for the first few years but then it started.

What do you mean?

Well, in year eight, Uncle Creepo accidentally walked into the bathroom while I was having a shower. I mean, it really seemed like an accident because he apologised and left – there weren't any locks on the doors in the house, probably so that my aunt couldn't get away from him. But then he did it again the next day and the next day after that, and even though I quickly covered myself with my hands, the third time it happened he just stood there staring at me. His disgusting, pervy eyes roamed up and down my body. And he was grinning. The fourth time it happened I yelled at him to get out, but he said that it was his house and he could go anywhere he liked, including my bedroom, which almost made me vomit. The sixth time he did it I was wearing my swimming costume and I just smiled at him, a 'tricked you' smile, and he said that if I ever wore my swimming costume in the shower again, he would come in and rip it off me. Which wiped the smile off my face pretty quickly.

By that time I'd started my period, but the rest of my body hadn't really caught up yet. Compared to Aunt Serena's watermelons I had a couple of fried eggs stuck to my chest, so I couldn't see what the attraction was.

In the end I stopped having showers and eventually the kids at school refused to sit next to me because I smelled like a wino. When my teacher sent a note home about my 'personal hygiene choices' – that was how she wrote it – I plucked up the courage and told my aunt. She got really angry and called me a liar and a home wrecker and a slut and accused me of trying to steal Uncle Tony away from her. She said it was a teenage fantasy and that I was making it all up. Anyway, she must have said something to him because the next day I noticed that she was wearing more makeup than usual and I thought, here we go again, and so Serena came up with a solution. She acted like it was all just a coincidence and said I should shower in the morning because my uncle left for work really early and he would be out of the house and so he couldn't accidentally walk in on me. It was so obvious that I could have kicked myself. It was just that at home we always had showers at night, after school and stuff because, well, how dirty can you get in your sleep? The first time I did it I waited until I heard Creepo's car backing out of the drive, then I raced into the bathroom. I was having a really nice hot, soapy shower and the door opened on me again. Only then I realised that it wasn't him but her. It was Serena and she said, 'Oh sorry,' but as she was washing her hands I noticed that she was staring at me just like he did, only she was being a bit more subtle about it. She was checking me out. Not in a leso sort of way, more like checking out the competition. Like she really thought I'd want to steal Creepo away from her. And when I came home from school that day there was a brand new exercise bike in the lounge room as well as some Pilates DVDs and I knew that I had to get out of that place. Away from their psycho little world. Only I couldn't. Things had settled down since Mum had hurt my father and they'd gone back to live in [deleted from transcript], but they still hadn't sent for me. Aunt Serena and Uncle Creepo had sold our house, but they'd either sent the money over to my parents or kept it themselves.

Wait a minute. How did you know that they sold the house?

Because I used to walk past it every day on the way home from school. It was a longer way but I used to do it, sort of hoping that I'd see Mum round the back hanging out the washing or something. But one day there was a For Sale sign out the front and a few weeks after that there was a Sold sticker plastered across it. But then things started to get really dangerous with Uncle Creepo and I knew that I had to do something.

[Pause]

In what way?

Hmm?

How did things get dangerous?

It was late. About eleven o'clock. I was reading in bed but I was tired and my head kept dropping into my book. So I turned off my bedside light and snuggled down into my doona. I thought they were still up. Watching a movie or something, because I could see that strip of faded light at the bottom of my door. Anyway, a bit later – it could have been ten minutes, it could have been an hour – I must have been in that place where you're technically asleep but still partially awake because, and I don't know how, I felt a presence in the room. I had it at my house later, with the ghosts and everything, but this felt solid.

I couldn't see anything. It was pitch black. Even the faded strip of light at the bottom of the door was gone. But there was something there. Someone. And then I felt the pressure at the bottom of my bed and my heart was pounding against my rib cage. I was so terrified I couldn't even speak, but he must have heard me breathing heavily because he said 'Ssshhh'. And I was even more terrified because I knew that it wasn't a ghost, or my aunt, it was him. It was Creepo. He told me to shush again and then he said that he was sorry. That he shouldn't have kept coming into the bathroom while I was having a shower but he couldn't stop himself because I was so beautiful and he couldn't help it and that it was all my fault for tempting him and I was deliberately having a shower in the afternoon so that he would come in and check me out and all the usual bullshit that paedos go on about so that they can blame the victim. And like the idiot that I was I told him that it was okay. That I understood. That I was sorry.

[Pause]

I can't even begin to imagine how terrified you were.

I was practically pissing myself by that point, but I had to think. I mean really think because that was all I had going for me: my brains. I'd read enough books, so some of them must have seeped in. Some of the smarts, I mean.

I didn't scream. At first I couldn't, and then I thought if I screamed, he could just cover my mouth with his hand, or worse, my pillow. And then he'd do stuff to me and kill me, or the other way round, and then he'd kill Aunt Serena too and bury us in the backyard or out in the forest where he'd stashed all our money.

Suddenly he stands up. He asks me not to tell Aunt Serena about his visit. That it will just be our little secret. Then he bends down and kisses me goodnight; on my cheek, with his sandpaper face and his cheap bourbon breath. He tells me again that I'm beautiful, that I'm going to make some lucky man a spectacular wife one day and then with a whispered 'goodnight, princess' he slithers out of my room. I knew that he would be back the next night and the one after, pushing things a little further each time, and I knew that I had to do something.

[Pause]

So what did you do?

I wrote that story.

A Visit in the Night

'GET IN, YOU LITTLE BITCH!'

'Tony!'

'How could she do that after all we've done for her? I open my home to her and this is how she repays me.'

'She's confused.'

I climb into the back seat and try to stay quiet. At least he won't come to my bedroom tonight. He hates me right now, which is how I want it.

'She'll have to go!' he spits and the blood freezes in my veins. 'Do you hear *that*?'

'But she's happy there.'

'I don't give a shit about her happiness. She's not staying there. That Kelliher is a wily old dog. I don't want him sniffing around our affairs.'

I relax a bit when I realise that he's talking about me leaving the school. Not shooting me and dumping me in a shallow grave out in the forest.

'Where will she . . .?'

'Take her up there tomorrow with a letter. Tell them that she's going to a professional psychiatrist, or whatever they are. Say that she's caused enough trouble and that she will be going to the local public school for the rest of the year.' He pauses and glares at me in the rear-view mirror. 'If they'll have her.'

After dinner I tell them I'm not feeling well and I'm going to bed. They don't say goodnight. Too pissed at me. They're in the lounge room murmuring. Discussing what's to be done. I try to listen in around the corner, but I can't make anything out.

I go up to my room, lie on top of my bed and try to figure out what to do. The cold wakes me a few hours later. I can see my breath through the dim glow of streetlight stealing in through my curtains. I get up to turn off my bedroom light. I hear their bed creaking and she's gasping his name. He'll leave me alone tonight. Maybe this is Aunt Serena's way of protecting me. Or maybe she's protecting herself.

I crawl into bed and pull the covers up to my eyes. Their bed eventually stops creaking and the strip of light beneath my door is illuminated. There's someone in the bathroom. I hope it's her. But then I hear the double flush and I know that it's not. It's him. He always double-flushes.

I close my eyes, but not seeing makes my heart thump even harder. I swear one day it's going to just explode. I look back across to the strip of light. It's punctuated by two black lines. He's standing outside. Waiting. Thinking. I can't see the handle turn but I hear it. Slowly, like the second hand of a clock and softly, like the dial of a safe being tricked open. And then he's pushing. Gently at first, then harder and harder. But he can't get in. He tries to shoulder it open but only the top half moves and it bounces back against the frame with a loud clunk.

'What's going on, Tony?'

Thank you, Saint Serena.

'Nothing. I was just checking if she's warm enough.'

'Well come back to bed, I'm getting cold.'

The top half of the door bends again. It doesn't bounce back this time because he's using all his strength to hold it there.

'You little bitch!' he hisses. 'This is *my* house. Don't you ever block this door on me again! Do you hear me? I'll be seeing you tomorrow.' Then he eases the door back into position so that it doesn't clunk again.

I crawl out of bed and scramble over to the door. I reach down and feel my lifesavers. I could kiss them. Two little rubber door wedges. Two-fifty each from the hardware store. I snuck out of school at lunchtime – just after writing my story, before things kicked off in another direction and I was summoned to the principal's office. It's the best five bucks I've ever spent. Actually, considering I took the money from Creepo's wallet (which even as a good Catholic girl I figured was okay because I was spending it on *him*), it was the best five bucks *he* ever spent.

The wedges have moved a little bit during Creepo's onslaught so I reposition them, shoving them so firmly under the door that my fingers are almost at breaking point. But he won't be back again. Not tonight, anyway. Aunt Serena will hold onto him.

I crawl back into bed and snuggle down deep. This will probably be my last night with them. Tomorrow when I take my letter up to school and see Father Kelliher, things will start to get serious.

And tomorrow night I will either be very rich or very dead.

CAFÉ

So remind me. Why did you think you were going to be rich?

Remember I told you about Creepo and Serena stuffing those big bags into the back of his car and then I had that dream that we all went for a drive out to the forest? At least, I thought it was a dream.

You thought he'd buried all your parents' money out there? Why would he do that?

Well, he couldn't just put it in the bank. Even I knew that. It'd look too suspicious.

Hold on a minute, I'm confused.

What about?

He can't have buried any money from the sale of your parents' house, because he didn't sell that until later.

Glad to hear you're paying attention. My parents had other stuff. Jewellery, cash. So I figured that's what he's buried out in the forest. And then when they sold the house, he could have added that money to the hoard.

So you wanted him to lead you to it? How?

My plan was to make him think that the police were going to come and start sniffing around. I reckoned if I could get him to move it to another place, even another place further out in the forest, then all I had to do was remember where he'd put it and come back later and take it. It was mine anyway. So then I could go off and live somewhere else, in a hotel or something, and not have to worry about him coming into the bathroom while I was having a shower, or having to stuff rubber wedges under the door.

But how were you going to follow him? On a bike or something?

A bike? I didn't have one. I was going to hide in the back of his car, out of sight.

But why on earth would he move the money if he thought the police were going to come around? If anything, that's the one time he wouldn't.

I didn't say it was a great plan.

Even if you somehow got hold of the money, where were you going to go?

I had no idea. The plan just involved getting the money. After that, who knows? Rent a granny flat or something. Con some old dear into letting me move into her garage.

But you were thirteen.

Well, I couldn't stay in that house. You know that. I thought maybe I could go to a refuge or even foster care. Maybe even an orphanage if they still existed. Could even pretend that I was anorexic. I was skinny enough. Go and live in a psycho hospital with my eyelids sewn shut and be fed through a tube. Anything would have been better than staying with Creepo.

Why didn't you just go to the police?

And say what? I tried to tell the school that something was up and where did it get me? I tried over and over to figure out what I'd say to the police and it sounded sillier – more fanciful and paranoid – each time I practised the words. I had no proof that he'd done anything wrong. The cops couldn't do anything until I could prove it.

That's not strictly true. Not when it comes to child protection. Your safety would have been paramount, and your uncle's rights and reputation a minor consideration. If there was just the slightest doubt that you were in danger, they would have removed you immediately.

I didn't know that then. I'm not sure I believe it now. But if it *is* true, I'd have lost the money. I had to stay close to have a chance of getting it. I mean, I'm not stupid. I reckoned it would have taken more than a few rubber door wedges to stop him the next night, so I figured that I had one more chance. If he didn't panic and move it that night, then I'd go to the cops or Father Kelliher or Mrs DeSnooza or the principal because no way in hell was I sleeping in that house again.

The Forest

HE LEAVES EARLY AS USUAL. SAY WHAT YOU LIKE ABOUT CREEPO, HE'S got a good work ethic. Though I suppose if he's ripping people off, it's easier to get to his 'business associates' when they're coming out of their homes, yawning and stretching on their first coffee and smoke rather than later when they've woken up a bit more

Even though my rubber wedges were doing their job, I didn't really sleep for the rest of last night. The sound of the trains was carried to me on the wind. I fantasised about where they were heading. To white sandy beaches where you could sit in the shade with a cool drink and read all day. To bazaars with intoxicating smells and maybe just a faint whiff of danger. To tree-lined boulevards with cafés and restaurants and book-shops that never closed. Of course, the trains were probably just crawling around the suburban rail network, marking their departure with that electronic burping sound. It's not easy to conjure up romantic fantasies when the steam train age is ancient history and the only thing stopping your uncle slithering his way into bed with you is that your aunty is hanging onto him, still trying to hold on to dreams of her own.

After breakfast I spend the morning packing. One way or another I'm gone tonight. I stuff my backpack full of warm clothes but they're bulky and don't leave much room for my books. I decide to limit myself to two, my old favourites *Matilda* and *The Old Man and the Sea*. I'm a bit sad at having to leave *Bleak House*. Even though technically it doesn't belong to me, I'll miss hiding out in its labyrinth. My imaginary grandmother will have a whopper of a fine to pay when the library catches up with her. Maybe I should write a letter on her behalf. Kill her off like they do in soap operas.

Aunt Serena gives me a letter to take up to school and then goes out for coffee with the girls. She tells me not to tell Uncle Tony that she's making me walk up by myself because he wanted her to take me. I give her a hug and tell her thank you. She says that she doesn't know what I'm going on about. But she does. The elephant enters the room, so I let it pass.

She looks nice today. Spectacular in fact. She always looks gorgeous when she goes out for coffee with the girls.

When she's gone I have a bit of a snoop around their bedroom, but there's no incriminating evidence. No maps of buried treasure with the edges all burnt and a big X marking the spot. I open up Serena's bedside drawer. There are credit cards and some cash, which I think about taking but then change my mind. She's been good to me – well, she's been okay – and I don't want to be responsible for her landing in it when Creepo finds out that I've taken some of their cash. And of course if everything goes to plan I'll be rich later tonight. Or dead. Either way my life is about to change.

I take the letter up to school and hand it in at the office. Father Kelliher emerges from the inner sanctum trying to make it look like a coincidence, as if he was on his way somewhere vitally important but he can spare me a moment if we hurry. We sit down and have a chat and everything he says is comforting. He has no reason for saying anything to me. I'm no longer his problem. His student. His parishioner. But he says it anyway. Talks to me about life, about education, about books. About Shirley Jennings coming to school today but then suddenly remembering my story – the knife, the spurting blood – and having to go home again. And although he could benefit from a little geography revision, particularly as far as the Americas are concerned, it's obvious that he is an intelligent man. I know I've been a bit hard on him. I also know that if I don't get hold of the money tonight, I'll be out on the streets without a cent and he will be the first person that I'll turn to for help.

When I get back, Aunt Serena is still out having coffee with the girls. Creepo might come home unexpectedly, but I risk having a shower anyway. A quick one. It might be my last for a while. Then I take my backpack and hide it the garage cupboard for later.

We have dinner together. Happy families. As usual it's Serena's and my job to serve him. He wants another beer: one of us has to get up. Wants more sauce, a second helping: one of has to leap into action. We never know which. He decides on the spur of the moment. Mind games. Power games. Bullshit.

I have to wait until they start talking. I can't just leap in or they might suspect something. My comment has to be in passing – a 'by the way' sort of thing.

'Did you take the letter up to school?'

Finally.

'Well? Did you?'

'Yes. Yes she did.'

'*She* did. You didn't drive her?'

'No, but she did. She went.'

'Then how do you know, stupid? Jesus! I told you to take her. Do I have to do everything round here?'

'I did it. I got there just before lunch. You can check if you want.'

'Don't get smart with me, girl!'

The tension is building. In a minute I hope to crank it up a notch.

'Get me another beer.'

Aunt Serena and I look at each other. I start to get up.

'Not you!' he snaps. 'Serena.'

While my aunt is rummaging around in the garage fridge, Uncle Creepo reaches over and grabs my wrist.

'You didn't say anything to anyone, did you?'

'About what?'

He squeezes my wrist harder, his thumb digging into the bone. I wince but try not to show it or scream out. Any harder and it might snap. 'I told you not to get smart.'

But I'm not. There are so many things I could tell someone about, I'm genuinely unsure which one specifically I'm not supposed to mention.

'About . . . you know.'

Fortunately Aunt Serena is on her way back, coldie in hand, which she twists open for him. He lets go of my wrist but there are red burn marks on my arm and a sharp pain deep in the bone. I put it in my lap. Rub it with my other hand.

'Did you speak to anyone at school?' He asks this like it was a social call.

'Just the office ladies.' I let his relief hang out there for a while. 'And Father Kelliher.'

I swear I can hear the adrenaline shooting through his system. His sphincter tightening.

'What did you talk about?' asks my aunt who, for all her help, has a different agenda from me.

'The usual stuff,' I offer, loving this more than I ought to despite my sore wrist. 'Grades, friends, church, school, books.' Buried treasure, wife beating, paedophilia, I add to myself.

I can feel him relax a little. He takes a long pull of his beer. In the clear. But I haven't finished with him yet.

'And then, just as I was leaving, two cops walked into the office.' From the corner of my eye I watch Uncle Creepo turn a ghostly white. Your turn to squirm, you slimeball!

Aunt Serena tries to act all casual. 'What did they want? Was there a break-in or something?'

'I don't know, but as I was walking out the door, I heard one of them say to Father Kelliher, "Is that her?"'

Aunt Serena gasps.

'Go to your room!' snaps Creepo.

Even though I've stabbed the beast and am in mortal danger of it lurching in retaliation, I have to twist the knife a bit further. 'Geez, do you think it was something to do with my story?'

'I SAID GO TO YOUR ROOM!' He bangs the table and the cutlery leaps into the air. His fork does a triple somersault. I desperately want it to spear the back of his hand, pinning him to the table. But life's not like that. Not fair. It just clinks harmlessly to the floor.

I practically skip over to the stairs and run all the way up. Then I tiptoe back down again.

'What are we going to do?'

Here we go. Game on.

'Shut up, woman! I have to think.'

There's a lengthy silence.

'I told you she was a loose end,' he says. 'I wished I'd had the guts to do it before.'

'Can you remember where you buried them?'

'Ssshhh!' hisses Creepo.

Yes. He's going to move the bags. I've done it.

I slip out to the garage and crawl into the back of Serena's car. Creepo wouldn't take his car for this. Not his bloke bling. He'll take Serena's, just like last time.

I wedged myself down behind the driver's seat, in his blind spot. There's almost nothing of me and I could probably cram myself into one of the seatback pockets if I had to.

He'll be in there now telling Serena to keep an eye on me, but unless she goes up to my room for a little chat, which in her current state of mind I seriously doubt, I'll be okay. If she checks on me from the doorway she'll see my doona bulked up with blankets and spare pillows and assume it's me. Asleep.

It's uncomfortable in the back of Serena's car, and not just because it's cramped wedged down behind the front seat. It makes me think about that dream I had about that trip out to the forest with them. Them and their bags. And now I know that I wasn't supposed to come back. That it wasn't a dream.

*

Everything's been a bit of a blur since Mum hurt my father. Serena's taken me home and put fresh sheets and blankets on the spare bed and tucked me in, but she's been crying the entire time. And then she leaves but I can hear her downstairs talking on the phone.

Uncle Tony comes back about an hour later. I look out the window as he backs his flashy ute up the driveway and then I hear the garage door clunk open. Serena is down there with him and I watch through a split in the curtains as they lift two bags from the back of his ute and into Serena's boot.

Serena is still upset – I can see her wiping her eyes when they've finished. Uncle Tony hugs her and rubs her back. I can hear him saying something to comfort her but I can't make out what it is. He then gets back in his ute and drives off.

Serena comes back up to me. I pretend to be half asleep and she pats me on the leg and tells me that everything is going to be okay. I ask her where Uncle Tony went and she says that he's just going to the chemist because he has a bad headache.

She strokes my face until I fall alseep.

It feels as though I've just drifted off when Uncle Tony is standing over me with a mug in his hand.

'Drink this,' he says, offering me the mug.

'What is it?'

He smiles at me and says that it's hot chocolate.

I think I'm going to like living with them. My father never made me a hot chocolate in my life.

I sit back and sip the hot chocolate. When I've finished I want to go back to sleep but I feel him gather me up in his arms. I'm lying over his shoulder as he hobbles down the stairs. He carries me through to the garage and lies me gently on the back seat of Serena's car. I hear them get in the front but I'm too fuzzy to open my eyes.

'She's cold,' says Serena, her voice breaking. 'She's only wearing a nightie.'

'She won't be cold for long,' he says.

'That's right,' I slur. 'You gave me a hot chocolate and I'm all warm inside.'

'Good girl,' says Uncle Tony, and I know I'm going to like living with him, even though Serena is blubbing again.

'And she's not wearing any shoes,' sobs Serena.

'Relax will ya!' snaps Uncle Tony. 'I'll carry her.'

He's so nice.

I don't remember much after that because everything was just a blur. I sort of remember them dragging the bags away from the car and then it all went quiet for a while. And the next thing I know he's carrying me through the forest and he stands me in front of a hole that he's dug and I know that this is where I'm going to be sleeping tonight. But my nightie's all white and it'll get muddy.

I turn around to tell him this but now he's crying too.

'Don't look at me,' he pleads.

And then Serena comes clattering through the trail.

'No, Tony. Not like this.'

'Shut up! We have to.'

'We can't,' she says.

'I told you to stay in the car.'

'Please,' I say.

'Turn around!' he snaps.

I do as I'm told. He puts something against the back of my head. It feels cold.

'Tony.'

And then he's on the ground crying. I turn around and pat him on the back like you're supposed to do when someone's upset.

He doesn't carry me back to the car, they're too busy holding each other up. The mud oozes betweeen my toes. It tickles but it feels quite nice. Cold but nice. I can't keep up with them because my head's still all fuzzy but they wait for me by the car. I climb in the back and lie down across the seat. He gets an old blanket out of the boot and throws it on top of me. I'm soon drifting off.

'I just couldn't,' I hear him say.

'Of course you couldn't,' says Serena. 'You're a good man.'

'She's a loose end,' he says. 'But she won't remember. I gave her enough to put out a horse.'

When we get home he carries me into the bathroom and washes my feet. Well, *she* does. After that she puts me to bed. She tenderly strokes my face while I drift off.

'It was just a dream,' she says. 'It was all just a terrible dream.'

*

I look at the garage door. The one that leads into the kitchen. But he's not coming. Of course he's not coming. It's not our cash out there in the forest. It's not mum's jewellery or buried treasure. How could I have been so stupid? God knows what he drugged me with.

I climb out of the car, open the cupboard door and there it is. My lime-green backpack and matching sleeping bag.

I slip it on and hit the switch that operates the garage door. It slowly clunks open. I could have slipped quietly out the back door and disappeared. But I want him to know that I've gone. I want him to know that I know. I want him to feel the butterflies squirming all over each other in his stomach.

As the door is clunking open, I take out my diary and rip out a page and leave him a note on the boot of Serena's car.

I walk out of the garage and slip away into the night.

CAFÉ

WHERE DID YOU GO?

Nowhere. I just ran for ages. Must have been about half an hour. Maybe more. You know that dream where you're being chased by a monster and you scream but you don't wake up? I have that dream all the time now. He couldn't chase me. He was born with one leg slightly shorter than the other. Or slightly longer, I suppose. Anyway, you know what I mean. I didn't even know where I was or where I was going, but I ended up in this park, slumped on one of the swings. Trying to catch my breath. Trying to think. What to do. Where to go. It was getting late by then. I suppose my master plan had been to get the money, catch a train to the airport and just go. To Europe. To see my parents.

Did you have a passport?

No. Not on me, anyway. I didn't say it was a great plan. Though I did have a passport because we were supposed to go on a holiday to the old country before . . . well, you know.

But life took a different turn after that. Creepo hid all our documents away somewhere. Probably in his safe.

Okay, so you got away.

I ended up in the park. And as I was sitting there, thinking, I saw Creepo's car turn into the street – not the paddock basher that my parents were in, the one he made Serena drive, but his good car, his four-wheel-drive ute, his pride and joy: the beast. He cruised slowly down towards me, scoping the park. The car stopped and the window slid down and he looked over. He was staring straight at me. And as he was staring at me I started to feel light-headed because I'd stopped breathing. But the glow from the streetlights didn't quite reach the play equipment. Not much anyway. There was also no moon. So something was going for me. So there I was, sitting on the swing and he was looking right at me and my heart was thumping so hard I thought that he had to hear it.

How close was he?

About thirty metres, I'd say.

Why didn't you hide?

I was hiding. I just wasn't hiding behind anything. A couple of months before we were doing poetry in class. One of the boys did this one about the war. The nobility of battle, sacrificing one's life that others might live, King and country and all that bull; pick your cliché. After he'd finished, the teacher, who was a casual because Miss Feathershaw was away stoned or shopping or something for the day, told us some stuff about World War I. Talked about the trenches and mustard gas and duckboards and bombs called whizz-bangs. And he said that at night, in no-man's-land – that was the bit of land between the German and our guys' trenches –

I know about no-man's-land.

Well, anyway, he said that at night, when snipers and stretcher bearers and sappers were out in no-man's-land

and an exploding shell lit up the sky, rather than duck for cover or crouch down, the soldiers used to just stand still so they looked like a rock or a tree. I figured that there wasn't much light reaching me from the street, so all I had to do was stay still and he wouldn't be able to see me.

Not a lot of swings in no-man's-land, I imagine.

Same thing though.

Did it work?

Am I here?

Okay.

I don't know why he picked that park. Maybe he'd scoped all the parks in the area, figuring that I had nowhere else to go. No other relatives. No friends. Not close ones anyway. He was looking straight at me but he couldn't see me. Eventually the window slid back up and he slimed away, and my heart stopped bouncing up and down like a basketball. And all the time I was thinking, *my parents are dead, my parents are dead*. And I couldn't even remember what they looked like.

But as I was thinking about my parents and not being able to escape to Europe to see them, I knew that I couldn't stay in the park. Friday night and all that. Gotta be some homeboys turning up eventually with a bottle of something cheap and a bunch of bad news for any girl who happens to be around.

Why didn't you just go to the police? I don't really understand.

I did. Stop interrupting.

Sorry.

As I was sitting there on the swing it was getting colder and colder and my wrist really started to hurt. I pulled up my sleeve and although it didn't feel swollen, when I pressed my fingers against it, a jolt of pain shot through my whole body. After he left, I picked up my backpack and started walking. But my wrist was hurting so much that I had to

stop. I took my spare jumper out of my backpack and made
a sort of sling. It felt better not having to carry it by my side
but it still hurt like hell and I knew it would be hard to run if I
saw Creepo's car again. This might sound weird but I actually
started heading towards home. To their place. I wasn't going
there, obviously, but there was a cop shop in [deleted from
transcript] Street. Problem was, I didn't know how to get there
from where I was without getting pretty close to their place.

It took about forty minutes to walk there and the only
thing open as far as I could see was the chemist. I wanted to
go in and get a proper sling and maybe some painkillers, but
I didn't have any money. Not much, anyway. I doubt that a
chemist would go to uni for all those years and then stay open
all night just so that he could give stuff away.

The cop shop was open of course. Always plenty of
business in this area. The chemist, the cop shop, and Maccas
a bit further down the road. Maybe they fed off each other.
I'd heard that the cops get cheap food if they go into Maccas
wearing their uniform. Maybe the chemist gave the same
deal.

Creepo's car was outside the cop shop. I didn't notice it
at first because it was parked behind a police van, but when
I caught sight of it I threw myself up against the wall and
into the shadows. He was probably inside reporting me as a
runaway, in which case they'd hand me straight back to him
no matter what I said, and from there it would have been be a
quick trip back out to the forest. He once told me that a couple
of his friends were coppers, so the other possibility was that
they'd tear up any statement I made, call him over and from
there it would be a quick trip back out to the forest. Either
way I was dead.

What did you do?

I went to church.

God Sux

FATHER KELLIHER IS ONE OF THOSE PRIESTS WHO RECKON GOD'S HOUSE should always be open. I remember him saying that once and I kind of locked it away in my mind. Now that I'm a runaway I just hope he was telling the truth and not talking in that obscure symbolic way that religious people do – I still don't know if Mohammed's people had that mountain dismantled and carted down to him.

As I wait in the shadows in the police station car park for Creepo to emerge and either go home or shoot me, it starts raining. Thank you, God. A gentle pitter patter that built to a heavy blatter before culminating in a deafening onslaught as a close approximation of Armageddon swept in from the south. I'm not big on the whole doomsday thing, but if four skeletons on horseback had gone galloping and sloshing down the street at that moment I wouldn't have been a bit surprised.

I scurry into the doorway of a closed Chinese restaurant but the rain just bounces off the ground. It's literally raining upwards. I'm desperately trying to think of somewhere that would be warm and dry and open. Then the image of the church flashes through my mind. A miracle? A sign from God? A stored memory? I couldn't care less. It was somewhere to go. Twenty minutes later the outside foyer of the church is providing some shelter, but I would give anything to be inside. Warm and safe. Dry. Asleep. Even Creepo wouldn't shoot me on consecrated ground. At least I don't think he would.

I push against the huge oak doors of the church, which must weigh about a tonne each. They don't budge a millimetre as my feet slide backwards away from them.

I try again by positioning my feet and shoving against the doors with my shoulder. They give a little bit but as soon as I stop shoving and try to slide in, they clunk back against the frame. God's house may always be open, but He doesn't make it easy to get in. Maybe there's a metaphor in there somewhere. Or maybe the hinges need oiling.

Then it dawns on me that I'm being mind-meltingly dumb again. I don't need to open both doors. It's not as if I've turned up with the Israelites fleeing their homeland. It's just me, my backpack and my rolled-up sleeping bag. Living with Uncle Creepo and Aunt 'don't act too smart' Serena has obviously had an impact.

I reposition my feet against one door and push with everything I've got, which isn't much. It gives just enough for me to slide my backpack and my sleeping bag in with my foot and, heaving against it again, I manage to slip in after them. The door clunks satisfyingly shut and the church folds itself around me. I feel safe. I feel loved. I feel protected. And although I realise that this is all probably taking place in my head, it still feels good.

I thank God for Father Kelliher. He keeps the big house open even though a couple of vandals got in last year and graffitied 'God Sux' on the wall behind the altar. They were probably looking for something to steal, but they were out of luck. God's house might have been open, but the silverware had been locked away. It happened on a Saturday night, but the next morning in mass, rather than covering up the image with some paint or a shroud, Father Kelliher preached on declining societal values and the availability of spray paint.

Now that I'm safe inside, I realise just how wet I am. I'm leaving pools of water on the ground.

Fortunately the church is newish, or at least it is by church standards. Not only does it have a crying room but it also has toilets. His and hers. I always found it a bit odd that the men's toilet has a top hat and a monocle on the door, while the women's has a picture of some bimbo's big hair from the 1980s. You would have thought that in church they might go for a picture of Moses and Mary or something. Is that being sacrilegious? Or are they trying to convince us lowly parishioners that mega-holy people don't go to the toilet? The first time I thought of it was during a school mass. My shoulders were convulsing so much as I imagined Moses ducking behind a tree for a wee and accidentally dousing the burning bush that Miss Feathershaw told me off when we got back to class.

I strip off in the toilets and swivel the nozzle on the hand dryer around so I can dry off. I love the hot air blasting against my skin. I feel a little self-conscious about being naked in church but I'm not technically in the church yet and won't be until I go through the inner doors and into God's house proper.

After I've hung my wet clothes over the shower rail and changed into my tracksuit and spare jumper, I make my way through the inner doors and into the church itself.

Even though I don't think He's there any more, I dip my fingers in the holy water and make the sign of the cross. Some things are just automatic, I guess. Besides, Father Kelliher thinks He's there and he's the one who's left the doors open (though he could probably put in a couple of lighter ones to make getting in a bit easier). So even if my sign of the cross wasn't automatic, I would still have done it out of respect for Father Kelliher.

Apart from the dim glow given off by battery-operated perpetual candles flickering away in the far corner, the church is completely dark. I walk down the aisle and slip into the second pew from the front.

I unpack my sleeping bag from its carrier and yawn like a hippo. I've never been this exhausted in my life.

It's cold in the church. Colder than I thought it would be. I put on an extra pair of socks and wriggle into my sleeping bag. In the rush of running all the way up here, of finding the church open, of getting inside, of getting dry, I'd forgotten all about my wrist. It comes back to me now as I try to zip up my sleeping bag. It's so sore that I can't do it. I have to improvise by pushing my feet against the bottom of the bag and then zipping it up with my good hand, then I practically have to dislocate my shoulder to get that arm back inside.

When I'm settled in I say a little prayer for my parents, though I don't even know why. Is anyone there? Is anyone listening? People pray for their sick children. Whole congregations and communities do. They die anyway.

After my prayer I wiggle down deeper into my sleeping bag, like a caterpillar into its cocoon. I thought the pew would be rock hard but I'm surprisingly comfortable. Surprisingly warm. Safe.

My eyelids are getting heavy but I try to stay awake a little longer. To think. To plan. To keep an eye out, to keep an ear out. For cars. For Creepo. Thank God all I hear out on the road are full Dopplers.

When I sleep, I sleep like the dead. Meanwhile, out in the forest, the dead roam the night.

ACT TWO

AFTER

Live as if you were to die tomorrow.
Learn as if you were going to live for ever.

— MAHATMA GANDHI

CAFÉ

Despite everything that happened, it still must have come as a shock when you realised that your parents were dead.

Not really. I sort of knew. In the back of my mind, at least. I mean, they had to be. I'd been told that they'd gone back to live in Europe. The old country. But no phone call? No letters? Emails? Not even a postcard? I knew something wasn't right. Apart from that, the last time I saw my father he was lying in his own blood. No one could have survived that. And Mum had done it to him. She couldn't have survived that. Not once Creepo found out. I mean, she could have escaped if she acted fast enough. I know that my father called Creepo when Mum had stabbed him, but he couldn't talk because the knife must have gone through his voice box. Creepo would have seen that the call was from my father, heard his gargling, his strangling, his death, and even he, as dumb as he is, must have guessed that there was some serious shit going down. Still, she had time. It would have been half an hour tops before Creepo and Aunt Serena turned up with guns and disinfectant.

Mum could have phoned the police, packed a couple of bags for us and bolted. Gone to a women's refuge or something. Even overseas. To the old country.

So why do you think she stayed? She must have known what your Uncle Tony would do.

Catholic guilt, I suppose. She wasn't that into the whole God thing, but when you're born into it, it kind of hovers over you for life. I mean, they make us do reconciliation, confession, when we're what, seven, eight years old? What mortal sin can you have on your soul when you're seven? You threw your brother's Lego block out the window of the car on the way to the beach? Cast that child into the pits of eternal damnation unless he repents. So you walk around feeling guilty for the rest of your life. God! No wonder we're so uptight. Catholics, I mean.

Did you have a plan?

Not at first. I just wanted to survive. When I woke up the next morning I was starving, and my wrist hurt like hell. I could have waited until mass started and then queued up for Holy Communion a couple of hundred times. Filled up on wafers. Stuffed myself full of God. But it was early Saturday morning, so God wouldn't be open for business until later on in the evening.

So what did you do?

I decided to evolve.

Darwin Sux

THERE'S THIS WORM IN AFRICA. OR MAYBE IT'S CENTRAL AMERICA or Bangladesh. No, I'm pretty sure it's Africa. And this worm survives by eating little kids' eyes from the inside out. And then when the kid's blind it just packs up and leaves. This worm doesn't serve any purpose. It doesn't compose symphonies, it's not trying to find a cure for cancer or come up with a workable solution to global warming. It's only reason for existing is so that it can eat little kids' eyes. There's no way a loving and caring God would have created something like that. Only evolution could throw up such an abomination. Darwin sucks.

Yet there are people who try to rationalise stuff like this eye-eating worm. Satan created it. Or God moves in mysterious ways. He has a plan. He's displeased. He's trying to test our faith. As if fifty million people dying in World War II wasn't enough to test our faith, he's up there sitting on his cloud, stroking his beard and thinking, 'Hmmnnn, I think I need to test their faith a bit more. An eye-eating worm ought to do it.' And why aren't there any dinosaurs in the Bible? Seems rather a big thing to have missed. Or maybe the dinosaurs weren't real at all and God just buried their skeletons in the ground to confuse us. What? The eye-eating worm not enough? The fifty million dead. The gas chambers. The shoes piled up outside the gas chambers. If there is a loving God, how could he keep out of that one?

So despite spending the night under His protective umbrella, I wake up thinking about this worm that eats little kids' eyes. Well, that and the noise of the cleaner out in the foyer. By the sound of her vacuum cleaner going back and forth across the carpet and then clattering over the tiles, she also moves in mysterious ways.

I check my watch. It's only seven-thirty in the morning. It occurs to me that the homeless don't get much of a lie in. They have to be up and gone before their hidey-hole, their sanctuary, is discovered. No rest for the wicked. But the cleaner is out in the foyer and hasn't come into the church itself yet, so I have a few moments to myself. I hit my mental snooze button.

As I'm lying there half-unconscious, I recall another story about evolution. This type of bird lived out on a remote island in the Atlantic Ocean and this bird's staple diet was eggs – lizard eggs, or the eggs of another bird, or whatever. And it survived by puncturing the shell with its beak and then slurping up the goo inside. Gross. During one particularly harsh year, the thing whose eggs it ate was missing something from its own diet. The missing thing wasn't enough to kill off the other animal but because of this missing dietary thing, the eggs that year were much harder than before. So hard, in fact, that the egg-goo slurping birds had heaps of trouble puncturing the shells with their beaks. But a few of them had really sharp beaks, so they didn't have any trouble at all. And the next year when the same conditions were repeated, it was only the birds with the sharp beaks that survived. Which left sharp-beaked birds to mate with other sharp-beaked birds and so every bird produced after that had a sharp beak to cater for the eggs that had become hard, and the blunt-beaked ones died out. So the theory of evolution is right there, proven in two generations of birds; and yet it's still called the *theory* of evolution. Go figure.

That's what I have to do to survive. I have to evolve. I have to become a sharp-beaked bird.

I ease the top half of my body out of my sleeping bag, trying to put as little weight on my damaged wrist as possible. I then reach into my backpack for one of humankind's greatest achievements – pen and paper.

I open my notebook to a fresh page but I'm forced to write with my right hand because my wrist is so sore. I press against the point where Creepo squeezed it and the pain almost makes me throw up, only I've got nothing in me to actually throw up. I think my wrist might be broken, and I know that I'll have to deal with it.

I suck on the end of my pen and then jot down my to-do list:

1. Get something to eat
2. Go to doctor's to get wrist fixed
3. Get some money
4. Find somewhere to sleep tonight
5. Develop bigger brain

In the end I decide not to go to Father Kelliher. I'd heard from other kids that you have to turn up at DOCS or the police station with a knife practically sticking out of your head if you want to be removed from your parents or guardians. And even then the parent/guardian could just as easily say that the child had done it themselves. Though just why a child would stick a knife in its own head is anyone's guess – to get away from the parent/guardian I suppose.

So even though I'm convinced that Father Kelliher is the one person who would go out of his way to help me, if the authorities can't find any trace of my parents (and there can't be much left of them after so many years decomposing out there in the forest) then they'll hand me straight back to Creepo and Serena. And then as I'm slowly decomposing and becoming part of the forest's ecosystem myself, all Creepo has to do is report me as a runaway and that would be that. So I'm going to the police, or Father Kelliher, or anyone else in authority, over my own dead body.

I wriggle the rest of the way out of my sleeping bag and pack it up one-handed. The cleaner has moved into Father Kelliher's change room (at least I've always assumed it was his change room. He can't arrive from the rectory already in his priestly robes) so I'm able to slip out of the church and into the bathroom without vac lady seeing me. I do some quick head maintenance (wash face, rub fingers over teeth, comb hair) with my unco right hand. I'm just about to leave when it occurs to me that I don't want to be lugging my sleeping bag around with me all day. I'll look like a runaway. Fortunately the bathroom has an old metal locker. Maybe it was installed in preparation for the day there'd be female priests. Ha! Fat chance. I open the locker, which is mercifully empty of the non-existent female priest's stuff, and wedge in my sleeping bag. My saturated clothes from last night's deluge aren't dry enough to wear yet so I drag them off the railing and stuff them in the locker with my sleeping bag and clank the door shut.

I'm wondering where on earth I'm going to sleep tonight when there is a gentle tap on the bathroom door.

'Is anybody in there?'

My heart thumps violently against my chest. Why had I messed around? Do I subconsciously want to be caught? I really don't know. That's why it's called a subconscious, I suppose.

I think about wedging myself into the locker – I'd certainly fit – but she'd hear the rattle of bone on metal or metal on metal as I clanked the door closed behind me.

'Hello,' she says again, but this time she knocks a little harder. 'Is anybody there?'

'Just a sec.' I decide to be honest and slowly, reluctantly open the door, hoping that vac lady will be so overcome with maternal love at the sight of my utter patheticness that she'll reach into her wallet and hand me a fifty to tide me over for a while.

She looks me up and down as if she's examining a stain on a priest's bedsheet. 'Who are you? And what are you doing here?' She's quite terse. Not at all maternal. Not in the least bit Christiany. She's certainly not about to go for that fifty. Fortunately she's attached to the church rather than the school and although I'd seen her pottering and doddering around before, she hasn't got a clue who I am.

She folds her arms and glares at me. 'Well? What are you up to?'

'I'm cleaning my teeth.'

'Why?'

'Because it's morning and they need cleaning. Only I haven't got my toothbrush . . .'

'But why are you cleaning them here?'

I hit her with my best mournful look. I try to think like a puppy. I go all wide-eyed.

'Because I'm homeless and I haven't got anywhere else to go.'

'Well, you can't stay here.'

I drop the puppy look. 'I thought this was a church and it's supposed to look after the poor.'

'That's nothing to do with me.' She turns on her heels. 'You wait there while I phone the police.'

As if anyone would ever do that.

'Bitch!' I shout after her.

I quickly grab my sleeping bag and damp clothes from the locker and race outside. Luckily she's latched the door open, so I don't have to haul it open myself.

The sun is so bright it hurts my eyes. I pause for a moment and struggle to heave my backpack onto my shoulder, blinking at the day and what it might have in store for me.

I don't have long to linger because the vigilante vac lady is soon hot on my heels.

'The police are on their way. You'd better wait there.'

'Why don't you blow it out your bum, you old bag?'

'Well, I never . . .'

'Maybe you should. Might stop you from being so uptight.'

I tuck my sleeping bag under my arm like a rugby ball and race off. And with that, I'm officially on the run.

My Paraguayan Aunt

FOR A SATURDAY MORNING THE MEDICAL CENTRE IS PRETTY QUIET. I suppose it's a bit too early for sporting injuries to have happened and anyone involved in a Friday night brawl will be at home sleeping it off or else slumped in the hospital's casualty department.

On the walk from the church, I used most of the few dollars I had to buy a couple of buns, then took the back streets to avoid Creepo and vac lady's riot squad. As I walked, I came up with a cunning plan to get in to see a doctor despite not having a parent or guardian with me or any money or even a Medicare card. The plan was that my mother, who would be mentally deranged for the exercise, had sent me along to register and queue up, while she did a bit of shopping for mad women's things. I didn't quite know how, but I intended to make the receptionist scared of my mother so that when she didn't show, the receptionist would be relieved and let me in to see the doctor out of pity. My name should still be on file from when I had the flu a couple of times, and a bout of tonsilitis a few years back. At some point while

I was waiting I was going to take a call on my non-existent mobile. The caller would sadly inform me that my mother, my poor widowed demented mother, had had a complete mental breakdown in the muesli bar aisle and been carted off kicking and screaming to a psychiatric hospital. My tears of anguish would be brushed away by the kind-hearted receptionist who would break medical centre protocol and allow me in to see the doctor. As it happened, when I went up to the reception desk, all she did was ask me my name and whether or not I'd been there before, and that was that.

So now I'm sitting in the waiting room silently breaking off bits of bun in my backpack and stuffing them into my mouth when the receptionist's not looking. Not that she would give a rat's anyway.

After a short wait I'm in with the doctor, the smell of disinfectant making my mostly empty stomach lurch and growl.

Dr Chen is a young, pretty, locally born Chinese woman and I'm a little jealous of her. Actually, I'm a lot jealous of her. I want her life. Though if I had her life, was a qualified doctor and everything, I wouldn't be working in a crappy little medical centre in a suburban shopping centre, looking after snotnose kids and flatulent grannies. I'd be a volunteer for Médecins Sans Frontières in Africa, trying to find a vaccine for that disgusting eye-eating worm. Still, I shouldn't be too hard on her. She only looks about fifteen and maybe she has uni fees to pay back to her parents and stuff before she's allowed to go out and be a real doctor and do worthwhile work.

She goes through her admin procedure, asking me my name and date of birth and everything, although it's obviously written in front of her. She's just ticking off my answers in her head, making sure that I am who I say I am. Seriously, though, who else would want to be me?

When that's over she asks me what I've done to myself. She seems so sweet and innocent, the way she puts it.

I tell her about my arm and point to where it hurts the most.

She examines it, but even though her touch is very gentle it still makes me flinch.

'That *is* sore, isn't it? You poor thing.'

My eyes are all watery now. Not because of the pain, which is bad enough, but because of her kindness. Her sweetness. I want her to take me home and look after me but of course that's never going to happen. Not in this life. A droplet of misery dribbles down my cheek. I'm falling in a pathetic heap and I've only been homeless for about twelve hours. I'll need to toughen up if I'm going to survive.

'How did it happen?'

My mind goes into meltdown. I'd been so caught up with cunning plans for getting past the receptionist, that it hadn't occurred to me that I might have to explain my injury to someone. An educated someone at that.

'I fell over.' Oh duh! I'll be using Mum's old trick next and saying that I've been walking into doors.

'This looks more like you've been hit by something. Or someone.'

'I hit something when I fell.'

'What did you hit?'

'A brick.'

'A brick?'

'That's right. I fell down the back steps and hit the ones at the bottom. They're made of bricks. The back steps, I mean. The front steps are too. But I didn't fall down them.' Shut up, will you!

'But you must have landed like this for the brick to have hurt you there.' She twists her own arm at an awkward angle and shows me the position she means. She's good all right. Smart. She should be working on the eye-eating worm vaccine, not listening to *my* bullshit.

'I can't remember, I was, er, drunk.'

'Drunk? You're only thirteen years old.' She pauses and then readjusts her attitude to deal with the modern teen. 'Do you really drink?'

'Not drunk. I meant asleep. I was sleepwalking.'

I can tell that she doesn't believe a word I'm saying, and frankly I don't blame her. Less bullshit comes out of an average cattle station in a whole year than what's sprouted from my mouth in the last five minutes.

She starts jotting something down on a pad. 'You'll need to have an X-ray.'

'Can't you do it here?'

'We don't have X-ray facilities. There's a radiologist centre across the road. Is your mother or father with you? They'll just need your Medicare card.'

And now I'm officially stuffed. Unless . . . unless I can run with the story I hatched to hoodwink the receptionist.

So I take a deep breath and launch my twisted tale of woe. About my widowed mother going bonkers and being spirited away by the men in white coats and how in my confusion and loneliness I'd got into her liquor cabinet and chugged down half a bottle of vodka and had fallen down the steps (back steps, not front) and hurt my arm, which is why I was too embarrassed to tell her the truth. But everything is going to be all right now because my aunt is on her way from Paraguay (I particularly like this bit. I mean, who would invent a relative from Paraguay?) to take care of me and make sure that I don't get into the liquor cabinet again. I should have left it there, I suppose, but I keep going, banging on about how I want to be a doctor too and how much I admire her and how I want to volunteer for Médecins Sans Frontières and come up with a cure or a vaccine for that eye-eating African worm. I'm practically hyperventilating when I finish.

I suppose I was hurling so much crap at her that she couldn't deflect it all. In the end she phones the X-ray place across the road and gives them a brief breakdown of my tragic circumstances, leaving out certain details like my future volunteer work and my Paraguayan aunt. She then reads out my Medicare number from the file and that is that.

I saunter over the road, wait for about half an hour – the first of the Saturday morning sporting injuries are turning up by this point – have my X-ray taken and I'm back at the medical centre before lunch – though just what I'm going to do for lunch, short of scrounging around the food court bins, is anyone's guess.

Dr Chen removes my X-rays from the envelope and sticks then up against the backlit screen.

'Mmnn,' she says. 'It's fractured all right.' She points to the painful bit on the X-ray and I nod, though I can't really tell which bit is fractured, apart from the pain of course. That's a bit of a giveaway. 'It's quite a nasty one too.'

I shake my head. 'Bloody steps.'

'Actually, it looks more like a compression fracture. As if you've had something heavy pressing down on your wrist. How are things at home?'

I gulp. She's fishing. I've got to get out of here before she calls the police too.

'I told you.'

She makes that 'mmnn' sound again. She doesn't believe me. I don't blame her.

'I'm going to have to put your forearm and hand in a cast. Are you left- or right-handed?'

'Left.'

'Well then, you'll just have to get by as best you can until your aunt arrives from Paraguay.' She actually smiles when she says that.

'My aunt *is* coming from Paraguay,' I mumble. 'It's one of the two landlocked countries of South America.'

'Hmmm?' says Dr Chen as she gets organised.

'The other is Bolivia.' I wish that I would shut up.

'What colour do you want?'

I ignore my own rambling and consider the options. I feel like being girlie and choosing pink. But in the end I go all emo, letting my hair fall down over my right eye. 'Black, please.'

She soaks the bandage in some water and starts unravelling it around my wrist. The water is very warm and it feels lovely as she unfolds the black bandage up and down my arm and my hand. When she's finished she tells me to wait while the cast sets. With the sun streaming in through the window, I could happily crawl up on the examination table and fall asleep. I feel safe here with Dr Chen. Or at least I do until she drops her bombshell.

'I was worried about you,' she says as she's washing the flecks of gunk off her hands and arms. 'So while you were over the road getting your X-ray I phoned your parents.'

I can feel the blood slowly draining out of my head. 'My parents?' I gulp and then come clean. 'My parents are dead.'

'Not according to them they're not. Their contact details were in your file.'

What has she done?

'Your mother isn't in a psychiatric unit. She sounds rather lovely in fact.'

'She's not my mother, she's my . . .' I trail off. I've painted myself into a bit of a corner here. I can't even keep track of all my lies. Maybe it's time to try the truth. 'She's my aunt.'

'From Paraguay? She didn't have much of a Spanish accent.' Dr Chen chuckles at her own joke.

'You don't understand.'

'I understand you've got a very active imagination. That's what your mum said. Told me not to believe a word you said.'

'Dr Chen. I need to tell you the truth.' Well, bits of it anyway.

Our conversation is interrupted by a knock on the door.

'Dr Chen,' calls the receptionist. 'Her parents are here.'

The door swings open and there's Aunt Serena and Creepo. Aunt Serena looks worried but Creepo just smiles, like a python at a cornered rat.

Freedom Vomit

My buns from the bakery tasted much better going in than they do coming out. Dr Chen quickly grabs a container and shoves it under my mouth. The smell makes me throw up even more, although there can't be anything much left in me.

'Could you wait in the reception area, please?'

'But we –' begins Creepo but Dr Chen cuts him off.

'Reception please! Can't you see that she's sick?'

'We're her parents,' complains Creepo as Dr Chen ushers them both outside and locks the door behind them.

I'm about to say that they're not my parents but Dr Chen seems to have a handle on it. I don't know how but she seems to have sussed things out. Why else would she lock the door? Maybe they teach this sort of stuff at uni.

Although Creepo has probably got his gun tucked down the back of his pants – he so wants to be a real gangster – he obeys Dr Chen's command. Maybe he respects her as a figure of authority. Maybe he's worried that she'll call security or the cops. Either way, I can hear them mumbling as they head back down the corridor to the reception area.

I spit bile into the container as Dr Chen tenderly rubs my back. It's been a while since someone comforted me like that.

When I've finished, Dr Chen wipes my mouth with a tissue. Then she smiles at me.

'You need to tell me what's going on, otherwise I can't help you.'

I look at her. I want to tell her everything.

'Those people aren't your parents, are they?'

'No.'

'Then who are they?'

'My aunt and uncle.'

'From Paraguay?'

'No one's from Paraguay. Except maybe Paraguayans,' I add, just to clarify things.

She smiles, even though I didn't mean it as a joke.

'Where are you parents?'

'They've gone back to live in Europe. It's a long story.'

'Hmmnn. I'm going to ask you a question now and I need you to tell me the truth. Okay?'

I nod, sensing what's coming.

'Are you being abused?'

I pause. That's the thing. I'm not being abused. Yet. I got out before it started. 'Not abused. But he was doing stuff. Getting ready. We saw a DVD about it at school.'

'Grooming? That's all I need to know.'

She picks up her phone. 'And your arm? Did he do that?'

I'm sick of lying. I'm sick of hiding. I've been homeless, on the run, for less than a day and I hate it already.

'Did he do that to your arm?'

'Yes.'

'There are people who can help you.'

She's finished dialling her number, but I haven't got any proof. Creepo will convince everyone that I'm lying and I'll be handed back. Let's face it, even Dr Chen knows that I'm a complete liar. If the police ask her she'll tell the truth – I'm a bare-faced liar.

I reach over and hang up Dr Chen's phone.

'What are you doing? I need to report . . .'

'If you do, I'm dead.'

'You'll be protected from him.'

'Yeah? For how long? You don't know what he's like. What he's capable of. Are the police going to guard me twenty-four seven?'

'No, but . . .'

'Then you've got to let me go. I can take care of myself.'

Dr Chen shakes her head. 'I can't do that. I have a legal obligation. It's called mandatory reporting. I could lose my job.'

'I could lose my life.'

We stare at each other.

'How did you know?' I ask.

'What?'

'How did you know that they weren't my parents?'

'I didn't. But I knew something was seriously wrong.'

'How?'

'Well, the sleeping bag is a bit of a giveaway, for a start.'

I stare down at my sleeping bag, which is tucked into its pink carry bag and sitting next to my lime-green backpack. Oh duh!

'And then when the door opened and you saw who was standing there, the look of terror in your eyes was not something you could fake. And then, you vomited, so . . .'

'Sorry about that.'

'Don't be silly. I'm a doctor.'

'You really have to report me?'

'I don't have a choice.'

'Is there a back way out of here?'

'There's a fire escape.'

'Let me escape down that and then you can still make your report and keep your job. You could just say that I ran off.'

'I can't do that.'

'What if I didn't give you a choice?'

'And how are you going to do that?'

'Easy.' I reach across her and pick up a scalpel from a round canister of scalpels on her desk. 'If you don't let me go, I'll stab you with this.'

She looks down at my scalpel and smiles. 'That's a paddle-pop stick.'

'Can we pretend that it's a scalpel?'

'You're that worried?'

'If you hand me over to the authorities, they'll hand me back to him and I'm dead.'

'No they won't.'

'Can you guarantee me, one hundred per cent, that they won't hand me back? That he'll never get to see me again?'

She pauses for a moment and that's enough. 'Well no, I can't.'

I'm up, scooping up my backpack and sleeping bag and racing for the door.

'Wait!' she says.

Something makes me turn back to her. 'You can't stop me. Not now.'

'I can't believe I'm saying this. I'll give you twenty minutes but then I'm calling the police.'

'Thank you, Dr Chen.'

'And here –' she jots something down on a card. 'This is my mobile number. I want you to promise to call me as soon as you can. I'll be worried sick until you do. Deal?'

I nod but it's not enough. I want to hug her and kiss her and tell her that she's the best person in the world, but I don't have any practice in that kind of thing. 'Thank you.'

I slip out into the corridor. You can see the reception desk from the corridor but not the reception area, which is around the corner. I follow the green 'Emergency Exit' signs to the fire escape door. I slowly turn the handle and push, expecting that it'll either be locked or alarmed. It's neither. Something is going for me. Even though I'm on tiptoe I can still hear the echo of my steps clattering back up the stairs to the medical centre, to Creepo and his gun. Amazingly I make it to the bottom of the stairs in one piece. I'm outside. I'm free. I'm gone. Racing down the hill to the train station.

I check my watch as the train pulls into the station. I check my pulse. It's racing. By the time Dr Chen is calling the police, I'm heading north.

CAFÉ

THAT WAS A CLOSE CALL.

Tell me about it. Too close. It was my first full day on the run and already I had vac lady and Dr Chen calling the police on me. I knew that if I was going to survive, I had to drop out of sight. But you need money to disappear and I hardly had any. A couple of dollars, if that. I had about two hundred dollars stuffed into a piggybank in my room, but I was so sure that I'd get my hands on Creepo's buried treasure that I didn't even think to take it with me.

I had to get away to think. You can't think if you're just trying to survive, jumping at shadows. So I got out of the city and headed north.

Did you keep your promise and phone Dr Chen?

Yeah. But it wasn't until a couple of days later. That was the first chance I had to get to a phone. And even then, when I phoned I sort of hoped that my call would go through to voicemail, but she answered it.

Did she call the police?

Well, she had to, didn't she? What's that thing called?

Mandatory reporting. It's the same for teachers.

That's partly the reason I called her. To warn her about Creepo. I said that if she had to work late, make sure that a security guard walked her to her car.

Why would he want to hurt her?

Because she reported him. About my arm. About his grooming me.

Of course. Sorry. Do you think she was okay?

I know she was. She told me that he came up to the medical centre the following day and threatened her. But he did it in the reception area in front of about twenty witnesses, because no way was she going into a consulting room with him. And so, get this, she slaps a restraining order on him. He's not permitted to go within two hundred metres of her. He can't even go to the shops any more. Not that he did much shopping anyway, but still. Creepo finally met a woman who stood up to him. She didn't go to uni for all those years to put up with his crap.

Didn't the police pursue the matter? With you, I mean?

What's to pursue? I was just a runaway as far as they're concerned. Dr Chen says that Uncle Creepo broke my arm and that he's grooming me, he denies it and says that I fell over. A report is filed, no one can prove anything. I'm on the missing persons database. Keep a look out for a thirteen-year-old girl, etc etc. I'll doubtless end up a street kid. Drugs, prostitution, dead before I'm fifteen. Another sad statistic. End of story.

But you didn't end up like that. A statistic.

That's right. I had brains. I had plans. I had a to-do list.

You headed north.

To my weekender.

Death Valley

AFTER ABOUT HALF AN HOUR THE TRAIN LEAVES THE SUBURBS BEHIND and we're snaking our way north. We weave through national parks, clackety-clack across old iron bridges before slipping down to the sea and following the contours along the coast.

When I arrived breathless and starving at the station earlier I had a simple choice. South to the city or north out of it. Although I suppose I am technically a street kid, there is no way I am going to let myself be chewed up and spat out by the red-light district and the leeches who lurk there. I know there are some nice parts to the city, some exciting parts, but whenever I went into town with Creepo and Serena, we always used to go to the dodgy parts for some reason, and they scared me. So it was north.

Now, with the remnants of my breakfast festering in Dr Chen's bin, I am just about ready to faint with hunger. I don't know how I'm going to get food. Or money. Could I fool anyone that I'm old enough for a job? I'm starting to panic at the thought, the bile rising up in my throat again. The only thing that matters right now, though, is getting through today. If I can take one step at a time to begin with, then maybe I can work towards getting my act together. No big picture stuff for now. Just get through each day. Each hour. Each minute. I need to get back to school, of course. Find a school that'll have me. I can't invent my eye-eating worm vaccine without an education. But that's big picture stuff and right now I need food.

I dig into my pockets and the dusty corners of my wallet hoping to find some forgotten notes. Nothing. I've got about three dollars in coins. That's it. I didn't plan this very well. Then again, Creepo was trying to blow my head off, so I didn't really have time to pass GO and collect the two hundred dollars from my piggybank.

Three dollars! Three *stupid* dollars. I don't even have a train ticket. If an inspector comes through, I'm gone.

This is good. Worrying about the inspector hurling me off at the next station has taken my mind off my growling stomach. Or it did until now.

If I can find a fish and chip shop I've got enough money for a few potato scallops. They're about eighty cents each and they usually throw in an extra one so you think you're getting a bonus and come back for more. I'm literally salivating at the thought of those hot, salty scallops. The crispy, crunchy heat of the deep-fried batter and the soft, juicy potato inside. I would seriously consider trading a kidney for one right now. Just one.

I look out the window at the trees and sand dunes and the ocean just beyond them. There should be plenty of fish and chip shops along the coast. This is where fish hang out, after all.

Now that we're well clear of the city, I decide to get out at the next stop, ticket inspector or not. Hunt down some scallops.

I pull out my notebook and look at my to-do list from earlier, crossing off my achievement(s):

1. Get something to eat
2. ~~Go to doctor's to get wrist fixed~~
3. Get some money
4. Find somewhere to sleep tonight
5. Develop bigger brain

Although I did get something to eat from the bakery earlier, I didn't keep it down for very long, so it doesn't really count.

Things aren't going very well. I have to get better at this. It's not so much a to-do list as a survival plan.

I'm trying to concentrate but there's a kid in the seat in front who keeps staring at me in that annoying way that bored kids do. Like you're supposed to entertain them or something. Play peekaboo for a few hours. The kid's mother has big, peroxide blonde hair and OMG floral leggings. The kid looks like one of those obnoxious little brats who could benefit from a clip around the ear. Not that I condone violence or anything, but still. He's definitely a snot eater, and probably not just his own. I know this because as he's staring at me he's got his finger wedged so far up his snout that he's in serious danger of digging out brain matter.

'Whad'cha do to your arm?'

'Leave the lady alone, Zac,' admonishes mother leggings.

Lady? Half a day on the streets and I've already hardened into an old lady.

He removes his finger and inspects the outcome. Nothing there, thankfully. I'm glad I didn't have to watch where it went if his fishing expedition proved fruitful.

He looks up and realises I've been looking disgusted at him. 'You're ugly.'

I lean forward. 'And you're the reason some animals eat their young.'

Snotface stares at me for a second and then scowls. 'Mum. She reckons you're gonna eat me.'

'Well, I will if you don't leave her alone.' Maybe old mother leggings has got a better handle on this parent/life thing than I gave her, or her fashion sense, credit for.

'Do you live on the train?' He obviously hasn't swallowed our cannibalism threat.

'No. Why would you think that?'

'Your dumb pink sleeping bag, stupid!' he says.

'Zac!'

'At least I don't eat snot.'

Then it dawns on me that snotface might be onto something. It's a real eureka moment. I could live on the trains. They travel all over the place. Some might even go all night; interstate or way out into the country. They might even have empty sleeper cabins. How cool would that be? And even the ones that don't go all night have to stop somewhere. In a yard or something. They mightn't have sleeper cabins or be all that warm once the heating's been turned off, but I've got my sleeping bag and spare jumpers to stop me from freezing to death. It'd be dry inside and safe once the guard had locked up for the night. Homeboys might come along and tag the outside, but they wouldn't be able to get in to tag me. They wouldn't know I was inside. I'd just have to keep quiet. It's definitely worth thinking about. I haven't got a clue where I'm going to sleep tonight. I can't go back to the church. It's Sunday tomorrow, God's big day in, so I definitely won't be welcome. The trains might be an option.

People start to stir as we approach the first of the towns dotted along the north coast. The whole region is just far enough from the city not to be commutable. On the weekend it's swollen by the masses exodusing the city for some peace and quiet, ignoring the obvious irony of the choked freeways, bursting hotels, bulging caravan parks and entangled fishing lines. By Sunday evening, when the hordes have dispersed, its pulse drops and it becomes once again the domain of retirees, committed layabouts and those who have ditched the frenetic pace of the city for a lifestyle that is just shy of a coma.

The train slows as we begin our approach to Death Valley. It's not really called Death Valley, of course. It's not even a valley. It's proper name is one of those made-up Mediterranean-sounding names like Bella Vista or Suburbia Sur Mer, as if the exotic name will make the place seem more interesting. It was nicknamed Death Valley when some journalist worked out that it had a higher death rate than Iraq or Afghanistan put together or something like that. It's not that there are suicide bombers wandering around, it's just that the average age of the residents is ninety-three or something. The Grim Reaper's got a timeshare condo up on the headland.

The stationmaster is checking and taking tickets. But he's doing it in such a half-arsed way that it's easy to sweep past him.

It's warm for this time of year. An off-shore breeze has pushed all trace of last night's storm out to sea. Cottonwool clouds dab gently at the sky, while the glint from the stainless steel tables outside the cafés practically pierces my eyes. A sneak peak at what looks like being a stormy and steamy summer. I take off my jumper and stuff it into my bulging backpack.

By the time I've walked down the street to the beachfront and dragged myself into the fish and chip shop, the lunch frenzy has passed, the shadows are lengthening, and with the wind from the south picking up, people are starting to pack up and head home.

The fish shop guy glances at my sleeping bag and then the cast on my arm. It's only quick but it's enough for him to sum me up. I'll have to do something about my sleeping bag. It's a bit obvious. Maybe I could get hold of a serious backpack to hide it in. Whack a couple of stickers on the outside and pretend that I'm a proper tourist from Sweden or Paraguay. I don't know what else I could do with it during the day. Maybe I could dig . . . I stop myself. A day on the run and I'm already burying stuff in holes like a hermit.

'Can I help you?'

As hungry as I am, it's still embarrassing. I mean, it's hardly worth the guy's effort to fire up the oil. But I've got to eat, otherwise I'll faint. And then it'll be a phone call, an ambulance, hospital, ID, Creepo, forest.

'How many scallops can I get for three dollars?'

The guy looks at me and then looks at my sleeping bag again. But he doesn't scowl. He has a pleasant face, though by the looks of his skin, he's spent a bit too much time standing over boiling oil.

'How many would you like?'

'I'd like four.' I look up at the price board. Just as I thought, they're eighty cents each. 'But I don't have three twenty.'

'I think we can stretch to four.' He gives me another smile and I kind of grin back but only half-heartedly. He's only giving me twenty cents after all and now that I'm on my own I can't go around smiling at strange men. If he'd thrown in a whole lobster and a bucket of chips then he might have got a smile.

Between the smell of the hot oil and the general oppressive heat of the shop I can actually feel my eyes starting to roll back in my head. There's a plastic chair that I'm forced to sit on before I collapse. And even then I can hardly hold my head up. My eyelids are getting heavy but I have to stay focused.

Alert. Creepo knows that I like the north coast. Sitting on the beach with a book. It was one of the few places that we regularly came to as a 'family' when my parents . . . went away. Creepo knows some people who have a penthouse apartment overlooking the beach and he used to send me and Aunt Serena over to the beach or for coffee while he conducted his 'business'. They even talked about moving up here.

'Would you like a drink to go with it?'

'I told you. I only have . . .'

'I wasn't asking if you wanted to pay for it.'

I'm half-inclined to say no to his charity. I need to learn to take care of myself. But I weaken. Although my water bottle's full, I wouldn't mind a caramel milkshake or Coke to go with my scallops. I could call it karma.

'A mineral water, please.' I'm proud of myself for opting healthy.

He waves his hand at the refrigerator, telling me to help myself.

I grab a bottle and look at the photos he's got around the shop. Suddenly I feel sorry for him. He might see me, but I see him too. He aches for the old country. His shop overlooks the ocean but he's pining for a different ocean. A different sea. The Mediterranean. His kids have probably left home. His wife dead or dosed up on something to see her through the day. He's giving me stuff not so that I'll feel better, but so that he will. That little squirt of joy juice through the brain.

God! I *am* turning emo.

'Would you like a bag?'

'For four scallops?'

'I gave you a bit extra.'

'If you think I need one.' I give him my three dollars and he hands me the bag. It's quite heavy. I can see that he's thinking of handing me back the money. But we both know that I have to save face. Being human is hard work at times.

'I've had a good day,' he says, explaining away his charity. 'And I'm closing up soon. Don't like letting good food go to waste.'

I smile at him despite myself. He's a good man no matter what his motivation is. I want to tell him to sell up and move back to Greece. But he'll never do it. He's a victim. Like the rest of us.

By the time I lug my parcel down to the sand, I've almost nothing left in the tank. While I was waiting I imagined myself ripping into the steamy bundle like a crocodile into a wounded wallaby and licking the grease and salt from the wrapper. But when I finally open it I'm like a child on Christmas day – there's too much happening to focus on one thing. Apart from my four scallops, my Mediterranean friend has thrown in fish, chips, two battered savs and a couple of those crabstick things. And even though I'm hungry enough to eat the bum out of a dead seagull, we both know that I'll never get through this lot in one sitting and he's given me dinner as well.

There's an old guy of about forty staring at me while I'm hoeing into my kill. He starts walking towards me but I turn my back on him hoping that he'll take the hint and piss off. And when I look back I'm grateful that he is walking away, though he keeps glancing back at me over his shoulder as he does. What a creep!

By the time I've scoffed down half my food and waddled back up to the shop like an expectant mum on a burger-only diet, my guardian angel is clattering the shutters closed.

'Thanks,' I say.

'It would have only gone in the bin.'

'You should go back,' I offer. 'If you miss it that much.'

'Back where?'

'To Greece.'

'Greece?' he says with a chuckle. I can feel myself turning red like I've just told a tampon joke to a bunch of nuns. 'I'm not from Greece.'

'But all those pictures.' I gesture towards the shop.

'Croatia,' he says. 'I'm from Croatia.'

'Well, wherever it is, you should go back.' I want to add, 'Before it's too late,' but I leave it as it is.

He fumbles with the padlock. 'The Croatia I knew is gone.'

'But still . . .'

'You can't go back.'

'Why not?'

He finishes locking up and looks up at me. 'Can you?'

He's not yearning for a place but for a time. A time that may not have even existed. There's a name for that I think. A simulacrum or something. I reckon only about one per cent of the population would know that word. Not that it matters. I'm still homeless.

He nods goodbye to me and walks away. Down on the beach, a wicked southerly buster has blown in. Even the life-savers are packing up their flapping flags for the day. I have to dig out my tracksuit pants to stop the sand whipping at my legs. I sit there dragging on my pants and watching the families heading for home. For safety.

Back in the city I suppose the birds and the homeless will be staking out their territory for the night, screeching or squawking at anyone who encroaches on their space. I've got to find somewhere to stay. I think about heading back to the station and finding a train to sleep on. But it's Saturday night, probably the worst time on the trains. The more the night drags on, the more leeches, lechers, drunks and thugs will pile on. Not the safest place for a teenage girl. Or maybe I should just go with it and see what happens.

No! I'm not going to give up. I don't believe in fate. Everything I do, every decision I make from this point on is down to me. God's not going to look after me. Neither is Allah or Krishna. Buddha, for all his peace-loving navel-gazing, couldn't give the remotest shit about me. When are we going to wake up to the fact that we're on our own? Look at that couple in America. Their daughter was sick, so all their friends and church buddies came over and prayed with them. They were still praying when the poor kid died in front of them of dehydration. An inquest found that if she'd been given fluids she would have been fine. She needed Gatorade not God.

I've wandered back to the beach, which is practically deserted. Families all off to restaurants. To home. It's just the seagulls and me now. The tide is coming in and reclaiming the beach. Washing away the sandcastles and memories of the day.

I notice a flash in the distance. A silent sentinel is guarding the rocks at the far end of the beach, which appears to stretch for ever. The lighthouse seems minuscule hiding there among the rocks, peeking out occasionally to warn sailors not to get too close. Hopefully no one is there because what I want most of all right now is to be where people are not.

I pull on my jumper, hitch up my backpack and begin the long trek north.

CAFÉ

TOUGH FIRST DAY.

You think?

But it must have got easier. Being homeless, I mean.

It did. But not until it got worse.

So you went to the lighthouse?

I tried. I know that they're not manned any more. That they're automatic. But I thought there might be an old cot bed or a hammock or something. Maybe tea-making facilities, like in the old days.

Tea-making facilities?

Don't laugh!

Sorry.

I was new to all this. For all I knew every lighthouse came with a freshly made bed and fully stocked pantry.

Did you make it to the lighthouse?

About halfway, I reckon. Have you ever tried walking along a beach when the tide's coming in? The surges drive you up to the dry sand and then it's like trekking through the desert. It's also sloped, so you end up walking at a funny angle.

So where did you spend the night?

Out in the open.

Wasn't that risky? Or scary?

As opposed to lying awake waiting for Creepo to slither into bed with me? I didn't get much sleep, but it was still one of the most peaceful nights I'd had for a while.

Weekender

I PASS A FEW OLD SURF SHACKS AND SOME McMANSIONS AS I TREK out of town along the beach. The surf shacks are crumbling to driftwood, while the relentless pounding of the ocean is reclaiming the yards and value of the McMansions. Beach fishermen are setting themselves up for their evening cull – hooks, bait, knives, thermoses. There's going to be blood spilled and coffee sipped tonight.

I walk for ages, not thinking, not planning, just enjoying the feeling of being safe. Of freedom.

After a while I stop and look back along the beach. The lights from Death Valley are flickering faintly through the sea mist, while up at the far end of the beach the lighthouse continues its relentless sweep. The night is fast drawing in and I'm still only about halfway there.

I clamber up the incline into the sand dunes. I look at the distant road and follow the headlights of a car heading north out of Death Valley and notice that the road veers inland once it passes the houses. It's just beach and bush this far up. I slip down into a hollow in the dunes which will keep me out of sight if anyone happens along. Though the chances of that seem pretty remote. I dig a small hole for my fish and chip parcel, hoping that the sand will still contain enough heat to keep it warm, then I scamper up out of my hollow, park myself on top of the dune and stare at the view. Out at sea, ships waiting to load their cargo are lit up like Disneyland. Soon they'll be hauling up their anchors and sailing off over the horizon. To somewhere exotic. Somewhere else. Maybe somewhere safe. I wonder if it would be possible to swim out to one and stow away. Though, when I think about it, a cargo ship is probably not the safest place in the world for a thirteen-year-old girl. The closest ship looks to be about five kilometres away. I couldn't swim that in a year, especially with a fractured wrist. I also read somewhere that sharks like to feed at dusk. The idea of going for a five-kilometre swim with a broken arm while being circled by a pack of ravenous sharks kind of takes the wind out of that set of sails.

I dig up my parcel like a dog with its bone but my dinner is stone cold. I'm not in the least bit hungry after my earlier blowout and the remnants have congealed into an unidentifiable greasy lump, but I have to eat to keep my strength up. I don't know when I'll get to eat again. I also have to read or my mind will congeal into a greasy lump too. It's my second night on the streets (okay – the church and the beach) and apart from the fish and chip shop menu, I haven't read a single sentence. I'll have to watch that. I can't invent that eye-eating worm vaccine, or keep one step ahead of Creepo, if I don't have my book smarts about me.

After dinner I climb up out of my hollow and lie high on the dune, staring out to sea. The moon has just peeked over the horizon like God with a lantern. The backlit cargo ships fade into irrelevance against the lightshow from the heavens.

People think they're so important, but we're just bacteria under a microscope compared to the infinity of space. No wonder we invented God to explain it all – the universe, life, everything, I mean. And maybe God's existence is proof that we're not as smart as we like to think we are. Because what we can't explain, we put down to an invisible magic man hiding in the sky. That doesn't seem enough somehow.

The smell of the ocean – that intoxicating mixture of salt, seaweed, waves and air – makes me opt for *The Old Man and the Sea* rather than *Matilda*. If I tilt the pages towards the horizon and squint slightly, I can just read in the moonlight. I feel bad for Santiago and the marlin, whom Santiago refers to as his brother. Bit of a harsh way to treat your brother if you ask me: stick a spear through his head and lash him to the side of your boat. Still, Creepo buried *his* brother out in that forest in a big garbage bag, and he was the same species. Well, near enough. If there's a lesson in *The Old Man and the Sea* it's about not getting in too deep. Going out too far. Venturing into unchartered waters. Swimming out to cargo ships.

I leave the sharks to it and crawl into my sleeping bag. The cold had crept up on me while I was out in the Gulf Stream with Santiago, and it's nice to snuggle down deep where it's warm. I don't know what I'll do if it rains. Lug my stuff back to Death Valley, I suppose. Find a bus shelter or a train. Head back into the city.

I look up to the heavens and the billions of twinkling stars. How are they possible? How is anything possible? The ancients explained the night as the gods throwing a blanket across the sky; the stars were tiny holes in the blanket. It seems pretty dumb now but at least they were thinking about it. Trying to understand and explain things. Now it seems as though we've just stopped thinking. We laugh at the people who thought night was caused by God's blanket having holes in it, but if you told those same people who were doing the laughing that everything in the universe, the stuff that we're made of, everything that is around now or has ever been – sand, sharks, scallops, beach fishermen, cargo ships, books, Frisbees, Father Kelliher, Dr Chen, my parents (what's left of them), Creepo's forest, Madagascar, Roald Dahl, Ernest Hemingway, toast, sea monkeys, Charles Dickens, everything that has ever been, everything that ever will be, the stuff that we're made of, matter, time itself – was once compacted down into an area the size of an orange, well, then they'd probably just smile at you and go shopping or start watching game-shows. Because that's way too much to have to think about.

So as I'm staring at the stars, I think about the Big Bang and how everything that ever was and will be was already there at the moment of creation. And I think and think and think and it doesn't do any good because although I kinda get the Big Bang and the idea that everything was there when it went off, what I can't get my head around is 'why?'. Why it went off. Why it exploded. And you can almost understand why we invented an invisible magic man in the sky lighting the fuse. But if you put the invisible magic man there with his box of matches, then you have to start thinking about where he came from. His being here for ever, as most religious people reckon, doesn't cut it because we can't get our minds around for ever. It's like when you try to think about the edge of the universe and you can almost get there (there are no more stars, no more anything, just an empty void) and then someone says, 'Okay, we'll build our brick wall here because this is the end of the universe', and then someone else says, 'Okay, so you've built your brick wall at the end of the universe, now what's on the other side of it?' And you say, 'Well, nothing,' but even as you're saying it you realise that nothing is something, and the more you think about it the more you realise that you'll never have an answer even if you think about it for ever, so you go shopping or start watching gameshows. The comforts of a mindless life.

A breeze whips off the ocean, bringing with it the odours of distant lands. I decide that's where I'm going to go as soon as I can. I'm going to get away. Properly. To distant lands. Asia. Europe. Somewhere else.

It's been a long day and my eyelids are getting heavy and so I abandon myself to dreams.

In the dead hour the ghosts creep out of the bush and go howling across the dunes, screaming their unfinished business to the night. But I'm nothing to them so they ignore me.

CAFÉ

YOU WERE TURNING INTO QUITE THE PHILOSOPHER.

That's the thing when you spend so much time on your own. You do a lot of thinking.

That's pretty intense stuff for a . . .

For a what? For a girl?

No. I was going to say a thirteen-year-old.

I was almost fourteen. Anyway, I didn't think exactly like that. But that's the sort of stuff that I was thinking about. I can put it more into words now.

So you became an atheist?

No. I never said that I was an atheist.

Agnostic?

That's just a chicken-shit atheist. You die and go up to heaven and say to St Peter, 'I never said that God didn't exist. I said that he might not.' 'Well that's okay, then. In you come.' Either we all turn to dust or we're all welcome. Except Hitler, of course. He's stuffed. And the rest of the Nazis.

Anyone else?

People who appear in infomercials. And television evangelists, of course.

Now you're talking.

They just make it up as they go along. They all do. Everyone thinks that they're the chosen people. The saved. Catholics, Protestants, born agains, Muslims, Mormons, Jews, the Amish, the Brethren; you name it. They can't all be right. God I hope it's not the Brethren. Imagine spending the rest of eternity wearing beige and not being allowed to log on to Facebook. It mightn't be hell, but it'd be close.

So what were you?

I don't know. Do I have to have a label? I wasn't anything. I was just trying to understand things. I had more questions than answers. Still do. It's hard to look up at the night sky, to see the glow from the white hot gasses at the centre of the Milky Way, to stare at infinity and come to the conclusion that it's all random. That there's no point. I could see all this beauty and I kept coming back to 'why?'.

Maybe there is no why. There just is. And people need to find a why because we require order, without which there's just chaos.

You know why I turned against religion? Organised religion anyway?

I've no idea.

God's beard.

His beard? You're going to have to explain that one.

Think about it. Every time you see an image of God he's got this long, flowing beard. Why? Isn't he just made of light? Why would something that's only made of light have a big bushman's beard?

I . . .

I'll tell you why. Because the guys who made him up didn't have very good razors. They didn't even have those el-cheapo yellow plastic ones. So these ancient dudes think that the symbol of authority is a beard, because they've all got one. So they naturally give God one. The biggest one they can think of because he's like *the* authority figure so he has to have the biggest beard. God didn't create us in his image, we created him in ours.

So you think the beard's the ultimate symbol of masculinity?

Well, no, obviously it's not. But we're talking religion here so it's not as if they can give him the biggest d–

Yes, thanks for that. Could you keep your voice down a bit, there are ladies present.

Okay, then. What about angels?

What about them?

You've seen paintings, sculptures, images of them. What do they always have in common?

They always turn up with a sheep.

I never thought of that. You're right, they do. Okay, so what else do they have in common? Apart from the sheep.

Wings?

Exactly. They always have wings? Why? Why would something made of light, an ethereal presence, need wings?

To look good.

Exactly! They gave them wings because they weren't thinking it through. Of course, now we could just give them a jetpack, a boarding pass, or a set of rocket pants, but we're stuck with tradition.

Rocket pants? Maybe we should get back to that night. You said before that it was peaceful until you heard ghosts.

Have you ever slept in sand dunes at night?

Camping. When I was about ten, I suppose.

If you heard the wind whipping across the dunes you'd swear it was ghosts. Despite that, it was peaceful because I knew that Creepo wasn't about to slide up beside me.

But it must have been unsettling in other ways?

It was surprisingly noisy. There's the waves breaking. The wind. The ghosts. And there was all this scurrying and scampering in the bush.

Rats?

That's what I thought. All through the night I imagined these rats twitching their little whiskers and staring down at me from the edge of the hollow and wondering if one of them would venture down to see if I was still alive and whether it was worth taking a chunk out of me.

In the morning I knew that I had to go back. Back to the biggest rat of them all.

Bleak House

WHEN I WAKE UP THERE ARE ALL THESE BEADY LITTLE EYES STARING down at me in my hollow. I could hear them scurrying and scampering around in the dark last night, but now there's a bit of light I can see them for what they are. Rats. About five of them, twitching their filthy noses and whiskers at me. I gasp and quickly draw my sleeping bag up over my face with my good hand so that only my eyes are visible.

I scoop up a handful of sand and hurl it at them. 'Piss off!' I scream through nylon at the filthy things.

And then, as my eyes adjust to the early morning light, I notice that these rats are much bigger than ordinary ones. They also have long floppy ears and are nibbling on vegetation.

I lower my protective sleeping bag. Unless Flopsy, Mopsy and Cottontail have turned carnivorous overnight, my fear has been misplaced.

I ease myself out of my sleeping bag, walk down to the water's edge and dip my good hand in the foamy surf, scooping some up to wash my face. It's wonderfully refreshing.

There's nobody about this far up the beach, apart from me and the oversized rodents. I can see a couple of specks of life down where the fisherman were last night (surfers, swimmers, demented joggers) but it's pretty isolated all the way up here. I think I'll make this my weekender. Maybe I could get hold of some driftwood and palm fronds and cobble together a sort of shelter, like that movie about that castaway bloke. My teeth feel all slimy and in desperate need of cleaning but I forgot to pack my toothbrush. It's funny, when you're little you think that when you're grown up you won't bother cleaning your teeth any more, because that's just dumb grownup stuff. After two days on the run on a largely fish and chip diet and I'm desperate for a fang polisher. I dip my finger back into the surf and brush them as best as I can with the salt water, running my tongue over each tooth to try to get rid of the slimy texture. My fractured arm is starting to itch beneath the cast, but Dr Chen forgot to give me a chopstick to scratch it with so I'll just have to try and scratch it mentally.

After I've combed the knots out of my rats' nest hair, I pack up my sleeping bag and begin the long, slow slog back to Death Valley.

I need food. I need sleep (proper sleep). I need money. None of which are available to me in Death Valley. So I head back to the station. It's still early so it's just joggers, surfers, the elderly and the homeless who are up and about. You've got to admire them – the old people, I mean. Here they are, their lives nearly over, but they're up and embracing the day rather than curled up in a corner somewhere screaming at the nothingness that awaits them beyond the grave.

I shake my head and slump down onto one of the platform benches at the station. I've got to stop having these negative thoughts. Suicide lives down that road. I'm alive. I'm safe. And life's a gift. Okay the gift sucks a bit at the moment, sort of like getting a pair of oversized pyjamas for Christmas when what you really wanted was an iPod, but I need to make every moment count. The train slides languidly into the station like a python down a rabbit hole. I haul myself on board and collapse onto one of the long seats. I didn't know that being homeless would be this tiring. At home, even at Creepo and Serena's, when I was tired or just wanted to be by myself to laze about or read, I would disappear into my room. Now I don't have a room.

I pull out *Matilda* to see if she's got any advice but she's too busy trying to suck up to Miss Honey. I need a Miss Honey in *my* life. More than Matilda did, anyway. Matilda's dad might have been a bit mean to her, but he didn't try to shoot her in the back of her head. At least I don't think he did.

When Matilda comes up short of advice I ask God, but he's obviously still pissed at me for the whole beard thing.

The train slips past an abandoned country church whose parishioners are now termites and bush rats. It's sad to see it all rotted and falling down. It's as if the church is slowly leeching back into the wilderness, taking along the hopes and prayers of those who gathered there with dreams of a better life – if not in this one then at least the one hereafter.

Oh my God! That's it. Creepo and Serena go to mass on Sunday morning. At least, they do if they can drag their lazy arses out of bed in time. There's a spare key buried under the garden gnome out the back. I could steal in and grab my piggybank while they're out. Two hundred dollars buys a serious amount of scallops.

I settle back in the seat and close my eyes, content in the knowledge that I have a plan for the day, dangerous as it is.

God knows why Creepo bothers going to church. In his psycho little world he probably thinks that there's absolutely nothing wrong with murdering his sister-in-law, going paedo on his niece, breaking her arm, trying to shoot her in the head, and then sticking his tongue out for holy communion on Sunday morning. Probably thinks he's wiping the slate clean. Squaring the ledger. I reckon he just goes so that he can watch all the other men drooling over Serena. And yet wasn't one of the commandments something about not coveting thy neighbour's donkey? Or was it his ass? Or maybe it was his wife. Maybe it was his wife's ass. Whatever it was, whenever I went to mass with them there seemed to be a whole lot of coveting going on: cars, 4WDs, houses, wives, bling.

By the time we're crossing the river my head is feeling fuzzy. As I'm lying there nodding off, I try to think like Creepo. He knows that I haven't gone to the police yet because if I had they'd have come around and arrested him or else returned me to him as a runaway. He doesn't know that I know that *he's* been to the police, but there's nothing that I can really do with that knowledge except use it to *not* go to the police myself. He doesn't know any of my friends from school, so he wouldn't go around to their houses to look for me.

I actually slump when I weigh it all up. Creepo knows that I've got no one to turn to and nowhere to go. I wonder if he knows about the two hundred dollars stuffed in my piggy-bank. If he does then he can only come to one conclusion. Eventually I'll have to come back.

After a fitful nap I'm woken by the train slowing as it reaches the outer suburbs. A squadron of butterflies descend to my stomach and get in a fight with the ones that are already there. I gather up my stuff and slap myself across the face several times. I can't venture into the lion's den half-asleep. I have to be alert. Focused. Or else I'll be chewed up and spat out, with my dismembered bits buried in the forest.

It's past nine by the time I stop at the end of the alley leading into their street. Mass will have started. Luckily I can see the house from the entrance to the alley. If they haven't gone to nine o'clock mass and Creepo comes out I will be able to escape back down the alley and he won't be able to chase after me because of his short (or long) leg. If any neighbours see me, they'll probably think I look a bit suspicious lurking about with my backpack and sleeping bag like this, but I'll just have to deal with it.

I summon up some courage and cautiously approach the house. My backpack and sleeping bag are weighing me down but I can't leave them in the alley because they'll probably have been nicked by the time I get back.

Fortunately for me the garage has been built slightly forward of the house, so even if Creepo and Serena are sitting in the lounge room, which they hardly ever do anyway, they wouldn't be able to see me cutting across their neighbours' front lawn.

I peer through the frosted side windows of the garage. There's only one car in there as far as I can tell. Serena's paddock basher – her ten-year-old Magna. The one Creepo used to dump my parents out in the forest. He wouldn't dream of using his you-beaut ute for that. Oh, no. Not the beast. It's his bloke bling. The roll bar and the chunky chrome exhaust pipes, not to mention the super-fat imported Yokohamas, are for show purposes only. It only goes off-road when he lets Serena take it to the shopping centre. That's the only time he lets her drive it. He wouldn't want anyone seeing her piling groceries into the Magna. Oh the shame.

I press my face hard up against the garage window and block out the glare with my hands. The fluorescent glow of the beast's metallic blue paint is definitely absent.

They've gone to church.

I toss my backpack and sleeping bag over the side gate. It's padlocked, so I clamber over it awkwardly, trying not to bang my arm in its cast. I ease myself down on the other side by stepping onto the wheelie bins.

I leave my stuff behind the bins, figuring that it will be safe there as it's out of sight from the road. Then I creep around to the back verandah.

I move the garden gnome aside and scratch at the dirt until I dig up the most unconvincing looking stone you could ever imagine. It's made of shiny brown plastic and has 'Made in Taiwan' stamped on the bottom. Presumably, like Serena, the Taiwanese are constantly locking themselves out, so much so that it's become an export industry.

With my tongue poking unattractively out of the side of my mouth, I dig my fingernail into the groove and flip open the stone's false bottom. I shake the key out, slide it quietly into the lock and I'm in.

Before I go in, I put the key back in its proper place. I don't want Creepo discovering that I've been in. I don't want him knowing how desperate I am.

I tiptoe through the kitchen and open the door to the garage, just to confirm that the beast isn't there. I'm relieved to see that it's not.

I'm tempted to raid the fridge on the way back through the kitchen but, again, I don't want to give anything away. I'll buy myself some buns at the bakery when I get hold of my two hundred dollars.

By sheer force of habit I step over the creaky eighth step (it was number six in my parents' house) as I'm making my way up the stairs and then cautiously push open the door to my bedroom. I thought that Creepo might have trashed my room in a rage by now but it's exactly how I left it.

On my bookshelves is the piggybank that my grandparents gave me when I made my first reconciliation. I didn't really have anything to confess so I made up a bunch of stuff (about swearing, about having bad thoughts) just to keep Father Kelliher happy and to give him something to feel superior about.

I turn over Noah's ark and remove the rubber stopper. Although it's noisy, I shake out all the coins and dig my fingers in for the cash. I don't know if it's exactly two hundred dollars but it was close enough the last time I counted it, which was a couple of weeks ago.

I twist the rubber stopper until its back in place and position Noah and his illogical ark back on my bookshelf.

I look at my books, which I miss so much – even the ones from the library which technically don't belong to me. I miss being with them; escaping, hiding out in them. On a whim I decide to take *Bleak House*. Although it will add some extra weight to my backpack, hopefully reading it again will add some extra weight to my brain.

I pull down *Bleak House*, stuff the money into my pockets and brush down the covers on my bed to remove all evidence that I've been here.

Just as I've finished patting down my doona, the toilet flushes. A double flush.

I stare at the closed bathroom door and literally have to cover my mouth with my hand to stop myself from screaming. A double flush means either Serena has dropped a large one or it's Creepo.

If it's Serena, she'll wash her hands, check herself out, probably squeeze a few blackheads, brush her hair, weigh herself and clip her moustache, all of which will give me enough time to slip back down the stairs and out.

If it's Creepo, I'm dead.

It has to be Serena. Creepo's beast has gone. And I've never known Serena to do the grocery shopping on Sunday morning.

I drop down just as I hear the bathroom doorknob turning. If I stay here and it *is* Creepo in the bathroom, he'll see me when he walks into his bedroom. *If* he walks into his bedroom. If he goes downstairs and then decides to come back up, he'll be staring straight at me from the stairwell.

I lift up the edge of the doona and wedge myself under the bed. I have to contort myself at an awkward angle to manoeuvre myself past the middle leg, but in the end I just about manage it. If I was any bigger I wouldn't fit. As it is there's just enough room under the bed for a mop like me. And even then it's still a tight squeeze. The bed is pressing against my chest. My face forced to the side. Luckily I've only got a couple of fried eggs for boobs. If Serena ever tried this, the bed would end up floating about a metre off the ground like something out of a paranormal movie.

The bathroom door swings open. It's painful but I'm able to crane my neck so that I can see past my feet who it is. I can only see the bottom part of their legs but, unless Serena has given up waxing, it's definitely not her.

Creepo slides past my door and into their bedroom. The way he's flopping around the house as if he's Lord Muck, he's probably in the nude. Hopefully, *hopefully*, he's in there getting dressed.

Maybe I can time my run for the exact moment he's putting his trousers on. By the time he realises what's happening, pulls up his pants and hobbles on his uneven legs down the stairs, he won't be able to catch me. I don't know where he keeps his gun though. The obvious place is his bedside drawer and that's just too horrifying to think about.

I'm not going anywhere.

Oh my God! A chill runs through me, turning my blood to ice. When I was stuffing the money into my pockets, I left *Bleak House* on the bed.

I edge towards the side of the bed and run my arm up, feeling around on top for my book. I freeze when Creepo comes back out of his room and stands on the landing. I can see his feet. If he turns his head to the left and looks into my room he'll see the book sitting there on my bed. He'll also see my arm. And then I'll be forest food.

Please, God. Make him go downstairs. It won't prove you exist. It'll just seem as though you suck a little less.

I don't know why he's standing there like that. Maybe he's thinking. Maybe if I listen intently enough I'll hear the mouse running around inside his brain.

And then he turns. I can see his legs and then eventually his greasy head as he disappears down the stairs. Thank you, God. Or thank you, Randomness.

I now have another problem. When Creepo or Serena walk back up the stairs, from the middle step they'll be staring directly underneath my bed. Directly at my feet. Directly at me.

Slowly, painfully, I heave myself out from under the bed. I'm positive that one of the floorboards is going to creak and give me away. I grab *Bleak House* and slide it beneath the bed and then creep around to the front and pull my doona down so that it's touching the floor. Then I crawl back under the bed to my sanctuary. It's darker than before and I can no longer see the landing outside their bedroom that leads to the bathroom and the stairwell. Oh to be at my weekender right now, being sizzled by the sun. That'd be heaven.

And then I hear the creaking eighth step. He's coming back up the stairs. He must have figured it out. I must have left a clue, like not closing a door or something? Maybe he's put in security cameras and he's got me in full colour skulking around the house and stalking up the stairs to my bedroom.

My door. It was only slightly ajar when I arrived and now it's wide open. Creepo must have registered this at least at a subconscious level when he was standing there on the landing.

He stops on the landing again. He hasn't gone into his bedroom. He hasn't gone to the bathroom either. He's standing in my doorway. I can't see him but I can sense him. Just like that time he crept into my bedroom when I was asleep and his presence woke me up. I couldn't see him then either but I knew that he was there.

I hear him close the door and for a moment I feel relieved. Then I realise that his presence is still here. He's in my room. He's closed the door behind himself. He's playing with me. He knows I'm here. My heart is thumping so hard I feel as though I'm going to black out.

He clomps slowly over the floorboards until he's standing beside the bed. His feet are just inches away from my face.

My face and chest compress even further. I feel the life being pressed out of me. I'm about to scream out but then it stops. He's sat down on my bed, the disgusting pig. And although I can barely breathe, I'm so close to him that I can smell his boozy breath.

'Where are you, you little bitch?' he snarls and I actually piss myself. I can feel the urine burning my crotch and trickling down my legs beneath my jeans.

Then I realise that he's not actually talking to me but asking himself a rhetorical question.

As if being trapped in a room with a sick, incestuous, murdering paedo isn't bad enough, I'm stuck under the bed wearing steaming wet undies. And I can smell them. I can smell my own fear. Surely it's just a matter of time before Creepo does too.

But he hasn't finished his rant just yet.

'I'm not going to jail because of you and your gutter whore of a mother!'

Charming.

But if he doesn't know that I'm in here, why has he closed the door?

Just as abruptly as it happened, the pressure is released and I can breathe again. I take in some short, shallow breaths, relieved to have oxygen flowing through my lungs.

The floorboards near my bookshelves groan. He's fiddling with something on one of them. Noah's ark by the sound of it. He's shaking it. Levering out the rubber stopper. He's trying to steal my bit of money, the creep. Beat you to it, psycho!

The he moves across and opens one of my drawers. He struggles with it a bit and from that I can tell that it's my top drawer. The one that is slightly warped. The one where I keep my pyjamas and undies.

Nothing in there for you, Creepo. No cash. No clues. Nothing but underwear. Sorry.

I hear him take a deep breath, like somebody sniffing a rockmelon in the supermarket. And then he walks over to the door. He doesn't open it though. He's obviously looking at himself in the full-length mirror on the back of the door. Why?

Then I hear him doing up his zipper. He obviously didn't finish dressing properly, the idiot, and now he's just noticed this in my mirror. But then he starts breathing deeply and there's a strange sound, like he's slapping himself across the face, the way I did this morning on the train to wake myself up. Only he's slapping himself in time with his deep breathing.

Downstairs in the garage I hear the door slowly clunking open. Creepo obviously hasn't heard it yet because he's still breathing heavily and slapping himself in the face.

Serena's back and Creepo's giving himself a pep talk about finding me or something. He must be because as he's doing his deep breathing, he's calling out my name over and over again. He's calling me some disgusting names too. But then, all of a sudden, he cries out like he's seen a huge spider or something. And downstairs I can hear Serena struggling into the kitchen with bags of groceries.

'Tony.'

'Oh shit!' He's heard her now.

'Tony.'

'Hang on,' he calls back, then mutters, 'Shit. Shit. Shit.'

He quickly stuffs whatever it was that he took back into my drawer.

'Shit. Shit. Shit.'

The eighth step creaks.

I hear him fumbling as he does his zip up again. Or is it down? I can't keep track.

'Tony?'

'In here.'

The door swings open.

'Hi.' He sounds guilty.

'What are you doing?'

'I was just seeing if I could find any clues where she might have gone.'

'Why was the door closed?'

'Because I was looking behind it.'

'Why?'

Serena sounds suspicious and I'm not surprised. She comes home and finds him hanging around my undies drawer. That's just dodge on so many levels.

My face and chest are compressed as he sits down on the bed again. If Serena plonks herself down next to him I'll burst.

'Can you give me a hand with the groceries?'

'Before you went out, did you go out the back?'

'No. I went through the garage.'

'No, before that. This morning. Did you hang any clothes out or something?'

'I haven't been out the back. Why, Tony?'

'Because when I got up, the back door was unlocked.'

I can feel my blood draining away.

'Maybe you didn't lock it last night.'

'No way. I definitely locked it. I don't want her creeping in here in the middle of the night and sticking a carving knife in my neck.'

'Tony.'

'Like mother, like daughter.'

'Are we going to ten-thirty mass?'

Please, please, please, please. Please, God, make them go to church.

'No way!'

You suck.

'There's something going on around here. Look at this piggybank of hers.' The pressure is released as he stands up again.

'Noah. It's kind of cute with the giraffe and the kangaroos.'

'It's empty,' says Creepo, giving it a shake.

'It can't be. I checked it yesterday. All her money was still there.'

'It's not now. Look.'

I can hear Serena levering out the rubber stopper.

'Did you take it?' asks Creepo.

'Me!' pleads Serena. 'Why would I take her bit of money?'

'Because I didn't.'

'Well, neither did I.' Serena sounds seriously pissed.

'Don't get all narky. I was just asking because I know *I* didn't take it. And if *you* didn't either then it can mean only one thing. She's . . .'

'. . . been here.' Serena finishes the sentence for him.

'And look. That house brick of a book that she's always got her nose in. That's gone too. We better have a look around to see if there's anything else missing,' orders Creepo. 'Check the gnome. She might've nicked the key.'

'What about the safe?'

'What about it?'

Of course. The safe. He's probably got my passport and our cash locked in his safe.

'You'd better check it.'

'I will, but she doesn't know the combination. Hell, *you* don't know the combination.'

He's right of course. I wouldn't have a clue what the combination . . . But then something buried deep in my mind registers and for the first time in ages, and despite the fact that my face is wedged up against the bottom of my bed and I'm wearing piss-soaked clothes, I smile. Because that's just where you're wrong, Mr Paedo! I do know the combination. I only heard it once but it's not a number I could forget.

Thank you, Serena. I wouldn't have even thought of the safe. Now I know that if I ever get out of here without being shot in the head, defiled and dismembered, I'll be taking more than my measly two hundred dollars with me.

If they don't go out today it's going to be an uncomfortable night, wedged under my bed like one of my rubber stoppers beneath the door. Unbearable even, especially in wet undies.

I have to hang tough, though. Just for one night. Because in the morning, Creepo will head off to work and Serena will go for her regular ritual – coffee with the girls. Then I'll be free. Free of their psycho little world. I'll never have to come back here again. Except maybe with a can of petrol and a match.

I'm in the clear. And then just when I'm positive that I can get out of this, I suddenly remember that I've left my backpack and sleeping bag outside next to the bins. And Sunday night is collection night.

CAFÉ

God! That must have been terrifying. My hands are sweating just listening to it. So how come Tony didn't see your backpack and that when he put the bins out?

He didn't put them out. That was my job. One of them, anyway. Obviously they hadn't adjusted to the new routine of not having me around. But I fretted about it all night, thinking that he might get up at any time and go and do it. Then he'd know that I was there. When I heard him snoring through the wall I actually considered creeping out of the house, but if I did that I wouldn't get my passport and any cash that Creepo might have stashed away in his safe.

So how did you know the combination?

Because Creepo makes a house brick look like Einstein. I was lying on my bed reading one day. It was the weekend, a while before he started walking in on me when I was in the shower. It was Saturday afternoon, I think, and Creepo came up the stairs whistling. But he wasn't whistling a song, he was whistling the Pizza Hut tune. You know the old one before they changed it – nine four eight one, double one, double one, Pizza Hut delivery.

Why?

Because Saturday was pay day. Scam day, or whatever you want to call it and he was cashed up. He was happy. Loaded.

So why was he whistling the Pizza Hut tune?

I didn't work it out until later. My mind just locked it away. The thing was, he always closed their bedroom door when he was putting things in his safe – in case me or Serena were around. But I suppose he didn't see that I was in my bedroom, and when he came back out he was actually singing the words to the Pizza Hut song but with a slight variation.

Which was?

Nine four eight one, double one, double one. Tony's cash delivery.

You're joking? The safe's combination was the Pizza Hut delivery number?

Well, I didn't know that when I was lying under the bed – not at first, anyway. But then when Serena mentioned that he should check the safe I remembered him singing that stupid song and it clicked.

So you had an uncomfortable night?

That's putting it mildly. I desperately tried to hold on but I had to pee a couple more times during the night, which was just revolting. I was worried they might smell me. I tried to pinch myself to stay awake, scared that I might have a nightmare and call out. But after spending the past nights in the church, then the dunes, and now wedged under my old bed, I was almost delirious with exhaustion. In the end I couldn't hang on any longer and fell asleep.

In the morning, when Serena went for coffee with the girls, things got really disgusting.

Ape Creature

IMAGINE WALKING THROUGH A GRAVEYARD AT NIGHT AND HEARING all these bells tinkling away. Only the tinkling isn't coming from the church but from below the ground. From the graves. How freaky would that be? Someone actually used to have that job.

During the bubonic plague – the Black Death – they used to bury the dead really quickly in an effort to stop the spread of disease. Sometimes they buried them too quickly. The story goes that grave robbers dug up this rich guy to see if he had any jewellery or cash stashed on him. They got a bit of a shock when they prised opened the coffin lid and found scratch marks on the inside and the guy gagging for breath. Rather than bury him again to cover up their crime, they brought it to the grave keeper's notice before disappearing into the night. When the media got wind of the story there was mass hysteria. People only calmed down when the government announced that in future plague victims would be buried with a bell. Even with this back-up method, the whole thing was pretty disturbing for everyone.

This is how I feel when I wake up. It's dark, I can barely breathe and there's something heavy pressing against my chest and face. For a split second I panic and think that Creepo has murdered me and buried me out in the forest, only he's been a bit too hasty on the whole burial thing. My kingdom for a bell.

Then I hear stirring in the next room and it dawns on me where I am. Creepo's alarm has woken me and he's in there fumbling around in the dark getting ready for work.

As my eyes adjust, I slowly become aware that the first essence of dawn is stealing into the room.

The first day of the rest of my life. People say that to try to coax themselves off their lazy arses and get out there and do something. But it really is the first day for me. When Serena goes out I'll get into Creepo's safe (I hope to God that he hasn't changed the combination) and get my passport and take a bit of cash to tide me over. After that I'll hole up somewhere for a while, catch up on some sleep and then when I'm rested I'll find myself a school. Start getting ready for uni, Médecins Sans Frontières, the vaccine for the eye-eating African worm.

Creepo goes into the bathroom, unleashing the sort of fart that, if anyone had struck a match in his vicinity, would have sent him hurtling into orbit.

'Tony,' admonishes Serena from her bed, as used to this morning ritual as he is.

'Better out than in,' he replies.

'Not for me.'

'Stop complaining or I'll come in there and give you a Dutch oven.'

'Don't be so gross.'

Creepo laughs and closes the door.

'Love you,' she calls after him.

There's no response.

And that's the thing that shocks me most in all of this. Serena knows that he's a sick, twisted, arm-breaking, murdering paedo, and yet she still loves the psycho. *Actually* loves him. Go figure. Maybe when you fall in love you go a bit warped. Your mind partially shuts down. I'll have to watch out for that. Luckily I've never been in love. Or at least, no one's ever loved me.

When Creepo emerges from the bathroom, for a horrible moment I think he's going to come back in here, do something with my undies drawer, but he just calls out to Serena to enjoy her coffee with the girls and that he'll see her around six.

Ten minutes later I hear the garage door clunk open, the guttural growl from the beast as it's stirred into life, and then finally he's gone, the beast purring down the street in the early morning sunlight. I'm especially scared at this point because he'll notice all the other bins and remember that it's collection day. The truck came in the early hours, clanking down the street like two tanks mating. Hopefully a few of the bins will have their lids flipped open so that even if he does notice them he'll see that it's too late.

It takes a couple of minutes before I can relax. He's not coming back. He's gone for the day. I'm safe.

I expect Serena to roll over for another three or four-hour snooze but instead she's in there mumbling on the phone. And she's not happy.

'Couldn't you get it serviced some other time?' I hear her say as she wanders across the landing and into the bathroom. 'You know Monday's our day. I need servicing too. Do you think about that? Tony's not interested in me any more. Too obsessed with . . .' she trails off. I don't know what she's going on about but it seems to me that she's got serious issues with Creepo – and yet didn't she just tell him that she loves him?

'No, I can't say.' I can hardly hear her now because, and this is really gross, she's doing a wee as she's talking on the phone. And she's backed up too. It sounds like Niagara Falls in the rainy season. Serena must have a bladder the size of a basketball.

'I could come and get you, if you want.' She's at the sink now, washing her hands.

'Yeah, really. I don't see why I should miss out on my coffee with the girls just because of your stupid car.' She laughs when she says this, though I don't really understand what's so funny about having coffee with the girls.

'Fine. I'll be there in about twenty minutes.'

She flushes the toilet, goes back into the bedroom and throws on some clothes and five minutes later the garage door is clunking open again.

When I can no longer hear Serena's paddock basher, I heave myself out of my coffin. Some of my muscles have seized up, my butt's raw and my back and neck ache like I've been stretched across a rack. I yawn and stretch and try to pump some blood back into the sorer bits. I can hardly believe my luck. I'm cramped up like a ninety-year-old with arthritis, but I had expected to be stuck under the bed for another few hours. Was prepared for it, in fact. Serena is not exactly a morning person. I can't imagine what she's up to. Despite what she said on the phone, it's far too early for coffee. None of the shopping centres will be open yet.

I grab a fresh pair of underpants, making sure that I dig down to an old pair buried deep in my drawer. The pair on the top – obviously the pair Creepo had out – have a gooey stain on them. Eeerrrkkk! If Serena ever goes through my undies drawer she'll think it was me. I pick up the pair of stained undies like it's a rabid rat and quickly run into the bathroom and flush them down the toilet.

Back in my room, I grab a pair of tracksuit pants. I'll wash my piss-soaked jeans later, when I get myself sorted. When I get away from this madhouse. I also grab another t-shirt. I remember it raining last night, absolutely bucketing down at one point, so my backpack and sleeping bag, sitting out there by the wheelie bins, will be soaked right through.

Even though I'm here alone, I still tiptoe as I cross the landing into the bathroom. I'm too scared to take a shower. I wouldn't be able to hear the garage door if Creepo came back unexpectedly. In the end I strip off my stinking clothes and give myself a good wash in the sink. My toothbrush has been symbolically removed from its place in their holder, so I use my fingers to give my teeth a good cleaning. It's nice to have cool minty breath flowing in and out of my lungs again. Considering all the crap I've been through over the weekend, it's nice to still be breathing.

After I've finished in the bathroom, I toss my musty clothes behind the door to pick up later and then make my way across the landing and into Creepo and Serena's room. The dragon's lair. They have a full-length mirrored wardrobe running along one wall, and I know from previous explorations that Creepo's safe is in the wardrobe. Before I get to that, however, I want to be able to protect myself against Creepo if he does suddenly turn up. I crawl across their unmade bed and slide open Creepo's bedside drawer. There's a bit of cash, which I help myself to, some watches and rings and a crucifix on a chain (ha!), a few car and 4WD magazines, and a gun with the silencer still attached. I've got no idea whether it's loaded so I'm just going to assume it is. I lift it out of the drawer. It's much heavier than I imagined a gun would be. I aim it at Creepo's pillow and fantasise about shooting him in the head, though I could never shoot another living thing. Not even him.

'Say your prayers, shower boy. Bang bang.'

The next thing I know I'm lying on the bed and there's a smoky smell all around the room and a high-pitched ringing in my ears. I sit up and reach over for the gun, which is also lying on the bed. I yelp as my fingers touch the barrel. I can't believe what I've done. I hardly even squeezed the trigger. I examine Creepo's pillow. There's a perfectly round hole right through the middle of it. I turn it over, but the hole goes all the way through and into the mattress. Luckily Serena sleeps with two pillows so I grab her spare one and shove Creepo's bullet-riddled one behind hers.

I crawl back across the bed and open Serena's drawer. Again there's a bit of cash, which I leave alone. There are also some credit cards which I don't. She has about five or six of them in a pile so I help myself to the one on the bottom. She'll never miss it and I'll only use it in an emergency. She also has a couple of dog-eared romance novels, which is kind of sad. Looking at the covers, I see she obviously fantasises about some swarthy Spanish dude with a ponytail galloping in on his stallion and sweeping her off her feet and carrying her back to his castle overlooking a vineyard. Instead she's stuck with Creepo beginning each day by peeling off the sort of fart that would show up on the Richter Scale. Ah, the romance.

I close Serena's drawer and turn my attention to the wardrobe. I slide open Creepo's side and am amazed by how orderly everything is. It's actually a little disturbing. His shoes aren't just placed neatly on their own rack, they're in colour-coded order. His suits and immaculately ironed shirts (which he does himself because Serena and I didn't do a good enough job) are all perfectly hung. And sitting in the corner is his safe. It's not as big as the one you see in banks heist movies, but bigger than the ones that you get in hotel rooms. It has an electronic access pad on the front laid out like a huge calculator. I take a deep breath, say a silent prayer, and enter the Pizza Hut number [9][4][8][1][1][1][1][1]. Nothing but silence. Instead a bunch of dashes replace the numbers that I've entered – [-][-][-][-][-][-][-][-] – and I know that he's changed the combination.

I could scream. Does anything work out for me? One little break. That's all I'm asking for. Then, while I'm busy mentally ranting, I notice that there are instructions just below the numeric pad. After you've entered the combination, you have to hit the # key. I enter the numbers again, more slowly this time, and then I press #. There's an electronic tinkling noise, followed by the sound of sliding metal and this time [-][-][O][P][E][N][-][-][-] comes up. I pull the door towards me and peer inside.

My jaw drops open when I see how much money Creepo's got piled in there. It's neat too. Just like his clothes. There are rubber bands around each bundle, just like you'd see in a bank robbery, and I wonder if perhaps that's where he gets his cash from. Maybe Creepo's an armed robber and his construction job is just a front. Although the cash bricks are neatly stacked, it's not so neat that he wouldn't miss a couple of them. I grab two, change my mind and decide that he wouldn't miss three, then I opt instead for eight, nine, ten and twelve, before realising that I am leaving a bit of a hole and revise my total back down to four. I toss them behind me onto the bed and then turn my attention to the small drawer that's in the safe. It contains a bunch of documents but also some passports: Creepo's, Serena's, mine and my parents'. So much for them going back to live in the old country. There are also some books tied up with an elastic band. I pull them out and examine them. They're my mum's diaries. I'm speechless. Flicking through to the beginning I discover that they go all the way back to high school.

Maybe she didn't have anyone to talk to so she confided in her diary. God knows why Creepo kept them. Maybe there's something in here about him. Something incriminating. Well they're mine now.

I toy with the idea of cleaning out the safe entirely. Maybe giving some money to charity or sending some over to Médecins Sans Frontières or to a hospital with a note saying that it's for them to use to invent a vaccine for the African eye-eating worm. But in the end I decide against it. If I clean out the safe Creepo will double his efforts to track me down. Maybe he'll call in 'the boys' or hire a private detective or even a hit man. But he won't miss a couple of bricks of money or my passport or Mum's diaries, surely. Not for a while at least. Unfortunately I've left enough evidence that I've been in the house, though he kind of suspects that already. There's no way he'll believe that I've managed to crack open his safe, though. And he'll only realise it if he looks for my passport or knows exactly how much money he's got in here.

I close the safe and hit the LOCK button. Inside, the steel bar slides across reassuringly. I'm in the clear.

Or at least, I am until I hear the garage door clunk open.

I climb out of the wardrobe and grab the money and Creepo's gun. I'm just about to race into my room and crawl back under my bed when I hear the door between the kitchen and the garage opening and Serena's inane laughter clattering up the stairs. I was so focused on what I was doing, I hadn't heard the garage doors when they opened, just when they closed. And now there isn't time to clamber back into my hidey-hole. Instead I crawl into the wardrobe and slide the door behind me. If Creepo is with her and he's got some cash to stash in his safe, I'm dead. I look down at Creepo's gun in my hands. Or *he* is.

They're coming up the stairs now. The eighth step almost shatters on impact with the two of them. What are they doing home? Creepo went to work and Serena went out for coffee with the girls.

'See you soon,' chirps Serena in a sing-song voice.

Then I hear a slapping sound – a sort of hand smacking a bottom sound, there's no other way of putting it – followed by more fits of giggling from Serena. She sounds like a cockatoo dangling upside down on powerlines.

And then Serena's in the bedroom. I can see through the small gap in the wardrobe doors that she's undressing. She's going back to bed. She quickly pulls off her tracksuit pants, jumper and t-shirt. I have to avert my eyes as she peels off her bra and undies. There are just certain sights that I do not wish to see, including Serena's boobs flapping about her like a couple of semi-deflated watermelons.

She said that she'd see him soon. That must mean Creepo is going back to bed too. With her. Oh no! They must be going to . . . I hope the sound of my vomiting doesn't give me away.

'Hurry up,' yells Serena. 'Get your hairy butt in here.' She practically explodes with laughter at this. Her sense of humour isn't all that brilliant. She thinks *Funniest Home Videos* is the height of hilarity.

It finally dawns on me that it's not Creepo in the bathroom. It's someone else. That this is her 'coffee with the girls'.

The guy, whoever he is, prowls into the bedroom like he's hunting wabbits.

'Where's my little kitten?'

I don't know who he is but he could clearly benefit from a visit to the zoo. Of all the animals that Serena could be compared with, a kitten doesn't exactly leap to mind.

'Where's my little kitten,' he says again, just to avoid any confusion. 'I'm going to make her purr.'

This makes Serena shriek with excitement.

Mercifully the guy is still fully dressed, though as he removes his shirt I have to do a double take. He's so hairy it looks like he's growing his own black singlet. His back has hair. His stomach has hair. His shoulders have hair. His neck has hair. His *hair* has hair. In fact, the only thing that doesn't have hair is his head – well, not much. It's as if he's used up his entire allotment on the rest of his body. To disguise this, he's gone for one of those comb-overs, which would only fool you if you were partially blind and irredeemably stupid.

Serena yearns for a Spanish dude to come galloping in and scoop her off her feet. Instead she's stuck with some sort of ape creature scampering across the room practically on all fours. I'm forced to avert my eyes again as the ape creature undoes his pants and slips them off.

Fortunately, when I pluck up the courage to open my eyes again they've covered themselves with a sheet.

They've only just started smooching when the sound of doof doof music comes blasting along the street.

No. It can't be. Not the beast. Not Creepo.

But then it screeches to a stop in the driveway, the horn blaring.

'Oh my God!' yells Serena, leaping out of bed like a frog on a barbecue.

'What?' replies the ape creature, his mind clearly elsewhere.

Serena pulls back the curtains and peers through the blinds. Unfortunately there's a window beam in her line of sight, so she's forced to bend over to see who it is, which exaggerates the size of her butt. And believe me, Serena has more than her fair share of butt. The ape creature reaches over and gives her a playful slap, sending out ripples of wobbling flesh. I don't think he's aware of how much trouble he's in.

Compared to those two, I feel rather safe in the wardrobe.

'Oh my God, it is!' screeches Serena. 'It's Tony.'

'What?' replies the ape creature, finally realising the gravity of the situation. He throws back the sheet. I quickly look away again. 'It can't be.'

'Quick,' gasps Serena. 'Hide.'

'Where?' pleads the ape creature, gathering up his clothes. 'In the wardrobe?'

Oh no.

'No,' replies Serena and I could almost kiss her. 'Next door. In the spare room. *Her* room.'

'Serena!' calls Creepo, bursting in downstairs.

The ape creature has only just closed my bedroom door when I hear Creepo bounding and hobbling up the stairs two at a time.

Meanwhile, Serena has crawled back into bed and gathered the bedclothes around her.

'What are you still doing in bed, you lazy cow?' gasps Creepo from the landing.

Serena smacks her lips together, pretending to have just woken up. 'What time is it?' It's not exactly an Academy Award-winning performance but it's enough to fool Creepo.

'Forget about the time, we have to go.'

'Where?'

Despite the fact she has a psycho in one room and her lover in the next, Serena is amazingly calm. I might have to rethink the whole Academy Award thing.

'Up the coast. Quick, get ready.'

'What? Why? Make me a coffee,' orders Serena. 'I'm not going anywhere without a coffee.'

She doesn't give a rat's about the coffee. She's just trying to get rid of Creepo so that he won't see she's in the nude and start asking questions, the answers to which he probably won't like. And will doubtless involve lots of yelling, lots of things being thrown, lots of sharp objects, lots of trips to the forest.

'And why are we going up the coast?' asks Serena, throwing in a fake yawn and stretch and barely managing to keep her boobs covered.

'Because *she's* up there,' replies Creepo. 'One of the boys spotted her on Saturday. Sitting on the beach, eating fish and chips. He thought it was strange that we weren't with her. Of course, I didn't tell him anything.'

'Why would she go up the coast?'

'She doesn't have anywhere else to go, obviously.'

'Can't we just leave her?' Thank you, Saint Serena. 'She hasn't gone to the cops yet, or we would have heard something from your mate.'

'We can't risk it. If she does we could both be in jail for a long time, probably life, you know that.'

'Okay. But if we find her, promise you'll make it quick.'

Saint Serena's halo slips slightly.

'Fine,' says Creepo. 'Come on. We've got to go.'

'Coffee first.'

'Okay, but it's only going to be instant.'

When Creepo heads back down the stairs to the kitchen, Serena clambers out of bed and throws on the same clothes that she went to collect the ape creature in. Then she goes into the bathroom and cleans her teeth. She is one cool cookie.

'Serena!' yells Creepo. 'C'mon.'

'Coming!' snaps Serena, flinging open the bathroom door and clomping downstairs.

And with that they're gone. Creepo must have made her a coffee to go in a thermos, because two minutes after she emerges from the bathroom I hear the guttural growl of the beast backing out the driveway and heading up the coast. Up the coast looking for me. Leaving me alone in the house with a naked ape creature. It's probably not my worst day on the streets so far, but it's definitely the weirdest.

A couple of minutes later I hear my bedroom door opening and the creak of the eighth step as the ape creature slinks back to his jungle.

I decide to give him twenty minutes just to be on the safe side. When that's up, I gather Creepo's gun and my cash, my piss-soaked clothes and *Bleak House* from behind the bathroom door and head off down the stairs.

I turn the corner into the kitchen, only to find the ape creature staring straight at me.

'Ah. You must be the missing niece.'

I'm so stunned that I almost drop the gun. I falter, then point it at him. The kettle is about to boil and he's fiddling about with his mobile.

'Oh, put that down,' says the ape creature. 'I'm no threat to you. Would you like a coffee?' He's very calm for someone who came within a whisker of dying.

I lower the gun. It was getting heavy anyway. 'Hot chocolate.'

'This isn't a café.' Then he looks at me and smiles. 'Then again, you have got a gun. A hot chocolate it is.'

The ape creature takes the milk out of the fridge and scrounges around in the cupboard for a pan.

'Do you speak?' he asks as he pours the milk into the pan.

'Probably too much.'

'Serena told me you'd gone AWOL.'

'Ay-wol?'

'Absent without leave. It's a military term. That's pretty clever you running away like that but hiding out in the house.'

'I'm not. I only came back yesterday to get some money from my piggybank but they came home.'

He nods at my four bundles of cash. 'It must have been bursting at the seams. Your piggybank, I mean.'

'I borrowed some from . . .' I trail off. 'From him. It's probably my parents' anyway.'

'Ah. A tragic accident.'

'Yeah, right.' I glare at him. 'What do you know about it?'

'Let's just say that I assisted with clearing up the financial side of things.'

'You're a crook.' I try to think of a better word but come up short.

'I operate within the grey areas of the law certainly.'

'So you know that my parents didn't go back to live in the old country?'

'I know that's the official line.'

'I don't understand how that's possible. Someone else must have sussed that something was wrong. What about their friends or my mum's parents? They must have . . .'

I trail off because he has a weird look in his eyes.

'Your grandparents, your mother's parents, were killed in an accident.'

Although I didn't really know them that well, it's still a bit of a shock. No wonder Serena only took me to visit them once, right after my parents 'disappeared'.

'Sorry to be the bearer of bad tidings.'

'I didn't really see them much. They were a bit weird, to be honest. How did they die?'

'House fire, I'm afraid.'

'You mean he killed them too?'

'The official verdict is that it was an accident. Apparently your grandfather was smoking in bed.'

'He didn't smoke.'

'Well, he certainly did that night.'

Although I don't think the ape creature meant it to be funny, I can't help but snort out a laugh. It dawns on him what he's just said and he laughs with me.

'Sorry. I didn't mean it like that.'

'So you're one of the boys?'

The ape creature bristles at this. 'No. I'm not one of his *boys*. I don't go around barbecuing old people while they're asleep. I'm a professional.'

I snort back another laugh. 'A professional what?'

There's a pause while the ape creature licks his wounds. It's safe to say that his day is not quite panning out the way he'd hoped. One minute he's planning a bit of bed-top wrestling with Serena, and the next he's hiding butt naked from the resident psychopath. Now he's been ridiculed by a gun-toting street kid.

'Where are you staying?'

I think about lying, but given what he's doing with Serena, it's not as if he'll be having a heart to heart with Creepo any time soon. 'I'm living on the trains.'

'That's rough.'

'I can look after myself.'

'Yes,' he agrees, staring at the gun. 'It seems as though you can.'

The milk is simmering in the pan so the ape creature makes me my hot chocolate. When he's finished stirring it he turns around and offers me the mug.

'Just put it on the bench.'

He smiles and does as I order, then goes back to making his coffee. I gulp down the hot chocolate, feeling the heat and sugar flowing through my body.

'Take it easy. You'll burn your stomach.'

'Shut up!' I snap, refusing to be nagged by adulterous, crooked ape creatures; even ones that make a lovely hot chocolate. 'I haven't had anything to eat for three days.' It's not exactly true but it's close enough.

'Would you like me to make you some breakfast? The fridge is well stocked.'

'No thanks. I'll get something later.'

'You don't trust people.'

'People yes. Men no.'

'Probably wise given your domestic circumstances.'

'What do *you* know about . . .' I trail off, trying to think of a better word than 'stuff'. He might look like the Wild Man of Borneo but he speaks well. '. . . about things?' Brilliant. It's as if I've swallowed a thesaurus.

'I know something of your dear uncle Tony, and believe me, after I've seen some of his handy work on Serena's beautiful face, I've often fantasised about parting his hairline with a meat cleaver.'

'So why haven't you? Are you chicken or something?'

He sips his coffee. Despite his shaggy exterior, he actually seems quite nice.

'Alas, I fear that I wouldn't adjust too well to prison life. I'm a lawyer, you see.'

'So, you've put people in jail. Don't want to say hi to them there?'

'No. It's the ones that I haven't been able to keep out of jail who might have an axe to grind with me, or else insert it somewhere I have no desire to see an axe inserted.'

I actually laugh at this.

'So I hang around the edges of Serena's life, waiting for her to call. Pathetic I know, but what can you do? I love her, you see.'

'Why don't you just run off with her?'

'Dear, sweet Serena has become accustomed to the life-style that your uncle affords her. She keeps me around for a bit of an illicit thrill, I suspect. I suppose between the two of us we make her happy. Besides, I don't think you quite realise just how dangerous your uncle is.'

'I've got some idea.'

'Visits in the night?'

I look down and say nothing.

'Serena hinted that something was afoot. You poor thing.'

I want to shout at him that there's nothing poor about me. That I've got a plan. A to-do list. That I'm going back to school, to university, and then to work for Médecins Sans Frontières and come up with a cure for that eye-eating African worm. But I think we'd both know that that will never happen. The closest street kids get to Médecins Sans Frontières is being treated by them.

I give him a wide berth and take a plastic shopping bag from the cupboard and stuff in my wet clothes, cash, *Bleak House* and Creepo's gun.

'What are you going to do with that? The gun, I mean.'

'Chuck it out. In the river or something.'

'A wise course of action. Show me.' He makes a clapping gesture, meaning I should pass him the gun.

I give him an 'as if!' look but then hand it to him anyway.

'Now, I'm not much of an expert on these things but if you want to keep your head in the vicinity of your shoulders, may I suggest transporting it with the safety catch on.' He holds the gun up to the light and then flicks a small switch on the side. Then he points it at the wall and squeezes the trigger. Nothing.

'Unless you're planning on becoming an assassin, I suggest removing the silencer. May I?'

I shrug and he unscrews the silencer and puts it in his pocket. He hands the gun back to me and I stuff it back into the plastic bag.

I stand up ready to get the hell out of there. 'Why are you still here? You know how psycho he is but you're sitting here drinking coffee.'

'A slight problem with my departure plan, I'm afraid. Deadlocked doors. Front and back. Thought I'd have a cup of coffee while I wait for a locksmith I know. Though locksmith is a fairly loose term for this particular tradesman. Anyway, there's plenty of time. They've gone up the coast looking for you, from what I could gather through the door.' He looks over at me. 'Finished?'

I nod and slide my cup over to him.

'Better tidy up. Don't want to leave any evidence of our little confab.'

He actually seems quite sweet as he tends to our cups, rinsing then under the tap and carefully drying them. I really wish Serena would divorce Creepo and marry this guy, despite what I said about him being an ape creature. Maybe he is her knight in shining armour after all – okay, hairy armour.

'It's okay,' I say, getting up from the kitchen chair. 'We can get out.'

He follows me through the kitchen and into the garage. I hit the button near the door and the garage door starts to clunk open.

'Interesting,' says Serena's knight. 'Deadlock the doors but leave the garage open to all comers.'

'I've worn shoes with a higher IQ than his.'

'Ah. Don't underestimate your foe,' he admonishes. 'Your uncle may be lacking a little in the area of book smarts, but he more than makes up for it when it comes to the streets.'

He steps outside while I hit the button that closes the garage door and then I follow him out.

'I'll call a cab. Can I drop you anywhere?'

'No thanks,' I reply. 'I've just got to get my stuff, it's around the side.'

'Risky. Remember what I said about underestimating him.'

He reaches into his wallet and hands me a card. It reads:

Marco Rossini – Lawyer and Accountant

He *is* smart.

'You never know,' he says. 'You might come into some money that needs . . .'

'Dispersing?'

'Exactly. That's a much nicer word than laundered.'

I don't know what he's going on about but I thank him anyway.

'How do I open a bank account?'

'Do you have ID?'

I nod.

'Just go in and open one. Put my office address down to have your statements sent to if you need an address. Or ask them not to send you statements. The notes are not sequential, are they?'

I don't know what he means so I reach into the plastic bag and hand him one of the bundles. He flicks through it.

'It's fine. Don't dump it all in at once, of course; that might raise a few eyebrows given your tender years, but otherwise everything's okay. Banks want to take your money. It's what they do, after all.'

I thank him and say goodbye. He walks off down the street calling a cab on his mobile. I'm about to chuck his business card in the gutter but on second thought decide to shove it in my pocket.

I retrieve my bags, climb over the fence, and then I leave that horrible house for ever.

Five minutes later I'm back inside, creeping up the stairs with a bag full of dog poo.

CAFÉ

WHAT WERE YOU PLAYING AT?

I couldn't help myself. I was gone. That was it. Finished with them. The house. Everything. Time to get on with my life.

So why go back inside?

It was pretty childish, I suppose. But then again, I was a child.

Go on.

After I'd stuffed my wet clothes and everything into my backpack, I took off. Although I'd hardly slept a wink in the last three nights, I was buzzing. I'd survived another close encounter of the psychotic kind and I also had someone that I felt I could go to for help if I really had to. Anyway, as I was walking through the park towards the train station, I almost stepped on it. It was disgusting. A complete gross-out. I mean, what sort of person lets a dog take a dump like that and not clean it up? And this was a seriously big dog. Either that or someone had been taking their rhinoceros for its morning walk. And it dawned on me – Creepo was getting off scot-free. He'd done so many disgusting, shitty things and there was nothing happening to him in return. No retaliation. No consequences.

So what did you do?

I scooped the poop. I got the plastic bag for my wet clothes out of my backpack and, this was the really disgusting bit, turned it inside out and somehow managed to pick up that steaming pile of pooch poo. I could feel the heat it was giving off through the plastic. I was gagging the whole time. After I tied up the bag, I ran back to their house, climbed the fence, raided the gnome and crept upstairs.

What did you do with it?

I emptied the bag halfway down the side of his bed, between the sheets, and then I carefully remade the bed. He was going to cop it. Even if it was just on his feet.

It wasn't much really, was it? A bit of dog poo in his bed? They could have come back.

Yes, but they didn't. And you're right. It wasn't much. But it was something. Something that Matilda might have done. I wanted him to know that it was me. To put him on notice. I wanted him to know that from now on there were going to be consequences to his actions.

Herr Gel

By the time the train pulls into the station the peak hour is over. Adults are at work, kids at school.

I'm jealous of those kids. I can feel them out there learning. Getting ahead of me. I was going to try to find myself a school today but after what happened last night, that'll have to wait until tomorrow. At least.

Now that I'm away from Creepo's house of horrors my guard comes down and I can feel just how tired I am. I can barely keep my eyes open and I have strange pains in my chest and head, not to mention the back of my neck. The trouble is, I haven't got anywhere to sleep. I know that there are probably hostels for the homeless in the city, but I'm pretty sure they'd be locked up during the day to stop us from lingering. And besides, I've decided to avoid the city. The thought of being alone there, at night, with all the drunks and weirdos freaks me out. The bright lights might attract the homeless, but some of that glitter will undoubtedly come from the red-light district and I'm not going there. Never. There are leeches there who'll stick poison in your veins so that you'll stick strange men's things in your vagina to be able to *afford* the poison for your veins. Death lives down that road. And not a very pleasant one.

I get up and slouch over to the map above the train's door. We're coming to a junction station for a new line that services the leafy northern suburbs. That could be a safe option. I bet very few psychos prowl the ivy belt. I could curl up on the seat and go to sleep. Or else I could stay on this line and head back up to Death Valley. To my weekender. To Creepo.

Looking at the map again I notice that there's a mega-mall a couple of stops along the new line that now has its own underground station. I'm not really big on the whole shopping thing but at least there'll be food, crowds, anonymity.

When the train stops I pick up my gear and haul my exhausted butt down the escalator to the new line. I lug my stuff on board the train that's sitting there and slump down onto the seat opposite a young mother who's obviously on a day out with her daughter. Shopping maybe. Off to yum cha perhaps.

The kid smiles at me and she's so cute in her little tartan dress and geisha girl hairdo that I smile back. Mum isn't happy. She yanks the kid's arm and snarls something to her in Cantonese. Mum then glares at me and is unable to prevent herself from sneering and muttering under her breath. I give her my best 'Screw you!' look so she gets up and yanks the kid across the aisle to another seat, almost dislocating her shoulder in the process. She loves the kid so much she's actually abusive in her protection of her. I'll never figure people out.

With a grunt the train shoots into the tunnel and I'm able to see my reflection in the blackened window. I take one look at my bedraggled features, my hollow, sunken eyes, my pasty face, my greasy hair and am half-inclined to move seats myself. It dawns on me that I have all the drawbacks of looking like a crackhead without any of the benefits. Not that there are any benefits to being a crackhead, other than death maybe. But still.

*

It seems to me that a shopping centre's role is to stop people from thinking. About life. About the universe. About death. About the oblivion that awaits us beyond our last breath. Come to think of it I could probably do with a bit of shopping myself. Stop being so emo about the misery that's waiting for us in the afterlife and get on with the business of enjoying life while it's here.

I slide into a booth in one of the cafés just off from the food court. It's still early so there are plenty of spare tables. There are a couple of groups of cackling mothers. Free for the day now that the sprogs have been dropped off at school. Half of them are in lycra, either coming from or going to the gym, or maybe because they think they look good in lycra. They don't. It's not hard to eavesdrop because they're basic-ally yelling. They're discussing the shortcomings of someone who hasn't turned up yet. From what I can gather the missing woman's husband sucks. Maybe this is Serena's coffee group.

I look at the menu but nothing really grabs me. I'm so hungry that I'm not hungry any more. I must be like one of those marathon runners whose energy levels drop so low that their bodies start devouring them. I reckon my body has given up waiting for food and it's starting to eat me from the inside out.

A young guy emoed up in black and with about a kilo of hair gel sitting slimily on his head eventually swaggers over.

He gives me a sort of *why-aren't-you-at-school?* look, but he doesn't say anything. Playing truant officer would obviously cut into his grooming time so he decides against it.

'What can I get you?' asks Herr Gel, who I've decided is German, purely for the gag factor. *Herr* means Mister in German. I read that somewhere. And for some reason *Kugelschreiber* means pen, which seems like a lot of effort just to say pen.

I stare at the menu again. My heart isn't in it, but I can't let my body carry on devouring me. If I keep this up I'll simply cease to exist. Or else wind up in a psycho ward with my eyelids sewn shut like the other foodie freaks.

'A mango smoothie and a cheese and avocado toasted sandwich.'

'What sort?'

'What sort of what?'

'Cheese.'

'The yellow sort.'

Herr Gel finds this absolutely hilarious. He snorts like a Colombian airport beagle. 'Swiss? Cheddar? Plastic? Edam?'

'Swiss.'

'Bread?'

Who knew ordering a sandwich would be this difficult?

'Whatever.'

'White? Wholegrain? Brown? Low GI? Thick crust?'

'White!'

Herr Gel jots down my order with his *Kugelschreiber* but mercifully they obviously only have one type of mango so with a 'back soon' he smiles at me and walks off.

'Samsung.'

'I'm sorry?' he says, turning back.

'I'd like my sandwich to be made in a Samsung toaster. I'm assuming we get a choice.'

Herr Gel points at me in that ridiculously uncool way that some guys do. 'You're funny.'

And you care more about what's on your head than what's in it.

I pull out *The Old Man and the Sea* just to give myself something to do while I'm waiting. Try to shut out the cackling mothers.

Eventually, just as the marlin makes a last, desperate bid for freedom, Herr Gel swaggers back with my order.

He places the toastie and smoothie in front of me and then undertakes an elaborate bow. 'Madam.'

I flash him a smile on and off and then take a long sip of my smoothie. One sip, that's all it takes and I can feel the energy flooding back into my system. My body backs off cannibalising me.

'Good book?'

I'm busy hoeing into my toastie like a shark into a marlin, so even though my mouth is half-stuffed with sandwich I tell him that it's a classic, which comes out more like 'cwassic'. I also spray some flecks of toast across the table. Charming.

Herr Gel picks up my book and examines it like it's a dead fish. 'Pretty boring title if you ask me.'

'I'll tell Mr Hemingway next time I see him.'

'He should have called it *The Old Man and the Sea Monsters*. That would have been more interesting. Would have sold more too, I bet.'

I haven't got a clue if he's joking or not. I'll have to get better at this sort of stuff.

'I'll leave you to it.'

I flash him another smile.

'Hey, listen. There's a toga party at uni on Friday night.'

I almost choke on my sandwich. '*You* go to uni?'

'Yeah. Why shouldn't I?'

'*The Old Man and the Sea Monsters*?'

'I was,' Her Gel pauses for effect, 'joking. Anyway, I'm not studying English but economics.'

'Why?'

'I want to be an accountant.'

'Why?' Wait a minute. Why was he talking about toga parties?

'So what do you reckon?'

'About what?'

'About the toga party? You have to bring someone.'

'What's a toga party?'

'You dress up like Romans. Ancient Romans, anyway.'

'Why?'

'It's fun. You know, Socrates and all that. It was a riot.'

'Socrates was Greek, not Roman.'

'Same thing.'

'No, it's not.'

'So are you in?'

I'm about to say no, but I've just realised that Herr Gel might be able to help me. 'My toga's in the wash.'

'Ha, ha. Just use a sheet.'

I haven't got a sheet. 'I'll think about it.'

'Sweet.'

'Are there any hotels around here? Good ones, I mean.'

He gives me a suggestive smile. 'Why? What did you have in mind?'

'Sleep.'

'Wait a minute,' says Herr Gel, getting serious. He looks at the cast on my arm, then down at my sleeping bag and backpack which are under the table next to my feet. Then he looks back up at my hair which is so greasy you could fry scallops in it. 'Are you homeless?'

'Is it *that* obvious?' If I can't wash my hair at least twice a week, I'll have to go with dreadlocks, which would be okay, I guess.

'Cool. I've never met a homeless person before. Especially a chick.'

How can you *especially* not meet a homeless person?

'You could come and stay at my place for a bit . . .'

A bit of what? I give him my withering 'as if!' look.

'. . . though my parents would probably suss there was someone else living in my room. Unless you hid in the wardrobe when Mum makes my bed.'

His mum makes his bed. 'Hotel?'

'There's one up on the corner.' He makes a gesture towards the road. 'It's just past the uni. It's really nice. My aunt had her wedding reception there. Lot of corporate types stay there on business.'

I don't know what corporate types are but I nod anyway.

'How do I get in?'

'You want to break into a room and crash?'

'No. Properly.'

'Do you have any money?'

I nod.

'It's expensive.'

'I've got my aunt's credit card.' I pull it out of my pocket and show him.

He studies the card. 'Serena Sanchez. Are you Mexican?'

'Paraguayan.' I have to bite my lip when I say this.

'Anyway, cash might be better if you can't get her signature right.'

I shove the card away again. It was stupid to show him, to let him see the name. 'I'm good for cash,' I say as coolly as I can.

He raises his eyebrows at me, and I think of the money bricks nestled in the bottom of my bag. Next to the gun. God.

I knew I should have thrown it out. But I didn't just want to chuck it in the bin or the creek. I don't know how to take the bullets out and kids might have found it.

'You would have to be the coolest chick I've ever met.' Herr Gel pauses and gives me another suggestive look and suddenly I suspect where he's coming from. He obviously thinks that without my parents around, with me being homeless and everything, I'll be easy prey. And I'm happy to feed the delusion if it helps me.

'Well? The hotel. How do I get in?'

Herr Gel stares at me as if he doesn't understand what the problem is. 'Just rock up to reception and ask for a room. Tell them you're paying in cash. Advance if they want it.'

'You don't think they'd ask questions?'

'About what?'

'Well, my age.'

'How old are you?'

'How old do you think I am?'

'Sixteen. Seventeen.'

I must look like death warmed up. 'Try thirteen.'

'Oh shit, sorry. You look a lot . . .' He trails off. 'Listen. About the toga party. It's probably best if you don't, you know. I mean you're cute and everything, but I don't want to go to jail.'

I give him my sweetest look and then lay the sarcasm on with a machine gun. 'That's so romantic.'

And now that he can't get anything out of me, not without going to jail, he'll just walk away. Toss me aside like a dirty handkerchief.

'Look. I'm sorry if I creeped you out and everything. You look much older and, I mean, how many thirteen-year-olds read Hemingway and know that Socrates was Roman not Greek?'

'Other way round.'

'How many thirteen-year-olds walk around with credit cards and wads of cash?'

Herr Gel tells me to wait where I am, that he's on a break in ten minutes and we'll work out a way of getting me into the hotel. Then he winks at me, smiles and is off serving other customers. I give myself a mental kick up the bum. Not all men are like Creepo.

Ten minutes later, as promised, Herr Gel is back. He plonks down another mango smoothie, which he tells me is on the house. His way of saying he's sorry, I guess. He's got his mobile with him and he's written the hotel phone number on a Post-It note. He also tells me that his name is Alistair McAlister, which seems so unlikely that I can't stop myself from laughing.

Alistair McAlister phones the hotel and makes a booking for me and my mother. I start to protest and gesture madly but I don't know the sign language for 'my mother has spent the last few years decomposing out in the forest', so he waves me away.

'All done,' he says, hanging up.

'Done?' I snap. 'My mother's dead.'

'It doesn't matter.'

'It probably does to her.'

'No, that's not what . . .'

'I suppose I could try and dig up a thighbone or something . . .'

'No,' interrupts Alistair McAlister because I'm starting to ramble. 'You don't need her. Just the idea of her.'

'So why did you book it in my aunt's name?'

'You might have to leave a credit card imprint, for the minibar and stuff.'

'I'm not going to have anything from the minibar.'

'They don't know that.'

'I still don't know how I'm supposed to get in without my dead mother or my . . .'

Alistair McAlister taps his head. 'Listen and learn.'

He tells me his plan, and although it's got a couple of holes in it, I have to admit that it's pretty good, so good in fact that I take a few notes. And then I realise that I'm learning my first lesson of life on the streets. Learning my first lessons in street smarts from a trainee accountant called Alistair McAlister whose mummy still makes his bed.

I've got a long way to go.

CAFÉ

Yeah, he was cool. He even gave me his mobile number and made me promise to ring him and let him know how it went. So I had three people looking out for me. Who I could get help from if I had to.

Three?

Dr Chen, Marco Rossini and Alistair McAlister. I suppose what I learned from that is that people are basically good. Yes there are some psychos out there but not as many as we think. Paedos make the news because what they do is disgusting. The millions, billions, or whatever it is, of men who aren't paedos don't make the news. People are good but we don't really get to hear about them because the media is only interested in the freak show; it makes the world look much worse than it actually is.

So you went to the hotel?

Yeah. I had planned to slink up to reception and ask for a room and if they gave me a funny look I was just going to run off. But Alistair said that I had to be super confident and act as if nothing was wrong. He told me about this uncle of his who was like this total thief. What's that word for someone who can't stop themselves from stealing stuff? Klept-something.

Kleptomaniac?

Yeah, well this uncle of his would go into a supermarket or the hardware store and wheel out a trolley full of groceries or a new workbench or something and just casually walk through the checkout.

How did he avoid getting caught?

Because he was so obvious about it. He didn't try to sneak out. He'd just march through the exit with his trolley or chainsaw or whatever and say something like, 'That's all sorted, see you later', and off he'd go. Or he'd march up to the guy on the exit door and go, 'Bob in tools reckons that this'll cut down a gum tree no probs, what do you reckon?' And then they'd have a chat about it and after that he'd thank the guy and just walk out.

How did he have the nerve?

Practice, I guess. He used to carry around this old receipt, which he'd look at as he was walking through the checkout, and nobody thought to question him.

What's that got to do with you? You weren't planning on embracing a life of crime, were you?

God no. 'Thou shalt not steal'. It's ingrained. Number eight on the hot ten list of commandments. Besides anything else, I figured if I got caught I'd be shipped back to Creepo and Serena, especially since by that time I was probably registered as a runaway. And then Creepo would totally ignore commandment number six and get right down to a bit of murdering, while Marco Rossini was busy engaging in a serious bout of number ten – coveting his neighbour's wife (or her ass).

Did you get into the hotel?

It was hard enough just getting there. Alistair said that it was just up the road but it was about a kilometre away and because I hadn't slept for so long I had to stop for a couple of breaks along the way. I was sitting there in the gutter just about ready to pass out I was so tired and there were all these young, healthy-looking uni students walking past me. A couple of them said something to me and so I told them where to go and what to do when they go there. It was my first stereotypical homeless moment. Sitting in the gutter telling passersby to go and screw themselves. I realised that I was only a supermarket trolley and a serious case of BO away from being a bag lady.

But you made it?

Eventually.

Room Service

AT MY OLD SCHOOL WE USED TO HAVE THIS CHINESE TEACHER. I DON'T mean that she was Chinese (even though she was), but that she used to teach Chinese. It was a pretty heavy ESL area. We had an Arabic teacher for a while too, but he used to yell at all the Lebanese boys until they cried. Anyway, when I was in year three, just before everything kicked off at home, I asked if I could go and learn Chinese, mostly so I could hang out with my bestie at the time, Susan Wong. I told the teachers that when I left school I was going to live in Hong Kong (which is where Susan was from and where she went back to at the end of year six) and it was unfair that I wasn't allowed to learn Chinese just because I wasn't Chinese. So they gave in and let me join in the Mandarin classes. I was lucky that the principal bought my bullshit story about moving to Hong Kong, especially when Susan told me that most people speak Cantonese there, not Mandarin.

Anyway, Mrs Chiu started each lesson by telling a traditional Chinese story. Sometimes the stories were interesting.

Other times they were mind-meltingly boring. Some of the morals were also a bit dodgy. I remember one story I did like called 'The Axe'. This old woodchopper wakes up one morning but he can't find his axe anywhere. He searches all over for it but can't find the thing. The woodchopper immediately suspects his neighbour's son but he has no proof. But every time the woodchopper looks at his neighbour's son, he looks like a thief, he walks like a thief, and he acts like a thief. Then a few days later the woodchopper finds his axe behind the chook pen, in exactly the same spot he'd left it. And the next time the woodchopper sees his neighbour's son, he looks like a boy, he walks like a boy, and he acts like a boy.

I feel a bit like the neighbour's son when I walk into the foyer of the Shangrila Pines Resort. I haven't stolen anyone's axe. I haven't stolen anything (apart from a couple of Creepo's money bricks and his gun, but that doesn't count) but I bet I look like I have. And that's what the story taught me. I need to look like I belong in a five-star hotel, not like a homeless chick who'd steal your last scallop, because, let's face it, I'm both.

The foyer doesn't have a sign that reads 'If You Don't Have a Serious Amount of Money Then Go Away!'. It doesn't need to. It's all shiny granite floors, plush inviting lounges, fresh flowers and artificial fountains. It even has a smell. A smell of success.

Above the reception there are a bunch of clocks announcing the time in Sydney, New York, Tokyo, London, and Dubai, so that'll come in handy. I don't know how ordinary people make it through the day without knowing the time in Tokyo. Beyond the reception area there's a café, a couple of restaurants and a bar. But before I can get to any of those I have to make it past reception. As I'm walking over to the check-in desk, I catch sight of my reflection in one of the mirrored columns dotted around the lobby. I look like I've stolen someone's axe and gone on a homicidal rampage.

I bail out and duck into the toilets for a better look. I don't know what Alistair McAlister saw in me that would make him want to ask me to a toga party. I look like I'm as close to death as you can get yet still technically be alive. Apart from my emaciated face and greasy hair, my t-shirt's all crushed and I'm wearing tracksuit pants because my piss-soaked jeans from last night are stuffed down the bottom of my backpack.

I wash my face and run my hands through my hair, figuring that the wet look is better than the grease ball one. After that I look and feel marginally better. I think about hiding my sleeping bag in one of the cubicles or in the bin and collecting it later. But it's not a homeless girl who's going to keep me out of the hotel; it's my imaginary mother who's going to get me in.

I march over to reception with my head held high and shoulders pulled back. I feel completely unco. I notice outside that a coach has just pulled up and is disgorging a Japanese tour group onto the foyer. From the amount of luggage the harried driver's unloading, it looks like they've just come from the airport. This could work in my favour. If the check-in crew are about to be swamped, they'll want to get rid of me as quickly as they can.

'Can I help you?'

I take a deep breath and try to recall Alistair McAlister's script. Say her name. It creates a connection. A familiarity.

I glance down at her left boob. 'Yeah, hi Mia. We have a booking.'

'And the name?' Mia is quick and efficient. I like that in a check-in clerk. She's a career woman. My mother should impress her.

'Sanchez.'

Mia taps her keyboard. 'That's a twin single for one night.'

I don't know what a twin single is, it makes no sense at all, but I say yes.

Mia glances up from her screen. She looks doubtful. Unlike Alistair McAlister, she obviously doesn't think I'm sixteen or seventeen. It's time to wheel out the big guns.

'I must look like crap,' I say, and giggle. I look up at the clocks on the wall behind her. 'We've just flown in from New York. My mother had to go into the city but she had the cab drop me off first. Didn't want me hanging around her high-powered meeting.' Then I put away the guns and go nuclear. 'She's a barrister.' A check-in clerk is not going to mess with a barrister. 'She's meeting with the Lord Chief Justice.' I don't even know if there's such a thing as a Lord Chief Justice, but I'm betting Mia won't either.

Mia smiles. 'You do look tired.'

'Tell me about it.'

'What happened to your arm?'

My psycho, paedo uncle broke it. 'I hurt it . . .' I was in New York, think. '. . . ice-skating.' Brilliant.

'There's a slight problem,' says Mia. 'We can't release the room to you yet. You see, we need . . .'

I interrupt her. 'I understand. My mum's a famous barrister, but she's also a single mum and we go all over the world together.'

Mia stares at me, as if she's not really sure where I'm going with this. Maybe I've overdone it. I put her out of her misery. 'You need her credit card, right? Or a deposit.'

'That's right,' says Mia, brightening now that we're on the same page.

'Happens all the time.' I hand over the credit card and two fifty dollar notes.

'Oh,' says Mia. 'We only need one. Credit card or down payment.'

'I know,' I reply, 'but some hotels prefer one over the other. Take your pick. Mum said that it didn't matter as long as you let me have the room.' There's just a hint of a threat in there. 'She said that she'd call after her meeting to see if everything's okay.' Of course she isn't going to call, what with her not existing and everything, but that's not the point. Mia just needs to believe that she will. However, Mia's got what she needs and the queue is building up behind me; she's going to be run off her feet for the next half an hour checking this lot in and she can't be looking forward to it. Mia slides the cash back to me and swipes Serena's credit card. Then she hands me the key, which is not a key at all but another card, two in fact (one for me and one for Mum) and that's it. I'm in.

'Take the elevator or the stairs to the second floor and your room is just along the corridor. We hope you and your mum have a very pleasant stay.'

'Thank you, Mia,' I say. 'We will.'

I practically skip up the stairs.

Thank you, Alistair McAlister.

*

It takes three swipes with the keycard for the lock to flash green. After that I push against the door and enter my safe haven. I've stayed in a couple of hotels before with Mum and my father, but they weren't anything like this. My father didn't like spending money – not on us, anyway.

The heavy door closes behind me with a reassuring clunk. I flick the latch. Safe at last.

After three nights sleeping (or not sleeping) rough, this is heaven. Heaven minus the praising.

The bathroom fittings are seriously expensive. Gold-plated taps, yet more granite and a shower screen so clean it may as well not be there. There's a stack of plush towels, and behind the door two robes hang ghostlike on hooks. In the room itself there's a widescreen TV and two huge beds. I chuck my stuff onto one bed and go on a treasure hunt around the rest of the room. The minibar doesn't just have drinks, it also has chocolates. Although it's tempting, I leave the Mars bars alone. For now. I've got to eat properly when I can.

I pull back my curtains, unlatch the door and step out onto a small balcony that overlooks the pool. The water looks so inviting, but I'm too tired and hungry to float, let alone swim. I slip back into my room and latch the balcony door, shutting out the fresh air and danger. Although Creepo doesn't have a clue where I am, I'm not taking any chances. With anyone.

I run the bath and pour in all the complimentary cleaning gels and oils. I don't even know what they're all for. While the cauldron of foam is building up I phone Alistair McAlister to let him know that I made it. He seems genuinely happy and avoids an awkward moment by not asking for my room number, which I wouldn't have given him anyway. He asks me to call him if I need anything and even if I don't. I have to keep in touch or he'll worry about me, he says. After that I unload my backpack, which stinks of stale wee. My own. I put my books, writing pad and my backpack outside on the balcony table to air and stash the money in the room safe. After that I strip off and hang my tracksuit pants, shirt and sleeping bag over the rail and chuck the rest of the clothes from my backpack into the bubble bath and climb in after them. I lie back and rest my head as millions of tiny bubbles burst against my skin. I have to keep my cast out of the water, which is a bit awkward, but I'm still so comfortable in the bath. This is the first time I've been able to relax in God knows how long. Not just the four days that I've been homeless; all the way back to year three, now that I think about it. Maybe my entire life. No fist and knife fights downstairs in the kitchen. No perverted paedo uncles trying to slither into my room. Slither into me. I hadn't realised how stressed I was until now. I can feel the tension being drawn out of me and dispersed into the water. Apart from the small strip of light beneath the door, the bathroom is in total darkness. I don't want anyone to know that I'm in here naked. Force of habit, I guess.

*

Off in the distance there's a strange gurgling sound. The bathroom door swings open and Creepo's standing there with a 'gotcha' leer etched across his face. I'm too terrified to even move. To fight back. It's over. He stalks into the bathroom and slides his hands around my neck, slowly strangling the life out of me. I can feel my eyes bulging as my existence begins to leak away.

I sit up and gasp, sucking oxygen and life back into my lungs. When my pulse has dropped a little I look around the blackness, trying to figure out where the hell I am. Where Creepo has got to.

The water's stone cold and it seems that in sheer exhaustion my head had slumped to the side and slid underwater. I could have drowned.

I haul myself out of the bath and slip on one of the plush robes from behind the door. And, just because I can, I drag on my fake Mum's too. I simply couldn't be arsed washing my clothes so I leave them in the bath to soak.

Although my body craves sleep, I'm too hyped up from the nightmare. How horrible would that be? My last memory of life on earth, the image to accompany me to the great beyond, would have been Creepo. Note to self – no more baths when I'm exhausted.

It's not exactly healthy but I order some wedges and a hot chocolate. Comfort food. I decide to count the money while I'm waiting.

Fifteen minutes later there's a knock on the door, which coincides with the sound of my chin hitting the floor.

'Room service.'

What have I done? 'Could you just leave it outside?'

'You need to sign for it.'

One bundle would have been enough. 'My mum's not back from work yet.'

'That's okay, you can sign for it.'

One bundle. But oh no, I had to go and get greedy and take four. I should have just stuck with my piggybank and *Bleak House*, but, no, I seriously must have a death wish.

I stop my mental ranting and look through the peephole. The waiter's wearing black pants, a white shirt and a black waistcoat. More crucially she's a she. I race over to Mum's bed and turn the bedcover over the cash. Then I slip off the safety latch and open the door.

'Good afternoon.' The woman strides confidently into the room and places the tray on the table. She hands me a small black folder. I'm not sure what I'm meant to do with it so I just say thanks.

She smiles, opens it up and points to where I'm supposed to sign.

'No school today?'

I sign on the dotted line. I've got no idea how much the kitchen and reception staff tell each other but I decide to play it safe and opt for consistency. 'We just flew in from New York.'

'Oh, I love New York.' She takes the folder back from me. 'Which bit?'

'Which bit what?'

'Which bit of New York did you fly in from?'

Is this chick mad? 'The airport.'

She snorts then seems to remember her role. 'Sorry. I mean where were you staying?'

Oh crap! That's the trouble with lying. You've got to do your research. I scan my memory banks, looking for something to lock on to. Man something. Man . . .? Mad Hatter? 'Manhattan.' Phew.

'I love Central Park, it's just so . . . New York.'

I'm not sure what to do with this so I decide to leave it. 'Enjoy your meal.'

I'm not sure if the World Health Organisation would agree that wedges and a hot chocolate constitute a meal, but I thank her anyway.

When she's gone, I slip the 'Do Not Disturb' sign on the outside door handle and the safety latch back on the lock. And now I can get back to some more mental rambling.

EIGHT THOUSAND DOLLARS!

That's what I've been lugging around with me.

It's not good, it's bad. Really bad.

I didn't think Creepo would miss a couple of money bricks, seeing how he had so many to begin with. But I've got absolutely no doubt that he'll miss eight grand. Hell, anyone would. I thought there might be a thousand all up. Maybe even two. But eight? No way. I wouldn't have taken it if I'd known there was that much. Creepo's got enough reasons to hunt me down as it is.

There's nothing I can do. It's mine now. And besides,

Creepo should pay for everything he's put me through. The eight k is for screwing up my life and being a murdering bastard. I'll take his cash for that.

I put the stuffing-up-my-life payment back in the safe and lock the door. Then I take the food tray over to my bed and make myself comfortable.

After I finish my wedges and hot chocolate, I snuggle down into the crisp fresh sheets. I open up one of Mum's diaries and try to get to know her better. It starts when she's sixteen. It's full of her hopes and dreams and fears. Standard stuff, I suppose. She could be any teenager anywhere. I flick forward a few pages to where she starts talking about my father, about his life in the old country, about how *his* father treated him and Creepo. Their mother died young and it seems like their father took it out on them and the bottle. My head starts to drop into the page and so I put away her diary and turn on the TV to see what's happening in the world since I left it. I think about watching a movie but I'm asleep in seconds.

ACT THREE

LAST TRAIN TO KATHMANDU

We are all in the gutter, but some of us
are looking at the stars.

— OSCAR WILDE

CAFÉ

You must have slept all day and night.

I could have. But I forced myself to get up a couple of hours later because I had things to do.

Like what?

Just boring stuff like buying toothpaste because the tube in the hotel room was too tiny to bother stealing. Then I phoned Dr Chen, because I'd promised I would.

What did she say?

She said that she'd reported me and that Creepo had come and threatened her. That's when she hit him with a restraining order, which totally cracked me up. Creepo thought he was so tough, a gangster, and Dr Chen is the size of an Oompa Loompa and yet she gets right in his face legally.

What else did she say?

She said that I should come to the surgery, that I'd be looked after, but I couldn't risk it. Dr Chen thought Creepo was bad news, but she didn't know just how psycho he really was. I told her that I was sorry for bringing all this trouble into her life. She said it was okay and I should come in and see her in a few weeks, to take the cast off my arm, and that was that.

And did you?

Yeah, but she was away on holidays in Hong Kong, so another doctor took my cast off. So anyway, before I went downstairs to the hotel shop for my toothpaste and stuff I went into the bathroom to get my tracksuit pants and t-shirt and I saw that all my other clothes were still in the bath. I fished them out and hung them on the towel rails, but I knew they wouldn't be dry for ages and that I wouldn't be going off to look for a school the next day, which was a really bad habit to be getting into, and I sort of hated myself for it. It was like I was looking for excuses not to reconnect with the world. So I called Alistair McAlister and asked him if he could phone the hotel again and book me in for a couple more nights. I figured that I was kind of like a wounded animal that needs to hole up for a few days to lick its wounds and get its strength back. He phoned me back in the room about five minutes later and told me that he'd done it; said that he was my mum's personal assistant and that she needed a few extra days, and the check-in clerk had said to take as long as she needed. Alistair also said that I should come to the toga party after all, as a friend.

I had dinner in the restaurant that night. I felt a bit awkward at first, sitting there without my mum but I knew that if I was going to live this lie, I'd better start getting some practice at it and not rely on Alistair McAlister every time I needed someone to bullshit for me.

How did you do?

It was easy. When the waitress came over I told her that Mum would be down soon only she was on an important call to Tokyo and that I should start without her. And that was that. I had a delicious bowl of pasta and a side order of vegetables, because I had to start looking after myself.

Weren't you a bit self-conscious just sitting there by yourself? You were only thirteen.

I was at first. Though the waitress couldn't have cared less. But have you ever had dinner in a restaurant by yourself?

Plenty of times.

So you know the secret. The secret of how to sit there by yourself without looking like the loserest loser in the whole of Loserdom?

Take a book.

Exactly.

There's that kind of dead time between when you've ordered and when your food is delivered, so I ducked back to my room and got *Bleak House*.

Seems kind of appropriate.

What do you mean?

You spent the previous night at your Uncle Tony's . . .

Yeah, you're right. The real bleak house.

Did you ever go back there again?

To Creepo's? No, why would I?

Just wondering.

Well I didn't, okay.

All right. I'm only asking. No need to get defensive.

It's hard, you know, reliving this shit.

We can stop for the day if you want.

No. I'm good. Let's keep going.

Okay. Can we talk about how you got back into school?

You're gonna love this. Before I met Cinderella, I had a sort of skanky fairy godmother.

And she looked after you?

For a price.

One other thing: would it be possible to borrow your mother's diaries? I assume you still –

Why?

I'd like to get to know your mother a little better, that's all. Delve into her background.

There's stuff about my father in there too. Stuff he'd obviously told her about growing up in [deleted from transcript].

Even better.

It's awful but I only really got to know her through her diaries and the more I read the more I began to like her. As a person I mean. I loved her as my mum, obviously. This might sound a bit weird but when I stayed at the Shangrila Pines, I used to go to the cemetery, which was a couple of Ks up the road, and sit and talk to her.

But how . . .?

It wasn't her grave. I found someone around the same age and talked to her instead. Talked to both of them.

A surrogate?

I suppose so.

That's . . .

Pathetic?

No. It's . . . nice.

The Ghosts and Mrs Bennet

The harsh winter wind banshees in off the sea, causing him to lose control momentarily. What little daylight there was has long since vanished over the horizon, leaving him alone and shivering in the dark. He corrects the steering just in time. A moment later and he or the bike or both would have disappeared over the cliff and been dashed onto the rocks below. It's not even his bike; it's little Anthony's, and he doesn't know that it's been borrowed. He'll be angry if he finds out.

He'd finished his deliveries about an hour ago but he'd stopped off in the woods on the promise from the other boys that Maria would show him her knickers for a drag on his cigarette. She didn't turn up. And now he was hopelessly lost. If he could just find a familiar landmark, he could feel his way home. He was half-inclined to abandon the bike, but Anthony would find out, and who knew what that kid was capable of. Anthony would get that look in his eye that frightened his older brother. It was the look of the devil. The look of the damned.

He pulled up and stared into the valley far below. He could make out the dim glow from one of the old farmhouses leading into their village. This was it. He was as good as home. He pushed off and guided the bike down the hill towards the light. He was going at a good pace now. He pumped the peddles hard in anticipation of the upcoming hill but his geography was out. Where he was expecting a small rise there was in fact a T-intersection. He slammed into the ditch and sailed clean over the handlebars without ever touching the breaks.

He woke to what he hoped might be the breath of an angel but was instead greeted by the stench of hell.

'Come on, boy,' said a voice through the fog. 'Come back to me.'

'Hmmn.' That smell. It was like rotting apples and methylated spirits combined with sulfur. 'What? Where am I? What happened?'

'You've had an accident. Nothing broken. You'll have a bit of a headache though.'

He felt his head. There was already a golf ball-sized lump forming near his temple and he had a fight this weekend.

'You're Dragan's boy, aren't you?'

'Yeah.' He squinted his eyes. 'Mr Tomasich?'

'That's right.' Old man Tomasich leered. God, when did he last clean his teeth? Since the last war, when his wife had disappeared with one of the troops or into the forest, Old Man Tomasich and his stinking den of iniquity had been slowly rotting back into the foul pits of the earth.

And yet here he was, in all his filth, happy to lend a helping hand.

'C'mon. Up you get. Big strong lad like you can take a hit to the head and get up before the bell.'

Old Man Tomasich helped him to his feet and patted down his jacket.

'The front wheel's buckled, but old Dragan can fix that up as good as new. He's good with his hands, your old man.'

The boy felt his jaw. His old man was good with his hands, all right.

He picked up the bike and wheeled it back out onto the road, its buckled wheel taunting him with each revolution. 'Thank you, Mr Tomasich.'

'Tell everyone I said goodbye.'

'Goodbye?'

He looked around but Old Man Tomasich just smiled, turned around and stalked off into the blackness.

'Where the hell have you been?'

The house, lacking a woman's touch, stank of men.

He stared at his father, who was curled up in his chair like a dog ready to pounce.

'Well?'

'I had to finish my deliveries.'

'Don't lie to me, boy. I'm warning you. Don't lie to me. You should have been home hours ago.'

'I had an accident. I got lost on the way home and crashed coming down the hill by Old Man Tomasich's farm.'

His father mumbled something under his breath and made the sign of the cross.

'He's not as bad as everyone says.'

'Who isn't?'

'Old Man Tomasich. He –'

'What are you talking about, idiot?'

'Old Man Tomasich helped me up. Made sure I was all right.'

His father hoicked up a throatful of phlegm and spat it onto the fire. 'Liar!'

'I am not. He –'

'Don't you contradict me, boy! You're a filthy, rotten liar.' His father made a move to get up, then seemed to think better of it. One of these days the boy would fight back and when that happened one of them would be leaving the house feet first.

'Don't call me a liar, Father. I'm telling the truth.'

His father seemed to loosen up, just for a moment. There was even a hint of a smile playing at the corner of his mouth.

'They found Old Man Tomasich's body this morning. What was left of him. He'd rotted right through. Stomach must have burst with all the gutrot he guzzled. Judging by the state of him he'd been dead about a month.'

In the dark recesses of the house he could hear Anthony laughing. He felt a shiver run down his spine as someone, something, walked across his grave.

*

I wake around four in the morning. The dead hour. My father said that this is when the door to the next life is open and it was easy for spirits to slip through. Both ways.

Although he wasn't a very happy man, he was big on ghosts, and I just hope he's a little happier now that he is one.

I wonder if he's in hell because of the terrible things he did in his life. I wonder if Mum's in hell for sticking a carving knife through his neck. Or maybe they have justifiable homicide in the afterlife. If they do, I hope Mum hooks up with a good barrister, like my imaginary mum.

I wrap myself in the doona and step out onto the balcony. A Cheshire Cat moon grins down at me through the trees. In the absence of God, it's nice to have something watching over me, even if it is just a well-lit lump of rock. The air chimes with the cold but there are no ghosts about. Not here. Which is a bit weird if you think about it. I mean, if I were a ghost I wouldn't be hanging around a dilapidated farmhouse like old man Tomasich. I'd go for a five-star hotel. Kick back and watch a few movies. Loaf about by the pool.

I try to picture my parents but I can't get a fix on them. Mum was beautiful to begin with but her soul must have been damaged beyond repair. I didn't really get it at the time, but I can see it now. Her smile, which used to light up like a Christmas tree, ended at her lips.

My father is easier to remember for some reason. He always wore a moustache. I'd never seen him without it. He wasn't as bad towards me as he was with Mum. Just absent. Even when he was there he was somewhere else. Dreaming of the old country. Dreaming of ghosts. We only ever connected through stories. Unlike Mum, Serena and Creepo, my father was a great reader, and he always told me stories on long car drives. I suppose that's one of the things that he missed most about Europe. The history. The books. The ghosts. What with the wars and everything there must have been so many dead wandering his old home that there was hardly any room left for the living.

I gaze up at the stars, which are shining brighter than I've ever seen. I suppose I've never been up at this time before.

It feels as though I could reach out and touch them. I make a wish instead. The stars twinkle in the cold. It takes so long for their light to reach the earth that they could have all winked out by now. I could be wishing on something that no longer exists. Ghost stars.

I crawl back into bed but I've slept enough. I watch a movie until the sun starts to rise, then I head on down for the all-you-can-eat buffet breakfast. It's for gluttons at their worst. Breakfast is included in the price of the room, but really, a bowl of cereal and one and a bit slices of toast and I'm stuffed.

By the time I get back to my room the bed-making fairy has been in and tidied up, which is something I could happily get used to. Serena was always banging on at me to make my bed, which was pointless seeing it would only get messed up again. She never said anything worth listening to anyway.

I'm about to go check whether my other clothes are dry when I notice that there's a keyboard in front of the TV. My room has internet access. I don't have to go schlepping around the streets looking for my new school, I can do it from my bed right now. If only I could get educated the same way. I could get on with working on my vaccine for that eye-eating African worm instead of hanging around the fast-finishers' box waiting for the doofuses and durnoids to complete their work.

It's tempting to go for a school in the ivy belt, but with those you'd probably have to supply a certified history of your family tree plus a complete DNA profile.

I pull up a map of the rail network and trace a line to the outer suburbs. I'm guessing they won't be so picky out there, especially near the jail. They'll be used to kids like me. Broken homes. Broken bones.

I decide against going Catholic. The Catholic schools will probably be connected in some way, and not just through Jesus. I don't want to suddenly pop up on some-one's radar. If Dr Chen's right and I've been reported missing, the police or social services will have contacted my old school. I'll go public.

At nine o'clock I phone the school that I've chosen. From my research it's in a fairly tough area, though not so tough that'll I'll get stabbed through my kidneys for not giving up my pencil sharpener.

The woman who answers the phone has been on the compulsory surly-old-hag training course.

I tell her that I've just moved into the area and need to enrol at the school. She sighs so deeply I think she's having an asthma attack. When she's recovered she tells me that we need to come up to the school to fill out some forms. We? She clari-fies this by telling me that I have to be accompanied by either a parent or guardian. I tell her that it won't be easy. She asks why. I tell her that my father isn't around any more and that my mother is a junkie. Then she's mumbling something in the background. I think I hear her say 'Another one!' but I can't be positive. She eventually comes back on the line and tells me that I need a parent, grandparent or guardian; just one will do and also proof of address. Then she hangs up.

I grab the complimentary notepad and pen from the bedside table and crawl back into bed. This is going to be harder than I thought. No wonder homeless kids don't go to school. It's a huge effort just getting in to one.

I tap the pen against my teeth while I try to think. I consider phoning Alistair McAlister, Dr Chen, or Marco Rossini and asking them for some help. No. This is my biggest test yet and I want to – need to – sort it out by myself.

I look back at the TV screen. The hotel's homepage is still up. That's it. You're supposed to be able to get anything on the internet, so why not a parent? Even a temporary one.

I look up actors' agencies first but then I figure that anyone who'd take on a gig like this couldn't be a very good actor to begin with. I need someone who's fairly unscrupulous. Someone who'll happily take cash from a kid for doing something a bit suss.

And then I crack it. I trawl through several websites. It's staggering just how many of them there are. Most of them are pretty gross but then I find one in the right area. There's a list of phone numbers on the website plus the contact's details and a brief bio.

I try the first number on the list. She sounds tired when she answers. Perhaps her work is nocturnal and she's been up all night. Never really thought about that. I start to outline the proposal but I've no sooner started than the woman tells me I'm a sicko and hangs up. The second one is friendlier but tells me that she doesn't do kinky and also hangs up. The third one tells me I'm a psycho fantasist, which is a new word for me and one I'll have to look up. Thirteen calls and a major rewrite of my script later I hit the jackpot. We have an intelligent and productive conversation which costs me five hundred dollars. Her name is Narelle and her accent is so thick I'm positive she's putting it on. We agree on a time and a place to meet the following day and that's it.

After I've tapped some more questions into the omniscient being again – for train timetables and unknown words (I am *not* a fantasist) – I go for a walk to the mega-mall.

I start at Alistair McAlister's café but unfortunately he must be at uni so I go to the bookshop. I opt for *Pride and Prejudice*, so soon I make my way back to my hotel with the book, plonk myself in a sunlounge by the pool and spend the entire afternoon reading. Tomorrow my work begins, but for now – bliss. The novel is basically about this mother who's trying to marry off her five daughters so that she (the mother) can have a better life and not get thrown out onto the street like a dirty handkerchief when her husband croaks it. The mother, who's more or less a pimp, doesn't really care who her daughters marry just as long as the husband is rich and has somewhere for her to live, preferably a castle. Mrs Bennet even tries to get the two eldest daughters, Jane and Elizabeth, to marry this mutant slimy cousin of theirs because the cousin will get the house when Mr Bennet croaks it. I don't know why the daughters couldn't score the house. Some obscure, sexist English law, I imagine. Anyway, maybe because the book was written like yonks ago, they didn't understand genes too well back then; because if they had then I'm sure Mrs Bennet might have lightened up a little, as least as far as marrying the cousin goes. At my old school I've seen the results of what happens when close relatives marry, and trust me, you don't want to go there.

It's the breathtaking language of the novel that keeps me by the pool until it's almost dark. Some of the passages are so beautiful that I read them over and over again for the sheer poetry. *'An unhappy alternative is before you, Elizabeth. From this day you must be a stranger to one of your parents. Your mother will never see you again if you do not marry Mr Collins, and I will never see you again if you do.'* I wished someone cared about me that much. How could you read that and not want to move into a bookshop? Story-wise, however, it's a bit of a letdown. If Mrs Bennet's daughters had been five brainless skanks who went shopping every day until they maxed out daddy's credit card, then she might have had something to complain about. But really, hooking them up with a bunch of chinless wonders so that she won't become a seamstress? Give me a break. And, while we're on the subject, Mr Darcy, one of the great heroes of English literature? The guy's got about as much backbone as a quadriplegic jellyfish.

I close my eyes and try to imagine what it would have been like living in that era but I come up well short:

After a light supper my dear Aunt Serena and I repaired to the drawing room where we embroiled ourselves in our needle-work. Following a brief discourse on the trials and tribulations of our respective days we proceeded to accompany each other on the piano-forte.

Shortly thereafter my Uncle Anthony entered the room complaining of his privations.

'Bloody shit of a day,' he opined.

'Anthony,' chastised my aunt. 'Such profanity. And in front of the girl.'

'Put a sock in it, woman,' he interjected.

My uncle removed the twist top from his evening beverage, slumped down on the chaise longue and released from his poster-ior an explosion of wind of such velocity and odorousness that the wallpaper peeled.

'Anthony!' beseeched my aunt. 'A modicum of decorum please.'

'Better out than in,' he ejaculated.

See! It just doesn't work.

Back to School

THAT NIGHT, THE FIRST OF THE GHOSTS COME HOWLING INTO MY room, swirling around my bed in a vortex and trying to suck up my soul. I hang on tightly to the side of the bed but it's a close thing. I could so easily just slip away. The light beneath the door offers little protection against the spectres my memories have stirred. I tell them to leave me alone, that I have things to do before I can go with them. I flick on the light, hoping that ghosts are terrified of bedside lights. The inner curtain billows in the breeze, more ghost-like than any ghost. I get up and slide the balcony door closed.

The next morning, the room is bright and peaceful. The bedside lights are still on, their glow timid compared to the sunlight streaming in. There's no sign of the ghosts. I catch a train to the outer suburbs, changing at the north-west junction. I've never really been to the outer suburbs before, only zoomed through them on the freeway heading off on holidays. I was usually too absorbed in my father's ghost stories to look out the window at the high-voltage power stanchions and the crap graffiti on the freeway's anti-noise walls.

They've got malls out here too. Huge mega-malls just like the ones in the ivy belt, or maybe even bigger. I don't understand it. I can tell from the houses that some of the people who live out here don't have much money, but maybe that's the point. What they have, they spend.

I meet Narelle at the agreed place and am immediately disappointed. She doesn't look anything like me. For a start, she's white. Snow white. If she got any whiter she'd be transparent. Still, my non-existent father could have been from somewhere else, which would explain me. She's also covered in so many tattoos she looks more easel than human. I'm grateful tattoos aren't hereditary. There's nothing in this world, or the next, that I love so much that I want a permanent reminder of it burned into my skin. Not the flag. Not my parents' names or my star sign in Chinese. Not a mermaid, a scorpion or a flying horse. Nothing.

I assume the woman standing under the big clock is Narelle. She seems kind of jumpy and looks like she's waiting for someone.

'Narelle?'

She looks me up and down. 'That depends. You got the money?'

I take the five hundred dollars out of my pocket and hand it to her. She looks at the money and counts it out. It's hundred-dollar notes so it doesn't take her long. Even so, she checks it twice. Then she folds it up and stuffs it in her handbag.

'There's a slight problem.'

'What?'

'Any kid willing to sling me five hundred bucks to play mum for an hour would happily pay a thousand.'

Oh no. I'm being hustled. It's time to get streetwise and hustle her right back.

'Not this kid.'

'Fair enough.' She turns to walk away. 'See ya around.'

'Hey! Give me my money back.'

Narelle turns back to face me. 'What money?'

Damn she's good.

'First rule of life on the streets, kid. Don't stump up the cash until the service has been rendered. Unless you do *my* job, in which case you get it in advance.'

She's got me. Either I pay her another five hundred or I've got to find someone else who'll probably charge the same or maybe even more.

'Fine,' I snap. 'I'll pay it.'

She looks at me and folds her arms. 'Let's have it then.'

I manage a half-smile. 'You'll get it when the service has been rendered.'

Narelle grins. 'Good for you, kid.'

I might be learning some life lessons from Narelle. It's just not the sort of education I'm looking for. No advanced maths. No top English class. No science. Absolutely nothing about eye-eating African worms. Just some stuff about not getting ripped off by someone who looks like she's walked off the set of *The Jerry Springer Show*.

Speaking of which, I can't turn up to school with Narelle looking like she is, even out here. How she managed to wiggle her scrawny butt into her skin-tight jeans without a couple of warm shoehorns to help her I'll never know.

'Narelle,' I say tentatively, not sure how she'll take my fashion critique. Still, I'm the client. 'We need to get you some different clothes.'

'I thought you said on the phone that I was s'pose to be a junkie.'

'A junkie, yes. Not a . . .' I trail off. The elephant enters the room, and Narelle goes right ahead and mentions it.

'A prostitute?'

'Well, yeah.'

'Honey, I *am* a prostitute. That's how you found me, remember?'

'Yeah, but I don't want the school to know.'

'But it's okay if they think I pump shit into my veins?'

I see her point.

'Kid, if you think I'll be the only pro with kids at this school of yours then you're not just out of your league, you're out of your mind.'

She looks at me. I fold my arms.

'Okay,' she relents. 'But you're paying.'

Of course I am.

'What are you, anyway?' she asks as we head off to the shops.

'What do you mean?'

'Are you Middle Eastern? South American? South African? Part Asian?'

'Something like that.'

'Okay. If they ask, I'll just say your father was in the American navy or something.'

'They won't.'

'Be proud of who you are, kid. Sometimes it's all we've got.'

And so my temporary mum and I go shopping. I thought she might go for designer labels, but in the end she settles for a pink fluoro tracksuit from a no-name outlet. It's not exactly subtle, but somehow it blends in. And except for the dolphin and Yin and Yang on her neck, the tracksuit covers most of her tattoos.

The shops aren't far from the school, but we queue for a taxi. While we're waiting, Narelle chugs down a couple of smokes. For some reason she seems nervous. Perhaps it's the idea of going back to school. Facing authority figures. When we finally get in a taxi the driver complains about the short distance and the smell of smoke, but Narelle suggests that he get on with his job and stop effing complaining. She then offers him a bit of career advice, firmly reminding him that he's an effing taxi driver and if he wanted to be an effing brain surgeon, he should have stayed at school for a bit effing longer. I can't help thinking that the office ladies at the school had better effing watch out.

I thought the school might be in a bit of a war zone or prison yard. All desolate, cold concrete and huge razor wire fences to keep the vandals out and the students in. Instead it's lovely. Some of houses leading up to it are kind of run down and overcrowded, with rusted cars and broken furniture out on the front lawns. But the school is like an oasis. A bit like my old school. The neat front lawns at the entrance are bordered by flower beds. The trees provide a wonderful shaded canopy and someone has even installed some bird feeders and built possum houses in a couple of them. Whoever looks after the school cares a lot. This place isn't in the ivy belt. It's not even in the suburbs where you have to choose between the Bible or the Koran. Out here it's either Ford or Holden and supporting the wrong football team could see you on life support.

The woman at reception is terse with Narelle, who is terse right back at her. Though at least she's reined in the swearing. She's much smarter than I gave her credit for. She knows that if she rages on here, the only door that will open is the one to the exit and she's got five hundred dollars riding on this.

She starts filling out the forms so I whisper to remind her that she can't use my real name in case I pop up on a radar somewhere.

'No worries,' she says. 'Leave it to me.' Actually it sounds more like 'loive it to moy'.

As soon as Narelle has finished with the forms we're ushered through to the principal's office.

'Good morning, Mrs Beauchamp. Robert Thompkins.'

'G'day, Bob,' replies Narelle, bunging on the accent even more. 'And it's Ms. *Mz*.' Narelle really emphasises the 'Z'. Apparently cheating someone of five hundred bucks is all good, but being addressed by the wrong title is insulting.

'Duly noted, Ms Beauchamp,' says Mr Thompkins.

'Old man shot through as soon as I missed my period.'

Although Mr Thompkins seems unfazed by this, I want the ground to open up and swallow me – or, preferably, her.

Mr Thompkins turns his attention to me and I immediately relax. He has a kind face. The sort an uncle ought to have. He also has a moustache, but unlike my father's, his actually suits him. He looks down at the form and then back up at me and smiles. 'And you must be Tiffany Star.'

Oh, great. Why didn't she just call me Tinkerbell and be done with it? Tiffany Star Beauchamp! I'll get beaten up every day as a matter of principle.

I glare at Narelle.

'Say hello to Mr Thompkins, Tiffany-Star.' She's biting her lip trying not to laugh.

Every nerve and fibre. Every molecule and atom of my being is cringing at the moment. 'Hello, Mr Thompkins.'

'Hello, Tiffany. Welcome to our school.'

'It's Tiffany-Star,' corrects Narelle. 'Loike, with a hoifen.'

I don't even know what Narelle is banging on about at first because her accent is becoming more exaggerated the more she talks. But then it dawns on me that this skanky cow is insisting that my name be hyphenated. She's enjoying this way too much.

'So what's your favourite subject, Tiffany-Star?'

'She's, loike, royal smart,' says Narelle, ratcheting up the cringe factor, which was already running pretty close to critical.

'It's okay, Mum,' I say. 'I'll discuss my academic preferences with Mr Thompkins.'

'Soi what I moyen.'

'I like all subjects, really. But I suppose my favourite would be English.'

'And what would be your favourite book?'

I'm about to say *Matilda* but for some pathetic reason I want to impress him. I also want to show him that I'm nothing like Narelle. 'I would have to say *Bleak House*.'

Mr Thompkins' eyes widen slightly. 'Not the one by . . .'

'Charles Dickens. Yeah. I've read it a couple of times.'

Mr Thompkins recovers enough to jot this down on his notepad like it actually means something.

'And what are you reading at the moment?'

'*Pride and Prejudice*.'

He writes this down too. Then he glances over at Narelle, who looks like she could barely read the cancer warning on a packet of smokes.

I've overdone it. By miles. Kids out here don't read Dickens and Austen. They don't read full stop. Not at home, anyway. They get dumped in front of the Sony babysitter as soon as they've got neck support.

'And what is it you want to do when you leave school, Tiffany-Star?'

Again I speak without thinking. 'I want to be a doctor and work for Médecins Sans Frontières in Africa.' Although I leave out the bit about the worm vaccine, Mr Thompkins still looks at me as though I've just flown in from the Andromeda Galaxy. I should have kept everyone happy and said that I want to work in a clothes shop. Now the poor guy has to deal with an alien in his midst.

Mr Thompkins looks at Narelle's proof of address and summons one of the office ladies to make a photocopy. He then announces that the school doesn't have a Gifted and Talented program because, he says, *all* children are gifted and talented – some obviously a little more than others. But there is still a top English class, which he'll put me in.

'Now?' I say.

He gives me that big, friendly grin of his. 'You don't strike me as someone who enjoys being out of school, Tiffany-Star.'

I nod because it's true.

'By the way,' he says, matter of factly. 'What happened to your arm?' He glances between both of us as he says this. He's obviously fishing.

I reply without thinking. 'I broke it ice-skating.' Oh no! That was my New York, five-star hotel, barrister mum lie.

'She's smart,' offers Narelle in support, 'but she's a bit of a klutz.'

It seems as though Mr Thompkins doesn't have a problem with the ice-skating ruse. Then I remember that the mega-mall where I met Narelle has its own ice-skating rink.

Outside the office I say goodbye to Narelle but decide I want to pay her back for turning me into a target with the whole Tiffany-Star thing.

'I'll need some money for lunch, Mum.'

Narelle glares at me. 'What about that money I gave you earlier? At the mall.'

'I spent it. On books.'

'I don't know what's wrong with the library.' I'm sure she wanted to throw an 'effing' in there somewhere but she's on her best behaviour in front of Mr Thompkins. Instead she reaches into her pocket and pulls out five dollars. She hands me the money and gives me a hug.

'Have a great day, Tiffany-Star.' Then she whispers in my ear. 'I'll be waiting for you after school, with a fucking baseball bat if I have to.'

Then I turn and walk off with Mr Thompkins.

'Bye, mummy,' I say, looking back over my shoulder. 'Enjoy Oprah.'

My mummy. My dear, sweet mumsie, standing there in her pink tracksuit, her body crying out for a smoke, flips me the bird.

CAFÉ

DID YOU REALLY NOT PAY HER THE OTHER FIVE HUNDRED?

No. I didn't need a psycho prostitute after me as well. We both knew that she could have phoned the school and said that the whole thing was bullshit.

So how did you find her?

I didn't. She lived up to her threat. Came and met me after school, with all of the other parents. She didn't look too happy to be there and for a minute I thought she was going to charge me extra. In the end she just stuck out her hand for the cash. Luckily I had enough on me to pay her off. She said that it was nice doing business with me and to let her know when the parent/teacher interviews were on. She said she might even give me a discount.

How was school?

It was really good. I thought the other kids would look at me like I was from a freak show or something, but they hardly even bothered to look up when Mr Thompkins introduced me. I guess they were used to seeing kids come and go, especially with the jail being so close by. At lunch a couple of Islander girls told the teacher that they'd look after me. I was really nervous at first. I thought they might try to mug me or drag me into the toilets and flush my head down the bowl. But they just lined up in the lunch queue with me and afterwards took me over to the uniform shop. They couldn't have been nicer.

What were the teachers like?

Really lovely. My favourite was my year advisor and English teacher. Her name was Miss Taylor, not Mz like Narelle. I don't think she was long out of uni – really young and enthusiastic. Her eyes lit up when she marked the roll, like she was thrilled to see us back. They were about to do an assessment task when Mr Thompkins dropped me off and she said that because I was new and might not have been studying the same stuff as them, I didn't have to do it, but I said that it was okay and I was happy to give it a go.

How did you do?

Aced it.

Miss Taylor was so excited that I thought she was going to explode. I thought the other students would hate me after that. But they didn't. They were almost as encouraging as the teacher. Patting me on the back and everything. I don't know, going to school out there really taught me a few things. Not so much about them but about me. Afterwards it felt weird walking into the hotel lobby in my second-hand school uniform but nobody seemed to mind. There was another student there as well but she was a bit older and her uniform included a hat, a blazer and a flashy laptop computer. Still, no matter how much cash her parents stumped up to send her to school, I doubted if she had a principal who cared as much as Mr Thompkins or a teacher who was as enthusiastic or kind as Miss Taylor. You can't buy that sort of stuff.

When I got to my room I made myself a cup of tea and scoffed the free biscuits they give you. After that I read *Pride and Prejudice* for a bit and then, because I was so tired, just fell asleep.

It was after seven when I woke up the following day. I should have packed my stuff ready to check out the next morning for my first full day at school but it was so nice and safe in the hotel, I just couldn't leave. I phoned Alistair McAlister and got him to book me in until the end of the week.

Your bill must have been mounting up.

Yeah, it would have been, but it didn't matter anyway because I'd decided to use Serena's credit card rather than cash.

How were you going to do that?

Figured it all out. By myself, too.

Did it work?

That's another story.

Epilogue

I SLOWLY OPEN MY EYES AND TRY TO FIGURE OUT WHERE I AM. Somewhere safe. Somewhere comfortable.

'Sorry to disturb you, Dr Bennet. We'll be departing soon. Can I get you anything?' The young woman's smile is so wide it's like one face isn't big enough to hold it.

'A glass of champagne, perhaps? You have much to celebrate. And it is our finest French champagne.'

Why not? If anyone deserves a glass of finest French champagne, it's me. 'Okay, then.' I reply. '*Merci*.'

The woman returns with my champagne and then retreats to leave me alone with my thoughts.

It's been over twenty years since I was homeless and living on the trains. Fifteen years since Creepo was incinerated when someone torched his house. Following uni graduation, I did my internship and then volunteered to work for Médecins Sans Frontières. My team and I didn't invent a vaccine for the eye-eating African worm. We eradicated it. I wasn't entirely comfortable with the arbitrary annihilation of an entire species, but I consoled myself with the idea that it was a heinous mistake that evolution had thrown up.

And now, two years after the worm had infected its last eye, I'm travelling to the Nobel Prize centre to collect my prize. But on the way, I have one more thing to do. Something I had promised myself a long time ago when I was homeless and living on the trains.

I've just arrived at Edith Piaf Railway Station, Paris, and settled into my luxurious cabin aboard the Orient Express.

Because it's quite late, the bed beside me has been turned down and the linen smells fresh. I run my hand over the pillow, which is soft and inviting. It's been a long day and my eyelids are getting heavy.

I lift up my feet but they're practically stuck to the floor. Some selfish a-hole has spilled their fizzy drink and left it to turn into glue. I notice on the seat across from my bed someone called Davo has used a black marker pen to express his undying love for Shazza – he's gunna luv her 4-eva, apparently. Someone else is of the mind that Rita sux big ones.

'The train on platform six stops all stations to the city.'

Well, that does it. How many invasions can you handle? So much for my romantic overnight journey from Paris to Venice on the Orient Express. No crisp white sheets in my first-class sleeper cabin. No French champagne.

I realise of course that my fantasy needs a bit of work. If I'm going to drink the finest French champagne, I need to know its name at least. Plus if I am fluent in French, I have to be able to say a bit more than *merci*. I don't know where they hand out Nobel prizes, though I'm pretty sure it wouldn't be called the Nobel Prize centre. My mum used to listen to an Edith Piaf CD. She's the only famous French person that I know of. Still, I doubt they would have named a railway station after her. Still, it's a work in progress and I'm happy with the way that it's developing. Certainly better than being slumped on an electric train as it clatters its way around the suburban rail network with its sticky floors, illiterate graffiti and liberal sprinkling of sad, mad people going absolutely nowhere.

CAFÉ

SO YOU LEARNED HOW TO GET AWAY BY ESCAPING INTO A fantasy world?

Is that weird?

Understandable given your circumstances. Who wouldn't want to travel first class from Paris to Venice on the Orient Express?

I found this brochure on the train that someone had left behind – 'Exotic Rail Journeys of the World' or something. I took one look at it and decided that's where I was going. In my imagination at least.

I suppose a psychologist might say that the sleeper cabin represents the safety of the womb.

Oh, cut the psychobabble. It was just a happy place to go in my head.

Can we go back a bit? Your first week at your new school. Was it hard to leave the hotel? Especially since you had the money to stay longer.

Yeah it was. Really hard. But as much as I loved it and felt safe there, I knew I couldn't stay for ever. Eventually someone would have come knocking on my door looking for my barrister mum or a down payment on the bill. Besides, I wanted the option to go back there again later, if things got too hard or the weather turned really cold or stormy. So on Saturday morning at the end of the first week at my new school, I packed up my gear and headed down to reception.

I want to hear how you did this.

It was easy, really. I gave the clerk the room number and asked for the bill saying that my mum was still in the room but on an important call to New York. The clerk printed it off, I took it back to the room, then I came back with the credit card explaining that my mother was still on the phone and could I take the credit card charge slip back for her to sign. The clerk didn't have a problem with this and so I trotted off back to the room again and returned a couple of minutes later with the signed receipt – I'd spent an hour practising Serena's signature at breakfast that morning, which was some sort of bizarre couldn't-be-bothered-with-a-proper-signature scrawl anyway. And that was that. I told the clerk we'd be leaving via the car park and that my mother said thank you for a wonderful stay. The clerk said we were very welcome and that she hoped to see us both again. Then she gave me a copy of the receipt. I smiled, picked up my stuff and walked out of the hotel through the underground car park and headed for the station at the mega-mall. And with that I was officially on the streets. Or the trains. Whatever you want to call it.

How did you manage at school? Carting all that stuff around?

I'd arranged to drop off my sleeping bag and other excess stuff at Alistair McAlister's café on school mornings. And on uni days he organised for another waitress to mind it for me.

Lugging that to and from school, I would definitely have shown up on someone's radar. But on the weekend I was on my own. I'd got myself another bag by then, for the extra stuff that I was carting around, so I really was turning into a bit of a bag lady.

How did you manage to survive? What did you do?

Well, the first day out of the hotel it was pretty cold so I decided to go back up to my weekender, at the beach.

Why would you go to the beach if it was cold?

Fewer people.

Right. Sorry. Carry on.

I got some scallops and chips from my Croatian friend – paid for them this time too – and then I walked the rest of the way to my weekender, scoffing the scallops and chips as I went and enjoying the warmth of my hands on the greasy wrapping. I timed how far it was this time. Two hours, walking on dry sand. No wonder I was stuffed when I got there. But I wanted to be as far away from the houses as I could. As far away from people.

I climbed into the dunes and then when I got my sleeping bag and stuff sorted in a hollow, I went for a bit of a poke around to see if I could find any shelter. There was a storm building up down south, the clouds were starting to seriously churn, and I could see that unless the wind changed direction and pushed it out to sea, it was going to be a big one. If I couldn't find any shelter and the heavens let me have it, I'd have a two-hour schlep back to Death Valley in the lightning and rain.

Shelter? What were you looking for? A cave or something?

Just something to cover the hollow in the dunes that I'd set myself up in. Some driftwood or something.

Did you find anything?

A door.

A door? In the sand dunes?

It used to be somebody's front door. On their house. It even had number 4 on it.

So how did it . . .

Get there? Who knows? I knew it'd been there for a while because it was quite rotted. It was sturdy enough to sit over my hollow and keep out some of the rain if and when the storm kicked in. I even poured sand over it to keep it camouflaged, but of course it blew away. Duh!

I spent the rest of the day perched on top of the dunes near my hollow watching the clouds darkening and the storm gaining strength. I also carried on with *Pride and Prejudice*, and then did some extra homework that Miss Taylor had set me. She really was a fantastic teacher. A bit delusional in some ways but hey, nobody's perfect.

Delusional? What do you mean?

She wasn't exactly a local girl – the outer suburbs, I mean. She'd gone to some straw hat and blazer private girls' school. And here's the thing. She said she was going to put me forward for a scholarship at her old school and that with my current grades and her recommendation I had a good chance of getting it. Imagine me with my straw hat, blazer and laptop computer, spending the weekend in the rail yards or under some old dero's rotted door up at Death Valley Beach.

I'd like to get to the rail yards if we could.

I bet you wouldn't.

You know what I mean. So did she put you forward for the scholarship?

Yeah she did. But things kind of got out of hand before I got the chance to sit it. We'll get to that.

Okay. So did the storm hit?

Not until about three in the morning. Just before the

dead hour. But when it kicked off it was biblical. I don't know if you're into the whole wrath of God thing, but I seriously thought he was having a go at me for all the stuff that I'd been thinking about him. It was so terrifying, even the ghosts would have chucked a sickie. Stayed on the other side. But amazingly the door completely covered my hollow, so apart from a few drips and leaks I was dry. Uncomfortable with my legs curled up, but dry. The pounding of the rain on the door was deafening. It was like I was hiding underneath a castle's drawbridge while a thousand horses and knights thundered by overhead. I was also worried that those rabbits might go off their veggie diet and turn into a pack off floppy-eared, land-based piranhas.

The only really terrifying moment was when there was no gap between the flash of lightning and the pounding of the thunder because that meant that the storm was directly overhead, on the other side of my door. But my shelter protected me against the worst of it. And in the morning when the storm had blown itself out and I'd emerged from my nest, I was so happy with my door that I completely covered one end of it, so it would stay in that spot and I could use it again.

Sounds almost like a rebirth, you springing out of the earth like that.

That's exactly what I thought. For some reason when I woke up that morning I felt really good. Recharged. It was like the storm had washed everything away. I'd survived God's retribution and it was as if I could renew myself. It was like being a born again atheist.

I thought you didn't like labelling yourself.

I don't, but you do.

Okay, what did you do next?

I wandered down to the surf to clean my teeth and wash

my face. As I was pouring water over my head I noticed a plane high above. The wheels weren't down yet but I could tell from the sound of its engines that it was coming in to land.

It was then I had another eureka moment and I knew that I was starting to get a little streetwise.

Last Train to Kathmandu

SIR ISAAC NEWTON'S BRAIN POWER WAS SO IMMENSE, HE USED TO get a headache just putting on his slippers. Sir Isaac Newton, if you need reminding, is the guy who invented gravity. Okay, he didn't actually invent it, he kind of just . . . well, pointed it out. Gravity has always been around, it's just that no one really knew what to do about it. Even Ug the caveman understood gravity. He knew that if the hunt went spectacularly wrong and a mammoth chased you over a cliff then it would hurt like hell when you got to the bottom, especially if the mammoth was still behind you.

The problem with Sir Isaac Newton was that his imagination was so out of control and he had so many ideas coming at him all the time, even when he first woke up in the morning, that he barely had time to pull on his slippers before his mind was raging and whirling and churning with something new and extraordinary. Ideas. Ideas. Ideas. Hundreds of them. Thousands of them. Torrents of them. And that's the thing that will help me survive. I have to keep thinking. I have to keep generating ideas.

The train slows as it approaches the junction station leading to the city. I look out the window as the blinding sunlight glints off the windows of the countless carriages parked in the yards a little to the north of the station. Because the train system doesn't operate twenty-four hours a day, the trains have to be parked somewhere at night. And this is obviously one of those places. It's like a big carriage sleep-over party. A rich guy's full-scale train set. You could almost imagine Thomas the Tank Engine chugging up and down the line boring everyone rigid about timetables and the importance of thorough engine maintenance.

It's here the line splits. Left to the city or straight on to the suburbs before that line splits again to the south or to the outer suburbs and my new school. Luckily Narelle lives far enough away from school for me to qualify for a travel card, which the office lady said I could collect next week. Today, though, I've bought a ticket – a student day pass – because the last thing I want is to be busted fare-dodging.

I stare at the trains as we slide past the yards. All those empty carriages. Dry. Safe. Locked. All those long empty seats. I don't know how I'm going to do it, but tonight I'm going to be sleeping in one of those empty carriages.

The doors slide open and several families pour on. The kids are excited, leaping about from seat to seat trying to get the best vantage point for the bridge and the approach to the city. There are a couple of single fathers with backpacks and weekend kids, heading for the movies or the museum and then inevitably onto McDonald's. One of the married guys locks eyes with a weekend dad and looks away, snuggling up closer to his kids and wife.

A couple of the younger kids soon tire of the scenery and elbow each other about my sleeping bag. I snap my book closed and stare at them. They giggle at each other and look away. They obviously see me as someone to avoid. A dangerous creature that you poke with a stick and then run away from.

Once we've crossed the bridge the train disgorges the happy families and broken fathers into the city, while I carry on beneath it, heading to the subject of my eureka moment. My great idea.

I opt for international rather than domestic. It's only one more stop but it's about one hundred times more exciting.

I head straight to departures; I'm not here to greet. I'm here to go. It's Sunday morning but already the place is buzzing. *I'm* buzzing. This is the one place where no one will look twice at a kid wandering around with a backpack and sleeping bag. A place where I can relax and feel safe. Free from scrutiny. Free from danger. I haven't been this excited in years.

I wander over to the huge departure board and scan the destinations.

LHR. HKG. TOK. LOS. AKL. ROM. DUB. I don't even know where some of these places are or what the abbreviations mean but that just adds to the thrill. They all sound so different and other-worldly. It doesn't matter if they happen to be the biggest shithole on the planet. Anywhere's better than here. Because in all those places, there isn't a single person who wants to murder me and bury my dismembered corpse in a forest. Not yet, anyway.

I search for the old country. My parents' home. The land of ghosts. But it doesn't appear on the list. No national carrier. None of the abbreviations even remotely resemble the capital city. So I guess I'm not going there. There's also no mention of Paris or Africa either but I know that Paris is close to London and as it's British Airways that's flying to LHR, I figure that LHR must mean London. So London it is.

I wander over to the food court and gorge myself on a McBreakfast, then I follow the signs to the observation deck.

No sooner have I got to the top than the aroma of aviation fuel wafts up my nose and clatters around the inside of my head like a startled rodent. To hell with fresh sheets, cut grass, eucalyptus trees, road tar, and Serena's lavender scented candles, this is something else. It's the scent of escape. I could happily breathe this in for ever. If a perfume company could bottle the fragrance of aviation fuel, *Cologne d'aviation*, I'd buy it in bulk.

I spend the rest of the day moving between the food court, the observation deck and the duty free shops. The perfume counters don't have any *Cologne d'aviation*, which is a shame, but I buy myself a diary to jot down my thoughts and to-do lists. At the far end of the airport, near an out-of-the-way café, I find a quiet corner to sit and read. It's so peaceful compared to the chaos of the check-in section and general excitement that, using my rolled-up sleeping bag as a pillow, I curl up and am soon drifting off. Caught in that special place between dreams and reality.

I float over to the British Airways sales desk.

'A single to London, please.'

The sales clerk flashes a fake smile on and off like a torch and asks to see my passport.

'I've been here visiting my father,' I reply, handing over my passport. 'My barrister mother was supposed to buy my ticket at the other end but there's been a mix up.'

She tilts her head to one side in a sort of gesture of support. Fortunately everything seems in order with my passport so she hands it back. 'Return or one way?'

'One way.'

It's three times as much as economy but I decide to travel business class. I opt against using the same ruse as the hotel and pay in cash. The sales clerk gives me a funny look when I drop the money on the counter, but she takes it without any further questions. Maybe she works on commission. She tells me it's getting quite late and that I'd better get a move on or I'll miss my flight.

I gather up my stuff and hurry through the entrance to the departure area. It's a long way to the British Airways gate, so long in fact that I'm forced to run. I arrive panting like an asthmatic steam train and hand over my boarding pass to the flight attendant. She ticks me off her list and lets me on board, closing the door behind us.

The business class seats are enormous. Well, they are if you're thirteen years old and weigh about thirty kilograms wringing wet. I pull out *Pride and Prejudice* and stuff my backpack and sleeping bag in the overhead locker. Then I slump into my seat and get myself comfortable. To think, Jane Austen never flew business class. Jane Austen never flew. She probably never even left England. She never knew about laptop computers or even typewriters. Never thought to contemplate that Keira Knightly would eventually play her great heroine in a movie adaptation of her masterpiece. Never knew about movies. Time marches on. And I've spent enough of it living in fear.

I'm drifting in and out of consciousness as we taxi away from the gate. The engines rev and I'm thrust back into my seat as we power down the runway and slip gracefully up into the afternoon sky.

'Bye Creepo,' I sneer as we muscle our way out over the suburbs. 'You'll never find me in Paris.' I look down at the patchwork maze of streets and parks. I think we might be

approaching their suburb. I used to watch the planes overhead
when I lived with them and dream of another life far, far away
on the other side of the horizon. I think I spot the park near
their house but from this high up I can't be sure, so, just in
case, I flip Creepo the bird.

'Excuse me. Hello.'

In next to no time we land in Paris and before I know it
I'm in Africa, wrestling with a gigantic worm that's dragged
me kicking and screaming into a river.

'Wake up!'

The worm has wrapped itself around me like a boa
constrictor and is dragging me under for the final time while
telling me to wake up. My life flashes before my eyes as I
struggle to hold on to it. The highlight reel's rather lacking.

'Hey, you!'

Each time I thrash my way to the surface, the worm drags
me under again.

There's the sound of heavy crackling. 'Sector nine. Stand
by, over.'

At the intrusion of noise the worm releases its hold and I
struggle back to the surface, my things strewn about me. I sit
up gagging for breath.

'What do you think you're doing here?'

'What?'

I look around, trying to piece things together. I can see
through the window that it's dark outside. That's something,
I suppose. At least I know when I am – night. Though just
where I am is still a bit of a mystery. Chairs. Café (closed).
Lots of space. Shops (some still open). Counters. Ah. That's
it. The airport. I put my head in my hands trying to take
everything in. The security guard nudges me with his foot,
reminding me that he's still here and has to be dealt with.
'Well. What are you doing here? Are you lost?'

Now there's the million dollar question. Am I lost? I wonder if he means metaphorically.

'No. I know where I am. I'm here.'

There's more crackling from his walkie-talkie. He presses a button and leans into it. 'Copy that. I'm interrogating her now.'

Interrogating me? Could this guy be any more pathetic if he tried? What's he think I'm going to do? Hijack a plane? Fly a jumbo jet? I can hardly ride a bike

'Are you waiting for a flight? Where are your parents?'

Their bones are turning into dust somewhere out in the forest, I imagine. I decide against telling him this and go with barrister mum instead. I prefer her to Narelle, even if Narelle does have a distinct advantage over barrister mum by actually existing.

'My family?' I finally reply. 'My mum's in London. She's a barrister.' A pretend cop is not going to mess with a barrister, surely. Even a gun-toting, walkie-talkie using, hip-swinging, foot-nudging, interrogating pretend cop. 'I was supposed to fly out today but the plane was full so I'm going tomorrow.'

'Well, it won't be safe for you to stay here. There is a designated area where you can wait, but the airport closes at eleven because of the curfew.'

I'm not sure who has the curfew – me or the planes – but I decide to leave it. So much for sleeping here all night. 'Do you have a ticket?'

No. 'Yes.'

Passport.

Yes. 'Yes.'

'Show me!'

'No! I haven't done anything wrong,' I snap. 'I just fell asleep. Is that a crime?'

'Who dropped you off? Who's looking after you? How old are you?'

What is this? Fifty questions? I fire back just as quickly. 'Dad. No one. Sixteen.'

'So where's Dad now?' He says this in a sarcastic tone, as if Dad doesn't exist. I suppose technically he doesn't, unless you count his ghost. And pretend cop doesn't appear the sort of guy who'd happily debate meta-physics or the nature of existence. Not while he has a walkie-talkie, a gun, and really shiny shoes, anyway.

'He's with his other family. His preferred family. My parents split up.' If some violins kicked in right now they would be very welcome. But there's nothing but the dim drone of a distant vacuum cleaner. And besides anything else, I don't think his heartstrings would easily be tugged by a bit of maudlin music.

'I don't think you're sixteen at all.'

I stare up at him. 'And I don't think you're a cop at all.'

'You're right,' he says, calling my bluff. 'So why don't we call one?' He starts speaking into his walkie-talkie again while I quickly gather up my stuff.

When he's finished he tells me not to move. Being the obedient citizen that I am, I stand up and slip on my backpack.

'I told you to wait right there!' he commands.

I start to walk off but he holds out his arm to stop me.

'You touch me and I'll scream rape.'

He backs off for a moment, but clearly the level of professionalism required for a career in the police force doesn't extend to the private security sector. 'You're a little psycho bitch, aren't you?'

'And you're a big, fat, hairy wannabe cop,' I snarl back at him. 'So we've both got issues.'

'Wait a minute, I know *you*.' He pulls something out of his pocket and stares at it. 'I thought I recognised you. You're Tony and Serena's kid. The runaway.'

I can feel the blood draining out of my face, but I try to stay calm.

'What are you talking about?'

He grins at me. 'Don't try to deny it. I've been to your house. For barbecues. You always were a cute little thing, handing out cabanossi and cheese and spanakopita on your little serving tray. I do a bit of work on the side for your uncle. He's been saying he's worried about you, really wants to find you.'

'You've made a mistake.' I'm almost pleading now. 'I'm not who you think I am.'

He actually laughs at this. Then he grabs my backpack with me still in it. I try to stay calm because it's all I've got. I try to think. The only advantage I've got is my disadvantage. This guy is huge. It's like Godzilla versus a squirrel, so he'll underestimate me. Underestimate what I'm prepared to do. He's holding me with one arm while pulling out his mobile phone with the other. As he's paging through his contacts, I drive my knee straight up and through his nuts. He didn't expect that. There's not much of me but I use every ounce of strength I've got and the effect is immediate. Pretend cop squeaks. I mean literally squeaks. Like he needs oiling. Then he drops to his knees. I've heard that it's a man's most sensitive zone, but I hadn't realised quite how tender it actually is.

He's still clutching my backpack, with me in it, but I spin around and pull back as hard as I can. He's far too focused on the pain in his gonads to worry about hanging onto my backpack, so he lets go and falls over backwards, his hands still holding his crushed cashews.

I race over to the escalator and jump down the stairs three at a time. When I get to the platform there's a train already waiting, so at least something is going for me. I hurry on board panting and panicking but trying to find calm. It's all I've got going for me. I have to outthink him.

I'm begging the doors to close but, I don't know, maybe it's waiting for a plane to land or something. Come on! I look over to the escalator and swallow. Pretend cop is hobbling down, talking into his mobile. Talking to Creepo, probably. My heart is pounding like it was when I was hiding under my old bed and Creepo came into the room. I've got to stop putting myself in these situations. I'll give myself a heart condition.

I duck down as he looks up and down the platform. When I stand up he's no longer on the platform. He's either gone back up, or he's on the train.

Then I see his huge bulk barging through the other carriage towards the door that leads into this one. He pushes the door open and then he's in the carriage with me. We stare at each other and he smiles. He's obviously retrieved his testicles from the back of his throat or wherever they'd got to and now he's standing there leering at me. It's that 'gotcha' sort of leer that I've seen before. We're still separated by the length of the carriage – he in one entrance, me in the next. But it's over. He knows it. I know it. Or at least I want him to think that I know it. Defeated, I drop my sleeping bag onto the floor and hold onto the pole for support. Pretend cop is still staring at me but he's staying where he is. He's got that look in his eyes. The look of a predator.

Apart from a young Asian couple weighed down with bags and the grime of two hemispheres, the carriage is otherwise empty.

'Hey,' calls pretend cop. 'He wants to talk to you.'

'Don't you come near me!'

He holds up his hands to indicate that he's staying where he is and then shows me his mobile. He mimes sliding it down the aisle. I don't want to agree with anything this trained baboon says. Any friend of Creepo's is an enemy of mine. When he sees that I'm not going to respond he slides it down to me anyway. It sits there on the floor like a hand grenade. I feel like smashing the thing into a million pieces. Instead I tentatively pick it up.

I don't want to say 'hello'. That seems too polite. In the end I settle for, 'What do you want?'

'Enjoying life on the streets?'

'Enjoy the dog shit in your bed?'

'You're disgusting!'

'Disgusting? I'm not the twisted pervert trying to rape my niece.'

'That was you tempting me and you know it.'

Unbelievable. 'You're sick.'

'Look,' he says. 'We can have this pleasant little father–daughter chat for hours but we'll just go round in circles. All I want is the money.'

'Too late. Spent it.'

'You better not have.'

'What do you think I was doing at the airport when your goon spotted me?'

'You can't have been going anywhere. I checked. You're not allowed to without permission from your legal guardian. That would be me.'

I thought that was probably the case, which is why I didn't really buy a ticket to London. Just fantasised about it.

'Okay then, I gave it away to charity. It's dirty money, anyway.'

'I don't think so. I think it's still there in your backpack. But you can't really do anything with it. You can't rent a place, you can't buy anything, nothing big anyway, because that would look suspicious. You're stuck with a whole lot of money that you can't use.'

'I'll throw it away then.'

'I'd think really hard about that if I was you. Really hard about it.'

'Can't you just leave me alone?' I'm trying hard not to plead. 'I won't say anything. I won't go to the police.'

'You think you're so smart. I've already been to the police. Told them you stole from me. Told them you ran away. Told them that you're a complete liar.'

'What if I tell them about my parents and they decide to look for them?'

Creepo laughs. It's a cold bitter laugh that tells me he's thought about this too. Maybe Marco Rossini is right. Maybe I have underestimated Creepo.

'Your parents left here five years ago. It'll be on the Department of Immigration's records. True, no one has heard from them since then. Something must have happened to them when they got home. Something terrible. Serena and I reported them missing both here and back home and in some quarters we're considered saints for taking in their daughter and raising her as our own.'

I close my eyes and try to think. How could the Department of Immigration believe that my parents left the country? I trawl back through my mind. There's something there. Something about Creepo and a blonde woman. Just after I moved in with them he grew a moustache. Serena said it was to make me feel more at home because of my father's moustache. It actually creeped me out at the time because he did look like a younger version of my father. And then there was that blonde woman who came over with a suitcase. She was obviously wearing a wig but she was a dead ringer for my mum. Although Serena was crying, Creepo said that they had to go. It was the only way. I watched through the window as Creepo kissed and hugged Serena, and then the taxi driver helped put their bags in the boot. Then the blonde woman hugged Serena too. Hugged her like she was her sister-in-law, even though Serena just stood there like a statue. And for a while it was just me and Serena and then when I saw Creepo again about three weeks later, his moustache was gone and so was the blonde woman.

'I know how you did it.'

'Did what?'

'You and that bimbo left here on my parents' passports, and came back on your own.'

Creepo laughs. 'I don't know what you're talking about. Sounds like another one of your stories to me.'

God! I have underestimated him. Just like I underestimated Narelle's intelligence. There's book-smart and there's street-smart and I don't think Charles Dickens and Jane Austen would stack up too well against the LA Bloods.

Finally, the doors start to close. Better late than never. This is it. I have to hold my nerve. I don't even look at them. They're of no interest to me.

'No deal, Creepo. The money's burnt.'

I'm about one-third of pretend cop's size so I have to time this right. I wait until the last possible moment. Until there's barely enough room for a broom.

I can hear Creepo screaming down the line.

I hold up the phone to pretend cop.

'Catch!' I pull back my arm and hurl the mobile at him with all my might. Then, while he's fending if off, I snatch up my stuff and bolt for the door, tossing out my sleeping bag and backpack ahead of me. Although my trailing leg gets snagged on the door on the way out, I make it onto the platform with just a bruise. The doors close and the train moves off, sliding past me with pretend cop jabbing his finger on the window and yelling something that doesn't sound polite, even though I can't hear a word. I pick up my stuff and am about to flip him the bird but change my mind and give him a little wave instead. For some reason it seems even more insulting. Then I walk up the steps and over the line for the trains to the north.

My heart is still pounding as I slump onto the seat. I can't believe where the day went. I was having a wonderful time at the airport, fantasising about escaping, but when I found that quiet spot I must have slipped almost into a coma. Then of course Creepo's goon shows up. Or did he? I was on a plane and now I'm on a train and I've got no idea at which point I woke up. I don't know what's happening to me. Exhaustion? Stress? It's all getting too much. I think I might be starting to lose my mind.

By the time we pull in to the northern junction station it's well after ten. It's too late to get into the rail yards. There's no one around to interview about the procedure. The trains that were on day shift are all tucked up in bed, Thomas the Tank Engine singing them a lullaby and discussing further engine maintenance issues. The ones that are still out will probably prowl around for a while and then stop running after midnight.

The train I'm on is heading up to Death Valley and beyond. Even though I could probably manage a two-hour walk on the sand, in the dark I wouldn't be able to find my hollow or uncover my camouflaged door number 4. And it'd be an early start to get to school on time. I'd only get a few hours sleep, if any.

I'll head south-west, find somewhere to crash closer to school. I gather up my stuff and step off the train and onto the platform.

As I'm standing there I notice a broken old man shuffling along the platform towards me. He appears to blend into the darkness, more shadow than human. As he gets closer I realise that if I hadn't seen him, eventually I would have smelled him. Where's a bottle of *Cologne d'aviation* when you need one? Where's a peg?

'Evening,' he says, doffing his imaginary hat to me.

I try to smile but I catch a whiff of him and I'm forced to hold back vomit instead. His stench is so overpowering, so all encompassing, I'm starting to feel light-headed. His suit and jumper look as if he dug them out of a bin in the early nineteen-seventies and has had them on ever since, while his beard is so long and snarled it could comfortably house a flock of magpies, providing they've had their nasal passages hermetically sealed.

He steps onto the train and turns around. 'You coming?' he asks.

Despite his overwhelming hygiene issues, he seems friendly and pleasant and oblivious to his own repugnant reek. Oh how I wish he had a place for a little soap, toothpaste and deodorant in his life.

'Well? Are you? Are you coming?'

'Coming where?'

'Kathmandu,' he announces and then laughs like it's the most hilarious thing that anyone has ever said. 'Ding, ding,' he continues, ringing an imaginary bell over the door. 'All aboard. Last train to Kathmandu.'

Kathmandu? I close my eyes and pull up an atlas from my long-term memory. Kathmandu . . .? This train can't be going to Nepal. Not without a massive tunnel beneath the sea. The poor guy's obviously barking mad.

The old man grins at me and reveals his tombstone teeth.

As he dings his imaginary bell again I notice the dirt ingrained into his skin. The poor guy doesn't need a bath so much as a scrape.

'Last train to Kathmandu,' he announces again and laughs some more, though in my opinion this gag has run its course.

'The last train to Kathmandu?' I shrug my shoulders. 'I don't know what that means.'

'You homeless?' he asks.

I make to say something in protest but then decide against it. What's the point? 'Yeah.' I stare at the ground because it's the first time I've acknowledged it. 'Yeah. I'm homeless.'

'C'mon then.' He beckons me on board.

The recorded message announces the train's imminent departure.

'Hurry up, sweetheart.' He's so nice it's actually tempting. But I know that ten minutes surrounded by his inescapable stench and I'll be hurling myself at the window like a demented fly trying to get out. And by the time I've finished contemplating it the doors have closed.

I hold up my hand to say goodbye and again he doffs his imaginary hat and throws in an elaborate bow as well.

I don't know who the hell that was, but I bet he would have an interesting story to tell.

As the train begins its slow slide out of the station, I notice that despite the late hour, there's quite a few passengers on board, most of them sound asleep. And then I see the threadbare blankets, the bags, the shopping trolley, the bags, the clothes scavenged from charity bins, the bags. Just about everyone on board the train is like him. Like me. This is some sort of homeless special. The train of lost souls. The last train to Kathmandu.

*

My tears slide down my cheeks and splash to the floor. They're mine. They belong to me. I don't want to let them go. I don't want to let anything go. I move my feet so that my salty misery is absorbed by my shoes.

Despite Miss Taylor's straw hat and blazer scholarship plans, I'm going to end up like them. I just know it. Riding through the night on a ghost train bound for nowhere and smelling like a skunk's armpit, dreaming of what was, of what might have been. Where the only happy place to go is inside your head.

It's so easy to slip into my fantasy world, where it's safe, where it's warm, where no one wants to hurt me, where you can fly business class to London with British Airways, or escape to Venice in a first class sleeper cabin on the Orient Express. It's just not so easy to come back. I'm already starting to have trouble recognising the difference between fact and fantasy and I've only been homeless for a week, most of which I spent in a five-star hotel. God help me when things get really rough. I'll probably end up escaping into my head permanently. It's not the insane who end up homeless, but the homeless who end up insane.

By the time I lug myself the half-kilometre from the station to school it's starting to drizzle. It's that pathetic sort of misty rain that doesn't seem very heavy but somehow manages to soak you to the bone. Hopefully the rain, plus the fact that it's getting on towards midnight, will mean that most of the vermin have scurried back to their rat holes.

I know it's not safe, but where else could I go? Death Valley? A hostel? A doorway? A skip? My old school's church? A park bench in the ivy belt? The last train to Kathmandu? I don't think I could stand the stench. And no matter how much cash I have on me, I couldn't lie my way into a hotel at this time of night. No one would believe that my barrister mother would be at a high-powered meeting now, leaving me to fend for myself. So I guess here's as good a place as any.

I don't think any buses will be running now. I remember something in the news a few weeks ago about how the bus drivers in one of the outer suburbs had gone on strike. It just got too unsafe. Rocks, abuse, robberies, violence. I'm pretty sure it was around here somewhere.

I roll out my sleeping bag along the cold, hard aluminium bench. From the dim glow of the streetlight I can see that there's broken glass scattered about underneath the bench. Maybe I could use a piece in self defence if any human vermin turn up.

I squirm myself deep into my nylon cocoon, turning onto my side in an attempt to get comfortable. Unless the wind suddenly swings around, the bus shelter will keep out most of the rain. The shelter itself is made of toughened glass, but every panel has been shattered so that I'm encased in a sort of opaque spider web. It'd be quite artistic if it wasn't so damn violent.

Apart from everything that's happened, there's something about today that's bothering me. I can't quite connect it to anything, but it's been hovering over my head since I emerged from my hollow up at Death Valley Beach this morning.

I fidget restlessly and the streetlight glints off the face of my watch.

I look at it closely, squinting against the dark. How could I have missed that? Today's date. I've got about five minutes left.

Well, I'm not spending it here. Stuck in a rain-soaked, shattered bus shelter on a hard, cold seat surrounded by broken glass.

I close my eyes and join the flight somewhere high above South East Asia. I can't be me any more – not this version anyway.

I summon the flight attendant over.

'How may I help?'

'Would it be possible to get a glass of champagne?'

'Certainly. Anything else?'

'A hot chocolate and a cupcake.'

'Of course.'

She disappears and returns a few minutes later with my bubbling glass of champers and cupcake. The hot chocolate will take a little longer, she says. They're just getting the marshmallows and sprinkles from the galley.

'Celebration?' she asks.

'Yes,' I reply.

She's waiting for me to elaborate but I want to enjoy the moment by myself, and she's smart enough to recognise this.

'Enjoy,' she says, before moving off.

I pick up the champagne flute and stare out into the pitch-black night. There's nothing out there but my reflection, distorted by the spider web of shattered glass.

I hold up the champagne in a toast. 'Happy birthday,' I say and chug the glass in one swig.

ACT FOUR

NULLUM FATUM EST

What the mother sings to the cradle
goes all the way down to the coffin.

— HENRY WARD BEECHER

CAFÉ

IT'S GETTING HARDER TO DIFFERENTIATE REALITY FROM FANTASY.

That's the point. It was for me too. But think about it this way. Given the choice between spending the night in a broken-down, rainy outer suburban bus shelter or British Airways business class, what would you choose? I didn't even have to try to fantasise in the end. My brain just took me away. It was as if it was trying to protect me.

The giveaway was when you went to board the plane and you said the flight attendant ticked you off her list, when they actually put the boarding passes through an electronic swiper.

Well, I hadn't flown before so I was just making it up.

Also when you went from the check-in area through to the departure gates you would have gone through customs.

I know that. Of course they wouldn't have let a kid that age take off overseas by themselves; not without the necessary paperwork, anyway. But that's the thing with fantasy. Reality doesn't have to get in the way.

Was the security guard real?

Yeah. I should have known that Creepo would have people at the airport. What with all his scams and everything I forgot that he had some legitimate businesses too. One of them was a security company. I found out later that he didn't own it himself, not entirely, but he had a share in it. That pretend cop was one of his goons, one of the *boys*. But . . .

[Pause]

But what?

He wouldn't have shot me. I mean, I know I had the gun and everything . . .

At the airport?

I know. I just didn't think but I'm sure Creepo's goon wouldn't have shot me. It was too risky. No matter what Creepo told him, he couldn't have known for certain that I had the gun in my backpack. They were just trying to scare me. And boy did it work.

And that train. The last train to Kathmandu. Was that real?

Doesn't seem like it, does it? But it was. I heard more about it later, from my friend Cinderella. And I saw it again a few times. It was surreal. A train full of shadows. Of living ghosts. On a journey to nowhere.

Happy Birthday

I'M DRAWN UP TO THE NEW DAY, MY NEW YEAR, BY THE SOUND OF tinkling. It's late-night, early-morning and I need another few minutes so I turn over to face the early morning traffic as it Dopplers past. The bench is so narrow that I'm only able to sleep on my side and even then it's a balancing act that I've lost a couple of times throughout the night. Luckily I managed not to slice open an artery on the broken glass when I fell. But really, a bus shelter is about as uncomfortable as being homeless gets. Hiding beneath door number 4 at Death Valley is a five-star hotel compared to this.

That tinkling sound. It's closer now. Right beneath me.

I open my eyes and gasp. I pull my sleeping bag tightly about me.

'Sorry,' says the man. 'I'm just trying to clean up this mess before you cut yourself. Didn't mean to wake you up.'

He reaches underneath the bench and picks up the rest of the glass, scooping it up in his unprotected hands, which are as big and as leathery as baseball mitts. He then drops it into the bin on the other side of the bus shelter.

'There,' he says. 'That's better. We won't be slicing ourselves open now, will we?' He doesn't complain about the broken glass or offer any opinions on the character or racial background of whoever might have been responsible for it. It wasn't his mess. It wasn't even his problem. He could have just stood there waiting for his bus, but he cleaned it up anyway. He also seems to think there's nothing unusual about a four-teen-year-old girl sleeping in a bus shelter. His only concern was that he woke me up, not that I'm here to begin with.

I sit up and start getting myself together. I yawn, stretch, squirm my way out of my sleeping bag and slowly roll it up. My technique at squeezing all the air out of it is improving with practice.

As I'm stuffing my sleeping bag into its carrier, I notice that the guy is wearing one of those bright yellow shirts that you see a lot around the outer suburbs. The sort favoured by men in trucks. Men on building sites. Men digging up roads. Men who need to be highly visible so that they don't get squashed by industrial machinery. I once heard someone call those shirts 'fluorescent wife beaters', supposedly because labourers have a higher incidence of domestic violence than those working in other professions. It's probably not even true. And it certainly isn't fair on the millions, billions, of working men who don't beat their wives. My father never wore a wife beater – yellow, orange, blue, lime green or any other colour – which is kind of ironic. Neither did Creepo for that matter, yet he wasn't above hitting Serena. So there's the theory out the window. Women wear them too, I imagine. When they need to be seen on building sites. Though I suppose that's the point. They rarely are. And even then they wouldn't be called wife beaters, surely. Husband beaters? I doubt it.

The guy also has one of those mullet hairstyles that dropped out of fashion in the nineteen-eighties. They still crop up occasionally, on the covers of Serena's old, dog-eared romance novels or on Country and Western CDs. He's also wearing a big, thick gypsy earring. Another relic from a bygone era.

'Rough night?'

I consider ignoring him but he seems okay. I mean, he didn't have to pick up that broken glass. The world's a marginally better place because of what he's just done. People will be able to use the bus stop today and won't even realise that they've got this guy to thank for it. He doesn't seem to want any credit or acknowledgement. Not even from me.

'About as rough as it gets.'

'Parents kick you out?'

'Something like that.'

'That's rough.' He shakes his head. 'Any bloody idiot can have kids, but you need a licence to own a dog.'

The wisdom of the west.

'You're not getting into drugs, are you?'

I'm actually quite offended. Not all teenagers are druggos. 'No!'

'Good for you.'

I notice his yellowed fingers. The nicotine patch on his arm. The hypocrisy hovering over him. Just because his drug of choice is legal, he thinks it gives him the right to preach to others. Which bit of 'Smoking Kills' don't you get? Or do you think the picture of that woman with half her face chewed off by cancer is on the packet for artistic reasons?

'My son got into drugs.'

Oh.

'Not that hard stuff. Just a bit of mull.'

I don't know what mull is, though I'm guessing it's marijuana. Just because I'm sleeping in a bus shelter doesn't mean I automatically know about this sort of stuff. How streetwise can you get when you practically raise yourself on Roald Dahl novels? Matilda and Miss Honey didn't fund their extravagant lifestyle by dealing in the playground. Despite evidence to the contrary, George's marvellous medicine didn't contain a single ounce of cocaine. And although Willy Wonka wandered around the chocolate factory completely off his face, this was because he was injecting Hershey bars rather than heroin.

The guy carries on with his anti-drugs campaign, but he doesn't realise that he's preaching to the converted.

'Scrambled his brain,' he continues. 'He was at school, doing real well. Wanted to be a carpenter, maybe even go to uni, then he got in with the wrong crowd. Weed sucked out all his ambition. All his get up and go. Him and his moron mates lived by that stupid expression. You know the one – live fast, die young, leave a good-looking corpse.'

I nod in agreement, though I haven't heard that expression.

'They all went out to this party one night and got completely stoned. Then one of them, Danny his name was – not much upstairs but a really good footballer – well he ended up wrapping his car around a telegraph pole. There was nothing good-looking about *his* corpse, let me tell you. Closed casket funeral that one.'

There's a pause while he fumbles for the cigarettes he doesn't have.

'Anyway, it shook my boy back onto the straight and narrow. He's working up north now. In the mines. No qualifications but at least he's off the wacky weed. Giving it a go, anyway.'

This is all very interesting, in an Oprah sort of way, but I'm not sure why he's telling me.

'You still at school?'

Right. Here it comes. The school of hard knocks, the university of life lecture. 'Yeah.'

'Then you stay there as long as you can. Get yourself a trade or go to university.'

'I *am* going to university.'

'What? Really?'

My sleeping rough hardly bothers him. Tell him I'm going to uni and his eyes pop out on stalks like a cartoon character.

'Why shouldn't I?'

'It's just that you seem so young.'

Oh. 'No. I mean I'm *going* to go to university. After year twelve.'

'Good for you.'

'I'm going to be a doctor.' I hold off on the African eye-eating worm bit. He's fidgety enough as it is.

'A doctor? You've set your sights high.'

There's a pause while he considers me.

'Can you go home?'

I shake my head. 'No.'

'Why not?'

'I'd rather not say.'

'Father not . . .' he trails off. 'Not messing with you, is he?'

'Uncle.'

'Bastard!' He shakes his head. 'You need to tell someone.'

'I'm handling it.'

He looks around the shattered spider-web bus shelter. I'm obviously not handling it very well.

He reaches into his bag and pulls something out. It's a book. I didn't expect him to have books in his bag. Booze maybe. Racing guide perhaps. Nunchakus. But if I've learned one thing on the streets it's that not everything's as it seems.

He passes the book to me. 'You should read this.'

I take it from him and study the cover. *The Diving Bell and the Butterfly.* Interesting title.

'It's about this Frenchman. He's only in his early forties or something, when he has a stroke. Something to do with his brainstem, whatever that is. Maybe you can tell me when you become a doctor. Anyway, he gets locked in his own body. All he can do is blink one eye. Blink and dribble. They thought he was pretty much a vegetable, but someone eventually sees that he's trying to communicate by blinking. So they sat a secretary in front of him and she would read out the letters of the alphabet and he would blink when she came to the one he wanted and then she would write it down, slowly forming words, sentences and what not. Do you know what he asked for?'

'No.'

'He asked to write a book. So they set him up with a stream of assistants and off he went. Took him about two years and something like a quarter of a million blinks but he did it. Not long afterwards, he died.'

Good one, God! What? Have a plan, did you? Bit short on blinking guys in heaven? Why didn't you test his faith a bit more by giving him cancer of the eyelid or something?

'He died?'

'Of pneumonia, a couple of weeks after it was published.'

'That's really sad.'

'Still. He wrote a book. How many people can say that? How many people say they're gonna do this, they're gonna do that, and then never get round to doing it? Doing anything? This guy did it. He blinked a fucking book, pardon my French.'

I stare at the book. It's not very thick. About a tenth of the size of *Pride and Prejudice*. Then again, Jane Austen didn't have to blink it. Maybe if she did she might have cut back on a couple of characters. Edited out Caroline Bingley for a start, who is just weird

I hand it back to him. 'I'll get a copy.'

'No,' he replies. 'I want you to have it.'

'Oh no, I couldn't.'

'I've read it. Three or four times. Please. I'd like you to have it. Let's call it a birthday present.'

'How did you know it was my birthday?'

'Er, I didn't. Is it really?'

'Yesterday.'

'Well then, happy birthday. You've got to take it now.'

'Thank you.' I look down at my present, my birthday present, the nicest present that anyone has ever given me. More liquid patheticness wells in my eyes.

He looks at me and smiles. 'If someone who can only move an eyelid can manage to write a book, imagine what you can do if you put your mind to it.'

His bus wheezes up, coughing and spluttering to a stop, and with a nod and a smile he's gone, giving me a final thumbs-up through the window.

One of the maths teachers, Mrs Grimshaw, heaves herself out of the bus's rear door. She stops to catch her breath and stares. Glares at me. At my sleeping bag. Then she glares at me again. Sitting there with my book, my backpack, my weekend clothes. Oh no. The plan was to drop my excess stuff at Alistair McAlister's café and then make my way to school. But things went a bit pear-shaped yesterday, so here I am. It's only seven o'clock. I didn't think anyone would be here this early.

Of all the people to bust me, why did it have to be Mrs Grimshaw? While we're on the subject of *Matilda*,

Mrs Grimshaw makes The Trunchbull look like Miss Honey. No matter where you are in the school you can always hear Mrs Grimshaw ranting and raving about something or other. Something trivial. Even though Mr Thompkins initiated a no-shouting policy amongst the staff, she still goes off like an industrial foghorn. I swear one day she's going to go off so badly, she'll just explode. Lighting up the afternoon sky with her innards and entrails and erupted spleen.

'You're that new girl aren't you? Tiffany something or other?'

'Yes, Miss.'

'Well. What are you doing sitting there?'

'I, er.' Come on, think. 'I, er, had a sleepover last night. At a friend's house. She doesn't go to this school. They had to leave early so they dropped me off first.'

'Well, you can't stay here, it's not safe. Whole place is full of hooligans and ruffians.' Hooligans and ruffians? She sounds like a late-night black-and-white movie set in London during a dastardly German bombing raid. I didn't know people still spoke this way. I actually snort out loud. It's involuntary but it's loud so I quickly bring up my hand to cover my face.

'And use a handkerchief when you blow your nose, girl!'

'Yes, Miss.' And I'll keep a sharp eye out for those ruffians while I'm at it. Oh, no! Why did my brain have to do that? I'm practically convulsing now. A fountain welling in my eyes again. I quickly turn to the side to make it look like I'm getting my stuff (rather than my shit) together.

'Come on, then. Hurry up. You can wait in the staffroom with me until Mrs Lee opens the library.'

'Thanks, Miss.'

'And get a handkerchief for that nose of yours.'

'Yes, Miss.' I follow along behind Miss Grimshaw, trying not to explode with laughter. It's sheer agony but a great way to commence my fifteenth revolution around the sun.

*

Mrs Lee arrives early with her serious connoisseur café-bought coffee. I don't know where she's from originally but she just oozes class. She's so stylish and attractive that she could come to school wearing nothing but a sack and it would still work on her. Like everyone else in the school, she seems really lovely and caring. Even Mrs Grimshaw's got her good points. She refused to leave me outside with the hooligans and ruffians, after all.

Although the library isn't supposed to be open before school, Mrs Grimshaw hands me over to Mrs Lee, who doesn't complain. She calls me darling and tells me that I can either do my homework or help her shelve the returned books and when we've done that I'm quite welcome to stay and read in one of the big comfortable chairs.

I ask her if I can help her every day and she takes one look at my sleeping bag and says yes.

This is my second birthday present of the day. Working in a library where it's warm and dry, and where I can shelve and read books to my heart's content. Mrs Lee doesn't know it but she's opened the gates of heaven.

*

We're designing a book poster in English when the hooter goes for recess. No one moves, which is weird. We're normally like a pack of wildebeests tearing out the door and across the Serengeti plains to the canteen or the quadrangle.

Miss Taylor is in the storeroom so she obviously hasn't heard the hooter. She must be up to something in there that she doesn't want us to know about. Texting her boyfriend, perhaps.

Then slowly, cautiously, she steps out of the storeroom carrying something. It's glowing and I see that the glowing things are candles and they're on a cake. A birthday cake. It must be someone else's birthday as well.

The lights are dimmed and Miss Taylor starts singing happy birthday and the whole class joins in. I start singing too but then Miss Taylor places the cake down in front of me. We're singing happy birthday to me.

Halfway through the song there's a knock on the door and Mr Thompkins and Mrs Lee steal into the room and join in the song.

I'm so choked up I can hardly swallow. Following a deafening hip hip hooray, Mr Thompkins calls for a speech. I just about manage to splutter out 'thank you'. I don't even know why Mr Thompkins and Mrs Lee are here. Maybe they've heard something. Realised that I'm not going to be here very long. At the school. On the planet.

When I cut the cake and make a wish, Miss Taylor actually hugs me. I mean, really hugs me. I hold onto her so tightly, I never want to let her go even though I'm dripping tears onto her top.

'It's all right, sweetheart,' she whispers in my ear. 'Whatever it is. You'll get through it. You're strong.'

'What's the matter, Tiffany-Star?' says Janyce, one of the Islander girls who keeps a lookout for me. She hands me a slice of cake that has pink a 'Tif' on it – the icing sugar remnants of Narelle's stupid name. Miss Taylor still has her arm around me but my eyes must be blood-red. 'Aren't you having a nice birthday?'

'No,' I sniff. 'It's the best birthday I've ever had.'

Miss Taylor squeezes my hand.

Janyce hits play on Miss Taylor's CD player and pretty soon the whole class is bouncing around the room.

'Does this happen on everyone's birthday?' I yell to Janyce above the music.

'Yeah,' she replies. 'Miss Taylor is awesome. How many teachers want to see you actually have fun?' She pauses for a second. 'I reckon you really need it too. That's all right – we'll all make sure you have a good time here, Tiffany-Star.'

I tilt my head to one side. I'm not sure what she means by this. But Janyce just smiles.

And for a moment I *do* feel special. I feel like this is the happiest moment of my life.

CAFÉ

She was. I mean, she is. But everyone was at that school. Even Mrs Grimshaw. She shouted a lot, but she shouted because she cared. She knew the kids who didn't want to learn were hindering the ones who did. I could just as easily have picked a school in the next suburb when I was looking, but I'd heard it was rougher.

More hooligans and ruffians?

Exactly. Mr Thompkins didn't just know every kid's name in our school, he knew their hobbies, their grades, their home life – good and bad. Hell, he even knew their favourite football team. He encouraged us to get involved in everything. To give things a go.

Because he cared.

That's right. And he made sure that the school did. He didn't bully the staff into caring about us, he chose teachers who did. Even the office ladies were less dragon-like than at other schools. You know something, I only went to that school for about six weeks but I still miss it. Even now I want to make Mr Thompkins, Miss Taylor and Mrs Lee proud of me. They say you should choose your parents wisely. I think it's just as important to choose the right school, especially if you stuff up on the parent selection thing.

Okay. Back to you. What happened after your birthday?

I figured it was time to find somewhere to live. I was sick of not knowing where I was going to sleep at night. Moving around all over the place. It was so tiring. I had a fallback option for the weekend – beneath door number 4 up at Death Valley, but I had to find somewhere for the week. A regular place. I needed routine. I needed structure.

Rail yards?

Rail yards.

Nullum Fatum Est

IN MY THIRD WEEK AT THE SCHOOL MRS LEE ARRANGES FOR AN author to visit. First he gives a talk to the whole of years seven and eight, then a writing workshop for thirty selected students. I was so excited when Miss Taylor and Mrs Lee chose me to be one of the students. During the workshop the author gives us a copy of one of his short stories. It literally makes our jaws drop.

Miracle Child

No one expected the baby to live, least of all his mother. Her three other babies had all died in quick succession. First Gustav, then little Otto and then her daughter Ida. And now this frail, sickly little boy seemed sure to join his brothers and sisters in the cold earth.

The couple, although new to town, were held in high regard due to the husband's position at the

Customs House, although the talk among the towns-
folk was that he spent too much time at the inn and
often had to be helped home. The wife seemed pleasant
and pretty and much too young for the bearded ogre
that fate had lumbered her with.

The couple stared into the crib that contained
their tiny bundle. The woman held her soaked handkerchief to her face. Alois detested public displays of
emotion. If she lost her composure, she would pay for
it later when Alois returned from the inn.

'Is there any hope for my child?' begged Klara of
the nurse.

'Pull yourself together, woman!' snapped Alois.

'We're doing all we can,' offered the nurse. 'It's in
God's hands now.'

'God!' said Alois with contempt, as if he was referring to an equal entity. 'What does God care for our
troubles?'

The nurse, unused to such blasphemy, excused
herself and went about her duties.

'It's all your fault, Klara,' snarled Alois, staring at
his fragile little son. 'You only make runts. Otto was
even smaller than this one and Ida smaller still.'

'Not Gustav,' corrected Klara, risking Alois's wrath
once again. 'Gustav was twice the size of Otto.'

'He still died!' spat Alois at his wife. 'They all
died!'

When Alois had left for the inn, Klara curled up
on a chair beside her baby. If this one died then she
would go too. What was left for her in this life?

That night Klara prayed. Although she wasn't
particularly religious, she was prepared to ask for help
from any and all quarters. If God had an ounce of

decency then surely he would let this one live. Just this one.

The days passed with Klara holding vigil by her son's little crib, and her husband holding a vigil of his own at the inn. Fully aware of Klara's circumstances, the doctors and nurses did all they could to give her baby every chance.

Two weeks following the premature birth, Klara woke to find one of the doctors examining her precious bundle.

'Is he . . .?' began Klara.

The doctor removed his stethoscope from the baby's chest and smiled at Klara. 'His lungs are clear. The infection gone. It appears, madam, as though you have your miracle.'

The tears cascaded down Klara's cheeks. She made no move to wipe them away and so they fell onto her little miracle.

The nurses and doctors gathered around and shared their heartfelt joy with Klara. She cradled her beautiful bundle in her arms, never wanting to let him go.

'He's such a fighter,' said the doctor. 'I wager that he would make a fine soldier one day.'

'What will you call him?' asked one of the nurses. 'Have you picked out a name?'

Klara was so overwhelmed with love for her darling boy that she failed to hear the question.

'I said,' prompted the nurse, 'what will you call him, Mrs Hitler?'

'I think,' replied Klara, 'I will call him Adolf.'

And everyone present agreed that Adolf Hitler was indeed a fine name for the little soldier from Austria.

The author's point is that you have to get the audience to care about your character – or generate empathy as he puts it, because that sounds better.

After the workshop the author gives me a signed copy of one of his books. He says it's because of the questions I asked but really I think he saw through me. He saw *me*.

Although I'm excited about the book, that story gets me thinking about fate. As in, there's no such thing. I'm sitting alone in the library afterwards thinking: what if Otto Hitler had lived? He might have gone on to become a bigger lunatic than his brother. Or he might have sold flowers by the side of the road outside of Salzburg. Nothing is predetermined. Because if it is, then your life's already been mapped out for you. What you'll do. Who'll you marry. When you'll die. You're nothing but an automaton, wandering around like a zombified drone.

Of course you can use fate as an excuse for not getting out of bed in the morning. For doing nothing with your life. Or you take the opposite tack. There is no fate. *Nullum fatum est.* That's my English class's motto. Miss Taylor has it up on the whiteboard. She wears a cross around her neck and her favourite book is the Bible but she believes that we make our own destiny with or without God's approval. Although she has to be careful, what with parent/teacher night getting close, she hints that although we haven't had the best start in life, that doesn't prevent us from changing our destiny, because there isn't one. We start each day with a blank sheet of paper in front of us, and what we write on it is up to us.

I already know what I want for my life and this isn't it. I want to become a doctor, so I have to do certain things to make that happen. I have to work hard at school. I have to read. I have to learn. I have to study. Then I have to get good enough marks to get into uni, and then I have to study hard to pass my exams. Then when I've finished my internship I'll be able to apply to Médecins Sans Frontières. And while I'm doing all this I'll learn another language – French maybe. Because everything helps. I'm not just going to sit back and go with the flow and then blame fate when it doesn't happen. I have to make it happen.

*

After school I wander over to the office and pick up my travel pass from the head office lady. She flicks through various envelopes and then hands the pass to me. As I'm signing for it she smiles. Actually smiles. Maybe she's heard something about me. Or maybe she's just heard about smiling and is trying it out. I hope she doesn't strain any facial muscles.

With my travel pass I'm legal. I've got my licence to roam.

I make my way over to the ivy belt, to the mega-mall and Alistair McAlister's café. I don't want any more fuss so I don't tell him that it was my birthday. He gives me a free hot chocolate anyway and asks why I didn't drop my stuff off with him that morning as we had planned. When I tell him what happened, about Creepo's goon and the Last Train to Kathmandu and the bus shelter and the book-giving guy in the fluorescent wife beater with the mullet haircut, he just stares at me and shakes his head.

'You make my life sound so boring,' he says.

'Boring's good. I'd love to be bored, just for a while.'

I don't tell him about having the gun at the airport. He'll only get all preachy on me. I wonder what everyone at school would say if they knew I was bringing a loaded gun to school with me each day. Probably wipe the smile off the head office lady's face for a start. It might even throw

Mr Thompkins a bit. I should have thrown it away by now but I'm hanging onto it in case Creepo turns up.

When I've finished my homework, I ask Alistair to bring me a toasted sandwich and then I start planning for tonight. If I manage to get into the rail yards, I'll have a nice evening of reading with my new books. If not, I'll be back in the bus shelter or a park bench in the ivy belt. I write a list: a few snacks, a facecloth, a wide-rim drink bottle, a small torch, a book light and batteries. That's really all I need.

It's a little after four-thirty when I say goodbye to Alistair and catch a train to the junction station. It's too early to get shut in the yards yet. Too early for the Last Train to Kathmandu. But early enough for there still to be school students about. Mostly boater, straw hat, and blazer but enough public students for my appearance not to raise any eyebrows.

I step off the train and when the stationmaster blows his whistle, I bound up to him like a six-week-old puppy.

'Oh, hi. I was wondering if you could help me please.' I'm so doe-eyed in my innocence that he can't possibly refuse.

'Yes. What is it?' He's not entirely happy about having to deal with me. There's a lot of him. A hell of a lot, in fact. His hips have disappeared beneath the rolls of fat. Although he's wearing a belt, it doesn't appear to serve any purpose, more a sort of leather halfway line. Merely standing there seems to make him wheeze. I hate to say it but he's sort of like the Fat Controller from Thomas the Tank Engine, minus the top hat and snazzy waistcoat. It's obvious he wants to get rid of me and get back to his doughnuts or whatever else he's got in his little office but I bound on regardless.

'Oh, great. Thanks.' I put my backpack on the ground and pull out my homework book to make it look official. 'I have to do a school project on a procedure. You know, how to make a poached egg, how to change a car's oil, how to blink a book, that sort of thing.'

He gives me a funny look when I mention the blinking book. He's obviously not up to speed on French literature by the physically impaired.

He leans forward and looks at me over the top of his glasses. I'm not sure if he's going to help me or eat me. 'And how can I help you?' Phew.

'I want to do something different from recipes and boring stuff about car engines, so I was thinking about doing something on trains. Like, say, how do they get over there?' I point over to the parked trains, which are about a hundred metres past the end of the platform.

'The yards? Well, they're driven over.'

I burst out laughing. It's so fake I could almost be a studio audience member for a comedy show about an American family and their amusing pet. 'Silly me. I mean, what happens before they get there?'

He looks vacant. Geez, keep up, dude! I push on. 'Like, how do you make sure that no passengers get left on board?'

Finally we get a bit of electrical activity upstairs. 'Oh, right. Well the train guard does what's called a walkthrough.'

I jot down some pretend notes in my homework book. 'A walkthrough?'

'Well, he . . .'

'Or she.' Oops. Couldn't help myself.

'You're right. There are a few lady guards about now.'

Lady guards?

'He – or she – starts at the front and walks through the carriages, making sure that there are no carry-overs.'

'Carry-overs?'

'People left on the train. Someone might have fallen asleep

or haven't understood or heard that it's a terminating train. They could be deaf or not speak English good.'

I look up from my non-existent notes but let it go.

'While the guard's doing his walkthrough, there's an announcement about the train terminating, but in my experience some people are so stupid they may as well have rocks in their head.'

'Or, as you say, they might not speak English very *well*.'

'True enough. So the guard has to do a walkthrough just to be on the safe side.'

'But the carriages are all double-decker. How does the guard make sure that they're empty?'

'Well he ...

Or *she*.

'... is supposed to walk through the top section and then go down the stairs and walk through the bottom, or visa-versa.'

Vice-versa.

'But most of them are pretty slack and once they've done the top they usually just pop their heads down the bottom and have a quick look. No one wants to get stuck on the train though, so it's not as if anybody would be hiding.'

'What about homeless people? Don't they ...'

'Nope. Not interested.'

'Who isn't?'

'The homeless.'

'Why not?'

'They don't want to be stuck in the rail yards, do they? They might be stupid to end up like they have ....

GGGRRRR!

'... but even they've got more sense than to let themselves got locked in a train all night.'

Another train is just pulling in. 'Hang on a sec, darling.'

I roll my eyes at 'darling', but he's busy watching the passengers get on and off. When it's all clear he blows his whistle and waves to the guard. The doors close and the train slides out of the station, heading north to Death Valley and beyond.

When the train has completely cleared the station, he waddles back over to me. 'Where were we?'

'You were saying something about how homeless people don't try to get into the rail yards at night.'

'That's right.'

'Why was that again?'

'Well, they're locked in, aren't they? Once the heating gets shut off it gets pretty cold in there. Freezing. And they can't let themselves out. They're stuck in there all night. No one to talk to.'

Who cares?

'Nothing to do.'

Book light.

'Nothing to eat.'

BYO.

'Nowhere to pee.'

Wide-rim drink bottle.

'I don't think even homeless people would pee where they sleep.'

Double GGGRRR!

'So then what happens? After the guard has finished his or *her* walkthrough?'

'Then the driver and the guard take the train over to the yards and together they shut it down for the night.'

'What if there is a carry-over?'

'Well, if the guard notices one, he's supposed to report it but really . . .' He leans closer to me like we're in on the great guard conspiracy. '. . . it's not worth the hassle or the kick up the bum from management if they find out, so what they generally do, and you didn't hear this from me, is the guard gets the carry-over down off the train and then he walks them over to a hole in the fence and turfs them out.'

'What about at night? Are there any security guards about?'

'A private security firm patrols the yards, but they're not interested in carry-overs. Not their job. They're there to keep out vandals and them graffiti morons.'

'What if the security guards did spot a carry-over?'

'I've never heard of it happening but I suppose unless the carry-over is smashing the window to get out, security'd just ignore them.'

I finish writing my pretend notes and close my book.

'Thank you. That's been really helpful.'

'Stick around,' he says. 'There's a terminating train due in fifteen minutes. You can watch the guard do his walkthrough.' He smiles at me and ducks back into his little office.

I sit on the one of the benches and wait for the terminating train. When it arrives the fat controller emerges wheezing from his cubbyhouse and waves to me to let me know that this is the train I'm interested in, as if the announcement being played repeatedly has somehow escaped my attention, or suddenly I don't speak English good.

No sooner has the lady guard started her walkthrough than the fat controller disappears. Although I didn't ask him I sort of get the feeling that he's supposed to stay on the platform while she's doing the walkthrough to make sure that nobody slips on board. But like he said: who would want to?

I pick up my stuff and wander up to the far end of the platform, to the front of the train. I stroll past the driver's cabin and glance inside but he just ignores me and carries on reading his paper. I look back along the platform and notice that it curves slightly. Even if the guard steps off the train once she's finished her walkthrough, she won't be able to see me until she's halfway back along the platform because of the way that it curves. I've found a blind spot.

I had planned to wait until it started getting dark before I made my first attempt, but the opportunity is too good to pass up. I step on board and dart up the steps to the top section. When the guard walks past on the way back to the driver's cabin, she would need to be about four metres tall to see me up here. Even so, I lie down on one of the long seats, which is still warm from either the sun streaming in through the windows or the previous passengers' butts. I hope it's the sun.

The doors close and the train moves off, slowly clackety-clacking across the points until we're over in the yards. After a few short, sharp shunts we come to a stop. A few minutes later the lights go off and the heating system shuts down. It's deathly quiet. Towards the front I hear what must be the driver's cabin door banging shut, and then the voices of the driver and the guard receding into the afternoon, back to their homes, their lives. And that's it. I'm in. I peer out the window and then duck across the aisle to do the same on the other side to make sure there's no one else around. When I'm positive that I'm alone I start getting myself organised. I'm still in my school uniform so I quickly change into my homey clothes. My train clothes now. I decide to have a little afternoon snack before I escape into *The Diving Bell and the Butterfly*. I'm proud of myself for buying some fruit. I peel my mandarin and then when I've finished I allow myself a comfort Tim Tam.

Now that I'm safe it's time to get bored. Blissfully bored.

It was easy slipping onto the train and hiding out in the yards where no one can bother me. Much easier than I thought it would be. In fact, I've only made one mistake, and that's the train itself. I should have waited for one of the newer trains. The silver ones with the yellow trim. Those trains have comfortable seats. They're made out of soft material, sort of like stretched velour. The train I'm on is older so the seats are covered in hard vinyl. But I'll get better at this. Better at working out timetables and what time they start yarding the newer trains – sometime after rush hour, I would imagine.

Dark creeps up on me slowly like something out of the woods. I didn't even notice it coming. It's only when I have to squint to read that I finally become aware of how dark it is.

I delve into my shopping bag and pull out my new book light. When I've inserted the batteries, I attach it to *The Diving Bell and the Butterfly* and switch it on. It illuminates the carriage like a sideshow alley at the circus. I gasp and flick it off again. I hardly even stirred when a couple of other trains were driven into the yards and parked alongside mine. But my book light terrifies me. It's giving away my hidey-hole. Signalling to the world: come and get me.

I take out my sleeping bag and unzip it completely so that it's a large square. I flip over the seat opposite me so that it has its back to me. Then I hang my sleeping bag over the backrest of both seats, erecting a sort of makeshift tent. I slide my backpack along the seat to use as a pillow. When everything is perfect I crawl inside, wriggle myself comfortable and switch on my book light.

I couldn't get any closer to heaven if St Peter was to turn up with a lamb and a couple of gates. I'm so comfortable I could almost weep. But I've blubbed enough already today, soaking Miss Taylor's top with a stream of birthday tears. Enough.

I finish *The Diving Bell and the Butterfly* in about three hours. It's really short, for obvious reasons. But every word, every syllable counts. Maybe authors should be made to blink their books. At least the first draft. Might cut down on paper. Save a few trees. The book, though, literally took my breath away and I was choked up when it ended because I didn't want it to finish. It's amazing what people can do if they put their minds to something. I wonder if Jean-Dominique Bauby would have even written a book had he not had that stroke. Would Stephen Hawking's genius have been so widely remarked upon if he hadn't been struck down with motor neurone disease? Would Anne Frank have written her diary had she and her family not been holed up in that wall cavity trying to avoid capture by the Nazis? Bauby, Hawking, Frank, Christ and a whole host of others might not have benefited from their suffering, but the world has.

Because I have time – no danger, no distractions – I check and double check both my homework and the extension work that Miss Taylor and Mr Singh, my maths teacher, have given me. When I'm positive that it's all correct, I flick off my book light and squirm out of my nylon chrysalis. I emerge a better person for having read *The Diving Bell and the Butterfly.* Jean-Dominique Bauby died in 1997 but he's still reaching out from the grave. That's a legacy worth leaving. Step lightly upon the earth, but leave a little ray of hope. I'd like to do that. But I've got to stop Creepo from killing me first.

I comb my hair and clean my teeth, swallowing the mixture of toothpaste and saliva. It's a taste I'm growing to like. After that I squat down and try to pee into my new drink bottle. I feel awkward and clumsy at first, like a baby giraffe bending down to drink at a waterhole for the first time, but I eventually mange to direct my steaming stream into the bottle while recalling the stationmaster's comment that even *we* wouldn't pee where we sleep. There's only a tiny puddle of pee on the floor when I'm done, but hopefully that will be absorbed by the floor grime during the night. The bottle is half full, or half empty depending on how ... no, it's definitely half full. And it's surprisingly warm through the plastic. The homeless person's hot water bottle.

I dismantle my tent, zip it up and slip inside. I stuff some of my excess clothes into my sleeping bag carrier and use it as a pillow, then settle down for the night. It's comfortable on the seat. Warm inside my sleeping bag. Safe in the carriage. Home.

This has been one of the best days of my life. It started with a birthday present, a birthday party, and finished with me finding a way into my new home. I made it into the rail yards because of my ingenuity. And if it didn't work at first, I would have tried again and again until I found a loophole. A blind spot. There was no higher force working with or against me. No predetermined path allowing me in or keeping me out.

Miss Taylor is right. There is no fate. Whatever I do from this point on is down to me. I choose my own path. Write my own story.

Nullum fatum est.

CAFÉ

So you found your place?

Yeah and it was great. I didn't have to escape into the fantasy world in my head any more. I had the rail yards. My books. And on the weekends when I wanted to get out of the city, I had door number 4 up at Death Valley.

Was it quiet at night in the yards? I'm trying to imagine it.

Deathly quiet. The first night I heard voices outside around midnight, but it was just a couple of teenagers tagging some carriages. I heard someone call out to them, a security guard probably, but they shouted at him to piss off and ran off laughing. The only other time I heard something was the most terrifying night of my life. It was even worse than when I was hiding under my old bed and Creepo came creeping around my things.

Did someone get in the train?

Someone. Or something.

What happened?

I'd been sleeping in the yards for about two weeks.

I really had it down to a fine art by then. After school I'd catch the train to the mega-mall for homework and reading with a hot chocolate at Alistair's café. Then I'd either have toasted sandwiches there, or something healthy or more substantial from the food court for dinner. Around five, five-thirty, I'd catch a train up the ivy belt to the junction station and then slip on board the first terminating train that came in. Then, when the train was safely tucked up in the yards and everything shut down, I'd set up my tent so that I could read and check my homework by book light or torch. I even found a brochure on the Orient Express that someone had left behind and so I tore out some of the pictures and stuck them on the back of the seat with Blu-tack. Then, when I'd had an evening snack of fruit and Tim Tams, I'd dismantle my reading tent, zip it back into a sleeping bag and go to bed. But that night was different. We'd had sport that day so I'd stayed behind shelving books for a while with Mrs Lee and then had a shower in the staff toilets when I was sure everyone had gone, so I was running late for everything. It was also raining and when I eventually got to the junction station there wasn't a terminating train for ages. I didn't get much reading done that night because when I finally got into the yards it was after ten o'clock and I was exhausted. At some point during the night I was sound asleep and then suddenly I wasn't. Something had woken me but I didn't know what. And then I heard it again. A door slamming shut. Somewhere off in the distance but close enough to wake me. It sounded like one of those connecting doors between the carriages. I was just starting to relax when I heard it again. It was closer this time and it was then I understood what was going on. Someone was walking through the carriages and banging the connecting doors closed behind them.

What did you do?

What do you think I did? I froze. I was literally paralysed. My heart was pounding away like a bass drum. Whoever was there was getting closer and the way they were slamming the doors sounded like they meant business. Then the door downstairs slammed shut and he was in the carriage with me. And it got cold. Deathly cold.

My heart's thumping just thinking about it. What did you do?

I was praying, begging, that he would go downstairs and carry on with his insane walkthrough, but of course he didn't. I could hear him climbing the stairs in his heavy boots. Slowly. Deliberately. And the carriage was like ice. My throat burned with cold just breathing. When he got to the top of the stairs he paused, just for a moment, like he was listening for something. Someone. I don't know, I was practically insane with terror by this point.

The thing was, now that he'd stopped, I couldn't even hear him breathing or anything. I just sensed him. Him and the cold that he brought with him. Then he was off again, stomping down the aisle towards me. Almost on top of me now. I had my sleeping bag pulled up so that only my eyes were visible. And there was enough external light for him to see me and me to see him because he was almost directly opposite me now. I heard his footsteps, felt his footsteps right in front of me, his hand reaching for the grip on the seat. The carriage was even colder now. My eyes were as big as beach balls trying to see who it was. But he kept on going. Walked right past me. Only there was no one there. He was a big guy by the sound of it. Huge. And he stomped past and I didn't see a thing. No silhouette. No shadow. Nothing. Just the sound of his feet, his heavy boots, clomping past. And then he was stomping down the stairs and into the next carriage, slamming the door behind him as he went.

What did you do?

Every muscle, every nerve and fibre, every sinew I've got was tensed up like steel. I slowly tried to relax, tried to breathe normally but it wasn't easy because I was absolutely petrified that he'd come back and find me. It was obvious that he was looking for something. Someone.

Who did you think it was?

At first I thought it must have been a new security guard. So new that he didn't know that he wasn't supposed to patrol the trains. And then I realised that it was Creepo. It had to be. He must have tracked me down. Put a private detective on my case or something. And he'd come to finish me off, only by some freak of nature, something to do with the light or, I don't know, a miracle, he hadn't seen me the same way I hadn't seen him. When I was sure that he'd gone, I checked my watch. It was just after four in the morning.

The dead hour.

I didn't think anything of that until the next morning. I mean, I tried to get back to sleep but I couldn't. Even though the cold had gone, I was just too worked up. I was lying there with my eyes wide open, my heart racing.

I bet you were glad when it got light.

It was one of the happiest moments of my life when the sun came up and the train kicked into life the next morning; when the lights came on and the heating exploded into warmth. It seemed like for ever before we were rattling over to the station to pick up the first load of passengers of the day, all business suits and corporate heels. As soon as the doors opened I tried to jump off but everyone just pushed past to bags their favourite spot.

That's not very nice. I mean, where's their train etiquette?

Well, there's not supposed to be anyone on board. The train's come over from the yards. I used to stand in the middle of the carriage and then sit down when the other passengers came pouring on so they'd assume that I was the first on and had come through the other door. And then if the announcement said that it was a city-bound train I used to jump up like I'd made a mistake and get off before the doors closed. Had it down to a fine art. But that morning I just got off as quickly as I could. I stood out in the open, staring up at the sun with my eyes closed, trying to thaw myself.

I found out later from my friend Cinderella the real reason the homeless didn't like the rail yards. About fifteen years before, there'd been a young guard who was a bit of a punk, though he couldn't have been a real punk, more early onset emo or maybe a goth. Anyway, this young guard didn't wear the normal guard's shoes apparently, but these big black Doc Martens. One morning he turned up for work a little worse for wear. The boss felt sorry for him and assigned him the express train heading north, which was a pretty cushy gig – long stretches between stations. Unfortunately, though, the young guard was still feeling sick as the train hurtled north, and when he stuck his head out of the guard's compartment to puke onto the tracks, he was decapitated by a south-bound freight train.

Oh my . . .

Lead item on the six o'clock news. Haunted the train ever since. Never finished his shift, so he's stuck doing walk-throughs for all eternity.

Are you serious?

Someone or something was in the carriage with me that night, storming right past me in heavy boots and the cold breath of eternity, but there was no one there. Nothing. It was absolutely terrifying. But you know what? Given the choice between Creepo and a headless ghost, I'd take the ghost every time.

Goodbye Tiffany-Star

It's Friday morning and Miss Taylor and I are meeting with Mr Thompkins. We've met like this a couple of times now; we talk about our weekends, the movies we've been to, politics, history, what we've been reading (she's been giving me books on philosophy and religion and World War I – I read *Fly Away Peter* and *Somme Mud* over the weekend up at Death Valley). But today she seems sad. Distant.

'Tiffany-Star,' says Mr Thompkins, in a weird sort of way. It's not the usual teacher-marking-the-role sound with the inflection at the end, more a 'What are we going to do with you?' tone.

'Yes, Mr Thompkins.'

'Tiffany-Star Beauchamp.'

This doesn't sound good. This doesn't sound like the 'good luck with the blazer and straw hat scholarship exam' meeting that I thought we were coming to.

'Do you know why you're here?'

Does anyone? 'Miss Taylor said it was something about the scholarship test.'

Mr Thompkins looks over at Miss Taylor. 'Well, yes, originally. Things have taken a slightly different course since I scheduled this little get-together with Miss Taylor.'

I look at Miss Taylor. She's staring off into space. I've never seen her like this. She looks seriously pissed.

Mr Thompkins is looking down at a piece of paper on his desk. Although it's upside down from me, I can see that it has a picture on it. A face maybe. Mr Thompkins picks up the paper and holds it towards Miss Taylor and me. Immediately all the blood flushes out of my face as if I've seen another ghost. A ghost of school years past.

'Does she look familiar, Tiffany-Star?'

It's my year three photo with MISSING plastered over it. Probably the most up-to-date picture Creepo and Serena had of me. It's the last school photo I ever got. Creepo and Serena never ordered one after that. Didn't seem to want any photographic reminders that they had someone else's kid living with them.

There's no point arguing. It's me all right. Younger. Cuter. Naive. Innocent. Taken just before I learned to shut everything out and read with my fingers wedged in my ears.

'When did you realise?'

'I should have twigged from the start. There was something about the way you interacted with your *mother* that just wasn't right. The look you gave her when she called you Tiffany-Star could have floored a horse, but I just dismissed it as a bit of mother–daughter tension. By the time we'd finished the interview, though, I thought to myself, if *she's* your mother then I'm Jack Kerouac's.'

I don't know who Jack Kerouac is, but obviously Mr Thompkins isn't his mother.

'I wished I'd followed my instincts and delved deeper, especially when Mrs Grimshaw found you out in the bus shelter. But you'd settled in so well I decided to leave it. I apologise for that.'

I don't understand. 'What do you have to be sorry about?'

'I'm worried that you've been sleeping rough and I could have done something about it. Got you home sooner.'

I look straight at Mr Thompkins. 'I'm happy on the streets.' I tell them I'm on the streets rather than the trains because I'm not finished yet. Not by a long shot.

'Oh, Tiffany-Star,' says Miss Taylor. 'How could you possibly be happy living in bus shelters and doorways and parks?'

I look at the door. Miss Taylor is blocking it slightly. I'm not sure if I can get round her quickly enough. My backpack is still in the classroom. I can't leave it. It's got my things. My money and the gun.

'The real giveaway was last Friday,' continues Mr Thompkins. 'I wandered down to the shops for a coffee. Do you know who I ran into while I was there?'

No, but I can guess. 'Narelle?'

'She was standing beneath the big clock like she was waiting for someone.'

Nature of her career choice. Always hanging around waiting for someone.

'I went up to say hello and she asked me if I was Trevor, which threw me a little. I told her I wasn't and she seemed confused. When I reminded her that I was your principal, I may as well have been speaking a different language. She told me where to go and believe me, her language was rather forthright.'

Despite the seriousness of the situation, I have to bite my lip at this point.

'It was only when I mentioned your name that the penny finally dropped. She apologised for the language and asked how you were going, but by then Trevor had turned up and I'd worked things out.'

'Who is this Trevor person?' asks Miss Taylor.

I turn to my teacher. God, she's so sweet. 'He was her client.'

'Client?' asks Miss Taylor. 'What does she do?'

I look at Mr Thompkins.

He shrugs his shoulders. 'Do you want to tell her or should I?'

I decide not to sugar-coat it. 'She's a prostitute.'

'Oh my go . . . odness,' Miss Taylor bails out of her blasphemy, but it makes her sound a bit wet, as if God is actually sitting up there on his cloud putting a black cross against anyone who mentions his name. That's one pedantic supreme being if he is.

'Your mother's a prostitute? Is that why you're on the streets?'

'She's not my mother and I'm not on the streets because of *her*.'

Miss Taylor looks at me and then at Mr Thompkins. 'I don't understand. You said this morning that Tiffany-Star was a runaway and that we . . .'

'She *is* a runaway,' interrupts Mr Thompkins. 'She hired this . . . this lady . . .'

You've got to love Mr Thompkins. Narelle might be many things, but she ain't no lady.

'. . . to pose as her mother so that she could get into school.' Mr Thompkins turns to me and smiles. 'I'd be asking for a refund if I were you.'

Miss Taylor reaches across and grabs my hand. 'What have we done to you to make you do such a thing?' There are tears welling in her eyes. Big I-don't-understand-why-the-world-has-to-be-so-cruel tears. I just hope that teaching, teaching out here, doesn't turn her hard. Turn her into Narelle.

'It's okay,' I say, trying to comfort my distraught teacher. 'I'll be fine.'

'Fine?' snaps Miss Taylor and it's as close to yelling as I've heard her get. 'Fine? You're reading *Pride and Prejudice*, writing essays on World War I, and doing year eleven maths, and you're sleeping in bus shelters? You're the brightest student I've ever met, and we've got you living on the streets. What sort of society does that to its young people?'

I don't think now's the time to tell her that I've finished *Pride and Prejudice* and that I've started re-reading *Bleak House*. I don't want to ruin the mood.

Mr Thompkins also ignores Miss Taylor's rant. 'Before I ask our guests to come in, is there anything you'd like to say?'

'Guests? It's not —'

'Police,' says Mr Thompkins and he can see that I'm relieved. If it had been Creepo waiting out there in reception I would have sung like a canary. Told them everything and just hoped Mr Thompkins had a taser or some mace in his top drawer to deal with Creepo's response. But with the police, I've still got a chance to get back to the rail yards.

'No,' I say. 'It'll all come out one day, I hope. But not today.'

Mr Thompkins gives me one of his looks. 'You sure?'

I nod, though it's probably not convincing.

'May I just say then,' continues Mr Thompkins, 'it's been an absolute joy and honour to have you as a student in our school.'

I shake Mr Thompkins's hand and promise to visit again when I've got things sorted out.

'One more thing,' he says. 'How much did Narelle charge you?'

I shrug. There's no point keeping it a secret. Not now. 'A thousand dollars.'

Miss Taylor gasps.

'It was only meant to be five hundred, but she scammed another five hundred out of me. On the day.'

'Is that why you were angry with her – during the interview, I mean.'

'Well, that and the stupid name.'

Mr Thompkins flashes his big, wide smile at me. 'I think I'll have a little word to the police on the way out. They might want to have a chat with her about this.'

Before we go out to face the music, Miss Taylor hugs me, but unlike at my birthday party, it's me who's comforting her. The world has got to her a bit today and I'm sorry that she had to witness the uglier side of things because of me.

The police are happy to wait while Miss Taylor fetches my backpack from class. She walks over to the police car with me, hand in hand. I don't want to say goodbye to my classmates. Not even Janyce, my temporary guardian angel. I don't think I could handle the looks they'd give me. The whispers. This is the second time this year I've left school without saying goodbye to my friends. It's sad, but better this way.

As I'm been driven out of school for the final time I wave at Mr Thompkins, Miss Taylor and Mrs Lee, who's obviously just been told and ventured out of the library to see me off. The hooter's just gone for recess, so there are also some students milling around and pointing at the police car while the teachers scamper over to the staffroom to bags the best seats and biscuits. Miss Taylor is crying on Mrs Lee's shoulder, but I feel nothing. Despite the Post-It note in my pocket with her phone number on it, she's already little more than a fading memory. They all are.

I'm proud of myself. I'm getting better at this. I can survive the streets, the trains, the rail yards. All I have to do is keep everyone else out.

Aunt Flo

'There are a lot of people worried about you,' says Senior Sergeant Morrison once we've driven out of school.

'I doubt that.'

She shakes her head and laughs. It's a cold, bitter laugh, like the joke's on me not with me. 'I've heard of teenagers running away from school to become prostitutes, but never, in all my years on the force, have I heard of a teenager hiring a prostitute to get back into school. I'm going to be telling this story for a very long time. What do you reckon, Danny?'

Constable Lang just grunts and focuses on driving. He's obviously not very good at multi-tasking. In fact, he hardly looks old enough to drive. He's probably got more pimples than arrests. I haven't quite figured out how, but he's going to be my way out.

'Your principal says you're very smart,' says Sergeant Morrison. 'The smartest student at the school.'

'I get by.' The fact is I'm not that smart, not naturally anyway. I've just had time to work at it. And given that the current theory doing the rounds is whether or not your eyeballs will pop out of your head if you sneeze with your eyes open, it's not as if there's a huge amount of competition.

'Which means you're probably very good at manipulating people.'

I'd be happy if they just stayed out of my way.

'Look. I know it's not easy being a teenager. Hell, I've got one at home, a son, not to mention my partner here who is only barely out of nappies himself, and if I can manage to get a grunt out of either of them I feel I'm doing really well. Right, Danny?'

Constable Lang grunts right on cue, though he does it with a smile as if he's used to being ribbed by his boss.

'So where have you been living?'

'The usual places.'

'And what *are* the usual places?'

'You know. Bus shelters. Parks. Doorways. Alleyways.' Anywhere but the trains or rail yards because I'll be back there again tonight while they're out combing bus shelters, parks, door and alleyways.

'That's not safe for a . . . how old are you, sixteen?'

'Fourteen.'

She shakes her head. 'How you haven't been eaten alive, I'll never know.'

'Maybe I've just been lucky.'

'If it was up to me I'd take every single runaway down to the morgue. Show you what happens to young girls when they choose life on the streets. You lot think you know it all.'

I stare out the window. Her lecture is valid for kids who take off because they want their freedom, or they don't want to do their homework, or they're sick of being nagged, sick of rules, of structure. It's wasted on me though. I took off because I chose life. Didn't want to be a victim.

'Just last week we had to take a young girl's parents in to identify her body. She wasn't much older than you. Sixteen, seventeen maybe. That's not something we'll forget in a hurry, right Danny?'

'You're right there, Sarge.'

'When the sheet was pulled back her mother made a noise like her soul was being torn out. Little girl lying there all bruised and beat-up like that. Autopsy revealed that she'd been pumped full of enough heroin to kill a horse.'

Now it's Sergeant Morrison's turn to stare out the window, trying to get the image out of her head. It'll probably be with her for years. For ever.

'She had to pay for her hits somehow. It's not cheap you know, that shit. Know how she could afford it?'

'Sarge.'

'I got to see the coroner's report. Not very pleasant reading, let me tell you.'

'Sarge.'

'Not when you've got kids of your own.'

'*Sarge.*'

'Shut up, Danny! She needs to hear this.'

I don't think I do.

'She was only a little thing. Not much bigger than you, really. Limbs like sticks. Plenty of sickos happy to cough up the cash for her services, especially if she wore her school uniform. You know what I'm getting at?'

Yeah. I get it.

'Autopsy report said that her vagina had prolapsed so far it was as if she'd had a freight train through her.'

'Jesus, Sarge!'

'She didn't OD accidentally with that last hit. She knew what she was doing.'

'C'mon, Sarge, that's enough. This one conned her way *into* school, remember? She gets it.'

I don't say anything because I'm not that girl. Poor thing. I will never be that girl. God, I hope I won't be that girl.

Suddenly Sergeant Morrison softens. Going from bad cop to good cop in the space of a breath.

'Look, we know about your parents. It must have been tough on you, them disappearing like that. But your aunt and uncle are doing the best they can. It can't be easy for them either, not having children of their own.'

She's obviously been to their house. Their mansion with its McParthenon supporting columns. She's seen their home. *My* home. She'll have been inside. Seen my room. Seen what I've given up for bus shelters, parks, doorways, alleyways and yet she still doesn't get it. I'm sorry for that girl in the morgue, but she hasn't done me any favours. Now because of her, and others like her, Sergeant Morrison is blaming the victims. Easy to do, I suppose, when your dreams are haunted by teenage girls laid out on cold, metal slabs like lumps of battered meat.

I could tell her the truth but she'd probably believe Creepo's version instead, especially with Serena backing him up. She already knows about my parents disappearing when they moved back to the old country. She knows how deceitful I can be – conning my way into school by hiring a prostitute and letting Miss Taylor and Mr Thompkins put Tiffany-Star Beauchamp forward for that straw hat and blazer scholarship. It's blatantly obvious that I'm a liar. But I'm a liar out of necessity, not by choice.

*

We don't enter the police station from the front like everyone else but through a side door, which makes me feel special, sort of like . . . well, a criminal.

Sergeant Morrison offers me a seat and then tells Danny to contact the Sanchezes.

'What happens now?' I ask.

'Well, you and I and Constable Lang, along with your aunt and uncle, and a case worker from social services, are all going to get together over a cup of tea and have a little chat.'

'You're not just going to hand me back?'

'We need to make sure everything is as it should be. There's a restraining order out on your uncle, and that certainly gets our alarm bells ringing. We've been in touch with the person who put the restraining order on him. Do you know who that might be?'

I shake my head. I want to see how this plays out.

'The doctor who fixed your fractured arm. She claims he was verbally abusive towards her. He says that's because she let you go, which doesn't seem unreasonable given the circumstances. Him being angry, I mean.'

Creepo's got everyone twisted around his disgusting little finger. Even the police.

'She didn't let me go,' I reply, because I look after people who look after me. 'I ran off as soon as the cast was set. It's not as if she had any choice.'

'She also claims that your uncle broke your arm. Is that true?'

'Yes.'

'So he *did* break your arm? It's not just another one of your lies?'

'You think I'm a liar?'

'I know you're a liar, *Tiffany-Star*. The question is how big a liar *are* you, and why?'

I feel pissed at her for this. Then again I am sitting in a police station with over five grand and a loaded gun in my backpack.

Constable Lang has finished his phone calls. 'They're on their way.'

Sergeant Morrison gets up. She seems edgy and keeps fidgeting and drumming her fingers on the desk. 'I've just got to duck out for a minute. Keep your eye on her.'

When Sergeant Morrison has disappeared out the side door, Constable Lang looks at me and makes a smoking gesture in the direction of his boss. We both smile.

'I've got to write up my report,' he says, turning on his computer. 'Will you be all right?'

'Yeah. I'll just sit here and read, if that's okay.'

I reach into my backpack and randomly pull out *Pride and Prejudice* as well as my hoodie. I don't know how Elizabeth Bennet would have handled this situation, but I think I can safely say that she wouldn't have dreamt, even in her wildest fantasies, not even as a way of getting out of marrying Mr Collins, of contemplating what I'm about to do. I actually feel a bit sorry for poor Constable Lang. But I'm not hanging around to chat with Creepo. No way.

I hope Sergeant Morrison has ducked down the shops for a packet of smokes rather than just outside to suck one down. Either way I'm on limited time, so I've got to get this right. I'll probably only get one chance.

I gasp deliberately and hunch forward, cradling my lower belly. 'Oh no.'

'Mmmmnnn?' says Constable Lang, who I can see is thoroughly distracted by his inability to spell Beauchamp.

'*Oh no!*' I say, a little louder this time. I'm actually thinking of throwing in a 'woe is me,' but decide to leave it.

Finally he looks over. 'What's up?'

I half-stand, tie the hoodie around my waist and make an embarrassed sort of face.

He looks at me blankly, so I pretend to stammer. 'I think I'm, um, you know . . . Aunt Flo.'

'Aunt who? Serena, isn't it?'

For God's sake. Do I have to spell it out for him? 'Time of the . . .' I keep hold of my hoodie with one hand and make an encouraging gesture with the other.

It takes him a little longer to register what's going on.

'Oh. Sorry!' he says. Obviously he has neither a girlfriend nor sisters in his life, so this is a big deal for him.

'Relax, Danny,' I say, trying to keep him calm because I don't want him to go looking for Sergeant Morrison. Not yet. 'Can you just let me run to the loo?'

He practically leaps up from his desk. 'Right. This way.' He starts leading me through the office and around the desks like I'm an expectant mum about to give birth. He's actually quite sweet. Maybe I should hook him up with Miss Taylor.

When we get to the toilets, I order Danny to wait outside in case I need anything. Fortunately there's no one else inside.

After a cursory search through my backpack, I open the cubicle door and peer out. Danny is waiting by the sinks.

'Everything all right?' asks Danny, apparently concerned that I might be bleeding to death.

I shake my head.

'Sorry, but I'm out of pads.' And then I hit him with the heavy artillery. God, I'm cruel. 'So I need you to find Sergeant Morrison and ask her if she's got any spare ones.'

I close the door and listen to Danny race off, then I hitch on my backpack, take a deep breath and open the door again.

Danny's not there. Probably running around like a

headless chook because, like a lot of men, he thinks that time of the month is a strange and dangerous thing not to be discussed under any circumstances.

I decide against using the side door in case Sergeant Morrison is out there chuffing on a deathstick. Instead I head down the corridor towards the front desk, where the duty officers look busy and harassed. I slip into reception unnoticed and make it out through the automatic front doors, then head down the street towards the train station with the sun on my face. It's hard not to sprint but I don't want to draw any attention to myself, so I kind of run with one leg and walk with the other, under some sort of insane delusion that this looks inconspicuous.

When I get to the station there isn't a city train due for seventeen minutes. Not good. Once the cops notice I've gone, the train station would have to be one of the first places they'd look. I'm stuffed.

Unless. Unless I head west. There's a train due in now. I could catch that and then make my way back to the city and the junction station later, when things have settled down.

There's an announcement over the PA apologising for the train's late arrival and saying that it should be here in five minutes. Great. The one time that I need . . . And then I see her, walking back up the street towards the police station from the shops. Sergeant Morrison *did* go out to buy smokes. She's probably one of those people who's always quitting but now, having given me the bad cop lecture on that poor girl, she's got herself all worked up and needs a cigarette or ten to calm herself down. She's going to be pretty excited with Danny in a few minutes. She'll need another packet. Maybe even a carton.

I actually feel sorry for Danny. He's probably hanging around outside the toilet and wondering if I'm okay, blissfully unaware that he's about to get his ear chewed off for letting me escape.

Finally the train slides in. It's not in any hurry or anything, it just sort of loafs into the station like, *chill, dudes, what's the big deal?* The doors open and I race up the steps through sheer force of habit. I always sleep upstairs when I'm in the rail yards. I grab a three-seater and slide over next to the window to keep a look out. If I were a real Catholic I'd be saying the rosary now, but as it stands I'd happily pray for whichever god will cast his magnificent radiance upon me and get me the hell out of here.

After what seems like fifteen hours, the doors close and we slip quietly away into the morning. And with no god putting his hand up to take credit for our departure, I'll put it down to CityRail's timetabling.

I look out the window as we slide past the police station but there are no sirens blaring, no one rushing outside with guns or tasers drawn, no riot squad abseiling down from a helicopter hovering over the train. Just the rhythmic clackety-clack as we pick up speed and head west.

CAFÉ

THAT WAS CLOSE.

One mistake. That's all it took. One mistake and it all very nearly came crashing down around me.

What was the mistake?

Narelle. I should have gone with my first choice – an actor.

A lot of prostitutes would consider themselves actors.

Yeah, well, Narelle wasn't a very good one.

When did you get back to the junction station?

It was still morning when I caught the train out west, so I just kept going until I was almost in the mountains. After a while I realised that I was standing out a bit in my school uniform and I started to worry that the police were on the lookout for that particular uniform, so I got off at the first station we came to, ducked into the toilets and changed into my normal clothes. Then I caught the next train heading back towards the city and got off at the mega-mall to collect my stuff from Alistair McAlister's cafe.

He wasn't on the afternoon shift because he had a lecture, but his friend was and he'd obviously told her more about my situation. She got all excited and went and fetched my things from the back room. I didn't tell her what had happened – I was a bit jealous of her to be honest, because I sort of figured that she was Alistair's girlfriend. I told her that I'd been feeling sick and left school early to go sleep it off. She was a bit of a ditz to be honest – bouncing around like Tigger when I told that I was going home to the rail yards, like being homeless was an exciting adventure.

Did you go to the rail yards?

No. It was far too early. And there was something I wanted to do. I'd been thinking for a while that Creepo was right about me not being able to spend his money. There was just too much of it. I was sick of carting it around, to be honest, and when I was in the police station, it occurred to me that if I was sent back with Creepo, he might somehow get the money back. He didn't deserve to get it back. I had to get rid of it.

What did you end up doing with it?

I was going to burn it, like I told Creepo, just so that I could piss him off, but I knew that would be pretty stupid. Someone could use it. Someone who didn't know, or care, where it came from. So I gave most of it away. I remembered that there was this chapel in the city that looked after and fed homeless people. I'd seen an item on the news about it when Creepo and Serena were out at a party one night. So I caught a train into the city and spent ages wandering about trying to find the place. I got some directions off an old Salvation Army guy. He told me that the chapel was on a side street in the red-light district, which freaked me out a bit, especially after what Sergeant Morrison had told me had happened to that poor girl who killed herself. But then I figured that the creatures who lurk there are largely nocturnal and as it was only early afternoon when I found it, I figured I'd be okay if I made it quick.

There were a lot of homeless people milling around a kind of front office when I got there, but I could hear music off to the side, so I followed the sound and walked into the chapel itself through a side door. By sheer force of habit I made the sign of the cross and sat down in one of the back pews. There was no one else there apart from me and this old bag lady who was up the front near the altar playing this white piano. She wasn't playing 'Chopsticks' or 'Three Blind Mice' either. It was a beautiful classical piece; really complex. I sat there totally transfixed, my jaw hanging open. Then I lost it. And I mean really lost it. Tears streaming down my cheeks. Strange noises coming from my throat. Huge body-wracking sobs. The works. I don't know where they came from or what was happening but I couldn't stop myself. Eventually the old lady stopped playing, came over and sat down next to me and just hugged me. She didn't say anything. She didn't need to. She just held me. Even when I felt a bit embarrassed and tried to pull away, she just held on tighter, which made it even worse. Because she got it. She got me. Even though I didn't.

Why were you so upset? I mean, I know the obvious reason . . .

I didn't really understand it at the time. But I thought about it later on the train back up north. It was because she played so beautifully. So perfectly. It threw me because what I was seeing and what I was hearing didn't fit.

So you're saying there was a juxtaposition between the way she lived and the way she played.

No no, it was because someone cared about her. Someone loved her. Once. She was a classically trained pianist. Even I could tell that and I couldn't play the rowboat song. Someone paid for those lessons, probably her parents when she was a little girl. She was once someone's little angel who wore pink dresses and ran out from her bedroom on Christmas morning and got all excited about her presents. She probably had family holidays by the sea and went for walks along the beach collecting shells with her father who explained all about the animals that had lived in them. She would have danced in the rain in front of the beach house and then got told off for almost catching a cold, and then she would have come inside, dried off and had dinner before curling up in bed and have a story read to her. And she would have had dreams. Hopes. Ambitions. And now she was . . . this. She was intelligent too. She understood what was happening to me before *I* did. But she was wandering the streets with her few bits and pieces stuffed in torn shopping bags and her manky old coat and her cat asleep inside the shopping trolley which was parked at the end of the aisle. I suppose I wondered what chance did I have if she couldn't make it. And so I lost it.

Did you recognise the piece she was playing?

No, but when I eventually pulled myself together she went back to it and it was so beautifully haunting that I walked up the aisle and I asked her what it was called. She told me it was by a composer called Philip Glass and the piece was *Opening*. That didn't mean anything to me so I wrote it down in my diary. It had this repetitive structure, and it made me think of the last train to Kathmandu. A train ride to nowhere. It made me think of my parents decomposing to mulch out in the forest. It made me think of the future and whether or not I had one.

When she'd finished the piece I thanked her and she held my hand and kissed it and ran it along her cheek. Then she went back to her playing and I made my way through to the reception area. I took the plastic bag out of my backpack and placed it on the front desk. The lady at reception saw the bricks of cash and gave me an odd look. I told her that it was a gift from my grandfather who had been homeless once but had made it rich out in the mines and had left a little bit of it to the chapel which had looked after him when he'd been down on his luck. I was actually crying again when I said this so it looked really convincing.

Still thinking about the old woman?

No. Well, yes, maybe, but not just that. There was a café and a games room just off from the reception area – I think that's what all the homeless people had been waiting for – and there were all these broken-down people shambling in and out. These wrecks of humanity. Ghosts. Shadows of people. I suppose I was crying because of everything that had happened since I'd arrived at the chapel. I got a glimpse of the future. Of how I would end up if I didn't keep myself on track. If I didn't get back to school. Something that everyone else seemed hell bent on keeping me out of.

Did she accept the money?

Yeah. I didn't wait around for her to count it or ask for a receipt or anything. She just said thank you and then I got the hell out of there as quickly as I could before she started in with the questions or offered me a bed for the night or a game of snooker.

How much did you give them?

I don't know. I didn't count it. Most of it. I kept some for myself for food and necessities and a rainy day at a hotel for when I was feeling really crap, like then, but I suppose I gave them about five grand all up.

Wow! That was pretty generous.

Not really. I figured it was bad money, so I could do some good with it. That plus the obvious fact that carrying around all that cash was seriously weighing me down. I felt so much lighter without it. Besides, I still had Serena's credit card.

When I left the chapel, I could see that there was a huge storm building up to the north. You could taste it in the cold air. So instead of catching the train up to my weekender and walking straight into a downpour, I caught a train to the mega-mall, walked up to the Shangrila Pines Resort, barrister-mummed my way in again with Serena's credit card and stayed for a week.

Must have been nice after sleeping on the cold trains with the ghost.

Don't laugh about the ghost. I felt it. And it should have been okay being back in the hotel but I couldn't enjoy it.

Why were you feeling down? You escaped. I mean, that was pretty ingenious what you did, escaping the police station like that.

I was feeling shit because it was the end of an era and I had no one to share it with. It was getting close to the end of the school year and so it wasn't worth trying to get into another school. In a couple of weeks' time all the other kids would be having farewell parties and making plans for the holidays. I ended the school year being driven away in a police car like a criminal. But I knew that I couldn't stand around moping. Not for long anyway. I had to figure out a way of getting into another school without showing up on anyone's radar.

I've got to ask. Did you ever see Miss Taylor again?

Yeah, I did. I called her just before Christmas. She invited me over for dinner. I was a bit hesitant at first in case it was a trap. She would have heard what happened with the police so I was really apprehensive when I got there. But it was cool. When she answered the door and saw me standing there with a bottle of lemonade and a couple of cupcakes in a bag she just burst into tears and hugged me. I thought she was going to cry for ever. But eventually we had dinner and talked. I told her everything because I was sick of being alone and not having anyone to confide in and also because I trusted her. I was also tired of lying. That's the thing with lying: you need to have a good memory just to keep track, and I was fed up with it.

What did she say?

She didn't judge me. She didn't judge anyone. Not even Creepo, which surprised me. She just listened. And she didn't offer any solutions. She didn't say everything would work out if I just had faith. She didn't ask me to trust in God even though she had pictures of Jesus in her hallway and over her bed. When we'd washed the dishes we settled back and watched a chick flick and we both ended up bawling our eyes out. It was such a girlie moment. I don't know what it was but being with Miss Taylor gave me hope. I could do it. I could survive. I didn't have to end up a piano-playing bag lady wandering the streets with my few bits and pieces and my cat in a shopping trolley. I had options. I had Miss Taylor.

Did she know that you were sleeping in the rail yards?

Yeah. I told her, but only after she promised not to tell anyone. She couldn't believe it but she was out of tears by then so she just shook her head.

Did she let you go to the rail yards that night?

What do you think? I slept on her sofa. Ended up staying there for a week. She refused to let me go. We were like flat-mates. I only agreed because by then it was the school holidays and she reckoned that school holidays were her time and she didn't answer to the Department of Education. I didn't want to push it though. I couldn't risk getting her in trouble and possibly ending her teaching career. But she was going overseas with a friend after Christmas, trekking in South America for a couple of weeks, so she asked me to house-sit for her, which, after the rail yards, was like the promise of heaven. She also helped me get into another school.

How? Did she pretend to be your mother?

No! But she got my assessment and report from school and told me about a loophole.

Okay, but before then, before you caught up with Miss Taylor, there was still a few weeks to go until the end of the school year. What did you do?

I read mostly. At night in the rail yards or, if it wasn't too hot during the day, up at my weekender. I also went to see a couple of movies and to the museum and art gallery. But I stayed away from the red-light district. Away from the homeless chapel. It was just too depressing. Mostly I just travelled around on the trains. I went bushwalking a few times when it was warm enough. I also used to go to the international airport and watch the planes taking off. I made sure I left my sleeping bag buried up at my weekender when I went to the airport so that Creepo's goons wouldn't spot me. That plus I always wore my baseball cap and sunglasses. I got to know the flight schedules and the livery of the planes so I knew which ones were going where. I really enjoyed watching the planes taking off to London and Paris and Hong Kong. I used to sit for hours up on the observation deck, breathing in *Cologne d'aviation* and dreaming of faraway places.

Then, on what was officially the last day of the school year, I met Cinderella, who saved my life. And it will haunt me for ever that I couldn't save hers.

My Emo Fairy Godmother

THE THING ABOUT THE OLD FAIRYTALES WAS THAT THEY ALWAYS contained a message. Once you had read the story and unravelled its moral core, you were meant to see the light and start living your life a better person. Sometimes the moral was blatantly obvious. *The Three Little Pigs*, for instance, is primarily about solidarity. About working together in the face of adversity to overcome what at first appears to be insurmountable odds. It also touches on the importance of sound construction principles and the benefits of hurling unwanted houseguests into pots of boiling water. The lessons derived from this porcine versus canine tale are obvious, even to a child. Others, though, are less clear. *Little Red Riding Hood* is about . . . well, the importance of being able to distinguish your bedridden grandmother from a cross-dressing timber wolf. *Rapunzel*, on the other hand, broaches the timeless topic of how imperative it is not to get lumbered with an evil witch as your primary guardian. The witch, who, in strict adherence to stereotype, was not only breathtakingly ugly, but also grossly unhinged. In the spirit of the age she was not confined to an institute for the criminally insane, but free to wander about locking girls in high towers and blinding handsome princes more or less at random.

Where do you even start with Cinderella? Let's ignore Cinderella's victim status and total lack of self-determination and head straight for the prince who was, let's face it, a bit of a jerk. Despite being captivated by Cinderella's radiant beauty for half the night, come the cold light of day he has completely forgotten what she looks like and only has her shoe size to go on. Either he was suffering from some sort of early onset Alzheimer's disease or else he was completely off his face during the big ball. The end result is that he goes trawling through the kingdom in some sort of perverted foot-fetish style quest for someone, anyone, who fits the glass slipper. Just how superficial is this guy? What if Cinderella had turned up at the ball looking exactly like she did only with a mole on her face that had a couple of twelve-centimetre hairs sticking out of it? What if a bearded troll just happened to have the same shoe size as Cinderella? 'Ah, well. Pucker up, bushy cheeks, it's snog time.' And no one ever bothers to question the sheer impracticality of Cinderella's footwear. Glass might be good for many things but it's not exactly malleable in its cooled state. If everyone turned and gaped when Cinderella made her big entrance into the ball, it's only because she'd have come staggering in like a drunken giraffe on rollerblades. Bit of a head turner.

What these fairytales teach us is that in order to live a rewarding life it's essential to be white and good-looking, preferably with royal lineage. And this is all before we even touch on the vital importance of being blonde.

But the real Cinderella was nothing like that. I should know; because she was *my* fairy godmother.

*

It's the final day of school and my plan had been to get away for a while. Head up north, load up on scallops and energy drinks and trek up to the lighthouse. Skim rocks into the ocean. Stare out to sea. Dream. After that I'd crash at my weekender for a while and then get down to the serious business of planning how to con my way back into school. There's a public high school a few stations up from the mega-mall that I would simply die to go to. It's not co-ed but the girls who go there seem happy and carefree. They wear pink dresses and sky-blue socks and when they get on the train in the afternoon they're not weighed down by life, more like they can't get enough of it. Even the emo girls appear happier than they'd like to be. Sometimes late at night in the rail yards, with the moon smiling down on me through the carriage windows, I fantasise about wearing a pink dress and blue socks to school.

The rain rules out my lighthouse trek so I dump my stuff with Alistair and, after a breakfast blowout of buns from the bakery, I head out west to my old school. I don't know what I thought I was doing, but by the time I make it to the bus shelter I'm soaked to the bone. Not my greatest moment of street life.

I stare at the school from the shattered shelter. I check my watch. I should be at English now. Miss Taylor will have them packing up the room, getting all her admin fina-lised and then organising everyone for the party with the other classes. For a moment I feel like gatecrashing, but the idea soon passes. Word would get out because of the way I left and then Mr Thompkins, the office ladies, or one of the other teachers would phone the police. They wouldn't want to, I understand that, but they'd have to. And I don't want to ruin the other kids' farewell party by getting carted off again. That's a memory burner that everyone could do without. Especially me. I don't think even Constable Lang would fall for the same routine again, no matter how much I embarrass him.

At ten-thirty the hooter sounds for recess and everyone comes pouring out to the quadrangle. Although it's still drizzling, there'd have to be an Armageddon-style deluge for the teachers to voluntarily hold recess in the classrooms on the last day of school. They're desperate to kick back with a party of their own in the staffroom. I can almost hear the champagne corks popping from all the way out at the bus shelter.

It's when I see a bunch of year seven boys hurtling down towards me like rabbits out of a sack that I realise I might have chance to say goodbye to my friends after all. I don't know what sort of game they're playing – something involving sticks and a lot of jumping up and down.

'Oi, boys,' I whisper over the fence, like some sort of delinquent drug dealer. 'Could you do me a favour?'

One of them looks over at me. 'Who're you?'

'I used to go to this school.'

'Oh, yeah,' says the kid with the biggest stick who appears to be in charge. 'Prove it.'

What darlings. Couldn't you just take them home and . . . and lock them in a cupboard under the stairs? 'Okay. Does Mrs Grimshaw still act like she's got a rock-hard booger stuck up her nose?'

This gets them laughing.

'Do any of you know Janyce Kirwan?'

They look at each other and shrug. 'Do you mean the one in year eight?'

As opposed to all the other Janyce Kirwans in the school?

'Yeah. That's her. Could one of you do me a favour and go and get her. She usually hangs out in the library . . .'

'What do you want her for?' asks this kid with a shaved head and rat's tail who, and there's no other way of saying it, looks destined for a career as an armed robber.

'I want to say goodbye.'

'Why? Where ya going?'

Geez. What do they want? My autobiography? 'I'm moving to Africa.'

'Cool,' says stick boy, brandishing his weapon like a light sabre. 'Heaps of animals and stuff there. Lions, giraffes, crocodiles, ostriches . . .'

For a minute I think he's going to list every single animal that has ever swept across the savannah plains. But fortunately his interest wanes and they go back to being Jedi knights again.

'Hello, guys? Janyce Kirwan.'

'Oh, yeah,' says stick boy. 'You go, Johnno. You know her sister.'

I don't even know what that means. 'Tell her it's Tiffany-Star.'

'Hey, aren't you that girl who got sent to jail for dealing?' says stick boy.

'It wasn't dealing,' I snap. Why does everyone automatically assume that street kids are druggos? 'And I didn't get sent to jail.'

'Still got arrested, but.'

I feel like screaming at them, but what's the point? As far as the rumour mill is concerned, Tiffany-Star got sent to jail for ever – might even get executed and stuff – for drugs.

'Just tell her I'm here.'

'I'll go,' says future armed robber. 'I'm the fastest.'

By the time Janyce and her posse have arrived at the fence the hooter has blared for the end of recess. I don't have much time. It'll probably take about two nanoseconds for the boys to spill the beans that the notorious fugitive, Tiffany-Star, is hanging around the school fence trying to sell everyone drugs.

'Oh my God,' shrieks Janyce. 'It *is* you. Come here.' She leans over the fence and gathers me up in a bear hug.

Growing up the way I did I'm not exactly a touchy-feely person, though with Janyce you don't get much of a choice.

'I thought the little shits were making it up. Kid came bursting into the library yelling that the druggo girl Tiffany girl was at the fence.'

I shake my head. 'I swear to God I've never touched drugs in my life.' Never will.

'Yeah, I know.'

'Did Mrs Lee hear him?'

'I think half the school did. But don't worry. She won't say anything.'

'She has to,' I reply, 'or she could get the sack.'

'Are you really homeless?' asks Perla, Janyce's bestie.

'Yeah.'

Janyce stares at me. 'Why didn't you say anything? You could have come and stayed with me.'

'What about your parents?'

'We're Samoan. There's eleven of us kids. They probably wouldn't have even noticed an extra one. We'd have to fatten you up a bit first. You look like a pool cue.'

I smile at Janyce. 'I'm okay. I've got somewhere to live.'

'Tell me it's not in a dumpster or something.'

'No. It's clean and dry.'

'And safe? Please tell me it's safe.'

I nod.

Janyce grabs me again. 'C'mon. Give Tiff a hug.'

Janyce's posse gathers around the boss in a sort of scrum. 'You remember this, Tiff,' says Janyce from the centre of the huddle. 'If anyone ever fucks with you, they fuck with the sisters.'

After a session of individual hugs from the sisters I pick up my backpack and walk away from the school for the final time.

'You can do it, Tiffany-Star,' calls Janyce after me. 'You can make it.'

I don't look back.

*

I schlep about two kilometres up to the next station, rather than the half-kilometre down to the one near the cop shop. With the rain still drizzling I spend the rest of the morning and most of the afternoon wandering around the rail system, staring out the window, going nowhere.

By the time school's out for the year my head is starting to loll about on my shoulders. I'm drifting in and out of consciousness almost oblivious to the train filling up with students on that school-holiday high. And by the time I notice that I'm on the wrong line, in the wrong seat, it's too late.

Even though I pretend to be asleep, it's their laughter that frightens me the most. Its cold taunt. It's as if they're saying that a little thing like a sleeping homeless girl is not going to get in the way of their fun. In fact she's going to play a major part in it.

'Kind of cute. But too skinny. Be like doing a broom-stick.'

More laughter. Forced laughter. They're not laughing at the quality of the gag but trying to wake me. Scare me.

I'm tensed up like steel when the first one kicks my foot. The butterflies in my stomach churning and squirming all over each other.

'Hey! We're talking to you!'

I can't ignore that. I open my eyes and look at them. Swallow. Year nine, I'd guess. Three of them. Sitting opposite me. Going backwards. The shortest one out for trouble. The two bookends for backup. A really bad combination, especially if you're a girl travelling by herself on the wrong line. Wrong cultural background.

'Are you Leb?'

I close my eyes, hoping that they'll disappear, but one of the bookends reaches across and tries to grab my backpack. I snatch it away from him. His laugh is to tell me that he's toying with me. That he could take my backpack if he really wanted to and there's absolutely nothing I could do about it.

'I said, are you Leb? You look Leb.'

I ignore them. I'm not admitting to anything. I don't know if being Leb is a good thing or a bad thing with these guys.

'Must be a leso.'

Keep quiet. Don't say anything. They'll give up and move on. On to some other poor girl. Oh crap! I can't have that.

'So I'm a Lebanese lesbian, is that right?'

If I thought that a gag might break the tension and make them back off then I was sorely mistaken.

'She's got a smart mouth on her,' says the short one. 'Maybe I'll give her a mouthful of this. See if that shuts her up.'

While the bookends fall about laughing, the little dipshit unzips his pants and lets it all hang out. I've never seen one before. Not up close, thankfully. Only a cutaway one in a school textbook and that looked all scientific with its tubes and bendy bits. This one's nothing like the one in the textbook. It looks a bit like a . . . well, a cashew. No wonder he's mad at the world. Still, no matter how small it is, I don't want it anywhere near me.

I look across the aisle for help, but there's none there. A couple of straw hat and blazer senior school girls are shut off from the world in their iPods, while a man in a suit is pretending that the only thing of interest in the carriage is in his newspaper, which he's taken cover behind. He'll be getting off at the next station, whether it's his stop or not. There's a scrawny older emo girl covered in tatts a couple of seats further up, but she's staring off into space out the window, too weighed down by her own baggage to take an interest in mine. I look back. The bookend closest to the aisle has his feet up on my seat, blocking any escape.

'Well,' sneers the little dipshit. 'What are you waiting for? Get on your knees.'

I'm not getting down on my knees for any man. Mortal or celestial. 'Go fuck yourself!'

The bookends think this is the most hilarious thing anyone has ever said. They're practically rolling about in the seat. Their laughter terrifies me because even they can see how non-threatening I am.

Dipshit just smiles. 'Or maybe I'll fuck you instead.'

'Oh, there you are.' The four of us look up, each equally surprised by the intrusion. 'I've been looking all over for you, Dom.'

'Sorry,' I reply, trying desperately to improvise. 'I got lost.'

She glares at the bookend next to the aisle. 'Get your feet down, you disgusting pig! You're not at home now.' And she's so forceful he actually moves them.

The scrawny emo girl with the tatts winks at me and sits down.

'I've missed you so much.' She reaches over and hugs me.

The bookend closest to the window practically explodes with laughter. 'She *is* a leso,' he says.

'Have you got anything sharp on you?' she whispers.

'Gonna put on a floorshow for us, girls?'

I nuzzle into her ear, playing the part. 'I've got a compass in my pencil case.'

'Hey! We're talking to youse slags.' Dipshit has recovered enough to attempt the dominant role again.

'You got anything to eat, Dominique?' she says out loud, reaching for my backpack. Dominique? I like that. It's a damn sight better than Tiffany-Star.

'Can you believe these lesos?'

Ignoring the little dipshit and his bookends, she opens up my backpack and ferrets around inside.

'How fucking rude is this bitch?' I don't know if he's referring to me or her, but I can't help but notice that he's still sitting there with his dick poking out.

'Hey, emo girl,' he says. 'If you hate the world so much, why don't you kill yourself –'

She moves with the speed and grace of a leopard. Before anyone realises what's happening, she's reached across, grabbed dipshit's cashew, and is now holding the point of my compass against it.

'One wrong move. One word from you or these two arse-holes and you'll be pissing sideways for a month. Do I have your attention now?'

Dipshit realises that he's encountered a dangerous animal – a highly volatile street girl. He'd have a better chance against Godzilla. He nods.

'Dominique,' continues my saviour, 'grab our stuff. We're getting off here.' I stand up and pull on my backpack. The train is just pulling into a station.

'My bag's a couple of seats down on the other side.'

Now that the tables have turned I push past bookend's legs and walk up the aisle and grab her backpack. She doesn't have much.

'Now you,' she says. 'Get up.' He does as he's told and as though his life depends on it, which I suppose it does. 'And if either of you morons move, I'll turn your mate here into a eunuch.'

The two bookends look at each other.

'Know what a eunuch is, you dorks?'

They shake their heads.

She glances over at me and shakes her head.

'Okay,' she says. 'One move and I'll be posting the family jewels home to his parents. You got *that*?' Fortunately she's hit upon a metaphorical construct they can grasp.

'And you, you little shit –' she gets right up into his face – 'I even want you to try something. Because I so want to stick you with this thing. Believe me. I will. And more than once. Your testicles will look like pincushions.'

'I won't do nuffink,' squeaks dipshit who, now that he's standing up and away from the bookends, no longer appears so threatening. In fact he looks pathetic. It's fair to say that his afternoon isn't panning out how he'd imagined.

'What would Mummy say if she could see you right now? I bet she'd be real proud. Treating women like shit. Like we exist solely for your pleasure and to serve you. Is that how it is in your culture?'

'No,' he squeaks.

'Really?' she acts surprised. 'That's how it is in most.'

I get the feeling that someone, some man, is responsible for the tatts and the attitude and her rage.

When we get to the carriage door I'm surprised by how little reaction there is from the people already standing there waiting for the train to stop. Hardly anyone seems surprised. I don't think I'll travel on this line again.

The train stops and the doors slide open. Several people push past as I step onto the platform with our backpacks. I look around. My emo friend has also backed onto the platform but she's still holding my compass against dipshit's manhood, and he's still standing in the doorway of the train.

'What happens now?' he pleads.

'We wait until the doors close and then I'll let go.'

'It'll get chopped off.' He's practically begging now.

'That's a risk you're going to have to take.'

'Please.'

'Please?' she mimics. 'I bet it wouldn't have made any difference if *she'd* said, "Please don't hassle me."'

The doors have a rubber safety seal on them to stop people getting their arms and legs and, though it probably wasn't envisaged in the design phase, their penises wedged in them, so he should be okay. *Should*. Whatever happens, I don't think he'll be taking it out in public again in a hurry.

The recorded message announces the train's imminent departure. The boy's eyes widen. The whistle blows. The doors start to close.

At the last second, my new bestie lets go and watches him tip backwards into the carriage.

'We'd better get going,' she says. 'Won't take them long to get the next train back.'

Luckily there's another train pulling in that's heading in the opposite direction. We grab our stuff, tear across the platform and jump on board.

We're still laughing when we sit down. In fact, we're practically falling over each other. We don't care how much attention we're drawing to ourselves. Right now we own the world.

'I haven't had that much fun in ages.'

'Fun?' I reply. 'That was terrifying.'

And with that we're off. We laugh so much that for a moment I forget just how much trouble I'd been in.

'Listen,' I say when we've recovered the power of speech. 'I just want to say —'

She interrupts my apology. 'Please don't. It wasn't your fault. Little arseholes were looking for trouble.'

'Well they certainly found it.'

She smiles and stares out the window. 'You were just sitting in the wrong spot. That's life. Just a random sequence of events.' She looks back at me. 'Think of all the moments, all the twists and turns of your day that led you to that seat. Someone was going to cop it from those a-holes this afternoon, which is why I followed them onto the train.'

'You followed them?'

'Yeah. They were being jerks on the platform. Shouting and swearing and calling out to girls what they'd like to do to them. Real subtle. You could see all these old people edging away from them. Stationmaster asked them to settle down but that short one told him to piss off.'

'You followed them onto the train. You're like a superhero.'

'Yeah. I'm Emo Girl.'

This sets us off again.

'I loved your line about being a Lebanese lesbian, that was a slam dunk. Beautiful. Wasted on them, but still.' She pauses. 'So are you?'

'A lesbian?'

She snorts like a horse. 'Lebanese.'

'I don't know,' I reply. 'I'm from everywhere.'

'Aren't we all?'

She stares at me but she has a distant, glazed look in her

eyes. The look of alleyways. And now that I'm studying her I can see that she's older than I thought.

'Can I ask how old you are?'

She looks at me and grins, turning her head to one side and letting the hair fall down over one eye – classic emo. I actually think she's taking the piss out of herself. 'How old do you think I am?'

I shrug. 'Mid twenties. Twenty-seven maybe.'

'Nineteen.'

Oh crap. 'Sorry.'

'What about you?'

'What do *you* think?'

'Seventeen? Eighteen?'

'I've just turned fourteen.'

'Girl,' she says, reaching across and grabbing my hand. 'We've got to get off the streets.'

'How did you know I was homeless?'

'You've just got that look about you, like you've seen more than you should have.'

Now it's my turn to gaze out the window.

She shakes my hand while she's holding it. 'Name's Cindy by the way. But everyone calls me Cinderella.'

'Can I ask why?'

'You could, but then I'd have to kill you.'

'Sounds like it might be worth it.'

She smiles. 'Okay. But only because I'm responsible for you now. Your life's mine.'

She speaks slowly, dreamily. 'When I was a little girl . . .'

I can't help thinking that despite the tatts and the attitude she still *is* a little girl.

'. . . my favourite bedtime story was *Cinderella*. Or at least it was until Dad hit the road and Mum hit the bottle. It lost a bit of its lustre after that. But when I was in year one we had a school book parade and I wanted to go as Cinderella because she was the only character I knew. Mum couldn't be arsed making me a real costume, she could barely be bothered getting out of bed most days. Just about managed to stagger into the bathroom to wash down some Prozac with half a bottle of vodka. I had this pink party dress that my grandma bought me. It was still in plastic because I didn't get invited to many parties and even when I did, Mum always said that I couldn't go because she couldn't get me there. So on the morning of the book parade I'm getting myself ready, making my lunch, packing my bag and everything when Mum puts in a rare morning appearance. She tells me off for wearing my grandma's party dress. When I tell her that it's the book parade and that I'm going as Cinderella she changes her tune. She wants to help. She wants to play mum again. She does my hair and makes a nice job of it too. Then she looks at my black school shoes that are all scuffed and scratched because we didn't have any shoe polish in the house. She tells me that I can't wear them. That Cinderella didn't wear black school shoes, she wore glass slippers. Said that I had to wear glass slippers or I wouldn't score myself a handsome prince. She didn't know that even back then, when I was seven, I would have preferred to score myself a handsome princess.'

'So you *are*?' I nod.

'Yeah,' she says. 'I *are*.'

'So what happened?'

'She sat me down, took off my shoes and socks and bound my feet in Gladwrap. She said it looked fantastic and she was so convincing that I believed her. I was able to cram my feet into my sandshoes for the walk to school but during the parade I took them off and there were all these Blinky Bills, Snow Whites and cats in hats rolling around on the ground laughing at my feet. Because she'd wrapped them so tight my toes began tingling and by the end of the parade I couldn't walk properly and so the school nurse had to cut off my glass slippers with a pair of scissors.'

She's staring out the window but I can see that her eyes are filling up.

'I've been Cinderella ever since.'

There is a lengthy pause while she collects herself. 'And you are?'

'Dominique.'

'Ah. A no-name. The mystery deepens.' She pauses again and then looks at me with glassy eyes. 'That's okay. Tell me, or don't tell me, when you feel comfortable.' Then she reaches into her backpack, takes out a small notepad and jots something down. She tears it off and hands me the scrap of paper. 'That's my mobile. If you're ever in the shit, you call me and I'll come and get you.'

'Thank you.'

'You don't have to thank me. In some cultures if you save someone's life you become responsible for them. I take that seriously.'

We're coming in to the major southern junction station. She picks up her backpack, reaches over and kisses me on the cheek. 'Take care of yourself. And if you can't, I will.'

I watch her scurrying along the platform towards a city-bound train. There's not much of her but people get out of her way when they see her coming. She's like an emo Moses parting the Red Sea.

CAFÉ

IT WAS LUCKY SHE WAS THERE.

Or unlucky *I* was.

When did you see her again?

The next day. When she left I was a bit scared those guys would come looking for us. But I figured, even if they caught the next train back, as long as I kept going forwards I would always be one station ahead of them.

Where did you go?

Straight to Alistair's café to lay low for a while. When I told him what happened he got angry with me and said that I was stupid travelling on that line by myself. He said even he wouldn't do it at certain times. Said that I wasn't as streetwise as I thought. It was like getting told off by my big brother after I'd been bailed out by my big sister, which, I don't know, made me feel all gooey inside. Pathetic, I know, but there it is. After that I bought myself a baseball bat.

Did you find out why Cindy was homeless?

Yeah, I did, though when we met technically she wasn't.

She lived in a squat near the university. Not the one that Alistair went to but the big one in town. She'd been on the way to visit her grandmother down south when I ran into her. Guess she changed her mind and went home after what happened.

When Alistair had finished chewing my ear off and brought me some dinner, I borrowed his mobile and called her. I just wanted to hear her voice again. They were having a big end-of-semester party at her place the next night and she invited me.

So you went?

She picked me up from the station and walked me back. Said it wasn't safe for a girl to walk those streets by herself, although she obviously had in order to come and get me. She and some friends were squatting in this run-down terrace house in that dodgy area just behind the uni.

Yeah, I know it. It's been gentrified a little since then but it's still pretty dark and dingy.

When we got back it wasn't like a rave party or anything. No one was dancing. There was some Indian music on a portable stereo and the place was lit with candles. Everyone was just sitting around smoking and drinking and talking. We sat down in a group and everyone said hi and then someone passed me a joint. I was actually going to take it just to be polite, but Cinderella said no, I was too young, which again made me feel special, like someone was looking out for me. I'd spent so long living outside of what was normal that it was kind of nice to have someone giving me boundaries, and so she took a drag and passed it on. I told her that it wasn't doing her any good either, that she was almost too young herself. She just told me to relax. Said it didn't matter what she did, because she would be dead soon. I was horrified that someone so strong could have just given up like that; thought maybe it was the dope talking. I felt my stomach lurch when she said that. It seemed so fatalistic and depressing. If Cindy couldn't survive the streets, I had no chance. Then she said that she'd seen a fortune teller at the markets a couple of years ago, when she was living on the streets. When the fortune teller first saw her palm she gave her this weird look. Cinderella made her say what was up, and although the fortune teller was reluctant she eventually told her that she wouldn't see twenty.

How old was she when you met her?

Nineteen, remember. I thought she looked much older, but that's the streets for you.

Seriously though. Why would anyone listen to some feral quack flogging nonsense about the future at a flea market?

She said it was the look in the fortune teller's eyes that frightened her. It was the look of Death. The Grim Reaper. The only thing missing was her scythe. Anyway, she's got this thing hanging over her and before I even asked, she told me that she would be twenty in about six months. She called it her Sword of Damocles.

We were just sitting there on this beanbag chatting and I'm lying in her lap and she's stroking my hair, like a big sister. She told me about the Last Train to Kathmandu, and I told her that I'd seen it a couple of times. Then she told me that the Last Train to Kathmandu didn't have to be a ride on the homeless special, although she'd travelled on it herself a few times when she first became homeless. It was about escaping. Going somewhere safe on the planet. In your head. She then told me that her fantasy journey was on the Trans-Siberian Railway, which was apparently the longest train trip in the world. It went from Moscow to Vladivostok, but for her it wasn't the destination but the journey. Almost ten thousand kilometres safely tucked away in your own private sleeper cabin where no one could get you, no one could bother you. That was her dream. I made her pinkie promise me that she would stay alive long enough to do it. Screw the fortune teller.

Eventually the guy who offered me the joint kind of just flopped down opposite us and joined us, which I was a bit pissed about at first because I wanted her to myself, especially after she'd just pinkie promised that we would take the Trans-Siberian Railway together. But when Cinderella introduced him he was actually really interesting. He was studying to be a microbiologist but he was also a full-on Christian.

Really? I thought most scientists . . .

So did I. But he said the deeper he delved into the mysteries of life, the more he saw the thumbprint of God. Reckoned that despite all our understanding of the natural world, the one thing that we couldn't get to the bottom of was life itself. Where it came from and why. Reckoned that without life to appreciate it, the universe, though breathtaking, was utterly pointless, so something, someone, must have created it. That plus the alternative was just too terrifying to contemplate. Of course it could have been the marijuana talking. He did seem to suck down a lot of it and so maybe he saw God through the haze.

Wouldn't be the first time.

Cinderella told him about my ambition to become a doctor and wipe out the African eye-eating worm, which I'd told her about when we took a short cut through the uni on the walk back to her place. He told me that it was called the Loa-loa worm and that it didn't actually eat eyes, though it could certainly cause blindness and encephalitis. When I asked him what that was he said it was a disease of the brain and that you certainly didn't want it.

Did Cindy go to uni?

No. She was smart enough. Later, when we decided to

crash, she took me into the bedroom that she shared with some other students and there were these huge stacks of books piled up behind her mattress, which was on the floor. She probably read more than me.

So why didn't she go to uni with everyone else?

Everyone else was living in the squat because it was away from their parents and it was free. A bit of adventure. First sign of trouble they could go scuttling back home. She *was* home. She'd left in year nine or something. Hit the streets with no way back.

Why?

You sure you want to hear it?

Yeah.

It's not very nice.

As opposed to what you went through?

It makes what I went through with Creepo look like a stroll in the park. Okay, maybe not a stroll in the park but it was worse.

It's not a competition.

I know.

Go on.

Her mother eventually dried herself out. Probably knew that she was killing her liver, killing herself, and then Cinderella would be on her own, only with no ball to crash, no handsome prince(ss) to whisk her away. She got some help apparently, from a neighbour, who belonged to the local church.

So she found God?

Say what you like about religion, I know I have, but looking up at Jesus is a damn sight better than looking up at the spinning room from the bottom of an empty bottle. Eventually her mum met some guy there. A church elder. He was a widower and they hooked up. They even went and got married and he was doing okay. Had his own business and nice house and so Cinderella and mum moved out of their housing commission flat and in with him.

I can see what's coming. Visits in the night, just like you.

And you'd be wrong. Stepdad was one of the good guys. He couldn't do enough for either of them. It was her mum.

What?

No, not in that way. She was full on. It's God wants this. God wants that. Jesus wants this. Jesus wants Cinderella for a sunbeam and all that seen-the-light crap. And when she fell off the wagon it's wasn't her fault but Satan's. He was tempting her because she was weak and blah, blah, blah. A real born-again arsehole.

Cinderella didn't do church. She reckoned there was something sick about that brainwashing, monotone chanting. You know, 'Lift up your hearts.' 'We lift them up to the Lord.' 'Let us give thanks to the Lord our God.' 'It is right to give him thanks and praise.' She couldn't stand it. No thought. No feeling. Just drone-like behaviour. But her mum insisted. Said that if Cinderella wanted to go on living under her roof, you gotta love that, then she had to go to church. Cinderella put her foot down. She was fourteen by then and old enough to make up her own mind about God and church and would rather live on the streets than be forced into doing something that she was dead against.

What did her mum say?

She didn't say anything. She just went up to Cinderella's room and packed her bag. Told her to get out. That she'd ruined her life by turning up in the first place.

And that was it?

No. Her stepdad stepped in. Refused to let Cinderella leave. It's a big, dangerous world out there and all that. Eventually, with her stepdad's involvement, they came to a compromise.

She didn't have to go to church but she would go to Friday evening youth group. That way she could hang out with kids her own age without having to go through that automaton chanting. First night there, though, she learned that she would have been better off going to church. The kids were okay. A lot of them went to the same high school. And although she had a reputation for being a bit of a loner, the other kids were friendly towards her. The youth minister, though, was a fruit-cake. His name was Justin Pembroke and he had a ponytail, a wife, and a mandate from God, or so he reckoned – one of those whack-jobs who really believe that God speaks to them. Cinderella said that looking at him gave her the creeps. There was just something about him.

Eventually he gathered them all together. Routine was that they had to listen to his bullshit for a while before they could get onto games and hanging out with each other which is what they were there for. When he started in on his sermon, a couple of the other kids looked over at Cinderella and rolled their eyes, kind of like 'Here we go'. You know what he started with?

No.

He held out his arms, like it actually means something, or, I don't know, he was channelling the heavens. Then he said, 'I love God.'

That seems fair enough. I mean, he was a minister.

You didn't let me finish.

Sorry.

He said, 'I love God.' And a couple of the more right-eous youths gave him the obligatory 'Amen'. Then he said, 'I love God more than anything in this world.' Again there were a few amens, though not as many this time. And then the clincher. He said, 'I love God more than I love my wife.'

I didn't know there was a ranking system.

Exactly. But do you know what really pissed off Cinderella more than anything? She was there. His wife. Standing just off to the side and everyone knew who she was. Even Cinderella knew her because that's how he introduced himself to her earlier in the evening – this is me and this is my wife, welcome to my flock. He was quite welcoming and friendly, apparently. But then when he said that, Cinderella could see that it hurt his wife. She had to put up with his crap because she was as devout as him and *he's* the man. But Cinderella didn't have to put up with it. She was into girl power, we all know that, and so she was going to do what wifey couldn't. She was going to hit back.

What happened?

She put up her hand and he kind of snapped at her because he wasn't used to having his weekly rant interrupted.

What did she say?

Well, she waited until she had everyone's attention and then yelled out, 'So what you're saying is that you love a being who may not exist more than someone who puts out for you?'

How did he respond?

Nothing at first because everyone was sniggering, trying not to laugh. She completely nuked him and he had no comeback. But he had to respond because it was his flock and so he told her that there was no place for her there and that she should go and clean out the storeroom and think about her attitude. And she did. She was still buzzing about having nailed him so she probably wasn't thinking straight.

Did she actually clean out the storeroom?

No. She said there was an old beanbag in there so she just kicked back and relaxed. Better than listening to Reverend Pembroke's mad tirade. But a bit later, when he sent the rest of them off on some quest or other, he slipped into the storeroom with her and, like me on the train with those guys, she realised that she was in serious trouble. He told her that she had a big mouth on her. So she responded by informing him that he was a pig. How was his wife supposed to feel about his public declaration? He told her that the only opinion that his wife would have was the one he gave her – she was the weaker vessel and man ruled the world and all that misogynistic bullshit that all the religious texts condone. And then, while he was undoing his belt, he told Cinderella that she needed to be punished. That God demanded she felt his wrath.

Oh no . . .

There was no one else there. He'd sent them all outside on some sort of hunt around the suburb, so that he could deal with her alone.

Why didn't she scream?

She did but he covered her mouth. Back then she wasn't the leopard that I met on the train. There literally was nothing of her. She was more like a punk kitten. So he turned her around and threw her up against this cupboard and . . . well, you don't need a graphic description.

God. I thought her reaction to that boy on the train was a bit excessive; now I see why. Did she tell anyone?

After he'd finished he literally threw her out of the church. The others were making their way back by then and he said that he'd caught her stealing and so he was chucking her out. It was bullshit of course but it was his word against hers and he was a youth minister and she was just some mixed-up teenage girl. Cinderella said that the worst part was that as he was dragging her past his wife, they locked eyes, and the wife gave her a look, like she sympathised with her but there was nothing she could do. Cinderella told me that the look haunted her because she knew that he was doing it to her too.

She arrived home hysterical and ran into the shower to try and wash him off. Then when her mum asked her what was the matter, Cinderella told her what he'd done, but her mum's back teeth were floating in vodka and she said that it was all the work of Satan, who'd obviously been tempting the minister through Cinderella. By that time her mum was onto her second bottle of the evening so Satan had been real busy that night.

The arsehole spread it around that she was a thief and not welcome back and if she turned up again he would be forced to press charges. And he comes out of it a hero because although she's stolen from the church, he didn't call the police because he has Jesus' love and God's forgiveness in his heart.

No one believed her version of events, of course, and she became a pariah at school because word filtered back that she stole the Poor Box from church to spend on drugs. When her mum sobered up she threw Cinderella out.

What an awful story.

She was a street kid. We all have them. And when she finished telling me hers I felt helpless. I was so angry but there was nothing that I could do with my anger and so it just weighed down on me.

She zipped us up in the one sleeping bag and we held each other all night. Protecting one another against the world.

In the morning she asked me to move in permanently so that she could take care of me. But I wanted to be on my own so that she could take care of herself. Her twentieth birthday wasn't all that far off and so she had to be on guard.

After breakfast I found Cinderella in the bathroom, down on her hands and knees scrubbing the tiles. It might have been a squat but it was her home and she liked to keep it nice, and besides, there wasn't going to be any fairy godmothers turning up for her. She, like the rest of us, had to look out for herself.

I left there later that morning knowing my enemy. The Loa-loa worm, and men who treat women like shit.

From the Cradle to the Grave

She takes most of the afternoon getting ready, although her natural beauty means that she doesn't have to try too hard. She could venture out in baggy overalls, sandals, and one of those caps with the woollen flaps over the ears, and still turn heads. Still, this could be the most important day of her life, and she wants to make it count. An impression to remember. Okay, she made an impression the last time she saw him. A permanent impression on the bonnet of his car which he told her he would need to get beaten out. They laughed as they rearranged their clothes and stumbled back into the party a discreet interval apart. He promised that he would see her again. He promised he would break things off with his fiancée. He promised her the world. Soon.

She'd been on the sharp end of wolf-whistles and catcalls from building sites since she'd been in braces. And now, in the second-last year of her teens, her face could open hearts the way her body could open wallets. Not that she would ever need to venture down that path. But still.

Her father had barely spoken to her since part-way through year ten when he'd lit a bonfire and fuelled it with her school reports and tunic. Her childhood gone in a plume of smoke, the flames of her reports dancing in her eyes. She might have become a nurse one day, but you needed good grades for that, and they'd started slipping as soon as she'd begun to escape down to the mall with her friends following rollcall. When her father found out he was apoplectic and stormed down to the mall and practically dragged her home by her hair. When he checked with the school and they reported that she'd been absent more than present, he'd started gathering the kindling. But now they were on speaking terms again because he finally saw her for the asset she was. And if he played his hand wisely, she could fund his retirement.

Everyone said she could be a model if she wanted to. Men mostly. Men in doof doof cars who bent her over their bonnets and slathered sweet nothings in her ear. Men who, if she was going to be brutally honest, probably had no contacts in the modelling industry whatsoever, but whom she would let take her for a ride anyway. Take her away. Her father would kill her if he found out that she was soiled. It was her greatest asset, he said. Her only asset. And it couldn't be stitched back together once it had been torn. You had to laugh at the old people who still clung to the old ways. The old values. The old country. What was the point in leaving if you brought everything with you?

But she had let her father play matchmaker, offering her body, her innocence, as the dowry for some rich, older guy. And he would pay through the teeth for something that she was giving away most Friday and Saturday nights. Men! They were so pathetic you just had to laugh. The way to a man's heart was through his stomach? It was a bit lower than that.

'Is he good-looking?' she'd pleaded when her father told her about the proposed dinner date after lunch, though it was part of their joke. The banter going backwards and forwards as he doled out nuggets of information. The five others hadn't worked out mainly because one was old, one was ugly, one was old *and* ugly, one was gay, and one already had a wife and kids back in the old country. Her father had coughed and told her this latest offering was a cut above all the others.

'He's a fine-looking gentleman.'

'Gentleman? You mean he's old?'

'Older than you, certainly. Worldly, yes.'

'At least tell me his name.'

Her father had just looked at her and smiled. It was funny, the only time they'd ever really got along was right now, when he was trying to negotiate the best price for her virginity.

'Please, Papa,' she'd begged, tickling him.

'Okay,' he'd finally relented. 'His name is Sanchez.'

For a moment she hadn't been able to breathe. She'd had to sit down to gather herself. Hide her excitement. Stop herself from screaming. Tony Sanchez – dashing and dangerous but with a great business mind. He and his brother had been cutting a swathe through their community ever since they'd arrived from the old country, although she could never remember the name of the older one, the dull one. He was quieter, sterner, smaller in stature than her Tony, but with fists of iron. He was not someone you said no to.

Even though she'd had a few secret liaisons with Tony, and he'd told her that he loved her, she almost didn't dare dream that he'd ever dump that lump of a fiancée and officially move on to her, just as he'd promised.

But Papa had made it happen. He'd finally come through. And so she hugged him like she hadn't done since she'd been a little girl and he'd taught her how to ride her bike.

She'd nuzzled into his neck, smelling his cheap aftershave and roll-your-own cigarettes, his hope that this one might be it. 'Thank you, Papa.'

'Start getting yourself organised,' he'd replied. 'He's not someone who likes to be kept waiting.'

That was her Tony. Always in a hurry. Always impatient. That was Serena's problem. She couldn't keep up with him. Couldn't keep him happy. Couldn't keep *him*. Now it was her turn.

When the doorbell rang a few hours later she practically sashayed into the lounge room. The only thing missing was the smoky saxophone backing track. It was the old cliché but today really was the first day of the rest of her life. She was wearing her backless cocktail dress that accentuated her hourglass figure. Tony would be putty in her hands and tonight she would be playing hard to get. No more free rides for Mr Sanchez.

As she glided into the room her mother looked up from her knitting and made the sign of the cross. Her father's jaw would have hit the floor if he hadn't been so busy beaming with pride.

'Aren't you going to show him in, Papa?'

'Yes, yes,' he replied, backing away from his daughter. Her mother shook her head and made another sign of the cross. She would be saying the rosary later. Twice.

She heard them mumbling by the front door. Exchanging pleasantries about the new country's weather in the old language.

Then they were walking along the hallway, past the small statue of the Virgin Mary, and around the corner.

'Bridgette,' said her father, completely ignoring his wife. 'May I have the honour of introducing . . .' But she didn't hear another word because her world was falling apart.

He took her to a restaurant from the old country where, in lieu of conversation, they'd danced. She like some wild creature born of the kasbah, he like he was made of wood. It was pleasant enough, she supposed, especially when all the other men watched her move, gyrating her hips like a professional belly dancer draped in a serpent. She loved that. She loved that all the other women hated her at that moment.

Afterwards he'd invited her back for coffee because his brother was away for the weekend with his fiancée, so he had the place to himself. Although she'd been feeling queasy, she still went up with her consolation prize. And, as she soon found out, he *wasn't* someone you said no to. To make matters worse, neither brother seemed to be familiar with the concept of chemists. That was obviously the woman's responsibility. So she was playing Russian roulette.

She arrived home a little later with her knickers stuffed in her handbag and her stomach churning. She spent the next hour doubled over the toilet. Her father stood at the door shaking his head, hoping that she hadn't had too much. Women just couldn't handle the drink. He hoped that Mr Sanchez had been a gentleman and hadn't taken advantage of the situation, but checking his watch and seeing that it was after two in the morning, he had his doubts. If it came to that he had a shotgun in his shed that would ensure Mr Sanchez did the honourable thing.

She just lay there with her face pressing down on the cool porcelain, oblivious to her father's presence. She'd been throwing up all week but had put it down to a virus. Now she knew she was in serious trouble and she didn't know what to do about it. She couldn't go to bed yet and disappear into dreams either because there was more to come up.

'You shouldn't drink,' chastised her father with folded arms. 'Women shouldn't drink.

Luckily she had alcohol to mask the terrible truth. Because what her father didn't know was that she'd been on lemonade all night.

*

Cinderella's squat empties out over the holiday period as the students slink back to the suburbs. Back to their own rooms with their racing car beds and boy band posters to tell everyone over plump turkeys and plum puddings how tough they're doing it. About life on the edge. Once the end of year exodus was over, it was generally just Cinderella and the rats. So I invite her to spend Christmas with me and my barrister mum at the Shangrila Pines Resort, courtesy of Serena and Creepo.

We don't want to snap Serena's credit card under the strain of too much room service, so we settle for takeaway blowouts from the mega-mall most nights. We swim in the heated pool and read on the balcony or in bed. I give her *The Diving Bell and the Butterfly*, hoping that she'll take the hint and stay alive. She gives me *Mansfield Park* because she reckons I'm a born romantic. I'm not, of course, I just like Jane Austen. So we read until we can hardly keep our eyes open and then, following a banana-split and hot chocolate from room service, we read again until our heads drop into our books. Then we curl up together, with me wishing the moment would never end.

Until the night of Cinderella's party I hadn't shared a bed with another person since I was tiny. That night I must have drifted off first. But last night she disappeared before me, twitching and flinching as she slipped deeper and deeper in to the dream world. I didn't know we did that – twitched, I mean. Maybe it's our bodies trying to ward off death. Even the temporary death of the night. Or maybe it's only junkies who twitch and Cinderella was fleeing the ravenous dragon that lurked in her veins.

Although we've been having the buffet breakfast, this morning I let her sleep. Tomorrow she'll be back in the squat by herself. Back to trying to think of a job that someone covered in tatts, with a year nine education, a serious drug habit and no ID might apply for. I have a few more days in the rail yards ahead of me before I start house-sitting for Miss Taylor. I would love to invite Cinderella to sit with me, try to help heal her scars, but a promise is a promise.

'No friends,' Miss Taylor had insisted as she handed me her spare key following our dinner a couple of weeks ago. 'I mean it.' It was risky enough just seeing me. If it became known that a street kid was living in her flat, she'd probably never teach again, and I couldn't risk that no matter how much I loved Cinderella.

I ask the doorman for directions to the cemetery and he draws me a map on the back of one of the hotel's glossy brochures. I know the way, of course. I've visited every time I've stayed at the Shangrila Pines, just to sit and talk. But he seemed so bored standing there in his uniform, I had to help him feel as though his existence wasn't pointless.

'Merry Christmas,' he says when he's convinced that I know which way I'm heading.

After about a kilometre, the semi-industrial area gives way to bushland. A reverential hush comes over the world as I turn off the road and enter the cemetery. There's a whoosh of wind and rustle of leaves high in the treetops, as if the angels are swooping down to guide the recently departed heavenward.

It doesn't take me long to find her plot. It's only small; she must have been cremated. I place a single red rose on her grave and wipe the plaque with a moistened tissue. I think mine are the only flowers she ever gets. When I started visiting, her plaque was filthy – battered by wind, dirt and time. Whoever left her here is either content with their memories, or has passed on themselves.

I wish I had been closer to her, then my sadness might be genuine. But I content myself with the knowledge that she was born in the same year as my mum, even if she died several years earlier, before her life had really started.

On previous visits I would like to have left a passage from Mum's favourite book, or rolled up her most treasured poem in a scroll and left it tied in a red ribbon on her grave. But she had neither. And leaving a copy of *New Idea* or a feature article from *TV Week* just wouldn't be the same.

However, I've decided that if Barbara Langdon is happy to play surrogate mum – and she isn't haunting me or anything, so she must be okay with it – then I can leave a favourite poem for her and my mum. And so this time, thanks to Cinderella's poetry collection, I've come prepared.

I pull the crumpled paper out of my pocket and try to decipher my own writing.

> I DREAMED that one had died in a strange place
> Near no accustomed hand;
> And they had nailed the boards above her face,
> The peasants of that land,
> Wondering to lay her in that solitude,
> And raised above her mound
> A cross they had made out of two bits of wood,
> And planted cypress round;
> And left her to the indifferent stars above
> Until I carved these words:
> *She was more beautiful than thy first love,*
> *But now lies under boards.*

I roll up Yeats's poem and place it on their grave, weighing it down with a rock, splashing the rock with sadness.

'I wish I knew you better,' I say to both of them. Then I might have something to cry about other than sadness itself.

Then I think of Cinderella and have to sit down on the grass.

Last night while we were scoffing down our KFC I noticed the scabs on her forearms. She always wore long sleeves, even to bed, but she rolled them up for the Colonel so that she wouldn't get grease on her peejays. When she was asleep I traced my finger gently along the marks on her arms. Faded tracks of desperate journeys. I had an inkling of what they meant. She was chasing the dragon. Heroin. I asked her once before, at the squat, if she did drugs but she got all defensive. Evasive. Said it didn't matter what she took because she was going to be dead soon. I told her that I needed her to stay alive so that she could look after me. Give me big sisterly advice. I reminded her that she'd saved my life and I was her responsibility. She just held my face and said that she would always watch over me. That didn't help, even if she believed it, which I seriously doubt. The moon always watched over me too, with its smiley face and Cheshire Cat grin, but it would be pretty useless if Creepo came hobbling towards me attaching the silencer to his gun or pulling a knife from his pocket.

If she is doing heroin I wonder how she manages to pay for it. I'd rather not know. The thought of my beautiful fairy godmother doing things with strange men in alleyways makes me want to vomit.

I look around the forlorn and forgotten headstones of some of the older graves. It would destroy me to leave Cinderella here, to scatter her ashes to the wind. But of course, she wouldn't be here. This is in the ivy belt. These are the graves of the rich. The loved. She'd be dumped in a paupers' grave. Three corpses deep in a plywood coffin. Left to melt into eternity with a couple of winos.

A chill wind is howling through the gravestones now as I hunch my shoulders against the cold and make my way back down towards the road, the gravel crunching heavily beneath my feet like soldiers marching. The wind screaming through the overhead powerlines sounds more ghostlike than ghosts, so I hurry along towards the exit before the skeleton trees reach down and grab me. There's no one about but me. Me and the lost souls who, like Barbara Langdon and my mum, I leave to wander forlorn among the empty eternities.

CAFÉ

I'M SORRY, BUT I HAVE TO ASK. ALL THOSE TIMES THAT YOU SLEPT together, did Cinderella ever . . .

Did she what?

Did she, you know, ever behave inappropriately?

Behave inappropriately? What is this, a church sewing circle? Do you mean did she ever try to bonk me?

Well, yes?

Don't be disgusting. I was fourteen years old. She was my protector. My fairy godmother. Do you think the original Cinderella's godmother ever tried to get it on with *her*?

Well . . . no. At least not in the versions I've read.

How do you think that one might have played out? 'You shall go to the ball, Cinderella; but only after we duck into the pantry for a quickie.'

All right, I get it!

If anything, I was the one who was in love with her. But that was probably abandonment issues. Missing mother-figure and all that. You know, Oprah 101.

So you stayed in the hotel?

About five days leading up to and past Christmas. We were going to stay longer but the hotel was booked solid on New Year's Eve and Cinderella had promised to spend it with her uni friends, and I had Miss Taylor's to get ready for.

What do you mean 'get ready'? Weren't you just minding the place for her?

Yeah, but I wanted to do it right. I had about a week to go before she went on holidays so I decided to live rough. Really rough. It was as if I felt I had to earn it. The comfort, I mean. I can't really explain it. I headed up to my week-ender. I'd only ever stayed there a couple of nights at a time max. This time I was there for six. And trust me, six nights living under a door in the sand dunes is enough to make anyone wilt. No showers and a mostly potato scallop diet and I needed a serious scrub and detox by the time I set off for Miss Taylor's.

Did you see her off or anything?

No. She told me to come and stay with her the night before she left but I didn't want to risk it. I mean, she wanted someone there to water her plants and keep an eye on the place, but the official line was that if anyone sprung me, I was a street kid who'd broken in and . . .

Watered the plants and kept an eye on the place?

Something like that.

What was it like after all that time living in the dunes?

Even Heaven couldn't beat it, especially because I was on my own and didn't have to go around praising my creator every five minutes.

Where did she live?

In the ivy belt, not far from the school with the pink dresses and blue socks. One stop up the line actually.

And is that where she went to school?

No. She went to some exclusive straw hat and blazer private girls' college up towards the junction station, remember? But where she lived is actually a small village – bakery, bookshop, cafés, and about three real estate agents because it's an expensive suburb. Not a shattered bus shelter in sight. There are a couple of blocks of low-rise flats near the train station and she rented one of those.

As soon as I got off at the station I went to the little grocery store in the village and stocked up on supplies. I got myself some herbal bath oils and candles to put around the bath. When I got in and unpacked I ran myself a bath and then stripped off. After six nights in the dunes I had sand everywhere. Sand in my hair. Sand in my clothes. Sand in my pockets. Sand in my sand. I ended up having a shower first to try to get rid of the bulk of it. I decided to listen to some music while I was in the bath. Talk about indulgent. But seriously, do you know what it's like to live the way I'd been living then suddenly have a home and be able to walk out to Miss Taylor's kitchen in the nude to get her CD player?

Not exactly. Not at Miss Taylor's place anyway . . .

Oh, shut up! You know what I mean. It was heavenly. To have a place of my own, even temporarily, where it was safe, warm and dry and where I could lock the door and keep out the world. Miss Taylor had her radio set to ABC Classic FM and so I relaxed in the bath with my herbal bubbles and absorbed. This one piece was so perfect that I actually climbed out of the bath and wrote down its name, which sort of defeated the purpose of relaxing in the bath to classical music, I suppose.

Do you remember it?

It was by Satie . . .

Gymnopédie Number One?

Smart arse. How did you know that?

It's an almost perfect lie-in-the-bath-while-it's-pouring-outside-day piece.

Almost perfect?

You should hear his *Gnossienne Number One*. It's even more haunting.

Trust me. After my nights in the rail yards with the ghost guard, I'd been haunted enough.

Fair point. So what did you do with yourself for the two weeks that you were there?

Nothing. I just repaired. All I did was sleep, eat, read, have long bubble baths and watch DVDs. Miss Taylor was a bit of a buff so I just kicked back on her lounge and watched movies. Got myself some microwavable popcorn from the village grocery store to help. After being on the streets, I knew I'd never take that sort of freedom for granted ever again. Still don't. I actually swung back towards spirituality again while I was staying at Miss Taylor's: there is a heaven, and it's right here on earth. It's being safe. It's being warm. It's being able to read and watch movies with microwavable popcorn and have long soapy herbal bubble baths while listening to classical music while the rain hammers down outside. It's being able to curl up in fresh sheets, knowing that you're not going to be subjected to any unwanted visitors in the night. I don't care what anyone says, that's heaven. No amount of wings, harp lessons, fluffy clouds and praising can beat that.

I didn't even have to worry about getting into high school either because Miss Taylor said that she had it all under control – she'd taken my reports and results from school – and she would finish organising it all when she got home from trekking. Though I did stress about whether I'd fit in. Would the other girls see through me? Spot that I was a fraud. It was the ivy-belt after all. But Miss Taylor convinced me that I

would be fine. Said that the school would be better for having
me there. So I had two angels watching over me.

Alistair?

More a big brother.

The only problem was that time went so quickly. It felt as
though I'd only just moved in and then it was all over and I
had to slump my way back to the rail yards.

Where you there when she got back?

Yeah. I hadn't planned to but I just couldn't bring myself
to leave. I helped her unpack and she showed me how to
download her holiday photos onto her laptop and then we
went through the enrolment procedure together. I would be
using her address as a base and for reports and everything. She
had it all worked out. She knew the loopholes. And because I
was getting more and more stuff than I could cart around all
the time, she let me start leaving some of it at her place. Like
Cinderella, she asked me to move in permanently. You don't
know how tempting it was to say yes. I was thinking it, but I
told her that it was too risky and I would rather die than see
her forced to stop teaching. I knew she loved it more than
anything.

Where did she think you were living when you weren't
with her?

I told her about the squat and Cinderella. I also told her
that I had another place up north but that I mostly stayed
with Cinderella.

But she knew about the rail yards?

Yeah, but she was horrified so I told her that I'd stopped
staying there. I think she would have even preferred to call
the police or social services rather than let me stay there any
longer. And that was the thing: after staying at Miss Taylor's,
the thought of going back to the rail yards horrified me too.
I'd experienced heaven and now I was sliding back down

to purgatory. On my first night back, when I strung up my sleeping bag across the seats so that I could read, I actually cried. Blubbed like a two-year-old. When I'd first got into the rail yards I was so excited and proud of myself, but at that moment I saw how pathetic it was. Even Cinderella's squat was a mansion compared to the trains. The hard, vinyl, vandalised seats, the cold metal bars, the dirty, grimy floors, the bone-chilling cold, the disgruntled ghost slamming doors at all hours. I knew that I had to find somewhere else. I wanted to be a doctor, for God's sake. I couldn't study for my HSC in the rail yards.

That was still a few years away.

Yeah, but I had to start planning.

But you got into school okay?

Yeah. Just like she promised, Miss Taylor organised everything and even bought my uniform, both summer and winter, as well as a jumper. She was also going to buy me some new school shoes but Cinderella beat her to it when she took me shopping at the mega-mall one Saturday morning. Even Alistair McAlister insisted buying me a new backpack. I couldn't believe how blessed I was to have those three in my life. They were so unselfish. So giving. There was nothing in it for them, but everything in it for me.

How was your first day at school?

It was okay. I didn't know anyone but I was buddied up with a couple of other newbies and that became our group, for the first couple of weeks, anyway. You know how everyone has a photo taken on their first day of the school year?

Yeah, I've still got my ones somewhere.

Well, Miss Taylor wasn't going to let me get away with not having one. The night before the first day of term, she insisted that I stay with her because she didn't go back until the following day. She got me up early, made us both poached eggs on toast, and while I was getting changed into my new uniform, she dug out her camera and insisted on a Kodak moment. Well, the digital version. I acted all teenager, like it was all so uncool, but when I was standing there in my pink dress and blue socks, I'd never felt so happy. Miss Taylor insisted on walking me to school. I didn't want her to, in case we got busted, but she wouldn't listen. She took me to the gates and gave me a hug and told me to make her proud. She held on to me for a while and I knew that she was crying.

When she finally let me go and I walked in with all the other girls I almost had to pinch myself. I wasn't just going to a school in the ivy belt, I was going to the school of my dreams. I was one of those pink-dressed girls, happy and carefree. The only bummer, the wake-up call, was remembering that I would be sleeping in the rail yards that night. And on that first day, when the hooter sounded and we poured out of the school in all our pinkness, I caught the train with all the other happy and carefree girls heading home. The only difference between them and me was that they were going home, whereas I *was* home.

What did you do?

I went househunting.

The Ivy Principle

If you spend a day travelling the length and breadth of the city you will notice a huge discrepancy between that haves and have-nots. The mansions of the bay and harbour areas would swallow, in one gulp, entire streets of desolation from the troubled zones of the outer suburbs, where disappointment hangs in the air like a wet blanket.

Although governments announce schemes to make life more tolerable for those occupying Struggle Street, it really is nothing more than a bandaid solution. And if the bandaid is removed too soon it leaves an open wound that is vulnerable to infection and disease like a dead cat on the side of the road.

The solution for this desperate disparity isn't to be found in politics but foliage. The stretch of dense, old-growth greenery between the mega-mall and the north-west junction station is locally and affection- ately known as the ivy belt. Although lacking the merchant banker/arms' dealer ostentations of the houses that mark our foreshore, the ivy belt's wealth is more consistent and stretches further.

The answer is glaringly obvious. Ivy. In suburbs where ivy flourishes, there seems to be a disproportionate number of old stone houses and well-kept gardens. In fact, apart from the odd abandoned place slowly being sucked back into the earth, there isn't a single sheet of fibro to be found, while asbestos roofing is an alien concept. Surely this cannot be a coincidence.

There is relatively little crime in ivy-cloaked areas. Armed robbery is virtually non-existent. And the only known case of car-jacking involved a tardy parishioner who, in sheer desperation, commandeered a Porsche at the traffic lights because he was running late for church. Apart from that one car-jacking, the only crime of note occurred earlier this year when a shopping trolley was left on the lawn of the Hills District Croquet Club, slightly damaging the playing service, and even then there are those who consider it an inside job.

Domestic violence decreases dramatically in areas where ivy manages to take hold, while year twelve retention rates are running at practically one hundred per cent.

This phenomenon needs to be investigated at both an economic and foliage level. Forget work-for-the-dole schemes and other public works drafted for the troubled zones; what is required is the immediate and mass planting of ivy.

Left unchecked, ivy has been known to crawl up the outer wall of small, single-storey, three-bedroom dwellings, turning them into four-storey, double-brick monoliths complete with atrium, vestibule, sun room, ducted air-conditioning, clay surface tennis court, and detached servant quarters.

To neglect the economic advantages of ivy any longer is not just socio-political oversight but criminally irresponsible.

There are empty houses spread out across the city. The main item of a deceased estate whose disgruntled beneficiaries refuse to accept the will of the deceased and take the corpse to court. These battles can drag on for years. Meanwhile the house sits forlorn and forgotten.

There was one near Creepo and Serena's. An old weatherboard place which, for some reason had a broken down phone box half-buried in the weeds and overgrown grass of the front garden.

Everyone said that an elderly couple had been murdered in the house. Battered beyond recognition by their deadbeat son who'd incurred some serious gambling debts and didn't have the patience to wait for his inheritance.

From front on it looked as though the house was frowning. The local kids used to throw stones at it, perhaps hoping that it would pick up and chase them down the street. And when there wasn't a single window pane left in either the house or the phone box, even the stone throwers admitted defeat and went away. It might not have been haunted, but after what had happened in there no one went near the place on Halloween. It was just too spooky.

I'm hoping for a place with a slightly less alarming history. I decide to start at school and work my way out in ever-increasing circles. Cinderella said that in the older, wealthier suburbs like the one my school was in, there were bound to be at least two or three abandoned houses. Squatters didn't usually bother with them as they didn't like to commute. They preferred the vibrancy, the alleys, the shadows of the inner suburbs and the city itself. What was the point of fleeing the domestic humdrum of suburban life, if you went and squatted down near the local hardware store? You couldn't reject western consumerism and embrace anarchy if you lived near a shopping mall. It just didn't sit right. Or that was Cinderella's take on it anyway. It sounded great to me.

The fields and courts shrill with the early morning whistles of vexed referees as I start my quest. Saturday is national sports' day so apart from a couple of geriatrics taking their fossilised pooches for their morning drag, I pretty much have the streets to myself.

I feel full of confidence as I stride past them. No one is going to mess with me. Not any more. I can take care of myself now. As the oldies pass me, their nervous glances seem to tag me as a serious sports girl or a lunatic street kid who's best avoided. I'm happy either way.

There's a reason they might think I'm sporty. If Cinderella hadn't stepped in when I'd been cornered by those trainee thugs on the train, God only knows what might have happened. I could have been beaten, raped, even murdered. Those scumbags might just have thought it was all a big joke, a bit of fun, but I couldn't know how it would end. I was totally vulnerable, outnumbered. Simply hoping that they wouldn't hurt me was a pretty pathetic defence strategy. And in future I can't rely on Cinderella to miraculously appear and turn into Emo Girl whenever I find myself in trouble. I have to be more self-reliant. So the afternoon it happened and I fetched up at the mega-mall to lick my wounds, I bought myself a baseball bat. I'd ditched the gun in the river by then, but now everywhere I go the bat goes too. Sticking out of my backpack like a samurai sword.

I trek the streets for over two hours without any luck. One house near the tennis courts seems promising so I scope it for a while from across the road. It's an old wooden place, probably dating back to colonial times. The wraparound verandah sags with the weight of time, the wood itself weathered back to resemble the logs from which it had been cut. I'm about to approach it when an old lady emerges from the front door and stares at me with her arms folded. Her skin's so pale she's practically transparent and even from where I'm standing her hands appear as gnarled as the roots of ivy that's tearing down rather than supporting the house. I suppose even ivy has its limits. I've already been standing there for quite some time, but the poor old woman seems so decrepit that it might be worth waiting a bit longer. The use-by date on her birth certificate must be getting close.

I give her a little wave and move on. After more wandering, I give up for the day and make my way over to Miss Taylor's place to recharge. For some reason it seems okay to see her outside school hours, as if she no longer reports to the education department and can meet up with whoever she liked.

While she makes me a hot chocolate I tell her what I was up to. She isn't impressed. We have our usual merry-go-round argument about my moving in with her or going to the police if my uncle is as bad as I say he was. I'd told her a little of what happened to me, she doesn't know everything. She knows about Creepo grooming me to be his private plaything. She doesn't know about my parents' bodies out there in the forest. As far as she's concerned I've just run away from my psycho uncle and I'd rather live in the squat with Cinderella than take my chances in foster care. I manage to prey on her innocence by telling some totally bogus stories about what had happened to other girls in foster care, and so we eventually come to an agreement. She won't tell anyone about me living rough provided that I stay in school, allow her to tutor me, and maintain an A-grade average on my reports. (Except sport. She would happily take a C for PDHPE.) I agree to the deal because I know two things. One: with my hard work and her help, I should be able to blitz all the assessments. Two: if I do get less than an A, I'll leave before she finds out. She won't see me for dust because no way in hell was I going to risk exposing me or her to Creepo.

She hands me the hot chocolate and gives me one of her teacher looks. 'So what does Cinderella think of you moving out? You *are* still with her?'

'She's not my mum.'

'Yes, but she is, for all intents and purposes, your guardian.'

'She has me on timeshare, with you.'

'Ha ha. Very funny.' Miss Taylor sips her coffee and stares at me as though she's weighing everything up. 'Okay. One more condition.' She says it like she actually has a choice in the matter. 'You let me buy you a mobile phone.'

'Why, Miss?' Although she isn't my teacher any more, I've chosen to keep to the formality of the classroom, so that she thinks she's in charge.

'So that if you're ever in trouble, or feel threatened, or just scared, you can call me or Cinderella or this Alistair person, and we can come and get you. Deal?' She holds out her hand, which I shake.

'Thanks, Miss.'

'Now,' she says, warming to the task. 'You're not having much luck, are you? Have you tried the Gardner place?'

I don't know what that means.

'It used to belong to Old Man Gardner. He was one of those dotty old buggers who if you kicked your ball over their fence would never give it back. Or if they did, it had punctures in it. He was creepy, or seemed that way when I was younger, but it was probably just us kids creating a bogeyman. We used to knock on his door at all hours and throw stones on his tin roof. Of course, he used to come screaming outside with his walking stick raised and we would all scatter to the winds. We were awful to him now that I think about it. He was probably just a lonely, slightly senile old man, and we treated him like he was the devil.'

'What happened to him?'

'He died. A few years back. He was ancient, probably getting on for a hundred. But it was one of those terrible stories: someone dies at home and no one discovers the body for ages.'

'So the house stinks of death?'

'I wouldn't think so. Though it's certainly run-down. It was when he was alive. Anyway, they have clean-up crews for when something like that happens.'

'Imagine having that job.'

'Well, you won't have to just as long as you stay at school. Anyway, he had a son, or perhaps it was a nephew, who tried to sell the place. But nobody was interested, not after what had happened there and all the rumours that followed.'

'What rumours?'

'Old Man Gardner's wife and daughter had gone missing, decades before, and we used to say that he'd killed them and buried their bodies under the floorboards.'

'And this is where you want me to live? Thanks.'

'Oh, it was just kids' talk. She probably ran off with some bloke or other. The daughter wasn't his anyway. She was from the wife's first marriage. Bit of a wild thing herself, if the tales are true. His wife, I mean, not the daughter. The daughter was a sickly little thing. Hardly ever went to school. Hardly ever left the house. My old neighbour reckoned she used to see her staring out the window, pale as death. Poor thing.'

Despite its terrible history the house sounds like it might be worth investigating. 'So where is it?'

'You just go past your school to the end of the street until you hit the rail line, then turn left and walk along next to the tracks for about half a kilometre.'

'What number?'

Miss Taylor smiles. 'Trust me. You'll know it when you see it.'

While Miss Taylor heads off to the mega-mall for my mobile phone, I sheath my samurai baseball bat and follow her directions.

She's right about my not needing the address. Compared to the rest of the houses in the street, the Gardner place sticks out like a bogan at the ballet. But it doesn't seem as threatening as I thought it might. The vibe isn't so much house of horror, more an absence of happiness.

Like that old lady's house a few streets away, the Gardner place also has a wraparound verandah, but because most of the boards have been cracked and warped by weather and time, a lap of the house proves impossible. In fact, the boards along the right-hand side of the house have all been removed. In their place are sheets of rusty corrugated iron and a metal gate that is attached to nothing and leads nowhere. You would need a tetanus shot before even venturing up this side of the house.

I try to heave up one of the windows but they've been painted or warped shut to the frame and don't budge so much as a millimetre. With the stealth of a ninja I tread cautiously towards the front door, noticing the ornate wooden doorbell and what looks like the skeleton of an old wind chime.

I turn the handle, just in case – against all odds – the door is unlocked. Amazingly it clicks, so I give it a push. When that doesn't work I shove my shoulder against it. On my third shoulder charge the frame splinters and the door swings open. The house lets out a twenty-year-old sigh and then seems to groan at the sudden intrusion of light and air.

I stand in the doorway, fanning away the musty odour of neglect. Stirred up by my invasion, dust motes dance about me in their millions. I'm dazzled by the sight until I'm forced to cover my face with my arm in order to breath.

I thought it would be full of mould but the house is surprisingly dry. A thorough inspection leaves me in no doubt. The rail yards are a place of desperation. But I know I could be happy here. Very happy.

The house is unfurnished apart from an old coffee table in the lounge room and a plastic swing bin in the kitchen. The kitchen itself is from a bygone era. Not that it matters. I can't cook. The bathroom is dark blue. It reflects the mood of the house but not mine. I don't think I've ever been this excited. The bath has a shelf running around it. Perfect for my scented candles. I try the sink tap which gurgles and spits air at first, then takes a deep breath and emits a deep, guttural disgruntled groan. Eventually a little water trickles out and, following a few more spurts, it becomes a steady stream.

I run all the way back to Miss Taylor's to get my stuff. Luckily she's back from the mega-mall and gives me a quick demo on how to use my new phone. She'll pay my phone bill, she insists, as long as I promise to phone her once a day.

She wants to come with me to the Gardner place, help me get settled in, but I refuse. I tell her that the neighbours look like the sort of people who'll take photos of trespassers before calling the police. She agrees that if she ever visits me, it'll have to be under cover of darkness.

After that I practically skip back to the house. My house. I slip up the path again and let myself in.

I have three bedrooms to choose from but settle for the lounge room instead. Things might have happened in those bedrooms. Things that might stir the restless dead, so I decide to leave them shut. Leave them to their memories.

I unroll my sleeping bag so that my head is against the wall but facing away from the door. Gotta have the Feng Shui in order. Then I light a couple of scented candles – lavender and ylang ylang. An ideal combination for driving away musty odours and evil spirits.

Later, following a fish and chips from the village shops, I settle down for my first night's sleep in my new home. I switch off my book light and am immediately enveloped in total blackness. No sooner have I drifted off than I am woken by something going bump in the night. Going bump in the ceiling. I smile and snuggle down deeper into my sleeping bag. It's either possums or the ghosts of possums past. Either way I'm not bothered.

A short while later when the wind picks up I'm woken by scratching on the tin roof. It takes me about an hour, lying there with my sleeping bag covering everything but my eyes, to realise what it is. A branch from the ancient gumtree in the front yard is trying to claw its way into the house.

In the early hours of the mornihg, I sense that the ghosts in the walls have come to visit, hovering above me in curiosity, but by then I'm too exhausted to care.

Home

OVER THE NEXT FEW WEEKS I SETTLE INTO MY NEW HOME. WHEN school's out for the day I can't walk up the street chatting like everyone else because the other girls would see me disappearing into the old Gardner place and start asking questions. So I head down to the village shops for a while and hang around the children's bookshop until it's safe to go home or I find a book that I want to buy. In fact, I become such a regular in the bookshop that the manager, Paul, offers me a job sorting out the stock, helping with customer enquiries, writing reviews. I don't have a tax file number, and I won't give him my address, so I suggest he pay me in books, which is even better than money.

I take a field trip to the local hardware store and am taught how to replace fuse wire by a man who looks alarmingly like Santa Claus. Although I don't use the house lights for fear of drawing attention, I manage to replace the fuses and get the electricity working so I'm able to buy myself a toaster and a kettle and some pots and pans.

The back verandah can't be seen from either neighbour's

house so at certain times of the day on the weekend I sit at the small, rusty wrought-iron table in the sun and read and do my homework.

*

About a month after I found my house, I'm summoned to the principal's office. Once more, just as things were working out I feel my world falling apart.

'What's this about?' I ask the girl who was sent to fetch me. 'Why does Mrs Cameron want to see *me*?'

'Dunno,' says my escort, who could use a refresher course in conversational skills.

I sit outside the principal's office debating whether or not to make a run for it.

It's a big school, about fifteen hundred students all told, so there are five office ladies, all of whom take it in turns to cast me their hateful glare.

I feel like flipping them the bird and making a break for it. But there are no police in the foyer and if this is something serious, surely my escort would be a teacher, like last time, and not some monosyllabic year eight mutant. I decide to hold on. For now.

Eventually I'm shown through to the principal's office.

It takes a certain type of person to oversee the educational and social development of close to fifteen hundred highly emotional and hormonally charged teenage girls, and I'm not entirely sure Mrs Cameron has what it takes. She spends most of the day bunkered down in her office, leaving the day-to-day running of the place to her deputies and of course the office ladies, and only ventures out to speak at assembly or to duck off down the road for 'personal reasons'; in other words, a smoke.

'Have a seat,' she says, her tone neutral, unlike her dress which clashes with practically everything, including, oddly enough, itself. Mrs Cameron insists on wearing the sort of floral creations that, if they were real, would give you severe hay fever. Today's subtle little ensemble is all oranges, yellows and purples. A real eye-gouger.

'Now then,' she says, looking down at my file. My heart thumps. This is exactly what Mr Thompkins did before I was carted off in the back of that police car. 'How are you settling in?'

'Fine,' I say, because I am. I've got a good group of friends who, unlike Janyce and her posse, treat me as an equal not someone to be looked after. That might sound ungrateful and I don't mean it to be. What I mean is that I want to be normal, whatever that is.

'Yes,' says Mrs Cameron. 'I'm hearing good things from your teachers.'

I bet she isn't. She's probably just killing time until the police arrive.

'Very good things indeed.'

This is torture.

'Do you know why you're here?'

Here we go.

I shake my head.

'Really?'

Oh, what's the point. I give up.

'When did you find out?'

Mrs Cameron looks at me over the top of her glasses.

'Find out what?'

'You know. Find out about me?'

I can tell by the look in her eye that she hasn't got a clue what I'm talking about. Either that or she's a good actor.

'About your what?'

And then I see what it was she was looking at. It's not my photo with 'MISSING' plastered across it, but last week's English essay on social justice. She's got my piece in her hands. I have to think quick because right now I've just asked an elephant into the room.

'About me . . . essay.'

'About *my* essay,' she corrects me. And for once I don't mind if someone don't think I speak English good.

She looks down at my work again. I called it 'The Ivy Principle'. It's not my best work and it's a bit clunky in parts, but I was happy with it.

'I've got to ask you,' she says. 'Are you serious?'

My look is all that's needed.

'Sorry. I had to ask. Well then, congratulations. It's an extraordinary piece of writing. Insightful, empathetic, original and thought-provoking. Funny too.'

'Funny?'

'Yes. It's a bit heavy-handed at times but the simile about the dead cat is hilarious.'

I didn't know I was being funny at that point.

'And the bit about the Porsche getting car-jacked and the supermarket trolley on the croquet lawn had us in stitches in the staffroom.'

They're talking about me in the staffroom? I wasn't even trying to be funny. Still, what with the house and everything, things are starting to work out for me and I'm happy to take a crumb from the high table.

'If I didn't know any better I would swear you lived out in the "troubled zones".' She tilts her head to one side, waiting for my response.

'Research. Books. Documentaries.'

She looks at me closely, but it's obvious she's getting fidgety and will probably need to duck out soon for 'personal reasons'.

'So what do you want to do with your life?'

Having shown up on her radar I need to drop off it again as quickly as possible before she starts digging into my past.

My African eye-eating Loa-loa worm plan is a memory-burner and will probably have her in stitches again – and get me another mention in the staff room – so I leave it. 'I want to be a writer.'

'A writer? Good for you. Keep at it and you'll get there. Work hard and . . .' She just sort of trails off. And I can see that as the nicotine withdrawal gnaws at her frayed nerve ends, I'm already slipping from her mind.

CAFÉ

THE HOUSE WAS A LUCKY FIND.

The first really big break I had. Once I'd settled in I had a feeling things were finally going to work out for me. Although I was seriously worried about Cinderella. Every time I met up with her she seemed even thinner than before. More wasted.

But didn't you say that at Christmas she rolled up her sleeves and tucked into a bucket of KFC?

Ate it, yes. Kept it down, I seriously doubt. After we'd finished dinner she said that she was going to have a bath. And although I did hear the bathwater running, I also heard the toilet flush a few times while she was in there.

Right.

And I suppose it was then that I started thinking about trying to get a place for myself. I figured if I could get some stability in my life, an attic to rent or even a squat somewhere quiet and peaceful, I could help Cinderella the way she helped me. I couldn't help much while I was staying in the rail yards, I could see that. I couldn't invite her over for

a girly weekend in the carriage. I knew I had to find somewhere else. And luckily Miss Taylor knew about the old
Gardner place.

Did *she* ever visit?

Who? Miss Taylor? No. She couldn't come during the day
because it just wasn't safe. One of my neighbours, this old bag
who lived by herself with about ten cats, was always snooping
around. Checking out the letterbox and poking around the
yard like she had a perfect right to. I actually bought some
plain curtains and hung them over the windows so that
she couldn't see me moving around. And of course at night
I couldn't use any light at all, apart from my book light, so
I couldn't really invite Miss Taylor over then. She taught me
how to cook though, at her place on the weekends. I also
learned some stuff at school, so I was getting it together.
Although the stove worked, the hot water system was cactus
so I had to boil water.

If the water and electricity were working, who was paying
the rates?

Beats me. Whoever owned the house, I guess. No one
came around looking for answers. I suppose I wasn't there
long enough for anyone to notice.

What about baths? You had a bath on your birthday,
remember, your last night in the house before the police
showed up.

I could have baths, but it was a hassle so I only did it on
special occasions, like my birthday. I used to boil the kettle
about fifty times and then mix the cold water in from the taps
until I got the temperature right.

Did Cinderella come and stay with you?

No. She liked it near the uni too much. She only visited
me twice. The first time she said that there was something
wrong with the house. Felt a presence. Like it was haunted.

She said the place felt like death. Ended up going home to the squat.

And the second time?

Do we have to?

It's your story. We don't have to do anything.

We've come so far, I have to tell you this bit.

Take your time.

Okay, the second time she came over, it was because she'd beaten her destiny. Her kismet. And I was such a piss poor friend, I didn't even know what day it was.

The Raven

THERE'S AN OLD TURKISH AND URDU WORD, KISMET, WHICH MEANS destiny. Although Miss Taylor didn't believe in it, she was always telling us twist-in-the-tale kismet stories, like the traditional Arabian one about the young sailor who, while fleeing Death, runs straight into its open arms.

I don't believe in destiny either, though I am battling it on two fronts, and not everyone is going to come out of it well. I can just feel it.

Firstly there's Creepo. I know that he wants me out of the way. Should I, like the young sailor in the story, run to face my kismet, or flee like a wild thing? That's the thing about kismet, whether you buy in to it or not: it'll be my attempt to flee that'll lead Creepo straight to me, and then it'll be a short trip back out to the forest of bones.

Cinderella worries me more. I don't know what she was like before she ran into that fortune teller, but now she's a mess. She doesn't take care of herself. She doesn't think right, she doesn't eat right, she doesn't exercise. She drinks, smokes and God only knows what that cut-down poison she's plunging into her veins is doing to her – body and soul. She says she can't embrace a future that isn't there. She's so convinced that she's going to die soon, she's killing herself in the process.

✳

I wake around two in the morning to someone or something whispering my name. The gum tree has been scratching at the roof all night but I'm so used to it that I hardly even hear it any more. If the ghosts in the walls know my name then they haven't used it until now, so I don't think it's them.

Through the haze of semiconsciousness I hear it again, only this time it's telling me to let them in because it's cold. I sit bolt upright when there comes a tapping at my chamber door, followed by a rap on the window. For a second I wonder if it's that raven that's been hanging around. Tapping at windows and doors is a funny thing for a bird to do, though. Even the bird of death.

I crawl out of my sleeping bag, flick on my book light, and scurry across to the door. There's more tapping at my widow.

'Who is it?'

'It's me, silly.' This is followed by a machine-gun burst of laughter. That's the raven out. At least whoever's out there realises that anyone tapping on the door and window of a seemingly derelict house at two o'clock in the morning is the silly one, rather than the occupant.

'Cinderella?'

'Who else? C'mon. Let me in, I'm freezing my tits off out here.'

I jerk open the door and she practically falls into my arms.

'What's happened? What's going on?'

She looks up at me with big puppy dog eyes. Big, glazed over, puppy dog eyes. 'Hello, beautiful. I've missed you.' Her speech is so slurred I can hardly understand what she's saying.

I pretty much carry her over to my sleeping bag, plonk her down on top of it and zip it up around her. She weighs almost nothing. The leopard that saved my butt on the train that afternoon is a memory. She curls up into a tiny ball in my sleeping bag and smiles at me.

'God, you're gorgeous. If you were ten year older . . .' She trails off. I don't know if she's drunk or what. She's definitely not herself. She's never talked to me this way before.

I stroke her forehead. 'What have you taken?'

'Nothing.'

'Don't lie.'

She snorts out another burst of laughter. 'Okay, I've pretty much had one of everything. We had a party, see, in the squat. God, it went off.'

'Do I need to call an ambulance?'

There's a pause while she stares off into space.

'There's a big black crow out there on your verandah. Did you know that?'

'Yeah. It's been hanging around for a few days. Actually I think it's a raven.'

'Ugly-looking thing.'

There's another pause.

'Cinderella. Do I need to get you an ambulance?'

'Nah. I'll be all right. Probably.' She bursts out laughing again.

'How did you get here? There are no trains at this time.'

'I took a cab. I just had to see you.'

'Why were you having a party in the middle of the week?'

She smiles at me. 'It's my birthday.'

Despite whatever it is that she's taken, and from her appearance it seems like plenty, suddenly I'm the one who's feeling shit. I can't believe I forgot her birthday. The one that she wasn't supposed to make it to. I'd written it in my diary and everything but I was too caught up in my own selfish pink-dress, blue-sock-wearing world and my principal's award for my stupid essay, that I completely forgot about Cinderella's birthday. What sort of crap friend am I?

'Well, happy birthday for yesterday.'

'No,' she corrects me. 'It's today.'

I look at my watch. She's been twenty for two hours.

'But why have a party the day before?'

'Because everyone knew that I was supposed to be dead, so they wanted to help me see it in. The new decade and everything. The rest of my life. Party kicked off about seven and it was still going strong when I left. But I wanted to see you.'

I bend down and hug her. She's trembling all over.

'I made it, girlfriend. That stupid cow at the markets was wrong.'

'See. Now you can start living.'

'That's right. As of tomorrow I'm getting my act together. No more drugs, no more drink, no more smoking, no more men, at least not professionally.'

I knew it.

'And no more vomiting?' I add.

She stares up at me. 'You knew?'

'Jesus, Cindy, look at you. I thought *I* was skinny. There are coat hangers fatter than you.'

'Not from tomorrow.' She flings her arms up and announces, 'In the morning you and I are going out for a huge breakfast.'

'Will you keep it down?'

She holds up two fingers. 'Scouts honour. Dib, dib, dib,

dob, dib . . .' She trails off. 'Dib.' Another burst of laughter. 'Oh, wait a minute. We can't go tomorrow. You've got school.'

'That's okay –'

'No!' she interrupts, suddenly donning her fairy god-mother guise again. 'You're not missing school.'

'I mean if we go early enough I can still make it to school on time. There's a café in the village.'

'Great. We'll get up early and power walk.'

'But I'm paying. For your birthday.'

'We'll see.' Cinderella closes her eyes. 'I'm so cold. Don't you have a heater?'

'Sorry.' I crawl into the sleeping bag with her. She's nothing but skin and bones. Even her tattoos have shrunk and appear less threatening than before.

I feel awful that I don't really know that much about her, apart from the abuse, apart from the sadness. 'Were you born here? In the city I mean. Or had you always lived down south?'

'No. I'm from Scotland originally. Inverness. Way up north. I came out with my folks when I was a wee baby.'

'I didn't know you were Scottish.'

'Aye, lassie. A wee bairn I was. A bonny wee bairn.'

Her affected Scottish accent makes me laugh.

'That means . . .' I trail off and look up the atlas in my mind. It's not today in Scotland yet. It's still yesterday. She won't be twenty for about seven hours.

'What does what mean?'

'Oh, nothing.' I'm being stupid.

I flick off my book light and gather her up. I gently rub her back, my fingers bouncing over her ribcage like a car over a cattle grid.

'No more heroin?'

'Promise. And no more E either. Not even pot. That stuff

blunts your mind. Whoever says drugs are cool obviously never takes them.'

No matter how tightly I hold her she just won't stop trembling. I suppose she's got no meat, no muscle to keep her warm.

'Tell me a story?'

'*Cinderella*?'

'Not that antifeminist shite. The Trans-Siberian Railway.'

'We're going on it remember? You pinkie promised.'

'Definitely. As soon as I get my shit together. Get a job and save up the cash, then we are so gone. Have to be during the school holidays, though.'

I have to bite my lip to stop myself from crying. Here she is, one of the most damaged human beings I've ever met, totally off her face on God knows what, and she's still worried about my education.

I take a deep breath to try and get *my* shit together. 'We get up early on the first day of the school holidays. We power walk to the village and have a big breakfast at the café . . .'

'Which I keep down because I'm not bulimic any more.'

'That's right.' I stroke her cheek. 'After that we come home and pack our stuff and catch the train to the airport.'

'And I've got a passport and everything's sorted out in my life.'

'Yeah. You're working as a youth counsellor. Helping street kids get *their* shit together.'

'Sweet. I'd fully give anything to do that.'

'Because of your great work the airline gives us an upgrade to business class and so we spend the entire flight eating, reading, watching movies and drinking tea and mineral water.'

'We can have a small glass of champagne, maybe, to celebrate. A wee snifter.'

I don't know what a snifter is but it sounds harmless enough. 'A really small one, sure.'

'Then what?'

'Well, we have a couple of days sightseeing in Paris to recover from the flight and then we catch another plane to Moscow where we take a taxi to the train station and pick up the Trans-Siberian Railway.'

'Do we have a sleeper cabin?'

'Of course.'

I close my eyes and breath through her hair. She's trembling so much she's practically rattling.

I just want her to go to sleep so that she can start recovering, but she's wants to know the details. 'One or two sleeper cabins?'

'What do you prefer?'

'Two, so we can stretch out, but with a connecting door.'

'Then that's what we've got. And they're both big –'

'But cosy?'

'Oh, yeah. Really cosy. And then the train sets off and we look out our windows as the snow-covered Russian fields flash past.'

'What do we do on the train?'

'We get better. We sleep. We read. We play board games. We repair. And at meal times we wander down to the first class dining car and eat until we're ready to burst.'

'And there's no one on the train to hurt us?'

'No. It's just us and some other travellers who are all really nice and friendly.'

'No dirty old men who want me to do things to them?'

'Absolutely not.'

'No youth ministers with ponytails?'

'No. He's been carted off to jail.'

Cinderella lifts her head. 'He's someone's bitch?'

'Barking like a dog.'

'What do we do when we get to Vladivostok?'

I'm glad it's dark because this way she can't see the tears streaming down my cheeks. She just can't stop trembling. It's so deep within that it's part of her. She probably doesn't even realise that she's doing it.

I pull myself together the best I can. 'The train stops here for a couple of days, so we do some sightseeing, but then we catch the train back and do it all over again.'

'It's cold outside, in Russia, I mean, but it's warm and safe on the train?'

'As cosy and as warm as it gets.'

'Yeah. That's great. I would have loved to have done that. With you.'

'Don't say that. We *will* do it.'

'Are you crying? Don't cry. I'll always be here for you.'

I would give anything just for her to stop trembling.

I stroke my tears into her hair. Her breathing is laboured as she slips down the levels of sleep. Her chest rattles as it rises and falls in rhythm with mine but each breath feels like a struggle. A battle to keep going.

I try to stay awake and keep watch over her, to keep the raven away, but eventually I slip into the dream world myself.

Cinderella died around four o'clock that morning.

CAFÉ

I'M SORRY YOU HAD TO RELIVE THAT. IT MUST HAVE BEEN HARD.

Not as hard as it was for her.

What do you think killed her?

Who knows? Drugs. Neglect. The streets. Life. All of the above.

How did you know she died at four o'clock?

I don't. Not exactly. But it was around then. I had this thing about four in the morning.

The dead hour? When the window into the next life is open, I think you said earlier?

I used to set my alarm for three fifty-five so that I would be awake for when it arrived.

Why did you want to be awake when the ghosts passed through? I thought you were frightened of them.

I was. I mean, I am. But I'd rather be haunted by one than become one. My father reckoned that at four o'clock in the morning we get as close to death as we could get and yet still come back. So I wanted to be awake for it.

You do realise that all this ghost stuff kind of contradicts your oblivion beyond the grave idea?

Sure. But like I said from the start, I had more questions than answers. Still do.

So what happened when your alarm went off that morning?

When I woke up I noticed that her chest wasn't moving up and down, and I panicked. I dragged myself out of the sleeping bag but she wasn't breathing. I tried to bring her back, mouth-to-mouth and CPR but she was stone cold. She was gone. I could hear someone screaming 'No. No. No.' over and over again. It was me.

I'm so sorry.

I don't think I want to do this any more. Talk about it. It's so hard. It haunts you, you know? Always will.

You tried to save her. To bring her back.

Not that, but what I did next. I couldn't risk ending up like . . . her, see, so I had to . . .

You had to . . .?

It sounds so awful, especially after she'd saved my life, but I couldn't call an ambulance.

That's understandable given the circumstances.

I had to get rid of her. God! It sounds fucked up just saying it. I didn't mean it like that. But I had to put her where someone could find her and tell her mum and everything.

So what did you do?

I ran out of the house. Down the street. I don't even know what I was doing. What I was looking for. But I ran all the way to the village, down towards the bookshop, although I had to stop a couple of times to throw up. But as I was vomiting into the gutter, I looked up and saw it. It'd been left outside in the supermarket car park.

What was it?

Fuck! This is so hard.

It's okay. You're doing great.

A shopping trolley. I wheeled it back home, up my path and . . .

Do you want a tissue?

No, I don't want a tissue. I deserve this. I should feel guilty about what I did.

So what *did* you do?

I went back in and carried Cinderella outside and put her in the shopping trolley. She weighed almost nothing. How messed up is that?

So there I was bawling my eyes out and wheeling my fairy godmother, my best friend, the *only* friend who knew everything about me, down the street like she was rubbish. Like I was just going to throw her away. And then I saw that one of her legs was wedged beneath her at an awkward angle and it took me some time to readjust her into a more comfortable position.

Where did you put her?

I was just going to leave her in front of the fire station and call triple 0 from the public phone on the corner. But across the road there's this church, so I figured that if the church couldn't look after her while she was alive, then they could bloody well take some responsibility for her now that she was dead. I also knew, despite my rage, that churches, synagogues, mosques and temples are packed full of good people, and for every Reverend Pembroke, there are about a thousand Father Kellihers, and what's more they *would* take care of her.

I wheeled her up the path and around the side because I didn't want her to be a freak show out the front or anything. I bent down to say goodbye and kissed her on her forehead and sort of hugged her. I didn't care if my fingerprints or my DNA were all over her. I loved her more than I've ever loved anyone and I wanted bits of myself left on her and her on me. The bars of the shopping trolley were icy cold. Cinderella hated the cold. She'd experienced so much of it and I couldn't leave her like that.

So I raced back home and got my sleeping bag. I was only gone for about ten minutes but when I got back a police car was out the front of the church with its lights flashing, so either a cleaner had turned up or someone had heard the noise I was making and called the police. I'd let her down again. She was going to be cold for ever. And because it was still yesterday in Scotland, she would be nineteen for ever too.

So the fortune teller was right.

No, she wasn't! Don't you see? She didn't foresee Cinderella's death, she caused it. You tell someone they're going to be dead before they're twenty, what happens? They go off and live life on a razor blade and, sure enough, they're dead before they're twenty.

Did you go to her funeral?

Yeah. I went to her squat that Saturday, like I was just dropping in to see her, and her housemates brought me inside, sat me down and told me what happened. It'd made the news, that's how *they* knew, and then one of them phoned her mother. The bitch.

Didn't they know that she'd gone to see you, the night before her birthday?

No. They all thought I still lived in the rail yards. According to them she just disappeared, which she did a lot, apparently. They took some comfort from the fact that she'd made it to twenty and they'd helped her celebrate it. There was no way I was going to tell them the truth.

The next week I took a day off school so I could go to the funeral. Her mum lived down south and I had to go on the same dodge line that Cinderella had saved my worthless butt on.

Her mother insisted on having the funeral at her church. The one where Cinderella had gone to her first youth group had run into that scumbag minister, Justin Pembroke.

He was there, the creep. I didn't need his nametag to tell me who he was. He was still wearing his ridiculous ponytail and a look of utter smugness. I found it hard not to run up to him and give his ponytail a yank. He was standing at the entrance to the church, offering his condolences to all the mourners, greeting everyone with a double handshake and a soulful she's-with-the-angels-now look. When he tried to shake my hand I pulled it away and told him to piss off. No way in hell was I letting that slimy bastard touch me. When I did it the creep just turned to his assistant and said something like, 'their grief is still raw'. What a dick!

And to make matters worse he was presiding over the thing. He knew what he did to Cinderella but was happy to stand up there on the pulpit preaching about taking the wrong path in life, about bad choices, about tolerance, about understanding. Then he changed direction and used Cinderella's funeral as an opportunity to preach. About how we all had to accept God into our lives or else we'd be doomed to spend eternity wandering through purgatory or worse. He honestly believed that the gates of heaven were closed to Cinderella but he'd just stroll in because, although he might be a rapist sack of shit, he'd accepted God into his life and Cinderella hadn't.

When he finished with his made-up madness, the mourners were given the chance to say a few words. Her mum chose not to. Probably too pissed to step up to the pulpit, so it was left to Cinderella's friends to see her off. One by one her housemates and street friends talked about her compassion, her humour, her sense of justice, of right and wrong, and while this was going on Reverend Pembroke just sat there with this big, stupid grin plastered across his face as if he was her closest friend in the world and they were just repeating stuff that he already knew. God, I hated him at that moment.

Eventually when the tributes stopped he sort of wafted back up to the pulpit. But as he started naming the hymn we had to sing, I knew I had to say something. I couldn't let her go without telling everyone what she meant to me. I had to say goodbye to my friend, my fairy godmother. So even though the organ music had just kicked in, I got up and walked to the pulpit.

Reverend Pembroke smiled at me as I approached and then whispered that there wasn't enough time and we had to move on. I just hissed at him to get the hell out of my way and I suppose the fire in my eyes told him he'd better not mess with me. He scurried back to his seat like the sewer rat that he was.

The organ kind of just petered out and I stood at the microphone and stared down at everyone. I hadn't realised how popular she was. There must have been a hundred mourners in the church. Maybe more.

I started by telling them that Cinderella had saved my life.

Reverend Pembroke sat there nodding like he knew it all along.

Then I launched into the full tale of how she'd rescued me on the train that day. I could see from the looks on her friends' faces that they knew that this is exactly the sort of thing that she would do. When I get to the bit about the compass point a couple of them burst out laughing. But not Reverend Pembroke. He got up from his seat and came over to shut me down. Apparently raping vulnerable teenagers is perfectly okay, but if you mention a penis in church then watch out.

Did he let you finish?

He didn't have much choice. I wrapped my hand around the microphone and told him that if he came near me I would insert it up his arse. He said that there was no call for that, so I told him to piss off again. Cinderella's friends were with me. They were shouting at him to let me finish. So he gave them one of his leers and went and sat back down.

Afterwards we all milled around outside, not sure what to do. Cinderella's housemates came over and hugged me and we all kind of cried on each other's shoulders. But as we were consoling each other I could hear that slimebag minister doing the rounds with his empty words. I overheard him tell someone that Cinderella had suffered because she chose drugs over God. That was it.

What did you do?

He was almost next to me by then. He turned to me and reached out to shake my hand – obviously he hadn't realised it was me. As he did I drove my knee into his balls as hard as I could. They'd have been pancakes when I was done. He collapsed onto the ground doubled up. And his wife was just standing there with her mouth hanging open, staring at me. Well everyone was. So I pointed at her and said that he'd raped Cinderella, and that she knew about it because she was there when it happened.

What did she do?

She gave me this weird look and then she turned towards where he was lying curled up on the ground and yelled, 'You said I was the only one. YOU SAID IT WAS JUST ME!'

Did you feel better after that?

No. Not really. But he felt worse.

What do you think she meant when she said that?

I don't really know. I thought about it later, on the train home. Either in her twisted little world she felt that he was being unfaithful, or else he was raping her too. And this guy thinks he's going to heaven.

Anyway, there was a church elder there and he asked me if what I said was true. I swore that it was, and that it was the reason Cinderella had become a street kid. He really didn't seem that surprised. He told us that they'd investigate the matter. It was a relief. Not that anything could be proved, but still, they might at least stop him working with children.

After I'd said goodbye to Cinderella's housemates and started walking down towards the train station I heard someone calling after me. It was Cinderella's mum. Her breath could have put *me* over the limit but I suppose it's not every day you go to your only child's funeral. She told me, slurred at me, that she hadn't been a very good mother. She didn't need to tell me that, obviously. I thought she was going to tell me off for messing up the funeral or swearing in church. Instead she asked me if I'd like to take care of Cinderella. I didn't know what she meant but I said yes. I gave her Miss Taylor's address when she asked where I lived. Three weeks later a courier delivered a parcel to Miss Taylor, which I collected from her after school. As soon as I got home I opened it. It was the urn containing Cinderella's ashes. She'd looked after me, so now it was my turn to take care of her.

Six months later, on my fifteenth birthday, the old bag neighbour must have sussed that she had a squatter living next door, so she called the police and the next day I was back on the trains, which sort of brings us full circle.

CAFÉ

NOT QUITE.

What do you mean, not quite? This is where we started. We've done the city loop.

It feels as though you're glossing over some of the details and skipping others. And there's a very big loose end still hanging out there.

Creepo?

Yes.

I knew you were going to say that.

Did you see him again? Did he find you?

Yeah, he did.

What happened?

Well, the morning after the police came to my squat – the day after my birthday – I packed up my stuff and took it around to Miss Taylor's place. I was keeping Cinderella's urn in a shoebox until I had a proper place of my own. Miss Taylor had gone to school by then but she'd given me a key so that I could come and go whenever I wanted to drop stuff off, pick it up or whatever. After school it was bucketing down and I couldn't face going back to the rail yards again so I checked in to the Shangrila Pines for a couple of nights, just to get myself organised. I figured I could start looking for another squat, maybe even move into Cinderella's old place. Her friends said I could.

I had dinner with Alistair McAlister at the mega-mall and then I trudged back to the hotel because I was feeling shit. I'd lost my home and even though I had Miss Taylor and Alistair, I still felt alone without Cinderella keeping watch over me. I'd been sort of numb since her funeral. I tried to keep it together, and Miss Taylor certainly helped, but there were times I felt as though I couldn't go on. I missed a lot of school because some mornings I just couldn't get up and others I just didn't want to. I'd spend the day staring at the wall. Barely had enough energy to get up and go to the toilet.

Depression.

You know about it then?

Yeah. I know something about the black dog.

I didn't realise it at the time because I didn't feel sad so much as empty. That everything was pointless.

That's the dog.

Miss Taylor arranged for me to see a counsellor at school, and that helped as long as I remembered what I could and couldn't talk about. Slowly I started to get my shit together. Only slept in on the weekends. Also my boss at the bookshop, Paul, started giving me more work. Insisted on paying me too, cash in hand. But no sooner had I come out of the fog than the police turned up and I lost the squat.

[pause]

I'm out of that now. I'm better.

Okay. So can we get back to Tony? You had dinner with Alistair and then went back to the hotel.

It was around ten o'clock. I was lying in bed watching a movie when room service knocked on the door. I wasn't thinking straight. It was only when I unlatched the door and turned the handle that I remembered that I hadn't ordered any room service. By then it was too late. He'd shouldered his way into the room and slapped me across the face. I stumbled and wound up curled up on the ground. He kicked me in the stomach. Luckily my arms absorbed most of it, otherwise he could have killed me there and then.

After I'd recovered a bit he told me to get up. That he was taking me home.

You didn't believe him.

I'm not an idiot. I had to get myself together. I had to think. And my arm hurt like hell where he'd kicked it. I figured he must have broken it again.

While he was pacing about the room I sort of eased myself up to lean against the bed and tried like mad to think.

I told him that he'd better listen to me because his life depended on it. He bent down and shoved his face in mine but I told him anyway.

Told him what?

That I'd written a letter and given it to a lawyer. The letter had all the details about how my parents had died, how he'd buried them out in the forest, and how they could still find specks of evidence on the car or in the garage. I really liked that bit. I also told him that I'd written that he'd been abusing me and if the police ever found out about it he'd be sent to jail as a paedo and he would be beaten up in the shower and worse every day.

What was the lawyer going to do with the letter?

There wasn't a letter. It had been Cinderella's idea ages ago when I told her how frightened I was that Creepo would find me. Pure genius. I told him that I phoned the lawyer each week and if he didn't get a call from me, he had to assume the worst and send copies of my letter to the police, the media and various underworld figures.

Various underworld figures?

I don't know. It sounded good at the time.

What did he do?

He kind of walked around for a while and then he came over and bent down and got right in my face again. Spat at me that I owed him money. I told him that it had gone on my lawyer's fees and the rest went to charity. Then he grabbed me by the front of my pyjamas and pulled me right up close so that I could smell his cheap bourbon breath. He said that I was a liar. That I was a deluded attention-seeker. If he ever saw me again, if I ever came to their house, he would kill me on the spot, which is bullshit because my lawyer had the letter. Or so he thought. Then he threw me back against the bed, got up and walked out.

That's it?

And we all lived happily ever after.

But that's not strictly true, is it?

What do you mean?

Tony and Serena didn't live happily ever after, did they? I did a little research. Well, I have a friend who is an investigative journalist and she did a bit of research. I didn't ask her to but she knew that I was writing this book . . .

So?

'Couple Slain in Shocking Killing'. That was the headline.

What are you talking about?

I've got a copy of the article here.

[Pause]

It was them, wasn't it?

So they're dead. I sleep better at nights.

When we first met you were adamant that I couldn't use any real names because you were scared, not just for you but for me as well. What was all that about if you knew that he was dead?

Okay, I knew, but he had some dodgy friends and business partners. I don't want any of them showing up at my front door.

Do you know what happened?

I suppose his past finally caught up with him. Or maybe one of his deals went bad. Crossed the wrong person.

I think he did.

What are you saying?

I think you know. We dug deeper. The coroner found an open verdict, which means that although the police are no longer investigating it, the file is still open. Apparently the evidence points to it being a murder–suicide, or an execution made to appear like a murder–suicide.

Wait a minute. Are you saying that I had something to do with it? I told you. I threw the gun away. In the river.

Did you?

I can't believe this. You're accusing me of what? . . . I thought we were friends . . .

We are. But I want to get to the truth. Who got their money? Their assets?

It seems to me like you and your little journalist girlfriend already know.

So you had something to gain from their deaths?

Hang on a sec. Are you an author or a detective?

Just trying to clear up this loose end. I mean, no one would mind too much if you did kill him. Slaying the dragon and all that.

I didn't do it, okay?

But you did benefit from their deaths?

Look. Serena was the beneficiary of Creepo's will and I was the beneficiary of hers. She hadn't changed it from when I was little. From when I first went to live with them. They didn't really have anyone else anyway. But I didn't know I was in her will. How could I? She never told me. Hardly ever spoke to me.

What did you do with all that money?

Remember Marco Rossini? Tony and Serena put him in charge of their estate. Their executor. I loved that when I heard it. Serena was having an affair with Marco, and Tony put him in charge of his affairs. Idiot. But it worked out for me. Marco calculated how much of the money belonged to my parents for their house and everything. All Creepo's is in a separate account and as soon as I turn eighteen, which is pretty soon, I can claim it all and then it's going to charity. His bad money can do some good. I'm going to keep just enough of his to take me and Cinderella and Miss Taylor on a trip. At the start of uni holidays we're going on the Trans-Siberian Railway.

So you got into uni?

Yeah. It wasn't hard once I got off the streets. I can't touch the money until I'm eighteen, but Marco sublet a flat for me in the same block as Miss Taylor's. He doles out enough for me to live off plus a bit of spending money.

So you *really* benefited from their deaths.

Okay, I did. But I still didn't kill them. I'm not like him.

Did you get into medicine?

No. I was a few marks short but I'm doing science and then I'll transfer to medicine later or else do it post-grad.

Everything worked out for you then?

Yeah. I suppose it did. In the end.

And you don't know anything more about how Tony and Serena died?

No, I don't.

Didn't the police find you and ask you some questions?

Of course they did, but I had an alibi. Proof that I couldn't have been there when they were killed.

Miss Taylor?

Exactly.

Wasn't she taking a risk? You being homeless and her being your ex-teacher. I mean, didn't you go out of your way to avoid being seen together?

The police were only interested in where I was and what time I was there. They didn't care why.

What about social services? Didn't they get involved? After all you would have still been listed as missing. Surely the police . . .

By the time social services showed up at school, Miss Taylor had applied to be my legal guardian.

Oh . . . was she able to get . . .

There was a lot of red tape but we got there in the end.

So she's . . .

Yep. She's my mum. Legally, anyway. I lived with her until I finished high school. After the holidays, when I started uni, I got a flat upstairs in the same block so that she could have some space. She's getting married next year. Now do you understand why I didn't want to use our real names? I don't want one of Creepo's scumbag associates showing up at Miss Taylor's door.

Of course. I'm satisfied. No more questions on that front. Thank you.

I suppose this is it. Thank you for trusting me with your story.

Far better than therapy. Cheaper too.

If there's anything else you think of between now and the publication date, give me a call.

Can I say it? Into the tape, I mean.
Sure. Go ahead.
THE END.
[End of Transcript]

CAFÉ

I THOUGHT I'D FIND YOU HERE.

I'm just going over our transcripts for the last few meetings. I've got a fair bit of catching up to do.

I see you've still got your Dictaphone. Is it recording?

Yeah. I switched it on when I saw you come in. If that's okay? In case you have anything to add?

Who's typing up the transcripts?

I'm using a service.

Not for this one.

What do you mean?

I mean you can record it but you have to type it up yourself.

Why?

Because I don't want to go to jail.

Okay. I'll do it myself.

Pinkie promise?

Pinkie promise.

You were right. There is more.

Go on.

The stuff at the hotel didn't happen like that. Like I said yesterday. Not quite, anyway. Cinderella did tell me to write a letter but, like I said, I never got around to it. Then when Creepo found me I never threatened him with it, at least not the way I said yesterday. I didn't even think of it until . . . well, kind of after, when he was messed up.

I figured it would be an okay way to end the story but I thought about it last night and I want to come clean. I need to tell you what really happened that night. Maybe it's the Catholic girl inside me, but I need to confess.

Like Father, Like Daughter

Tired of life on the desert plains, a young scorpion set out to see the world. After a while it came to a wide river and with nothing to float across on and not being able to swim very well the scorpion realised that its journey had come to an end. Unless. Unless . . .

'Excuse me,' said the scorpion to a frog that was sunning itself on a rock.

'Yes?' replied the frog, wary of this dangerous creature and ready to make a leap for the water if it reared up at him with its stinger.

'I'm on a great adventure,' replied the scorpion. 'Alas, however, I cannot cross this river because I am not a very competent swimmer and will surely be swept away.'

The frog was suspicious. 'And what has that to do with me?'

'If you could see it in your heart to ferry me across to the other side I would be eternally grateful.'

'What nonsense,' chuckled the frog. 'As soon as I come near you, you will surely sting me.'

'To do such a thing would display the greatest ingratitude, for you would have helped me continue with my journey.'

The frog could see that the scorpion had a valid point, so he gathered himself up and hopped down to the water and stood before the scorpion.

'No stinging,' reminded the frog.

'Of course not,' said the scorpion. And with that the scorpion climbed upon the frog's back.

The scorpion's claws made the frog wince when they dug into his soft skin, but eventually they were both comfortable enough and set off on their odyssey across the river.

The current was strong, making the going difficult, but the frog, with its muscular hind legs, was able to make good progress.

When they were about halfway across, the frog suddenly felt a searing pain in its back. He turned his head just in time to witness the scorpion removing its stinger from its tender skin. He could already feel the creeping paralysis spreading out across his body.

'You fool!' gurgled the frog, struggling to keep his head above water. 'Now we will both drown.'

'I'm sorry,' said the scorpion. 'I couldn't help myself. It's in my nature.'

And with that they both slipped silently beneath the swirling current.

The light from the passing cars steals in through the curtains (*my* curtains. I paid for them myself) and briefly illuminates the ceiling. I love the sound of cars as they pass. The Doppler effect, I think it's called. An incomplete Doppler means that someone has pulled up outside. Potential trouble. Like tonight. But a full Doppler means I'm safe. The car has gone on its way. I love full Dopplers.

You'd think that the ghosts in the walls would visit me tonight. To say goodbye. But they leave me alone. There's just the sound of the dying gum tree scratching on the tin roof to get in. The coming and goings of the possums in the ceiling. A storm brewing to the south.

Sleep creeps up on me slowly, like hypothermia at sea, and I'm happy to be carried away. This will probably be the last good night's sleep I'll have for a while, so I better make it count. Tomorrow I'll be back. Back on the trains.

*

By the time I've packed up my stuff and lugged it to Miss Taylor's, she's already left for school. I'm relieved she's not in. Although Cinderella is tucked safely away in her shoebox, I'm not sure how Miss Taylor would feel about having her as a housemate.

School's a blur and I keep getting in trouble for not paying attention. Our English teacher wants us to discuss that stupid frog and scorpion fable about human nature. I've never understood that story to be honest. There was absolutely no reason for the frog to help the scorpion. He had nothing to gain from it.

Some people could say there was nothing in it for Cinderella when she saved my butt on the train that day, but that's not strictly true. By intervening when she did she was making the world a better place for me, for her, for girls, for women, for everyone in fact. Everyone except little perverts who insist on hassling people and flashing their dicks in public.

At lunch my group tries to comfort me, to reach me because they can see that I'm somewhere else. But most of them live in homes covered with ivy. With swimming pools and atriums and vestibules and generally a full complement of parents; how could they possibly get what's going on with me?

The heavens open up in the afternoon so I catch a train to the mega-mall and have an early dinner with Alistair McAlister and then later, during a break in the storm, I slosh up to the Shangrila Pines Resort and check in with my absent barrister mum. I just couldn't handle the thought of the rail yards tonight, not the day after my birthday. I decide to stay for a few days and try to figure out my next move. If I can't find another empty house in the ivy belt, I might have to move into Cinderella's old squat for a while. I know it will be a long commute to school each day, but her friends have always said that I would be very welcome to stay with them. Be better than the rail yards, I suppose.

At ten o'clock there's a gentle tap on my door followed by a cheery 'Room Service'.

The latch is off and I've turned the handle before I remember that I haven't ordered any.

'Inside, you little bitch!' Suddenly I'm lying on the ground with a hand mark burning my face. While I'm lying there he lays into me with his foot. I take cover as best I can, curling up into a tight ball. There's a sharp pain deep in my wrist where he broke it before and has probably broken it again.

He pulls a chair up in front of me and sits down like he means business. Everything's happened so quickly, I haven't even had time to be scared. Yet.

'What? You didn't think I'd work it out?' He's calm now, which scares me even more. 'I was going through the accounts, ready for tax time, noticed the charges from the hotel. Thought she was messing around behind my back. I didn't confront her. Started staking out the hotel. Catch 'em in the act. Then they'd both see what happens when you mess with Tony Sanchez.'

'Only megalomaniacs refer to themselves in the third person.'

'What did you say?' he raises his hand to hit me again. 'I'd watch that smart mouth of yours if I was you.' He lowers his hand. 'Bribed one of the desk clerks instead. Saves waiting around. Five hundred bucks for tipping me off when she checked in again. He called me about half an hour ago, said that, according to the computer, my wife had checked in with her daughter around four. I thought, what the fuck? There must be some mistake because she was sitting right next to me watching TV and we'd both been home all afternoon. Then it twigged. It had nothing to do with her. You'd taken the silly cow's credit card and she hadn't even noticed.'

I stare at him. He's won. He's got me. Unless. Unless . . . I'm sitting on the floor leaning against the bed and Creepo is right in front of me. If I can just get him away from me for a moment I should be able to reach it. Luckily I put it on this side of the bed.

'What happens now?'

'I can't sleep,' he says, almost pleading with me. 'Hardly a wink since you shot through.'

Guilt? Is he finally admitting that he messed up my life? That doesn't seem like him.

'I keep imagining you creeping up the stairs with a butcher's knife. Coming to stab me in the neck while I'm asleep. Stick me like a pig. Do you know what that's like?'

I know what it's like to be lying in bed with the covers pulled up to your eyes waiting for your uncle to come creeping into your room for some special time.

I need to keep him talking. Need to find a moment so that I can grab it.

'But how could you kill my mum? Bury my parents' bodies? How could you do what you did to me?'

'Do what? What are you talking about?'

The amazing thing is he seems genuinely mystified as to what I'm going on about.

'Coming into the bathroom while I was having a shower. Creeping into my room at night?'

He leans forward, grabs me by my pyjama lapels and throws me back against the side of the bed.

'That was you. Trying to tempt me. Just like your mother.'

'What's my mother got to do with anything?' I reach behind me and feel beneath the mattress. Maybe I can grab it anyway.

'Like mother, like daughter. She was everyone's and anyone's. All you needed was a souped-up engine and a wallet full of cash.'

'But how could you even look at me like that? I'm your brother's daughter!'

He bursts out laughing. It's a cold, heartless laugh that chills my blood.

'Do you really believe that? Why do you think he had next to nothing to do with you?'

'What do you mean?'

'She was screwing some mall rat at the time she started seeing your *father*. That's why her old man pulled her out of school. Reckoned he had to get her married off quick, while she was still worth something and not damaged goods. My brother was the first poor sucker to come along. He figured out you probably weren't his but he didn't care if she came with a bit of baggage. Reckoned she'd be a nice docile little wife, give him lots of handsome sons. Of course, you screwed all that up for him. You and that big, fat head of yours, causing problems in your mother's plumbing.'

I put my head in my hands and am soon bawling like a baby, shedding a few crocodile tears of my own, convulsing my body in grief. But I'm only stalling for time.

'If it's any consolation, it'll be over soon.'

Now. Now that he's won. Now that he thinks he's hurt me, I might be able to catch him off guard. 'Can't you just let me go?' I plead through my tears. 'I won't say anything. Promise.'

'Too risky. You'll tell the cops sooner or later.'

'No. I'll go away. You'll never hear from me again. Ever.'

'Yeah, yeah, yeah. You say that now, but what about when you get older. You know what I did to your mum. You'll want revenge. It's in your nature.'

'I'll go away. To Africa. Never come back.'

'Africa. You wouldn't last a week in Africa. Even Africans have trouble staying alive there.'

That's because Africa has been raped by just about every other continent.

'I'm sorry. I really am, but it has to be this way.'

I smack my lips together, resigned to my fate.

'Could you get me a drink before we go? From the minibar.'

He looks at me like he can't believe what I'm asking.

'Please. I'm really thirsty.'

'Sure,' says Creepo. He gets up. 'Why not? As the Mafioso bosses used to say, "It's nothing personal. It's just business." We can still be civil.'

As he's walking over to the minibar, I reach further beneath the mattress and pull out my baseball bat. He's always underestimated me.

I stand up and slip across the room.

'What do you want? Coke, lemonade or –' That's as far as he gets. As he turns towards me to finish the question, I slam the bat into his face with everything I've got, obliterating his nose and shattering his jaw. He goes into immediate shock and just stands there with his hands covering his face and his mouth hanging open because he can no longer breathe properly. He doesn't fall down. Not at first, anyway. So I give him a hand. I draw back the bat and drive it into his kneecap. His leg snaps back at a sickening angle and he collapses onto the floor.

'Like mother, like daughter, hey, you arsehole!'

All he can do is groan and spit blood, along with a couple of teeth.

'It's nothing personal,' I mimic. 'It's just business.'

With his last ounce of energy he holds up his hand. 'Wait,' he pleads. 'I've got to tell you something.'

I raise the bat over his head. One swing and it will all be over. I'll be off the streets. I'll be out of the rail yards. No more squats, church pews, airport lounges or door number 4 up north. I grip the bat. Twirl it. Stare down at this man, this thing, who murdered my mother in cold blood and would have been happy to live out his sick fantasies on me.

But I can't do it. I'm not like him. It's not in my nature. I lower my weapon.

'Good girl,' he splutters. 'You always were a smart one.'

'Shut the fuck up, Creepo, and listen to me! I could kill you right now, you know that, right? Groan once for yes. Twice for no.' I press the bat into him.

He lets out a groan.

'Do you know what that means?'

A single groan.

'That's right. I'm letting you go. I'm saving your life. So now you can't hurt me.'

Groan.

'But because I can't trust you, I'm going to write a letter which will detail everything you've done in your grubby little life. About Mum, about me, about all your dodgy deals. And do you know what I'm going to do when I've finished writing my letter?'

Eventually, with a little further encouragement from my baseball bat, he emits a double-barrel groan.

'I'm going to give it to a lawyer with certain instructions. And do you know what one of these instructions will be?'

Baseball bat. Poke. Groan. Groan.

'I will call the lawyer once a week to let her know that I'm okay. That I'm alive. And if at any time she doesn't hear from me then the letter and all the shit you've ever done goes public. And you'll wind up in some paedo cell with a hairy biker who'll do to you what you were planning to do to me. Do you understand?'

Groan.

I wipe his blood off my baseball bat and start packing my stuff. Though I haven't got a clue where I'm going. No idea where I'll be sleeping tonight. And I hate him for this more than anything.

'Oh and by the way. You were right about Serena having an affair.'

Although Creepo seems close to death, he opens his eyes at this.

'You know *your* lawyer, Marco Rossini? They get together a couple of times a week and bonk each other's brains out.'

He closes his eyes, unable to take any more.

I pull on my backpack and sheath my samurai baseball bat. Then I pull out the key card from the slot and toss it at him, leaving Creepo alone and broken in a rapidly cooling room.

*

I can hardly believe where I find myself heading, but I have to put things right.

She's not exactly my favourite person on the planet. In fact, when I go to call her I realise that I don't have the number. It's not exactly one I'd put on speed dial. But there was that night when Mum and my father went away and she took care of me. She packed up my stuff and looked after me. My head was resting in her lap as she stroked my face and told me that everything was going to be all right, even though we both knew that nothing would ever be the same again.

I don't know if Creepo will go to hospital or just curl up and die. What I do know is that I need to get to Serena before he does. I need to get her out of there and over to Marco Rossini where she'll be safe. Where she'll be loved.

By the time I arrive panting at the end of the alleyway almost an hour has passed since I left Creepo in a heap on my hotel room floor. It's taken me two trains and a long run to get here.

It's quiet in the house. Too quiet despite the hour. I peer in through the garage window and notice the blue metallic glow of the beast. I don't know what this means. Either he took Serena's car to the Shangrila Pines and it's still there, or he took the beast and somehow managed to drive it back.

I scamper up and over the side fence and around to the garden gnome. I lift it up but the fake stone has gone. I shake the gnome in case they put it inside it but it's empty.

Although it'll be noisy, I have to risk it. I remove my

baseball bat and tap it against the window until the glass shatters. Then I reach in and turn the lock and slip inside.

'Serena,' I hiss. 'Aunt Serena.'

I notice the glow of light from the kitchen and hear a noise that isn't human. It sounds more like an animal in pain. I grip the bat tighter and raise it over my shoulder.

I turn the corner into the kitchen. Just like my father all those years ago, Serena is lying in a pool of what looks like tomato sauce, only she isn't doing the backstroke. She isn't doing anything. Her eyes are wide open but her soul is long gone. There's no light in them. Creepo is lying on top of her, blubbing like a baby.

My hands are shaking as I brandish the bat at him. 'How could you kill your own wife?'

Creepo doesn't even turn to face me. 'I didn't, she . . .' He doesn't seem surprised that I'm there. 'It's your fault. If you hadn't told me, I wouldn't . . .' He trails off, trying to find further evidence that I was responsible for shooting Serena through her heart. There's no sign of the gun, which is something.

'She laughed at me. When I confronted her about it she told me I was pathetic and laughed in my face. She didn't even care that I was hurt, she didn't even seem to notice. She just said that she was glad that I'd found out, and she was going to go and be with him. With a real man. And then she laughed at me again and said that I was ugly. You did this, you little bitch! It's all your fault.'

'It's always somebody else's fault.'

'She made me, don't you understand? She asked for it. Just like you did when you kept having showers in front of me.'

'Look at me, Uncle Tony.'

No response.

'LOOK AT ME!'

He manages to drag himself up to a sitting position and leans back against the fridge.

I keep my distance.

Despite everything that's happened, he still finds it in himself to smile at me. 'You're not going to kill me. You don't have it in you.'

'I don't intend to kill you. But I *am* going to wait until the police get here. Make sure you don't crawl away to some slimy rat hole.'

'You're not going to call the cops on me. I've got a cleanup crew on the way. They'll be here any minute.'

'No one's coming. It's over.'

'You wouldn't want to see you're dear old dad in jail, would you, my darling daughter?' He leers at me when he says this. He's just shot his wife through her heart and yet he can still sit there smiling.

'Don't call me that. Or I might just kill you after all.'

'You don't get it, do you? And yet the clues have been staring you in the face from the start. You think you're so smart, but really, you're just like your mother. As I've always said, like mother like daughter.'

'I don't know what the hell you're talking about.'

'Do I need to spell it out?'

He pauses, trying to breathe through his almost non-existent nose. 'Your father wasn't some mall rat. I made that up. Your mother was having an affair when she met my brother, all right. She was having an affair with me.'

No. Not that. Anything but that.

'She was pregnant with you when she hooked up with your *father*. He knew that you weren't his; what he didn't know was that you were mine. Well, you might be. I wasn't the only one.'

I turn around and vomit into the kitchen sink.

'There, there,' he taunts. 'Let it all out. Life's complicated, isn't it?'

I take a deep breath and try to pull myself together. 'But you used to come in the bathroom when I was having a shower. You used to creep into my bedroom at night. And don't say that I was teasing you. For God's sake, you would have raped me if I hadn't run away and yet all the time you knew that there was a chance that I was your . . . I might have been your . . .' God! I can't even say it.

He snorts out a laugh along with some blood. 'I didn't say I was a good father.' Again he laughs and it's cold, bitter, like he's finally got the better of me. He's won. Because he knew all along that he had an ace up his sleeve. But now that he's played it he's got nothing left.

'She loved me, you know. Always had. Right up to the moment I put a bullet through her head.'

I feel like throwing up again, but I keep the bat raised at Creepo in case he tries anything.

He stares at the baseball bat. 'You know something? I didn't really think you were mine. Well, we're nothing like each other, are we? But then tonight, I thought, you know what? Maybe she is and I kind of like how she's turning out. There was a moment in that hotel room this evening when you were beating the living shit out of me that I was actually quite proud of you. It was like, "that's my girl".'

I turn to the sink again, unable to look at this bastard, this bastard maker, any longer. I've got nothing left to throw up so I spit bile.

When I turn back he's pointing his gun at me.

He smiles. 'Put down the bat.'

I gulp. He must have had it beside him. How could I have been so stupid?

He's hardly got the strength to hold it up so he's resting it on his leg. 'C'mon. This is silly. We can work something out.'

Then I hear it in the distance. It's very faint but getting closer.

'What's that?' He's heard the siren too. I start to back away.

'It's over, Creepo.'

'What? You already called them? I thought you said . . .'

'On my way here. Told them everything.'

'You little bitch!' He raises his gun and points it at me, but he doesn't have the strength and his hand drops limply beside him, the gun clattering to the floor.

I move behind the breakfast bar to safety. If he goes for his gun again I can drop down out of sight.

'Do you know what they do to paedos and wife murderers in jail, Creepo?'

But he doesn't need me to remind him. He knows. With what little energy he's got left he reaches down for his gun once more.

He glares at me. 'Fuck you!'

'No,' I say. 'You didn't.'

I see his hand tremble as he stares down the barrel. The back of his head splatters against the fridge in an eruption of red. My ears are ringing and that smoky smell fills the room.

I wipe my fingerprints off everything I've touched and wash away the vomit from the sink, removing as much evidence of my being there as I can.

I hitch on my backpack and stare down at Creepo. The gun is lying on the floor with his hand limply beside it. His mouth is hanging open and his eyes are still glistening with the last electrical surges of life. His soul, if he has one, isn't about to soar off to the heavens. It isn't going anywhere. It'll rot with the rest of him in a cold, dark grave.

I've just watched Creepo shoot himself through the head

and I don't feel a thing. No guilt. No sadness. No joy. No remorse. Nothing.

Like father, like daughter? I don't think so.

It's then I notice that I can no longer hear the siren. The ambulance or fire engine or whatever it was has obviously reached its destination.

I turn off the kitchen light with my elbow and leave that house for ever.

The Beginning

BY THE TIME I FINALLY GET TO THE CHURCH IT'S ALMOST FOUR IN THE morning. Miss Taylor wasn't exactly thrilled about me turning up when I did and disappearing with my shoebox without so much as a word, but she'll forgive me. She always does.

The outside foyer offers some shelter from the deluge. I know it's just the weather cycle but it's hammering down so hard it feels positively biblical. I put Cinderella's shoebox on the ground near the door where it's dry and unhitch my backpack. I feel my arm where Creepo kicked it. It's probably broken again. I also notice some flecks of dried blood. I step out and let the torrent wash away the blood and the last remnants of my previous life. Even my arm doesn't feel as sore as it did before. I stand there with my arms out to the side, letting the heavens cleanse me. I open my mouth and let the water surge through my body, giving me strength so that I can begin again.

The door feels lighter than before as I push through and squelch my way over to the bathroom. I quickly pat myself down with a towel and change into some dry clothes. Even though my hair is still sopping wet I make my way through to the church proper.

I look at Jesus, hammered up there on the cross, a permanent reminder of all our human frailties, the guilt we're supposed to feel just for being alive, the sins that must be atoned for. I don't know if he was the son of God, a fraud, or just a delusional old hippy, but either way he was kind of cool. And I suppose if you're going to attach your belief systems, your hopes, to something, then his wagon is as good as any.

When I went to school here one of the more righteous teachers showed us a DVD about this creationist guy who was banging on about how the banana was the atheists' nightmare. His argument was that it fitted so perfectly in the human hand that it must have been created especially for us. It's sort of like the hermit crab who believes that the shell that it's taken over fits it so perfectly that it must have been created especially for *it*. Where the guy's argument falls down is in his referring to the banana as 'the atheists' nightmare' as if it's the one thing that we can't get past. The atheists' nightmare isn't a bit of bendy fruit, it's being atheist. I don't think there's a single atheist who doesn't want there to be something else beyond the night. Even the staunchest anti-creationist would surely be happy to spend eternity loafing around on a cloud plucking at a harp and praising the almighty rather than having to face the horrifying prospect of annihilation. All we're asking for is some proof, and I don't think the banana cuts it.

I start making the sign of the cross out of habit and respect but then I stop myself midway through. It's stupid. Do we even think about what we're doing when we cross ourselves? The cross is a barbaric execution device and I'm not going to acknowledge it any more. I prefer to remember how Jesus lived rather than the method of his murder.

I make the peace sign at JC and wander down the aisle to a pew near the front; the one where I spent my first night homeless. It was raining then too, I recall. Absolutely bucketing down. So I suppose in a way I *have* come full circle. And right now I feel the touch. The touch of being part of something greater. Something magnificent. That it's not just me against the world. Was God testing me? Was it part of his grand plan? If it was then it was a pretty crap one. Surely five people didn't have to die to make me see the light. Or maybe what I'm experiencing is simply a surge of chemicals through my brain released by the realisation that I don't need to be afraid any more. That I can come in from the cold.

I pull out my sleeping bag and snuggle down deep inside, zipping it up around the two of us.

My arm feels fine now. I won't even need to go and see Dr Chen, which is weird because I was positive that it was broken. Again.

I wiggle around trying to get myself as comfortable as possible, keeping Cinderella's shoebox firmly against my chest. Keeping her warm.

The battery-operated perpetual candle flickering away in the corner gives off just enough light to illuminate Jesus. I flash him a smile, flash him the peace sign again and settle back in the warmth of my nylon cocoon.

When I sleep, I sleep like the dead. Meanwhile, somewhere out in the forest, the dead can now rest in peace.

THE BEGINNING